O9-CFT-733

More Praise for *Galatea 2.2*

"I love and admire this book . . . but I cannot give an adequate sense of its many marvels. . . . One of the most beautiful and baffling dialogues in recent fiction."
— *Boston Globe*

"An ingenious, ambitious, at times dizzily cerebral work. . . . Much of it soars and spins."
— *New York Times Book Review*

"Richard Powers, like Bill Gates, is his own CPU, creating his own benchmarks for fiction. For all his cybersmart wizardry, he still writes about megahurts in a language anyone can understand."
— *Philadelphia Inquirer*

"One of the few younger American writers who can stake a claim to the cerebral legacy of Pynchon, Gaddis and DeLillo."
— *The Nation*

"*Galatea 2.2* is entertainment of a very high order, and likely to be remembered as one of the best books of the year, because its erudition is nourished by genuine feeling."
— *GQ*

"Powers' exposition of the linguistic and perceptual intricacies underlying consciousness is nothing less than brilliant."
— *The New Yorker*

"The kind of delicious novel of ideas that a computer-literate Vladimir Nabokov would have written. . . . With dazzling stylistic virtuosity and a keen grasp of character, Powers has reshaped the myth of Pygmalion into a compelling parable for the digital age."
— *San Francisco Chronicle*

"This book, however cerebral, embodies a lifelike vitality of movement, uncertainty and change. A brilliant torrent of knowledge, feelings, quotations and invention, it genuinely requires the reader to complete its sense."
— *Chicago Tribune*

BY RICHARD POWERS

OPERATION WANDERING SOUL

THE GOLD BUG VARIATIONS

PRISONER'S DILEMMA

THREE FARMERS ON THEIR WAY TO A DANCE

GALATEA 2.2

RICHARD POWERS

Harper Perennial
A Division of HarperCollins*Publishers*

This book was originally published in 1995 by Farrar, Straus and Giroux. It is here reprinted by arrangement with Farrar, Straus and Giroux.

GALATEA 2.2. Copyright © 1995 by Richard Powers. All rights reserved. Printed in the United States of America. No part of this book may be used or reproduced in any manner whatsoever without written permission except in the case of brief quotations embodied in critical articles and reviews. For information address Farrar, Straus and Giroux, 19 Union Square West, New York, NY 10003.

HarperCollins books may be purchased for educational, business, or sales promotional use. For information please write: Special Markets Department, HarperCollins Publishers, Inc., 10 East 53rd Street, New York, NY 10022.

First HarperPerennial edition published 1996.

Designed by Fritz Metsch

Library of Congress Cataloging-in-Publication Data

Powers, Richard, 1957-
　　Galatea 2.2 / Richard Powers. — 1st Perennial ed.
　　　p.　cm.
ISBN 0-06-097692-6
　　1. English literature—Study and teaching—Fiction.
　　2. Artificial intelligence—Fiction. 3. Novelists, American—Fiction. I. Title.
[PS3566.O92G35　1996]
　813'.54—dc20　　　　　　　　　　　　　　　　　　　　　　96-2117

96 97 98 99 00 RRD 10 9 8 7 6 5 4 3 2 1

The brain is wider than the sky,
   For, put them side by side,
The one the other will contain
   With ease, and you beside.

The brain is deeper than the sea,
   For, hold them, blue to blue,
The one the other will absorb,
   As sponges, buckets do.

The brain is just the weight of God,
   For, heft them, pound for pound,
And they will differ, if they do,
   As syllable from sound.

—EMILY DICKINSON

GALATEA 2.2

It was like so, but wasn't.

I lost my thirty-fifth year. We got separated in the confusion of a foreign city where the language was strange and the authorities hostile. It was my own fault. I'd told it, "Wait here. I'm just going to change some money. Check on our papers. Don't move from this spot, no matter what." And chaos chose that moment to hit home.

My other years persist, like those strangers I still embrace in sleep, intimate in five minutes. Some years slip their chrysalis, leaving only a casing to hold their place in my sequence. Each year is a difficult love with whom I've played house, declaring, at each clock tick, what it will and won't put up with.

My thirty-fifth trusted no one. As soon as I said I'd only be a moment, it knew what would happen to us.

Thirty-five shamed me into seeing that I'd gotten everything until then hopelessly wrong. That I could not read even my own years.

At thirty-five, I slipped back into the States. I did not choose either move or destination. I was in no condition to choose anything. For lack of a plan, I took an offer in my old college haunt of U. The job was a plum, my premature reward for a portfolio that now seemed the work of someone else.

I thought the year a paid leave of absence. A visiting position, where I might start again with the recommended nothing. House, meals, office, expenses, and no responsibilities except to live. I clung to the offer without too much reflection.

In fact, I had nowhere else to go. I couldn't even improvise a fallback.

It had to be U. U. was the only town I could still bear, the one spot in the atlas I'd already absorbed head-on. I'd long ago developed all the needed antibodies. When you take too many of your critical hits in one place, that place can no longer hurt you.

Nothing else remotely resembled home. Time had turned my birthplace into an exotic theme park. I could not have gotten a visa to live where I'd grown up. And I'd just spent the last seven years in a country that seemed exile already, even while I'd lived there.

But U. I could slink back to, and it would always take me. We were like an old married pair, at exhausted peace with each other. I did school's home stretch here, learned to decline and differentiate, program and compose. U. was where I took Professor Taylor's life-changing freshman seminar. Twelve years later, a stranger to the town, I passed through to watch Taylor die with horrific dignity.

U. was the place where I first saw how paint might encode politics, first heard how a sonata layered itself like a living hierarchy, first felt sentences cadence into engagement. I first put myself up inside the damp chamois of another person's body in U. First love smelted, sublimated, and vaporized here in four slight years.

I betrayed my beloved physics in this town, shacked up with literature. My little brother called me here to tell me Dad was dead. I tied my life to C.'s in U. We took off from U. together, blew the peanut stand to go browse the world and be each other's whole adulthood, an adventure that ended at thirty-five. The odds were against this backwater having anything left to throw at me.

Since my last trip back, I'd achieved minor celebrity status. Local Boy Makes Good. I'd never get my name on the city-limits sign. That honor was reserved for the native Olympic legend. But I now had the credentials to win a year's appointment to the enormous new Center for the Study of Advanced Sciences. My official title was Visitor. Unofficially, I was the token humanist.

4

My third novel earned me the post. The book was a long, vicarious re-creation of the scientific career I never had. The Center saw me as a liaison with the outside community. It had resources to spare, the office cost them little, and I was good PR. And who knew? A professional eavesdropper with a track record might find no end of things to write about in an operation that size.

I had no desire to write about science. My third novel exhausted me for the topic. I was just then finishing a fourth book, a reaction against cool reason. This new book was fast becoming a bleak, baroque fairy tale about wandering and disappearing children.

Even I could not fail to see the irony. Here I was, crawling back to the setting I had fictionalized in my sprawling science travelogue. The University put me up in a house, the seventies equivalent of the barracks where the hero of my book had lived on his arrival in town. Beyond a lone bed and desk, I left my rooms unfurnished, in my character's honor.

I bought a secondhand bike, perfect for the stretch from my house to the Center. The research complex had sprung up since my last visit. A block-long building in a town the size of U. cannot help but make a statement. The Center's architecture laid irony upon irony. It was a postmodern rehash of Flemish Renaissance. In the Low Countries, I'd lived in postwar poured concrete.

The Center had been built by an ancient donor couple, two people archaic enough to get through life still married to each other. They reached the end of that shared existence with nothing better to do with the odd fifty million than to advance advanced science. I don't know if they had children, or what the kids were slated to get when the folks passed away.

U. got a warren of offices, computer facilities, conference areas, wet and dry labs, and an auditorium and cafeteria, all under that jumble of Flemish gables. The small city housed several hundred scientists from assorted disciplines. Thankless Ph.D. candidates did the bulk of the experimental drudge work, supervised to various degrees by senior researchers from all over the world.

Work at the Center divided into areas so esoteric I could not tell their nature from their names. Half the fields were hyphenated. Creative play spilled over borders, cross-pollinating like hybrid corn in heat. Talk in its public spaces sounded like a UN picnic: excited, wild, and mutually unintelligible. I loved how you could never be sure what a person did, even after they explained it to you.

Most attention converged on complex systems. At the vertex of several intersecting rays—artificial intelligence, cognitive science, visualization and signal processing, neurochemistry—sat the culminating prize of consciousness's long adventure: an owner's manual for the brain. With its countless discrete and massively parallel subsystems, the Center seemed to me a block-wide analog of that neuronal mass it investigated.

The Center and two dozen similar places here and abroad would decide whether the species would earn its last-minute reprieve or blow the trust fund the way it intended. The footrace would photo-finish here, as life came down to the wire. Bio-chips, seeded to grow across the complexity threshold. Transparent man-machine interfaces. Control of protein folding. High-def, digital contrition.

The building teemed with job descriptions: theorists, experimentalists, technicians, magicians. Someone here had a probe attached to every conceivable flicker. One wing swarmed with scientists who proclaimed their transcendence over engineering. Another housed engineers who didn't even acknowledge the distinction. What one floor banished bred like mold in a nearby quarter.

The Center was big. So big I lost my office twice in the first month, the way you lose a rental in an airport parking garage. Sheer size was the Center's chief virtue. Even the embarrassment of talking to the same colleague twice faded in a place so huge. In such an expanse, I hoped, one year would be too brief for me to be of any but passing interest to anyone.

What's more, the complex opened onto virtual space, through a spreading network backbone. I had an office with my name on the door, and a computer cabled into the world web. No one suspected that I had no research group, that I could not tell a field-responsive polymer from a spin glass. I came and went in awful freedom, a complete impostor.

I found the dress-up weirdly pleasant, knowing I could go home nightly to a house both empty and rented. For a long time, I must have been aspiring to just this. Immaculate and cold-booted, a resident alien. Just passing through the old alma mater.

The Center had much to recommend it. Its doors knew me from a distance. They clicked open at the command of an infrared pass card that I didn't even need to take out of my wallet. I flipped backside to sensors, mandrill style. Anyone reading this by accident or nostalgia a hundred years from now will have to take my word for the novelty.

The parabolic front foyer concentrated sound. I liked to stand at the focus and hear the rush of my own breath, the throb of blood coursing through my veins. I listened to my body's roar, sounding for all the world like a message left on an answering machine by someone who died later that day.

I tinkered at my new novel, ticking at the machine keys with my door closed and the fluorescent lights doused. My office reveled in state-of-the-art, clean-room efficiency. The perfect place to tuck my millennial bedtime story in for the night. I'd click a radio button on my screen and eighteen months of work waited for me by the time I hiked upstairs to the network laser.

I browsed the world web. I fished it from my node on a building host that served up more megabits a second than I could request. By keying in short electronic addresses, I connected to machines all over the face of the earth. The web: yet another total disorientation that became status quo without anyone realizing it.

The snap of a finger, a satellite uplink, and I sat conversing with a mainframe in my old coal-mining ex-hometown seven time zones away. I could read the evensong schedule from off a digital valet in Cambridge, download Maurya painting, or make a Cook's tour of New Zealand. In seconds, I could scroll through dinner menus in languages I could not even identify. From my chair in the virgin Center, I revisited every city I'd ever spent time in and hundreds I would never get around to visiting in this life.

The town had been knitted into a loose-weave, global network in my absence. The web seemed to be self-assembling. Endless local investigations linked up with each other like germs of ice crystal merging to fill a glass pane.

The web overwhelmed me. I found it easier to believe that the box in Pakistan I chatted with was being dummied up in the other end of the building. I didn't know how my round-the-world jaunts were being billed, or if they were billed at all.

For a while, I felt a low-grade thrill at being alive in the moment when this unprecedented thing congealed. But after weeks of jet-setting around the hypermap, I began to see the web as just the latest term in an ancient polynomial expansion. Each nick on the time line spit out some fitful precursor. Everyone who ever lived had lived at a moment of equal astonishment.

The web had been a long while in linking up. It, too, was just a stopgap stage in a master plan drawn up on the back of the brain's envelope. A bit of improvised whittling, forever a step shy. A provisional pontoon in that rough pencil sketch for final triumph over space and time.

I explored the world's first network in embryo. After days of disappearing children, I spent my nights playing in the greatest virtual sandbox yet built. I'd stumbled upon a stack of free travel vouchers. I put up in U., but I resided elsewhere. I thought: a person might be able to make a life in all that etherspace.

Each day produced new improbabilities. I searched card catalogs in Kyoto or book reports from Bombay. German soccer scores and Alaskan aurora sightings filled my office E-mail pouch.

I eavesdropped on international discussion groups, ongoing, inter-active Scheherazades that covered every imaginable theme from arms control to electronic erotica. Notefile threads split and proliferated in meiosis. Debates flowed without beginning or end, through tributaries and meanderings, responses to responses to responses. Inexhaustible protagonists from every time zone posted to the continuous forum a dozen or more times a day.

Alone in my office, blanketed by the hum of the Center, I felt like a boy happening onto a copy of the *Odyssey* in a backwater valley library. I wanted to rush out into the hall and announce my each discovery. But who could I tell? Those lonely souls who stood most to gain would only shake their heads, dazed, locked out on every level. Those who had the wherewithal to see what the fuss was about had already habituated to the inconceivable.

Advanced science, of course, profited enormously from the web. The groups at the Center could now read journal articles months before they hit print. The data Autobahns had no speed limit. They plunked one in front of any results on earth before you could read the "Connect." Researchers peered into colleagues' labs on other continents, in real time. They shared data in 3D, as they gathered it.

On all sides of my cubicle, experimenters scoured the nodes. The net reduced duplication of effort and helped pinpoint crucial results they otherwise might have missed altogether. Instant telemessaging produced an efficiency that fed back into steeper invention. And invention accelerated the universal linkup.

But the longer I lurked, the sadder the holiday became. People who used the web turned strange. In public panels, they disguised their sexes, their ages, their names. They logged on to the electronic fray, adopting every violent persona but their own. They whizzed binary files at each other from across the planet, the same planet where impoverished villages looked upon a ball-point pen with wonder. The web began to seem a vast, silent stock exchange trading in ever more anonymous and hostile pen pals.

The web was a neighborhood more efficiently lonely than the one it replaced. Its solitude was bigger and faster. When relentless intelligence finally completed its program, when the terminal drop box brought the last barefoot, abused child on line and everyone could at last say anything instantly to everyone else in existence, it seemed to me we'd still have nothing to say to each other and many more ways not to say it.

Yet I could not log off. My network sessions, all that fall, grew longer and more frequent. I began to think of myself in the virtual third person, as that disembodied world-web address: rsp@center.visitor.edu.

How long could I show up at the Center and produce nothing of use to anyone? The productivity problem. The pure-research problem. The inspiration, the blind-trust problem. I could drift without limit and still not be reprimanded. I had the year gratis. I might do nothing but prime the pump, rest and recharge, and still I would not ruffle so

9

much as a mite's mood where it camped out on the eyelash of the emergent digital oversoul.

I meant to milk the new book for as many weeks of touch-up as I could get away with. Past that point I tried not to speculate. Three times before, the end of a long project had kicked off the start of another. I'd mastered the art of surviving narrative whiplash. No reason, in theory, why I couldn't regroup again. Go on and work forever.

But this time felt different. This time, after I paid my Pied Piper account, nothing waited for me on the far side of story's gaping mountain. Nothing but irremediable Things As They Are.

What little diversionary work remained I dragged out for all it was worth. Two Kbytes of new text or four of reasonable revision honorably discharged me of the day. Beyond that, I could indulge my remaining hours in good faith. A page and a half freed me to go and do as I liked.

Mostly, I liked to haunt the Center after hours. At night, the building thinned almost to empty. The community of night research emitted a sober thrill. The handful of sallow, animated faces at that hour could not help but be there. Their inquiries had them hooked, as levered to the intermittent payoffs as their lab animals. They piloted the halls, feverish, close to breakthrough, indifferent to clock time. They weaved from lab to lab in directed distraction, eyes combing every visual field but the corridors down which they moved.

Except for these addicts of the verifiable, I had the place to myself. That alone was worth coming in for: fifty million dollars of real estate filled with several hundred million in instruments, boxes that glowed with subdued purpose, abandoned like an electronic Rapture. No one could have a more profound sense of history than a night custodian of such a building.

Night brought open-endedness to the place. Through the machine on my desk, I could disappear down the coaxial rabbit hole to any port of call. I had a phone I could dial out on but which never rang. I had a white board and bright pastel markers that wiped off without a trace. I amused myself by writing out, in different colors, as many first lines of books as I cou_d remember. Now and then I cheated, verifying them on the web.

These nights were dead with exhilaration. Like battening down in the face of a major maritime storm. All I could do was stock the mental candles and wait.

On such a night, I met Lentz. From my first glimpse, he seemed the person I'd come back to U. to meet. While I stood by, this man prototyped the thing humanity has been after from out of the starting block. In the year I knew him, Philip Lentz would bring a life back from the dead.

The night in question, I'd diverted myself so successfully with bursts of null activity that I found myself still in the building well past midnight. I was prowling the corridors on the floor above my office. I stood outside a conference center, reading a posterboard entitled "Compliance of Neuronal Growth over Semiconductor Substrate." Someone had encouraged nerve cells to connect themselves in clean, geometric, living chips. And had electron microscopy shots to prove it.

I felt my perfect solitude. A few fluorescent highlights here and there kept alive the odd captive plant. As I do when I'm alone, I hummed to myself. Only now, in the distance, I began to hear the music I'd been humming. Mozart, the Clarinet Concerto, middle movement. The one that C. had thought the most pained palliative in creation.

Here, in the deserted, empirical dark, years too late, I heard that she was right. In the Center, where no birds sang, this sound, slowed to a near stop, resigned all hope of ever saying just what its resignation carried. At this impossible hour, when even the most inexorable researchers had gone home to whatever family they could muster for themselves, only music stayed behind to prove the ravishing irrelevance of research.

The clarinet and orchestra exchanged phrases, elaborating on the ongoing expansion, unfolding, inhaling beyond capacity like the lungs of a patriarch wedging open the air after being told of the death of his last great-grandchild. The endless phrase spoke of how you reach an age when anything you might answer would not be worth asking.

Who in all this restless measurement had time for so infinite an aside? The late-night auditor, whoever he was, must have thought he listened alone. Even the cleaning crew had gone. The earliest hard-core hackers would not stumble in to their predawn keyboarding for another two hours.

Ordinarily, any sound would have driven me to an emergency exit. Now I gravitated to the source, audiotropic, to secure the forsaken signal.

The tune grew more real. It approached the asymptote of live performance. The next turn of the corridor maze would flush out a covey of tuxedoed instrumentalists. The thread of sound led me to an office down a spur hallway I did not know existed. The cell door stood wide open. The phrase issued from it as if from the wellspring of all improvisation.

The music's hopeless peace emboldened me. I came alongside the door and looked in. Except for the sound, the room was deserted. I bathed in the emptiness. Heaps of equipment, much of it bare boards and components, shimmered in the dark. Some of these devices produced this ethereal interpretation, while others only absorbed and contemplated it.

From a cave of instruments in the corner, light glinted off two small surfaces. What I had taken to be two flat LCD panels flickered into a pair of near-opaque glasses. The creature behind them now gazed at me without registering anything. Archimedes looking up languidly at the Roman soldier about to run him through: Don't disturb my circles.

The head attached to these glasses peaked in a balding dome. From freakish frontal lobes it tapered away to nothing at the temples only to erupt again in a monstrous beak. Even after I oriented the image, the face shocked me.

The man stretched out on a reclining office chair. His head flung itself back against a flatbed scanner. His feet kicked up on a mountain of offprints. Even horizontal like this, he could not have been longer than five and a half feet. Yet his doe-colored jacket and white oxford button-down crept up his arms as if the knit were unraveling.

I'd never seen this man before, either in these halls or anywhere else. Not even I could forget such a figure. He must have been at least sixty, in earth years. To judge by his pallor, the fellow avoided all contact with natural light. His puzzled blink suggested that he avoided human contact, too, to the extent of his abilities.

Without taking his eyes from me, he continued his series of infinitesimal hand adjustments in the space in front of him. He pushed a suite of frictionless hockey pucks about the wired surface of his desk. The rink looked like a cross between an acupuncture map and a player piano roll. Between the music and these arcane hand motions, I couldn't decide who led and who followed.

The conductor gestured across his electronic score, locking stares with me until the slow movement played itself out. Discord and resolve, the devastating rasp of reed, the musical sequence pushing against the limits of my cranial sounding post, a grace too huge and slow for understanding.

The lemur-like man appraised me, unselfconscious. We made interstellar contact, paralyzed by the mutual knowledge that any attempt to communicate would be culture-bound. Worse than meaningless.

Silence, after such sound, grew unbearable. I broke first. "Mozart," I said. Having begun to make a fool of myself, I pressed on and completed the job. "K. # 622. What happened to the finale?"

The man's hands stopped and laced themselves behind his head. He snorted out the side of his mouth, as if flossing the idea from between his teeth. "No finale. We deal exclusively with middles here."

He picked up the hockey pucks and started to shuffle them again. Music rose from the aural grave. The clarinet recommenced its paralyzing simplicity. That perfect phrase breathed in and out just as before, steeped in stabbing acceptance. But something different unfolded this time. A slower, more forlorn rumor. Where the difference lay, there was no saying.

The owl-man made his mechanical adjustments, as if he dreamed this music himself, out of a computational hurdy-gurdy. He flicked switches and fiddled with sliders. My shadow must have snagged the edge of his retina, because he looked up, surprised to see me still standing in the doorway. "Thank you for the little chat," he said. "Good night."

I bobbed my head in ridiculous acquiescence and backed down the hall, dismissed to safety.

I don't know what I expected, really. Civility, perhaps. Acknowledgment. An exchange of names. All the social niceties that I'd avoided so studiously since my Dunkirk back here. I obsessed for a day and a half, inventing ironic, dry comebacks. In my head, I let the man know in no uncertain terms that I was neither a pest nor ludicrous.

Under cover of daylight, I returned to pinch his name off the office door. Philip Lentz: a name as Palladian as the man was misshapen. The Center's promotional brochure said he explored cognitive economies through the use of neural networks. The pamphlet withheld even the foggiest idea of what this might mean.

For years, back before I saw the photograph that led to my retirement from software, I'd made a living by writing code. But a neural net, I learned in browsing the web, resembled nothing I'd ever programmed in my coding days. Neural networkers no longer wrote out procedures or specified machine behaviors. They dispensed with comprehensive flowcharts and instructions. Rather, they used a mass of separate processors to simulate connected brain cells. They taught communities of these independent, decision-making units how to modify their own connections. Then they stepped back and watched their synthetic neurons sort and associate external stimuli.

Each of these neurodes connected to several others, perhaps even to all other neurodes in the net. When one fired, it sent a signal down along its variously weighted links. A receiving neurode added this signal's weight to its other continuous inputs. It tested the composite

14

signal, sometimes with fuzzy logic, against a shifting threshold. Fire or not? Surprises emerged with scaling up the switchboard.

Nowhere did the programmer determine the outcome. She wrote no algorithm. The decisions of these simulated cells arose from their own internal and continuously changing states.

Each decision to fire sent a new signal rippling through the electronic net. More: firings looped back into the net, resetting the signal weights and firing thresholds. The tide of firings bound the whole chaotically together. By strengthening or weakening its own synapses, the tangle of junctions could remember. At grosser levels, the net mimicked and—who knew?—perhaps reenacted associative learning.

Neural networkers grouped their squads of faked-up cells together in layers. An input layer fronted on the boundless outdoors. Across the connective brambles, an opposite squad formed the door where the ghost in the machine got out. Between these, the tool kit of simulated thought. In the so-called hidden layers lay all the knotted space where the net, and networkers like Lentz, associated.

The field went by the nickname of connectionism. Piqued, I subscribed to the web's discussion group on the subject. Reading made good counterpoint to my final rewrite. It was also a great day-waster and delaying tactic. Studying postponed the time when I'd no longer have any rewrite to counterpoint.

Now, whenever I logged on to the system, a new round of notes on the topic greeted me from all quarters. Several of my fellow visitors at the Center took part, firing messages back and forth to intercontinental colleagues. But unless this Lentz signed on with a pseudonym, he seemed to cut a wide side step around the citizens band.

I followed the exchange. The regulars took on personalities. The Danish renegade. The Berkeley genius provocateur. Slow and Steady, respected co-authors, in constant battle with their archrival, Flash-in-the-Pan. Some speculated. Others graciously deflated. I saw myself as a character in this endless professional convention: the Literary Lurker. Novice symposium dabbler, who no one knew was there. But even lurking left a signature.

I learned that networks were not even programmed, in so many words. They were trained. Repeated inputs and parental feedback created an association and burned it in. Reading that fact tripped an association in *me*. The man had been sitting in his office after midnight, playing the same five minutes of Mozart again and again to an otherwise empty building. To a bank of machines.

This Lentz, I reasoned, had a neural network buried in that mountain of equipment. One that he was training to recognize beauty. One that would tell him, after repeated listenings, how that simple reed breathing made and unmade the shifting signal weights that triggered souls.

Some days later, the beak thrust itself into my office without knocking. Dr. Lentz stood upright even more precariously than he reclined. Even standing still, he listed like a marionette on a catamaran, my office door handle his rudder. Again the summer suit, the last scientist not giving congressional evidence to wear one. His skin had the pallor of a sixties educational TV host. He looked as if he'd taken self-tanning cream orally.

"Reclusive novelist living in the Netherlands?" His voice held more accusation than question. An allusion to a photo caption that had run in a major news weekly. I'd been captured in front of a stand of palms imported into the Sonora. The text beneath gave my life in thumbnail, now wrong on all three counts.

I launched my screen saver, to blot the incriminating text on my tube. He might have read it, even from his angle. Those eyes seemed set out on stalks.

"Yep. That's me."

"*Yep?* This is 'dazzlingly brilliant'? So tell me. What is it about the Dutch, anyway?"

"Excuse me?"

"They hang around your writing like dung beetles around a cholera ward. At least a cameo appearance in every book you've written. I mean: fifteen million tulip-sucking, clog-carving water wizards. So what? That's less than the population of greater New York."

He'd done his homework. And wanted me to know.

"Search me," I countered. "Accident. Pure coincidence."

"Nonsense. Fiction doesn't permit accident. And what little coincidence it does put up with is far from pure. Why don't you write about real countries? The whole global community is out there, chain-dragging on its own economic exhaust pipe. It's North against South, you know. Haves versus have-nots. How about a swing through the tropics? The lands of the 6 percent population growths and the two-hundred-dollar-a-year incomes?"

I gestured toward the hard disk on my desk where my latest sat, all but finished. "There's a bit in the new one . . ."

He waved me off. "Doubtless the Dutch are in attendance as well."

Two words, right at the end. The little Frank girl's *Dear Kitty*. He gloated. I looked away.

"You and your precious bourgeois queendoms. Why should I care? Why should I pay twenty-five dollars—"

"Only thirteen in paperback." The joke fell flat. At that point I would have given him the complete works at cost, to get him out of my office.

"Twenty-five dollars to read about a negligible nation whose unit of currency sounds like something you'd use to pay the tinker or cobbler."

"Well, they did rule the world once."

"For what—twenty years? The Golden Age." He paced in place. The eye-darting edginess started to get on my nerves. I shoved the spare chair at him. He sat, smirking.

"The great middlemen, your Dutchmen. Bought and sold all races, colors, and creeds. Tell me. How does it feel to live in a country that peaked three centuries ago?"

"I haven't a clue." I hadn't yet decided how it felt to grow up in a country that peaked three years before I tried to bail out.

I didn't relish the idea of an insult match with a stranger. Besides, I'd already reached the same conclusion he had; this cognitive economist who had no more than browsed my novels, standing in front of the fiction "P"s at the University bookstore. He was right. It was time to give the Dutch a rest. After my latest, I planned to put them down for the count.

But then, my plan for the next time out was to pack in everything. Not just the exotic bits, the color travelogue. I meant to retire my whole mother tongue.

In the meantime, I figured I might at least bait this scientist. I wasn't doing anything else that afternoon anyway. Nothing but writing.

"They've had more than their share of world-class painters and composers, for a negligible country."

"Oh, please, Mr. Powers. European-class. The *world*, it may stun you to learn, is predominantly black-haired. A plurality of those live without adequate shelter and would use *The Anatomy Lesson of Dr. Tulp* as a canvas roof patch if they could."

"And your Mozart?" I don't usually like cheap counterattacks, but the man asked for it.

He shrugged. "The piece happened to be handy. A small fraction of the available repertoire. Replaceable, I assure you." He stood and strode to my whiteboard. Without asking, he erased the text I'd written there and began to draw a matrix of hollow boxes. "All right. I'll grant you the pretty pictures and a few good tunes. But they've never amounted to much in the novel-writing department, have they?"

"That's the fault of translation."

"Not the limits of that expectorant Low German dialect? An orthography to write home about. And crikey! How do you deal with that syntax? An even by native speakers not until the ultimate grammatical arrival capable of being unraveled word order that one's brain in ever more excruciatingly elaborate cortical knots trivially can tie."

His burlesque was note-perfect. He tore it off, at tempo. It chilled me. How much homework had the man done? Could a cognitive linguist parody a language he didn't speak? I didn't want to know. I wouldn't have answered him in kind then, even if he switched over.

I still dreamed in that language. It ruined me for English. Gone for over half a year, I still saw the spire of the Utrecht Dom each time I walked under the Center's tower. I could not shake free from a place I never felt at home in. And all because of some dead Polish kid who attended the next grade school down from my father's. A kid who didn't know the Netherlands from the East Indies.

I'd formed an impression of the place in a dank Chicago suburban basement late in winter at age eight. A child's account of the flood that ravaged Zeeland shortly before I was born turned real in my head. That's what it means to be eight. Words haven't yet separated from their fatal content. For a week and a half, I saw people camped everywhere on top of step-gabled houses, island traumas in ever-rising water.

This was my unshakable image of a place I thought would never be more than an image to me. The word "Holland" filled me with autumnal, diluvian disaster. And this sense persisted, even after living for years as far inland as reachable, high up in the Dutch mountains.

On the day I read that book, sixty-seven blocks north of the Loop, C. was sixty-seven blocks south, lashing fast another imaginary Netherlands altogether. Everyone has a secret low country of the heart where they should have been born. C. missed hers by a year and an accumulation of ripples.

C. was more Dutch when I met her in U. than she became later, after she expatriated. At twenty-five, she learned that she could claim citizenship anytime before the age of thirty. It was as if Belonging lay in some ivory-inlaid credenza in the Hague, waiting to be opened before expiration date. Hers for free, by virtue of being born of Dutch parents. Even parents who had halfheartedly jumped the schooner of state. Once she claimed her birthright, displacement became total.

I could trace the chain of dislocation back to a nineteen-year-old Polish boy I didn't know from Adam. A South Side kid who should never have left home. His name clustered with lots of recalcitrant Slavic consonants. To me, it was unique. For all I know, the same surname takes up a column and a half of the Cicero phone book. The boy's own dislocation must have begun at least a generation before. But I did not know his particulars.

His home, however transient, was not Chicago per se but that emulation of Kraków that interwar Poles ran on the southwest side of former Fort Dearborn. When Armageddon reached as far as the Back of the Yards, the boy volunteered. His family sent him back to liberate a native land he'd seen only in imagination. Before he went, he married. One married young in those days, quick and willfully, to preempt just what happened to him.

The boy was called Eddie. I named my father and a hybrid me after him in my second book.

Eddie and his war bride lived together for two electric bills at the most. Then he vanished. He was killed in that extended tank battle that ran from the forests of eastern Belgium up through Limburg into Nijmegen and Arnhem. He never lived long enough to be anything but a story. This one.

He left behind only one possession. That is, his adopted government left it: one of those pristine stone crosses in one of those endless diffraction-pattern cemeteries that roll across the forgetting countryside. The Low Countries specialize in them.

When war abated again, someone had to care for all the crosses. Cemeteries had proliferated faster than babies, and it came time to adopt them. Village women throughout Limburg enlisted to tend to Margraten. A still-young woman who had stood on a hill and watched Charlemagne's capital burn, who had once run out into the lane with a carving knife at reports of a village horse being strafed, adopted Eddie.

Instructions were simple. Keep the area trim, and perhaps place flowers on history's birthdays. The woman did this and more. She struck up a correspondence with the widow and the bewildered Gold Star mother. God knows in what language. The widow—who knew all along she'd be left with nothing but unreadable letters from foreigners—spoke English and Polish. The mother spoke only Polish. The volunteer grave-tender spoke only Limburgs dialect and that imposed foreign language, Dutch.

The Netherlands was as mythical to the Americans as the States were to the Limburger. But somehow they communicated. Widow and mother visited the grave. They stayed with the grave's adopter, her husband, and their two babies. The Chicago Poles told the young family that if they ever wanted to emigrate to the blessed hemisphere, they had sponsors.

Limburg had never been generous, and war payments, as always, fell on the already destitute. The gravekeeper's husband, a railroad man, declared that he belonged to any country that would feed him. And so a basement room in Little Kraków became the family's country.

After a year, the immigrant wife could stand the New World no longer. She fled back to her beloved Limburg, her two young children in tow. The railroad man stayed, refusing to return home in disgrace. He wrote her letters, in his newly acquired, schoolbook English: "I'm here working. You know where you belong."

After six months, the woman dragged home to her basement nation. C.'s birth was her mother's consolation prize, the one good thing in an unlivable locale. They named C. for the dead boy's widow, who never remarried. After that first death, no room for another.

The family rented a house in a Lithuanian ghetto not far from the stockyards. Lives later, I stranded another, imaginary, Dutch immigrant family in that house. I built my written copy from the descriptions that C. fed me from memory. For two decades, C.'s family lived in that city, speaking to each other in secret phrases. You could say anything, anywhere, in those words. And no one but the displaced would understand you.

They kept themselves alive as exiles do: with rituals and recollections no longer recognizable to those who never left. C.'s mother raised the baby on accounts of a magic village called E. The nether-nether land that C. grew up on was peopled by scores of aunts and uncles and hundreds of cousins with archaic names and fairy-tale histories. Never tie your life to a woman with ten dozen first cousins. Never try to expatriate to a country where the currency is called a gulden.

C. tried. She had to. The image her mother wove of E. was more painfully imprinted in C. than any neighborhood she'd actually lived in. C. tried to reclaim that fabulous nation. And I tried to follow her.

"Oh, Beau!" she told me. "It's so beautiful there. It's like a balm on your heart to see it." And so it was, still. Bits and pieces, anyway. Here and there, isolated half-timbered villages poked out between new industrial terrains, like traces of fresco from under annihilating renovations.

21

C. returned to her E., went back for the first time. On her arrival, a restored citizen, she became an instant curio. She learned that she spoke a dialect frozen in time, steeped in expressions discarded a generation before. And she spoke this dead idiom with a Chicago accent, equated, by the townsfolk of E., with gangsters who had all been shot thirty years before C.'s parents learned their first textbook slang.

I tagged along in C.'s wake. And my first textbook sentence: *Nederland is een klein land.* A negligible land. A minuscule country that most people in America think lies somewhere in Scandinavia. Ruled the globe once, for two decades.

Adventure ended in further exile. I came back to the States and failed to recognize them. That *klein land* came back with me, infesting my insides like a medfly slipped past customs. Its national anthem, the most beautiful in the world, with its absurd last line, "I have always been loyal to the king of Spain," hurt me when I caught myself humming it. The thought of those yellow trains, timed to the quarter minute, ruined me for further travel. The sight of an orange soccer jersey still cut into me with a boy's Goliath-killing hope, more cruel because not my boyhood. Syrup waffles in an import store hit me now like a wooden shoe in the chest.

Dutch was a shrapnel wound. Like C., I was a different person with that stranger's vocabulary in my mouth. I hated the sound of those words now. I would have forgotten them if I could. But I still said them to myself, when I needed the safety of secret languages. Each syllable aged me. I could no longer say what the simplest word meant. I'd never be rid of them, whatever my next book succeeded in killing off.

But I wasn't about to give Dr. Lentz the pleasure of this narrative. I didn't much like his type: the empiricist who thought the world outside his three variables worth no more than brilliant condescension. I had met too many of his sort at Center functions. They always ended up by telling me to adopt a pen name. It would do wonders for my sales.

Lentz stood at the whiteboard, connecting the hollow boxes with deft switchboard cables. I cleared my throat. "The Netherlands is one of the two or three places on earth where Western civilization almost works."

"Christ. Give me credit for a little intelligence." He answered without a moment's thought, without even turning around. "If you insist on harping on the Dutch, why don't you do the story of a handful of earnest Moluccan separatists who, lied to and betrayed by their old colonial whore of a mother, hijack a passenger train from Amsterdam to—"

"Don't worry," I told him. "They're history. I'll never mention them in print again."

After that, we left each other alone. When I next saw Lentz by accident in the corridors outside an unavoidable Center obligation, he greeted me in round tones. "Little Marcel! How are the words treating you?"

"Don't call me that. It's not clever."

"Who's being clever?"

"It's self-conscious and patronizing."

Lentz pulled back and pursed his lips. He contemplated finishing me in one swipe. Instead, he did a rapid about-face. "I'm sorry. That wasn't my intention. You see, I'm a bit of a social maladroit. We all are, in this pursuit. Comes with the turf. It's all of a piece, really." He swept his hands around himself the way a magician waves handkerchiefs over the body of a sequined assistant he is about to saw in half. "The myopia, the dwarfhood, the aggression, the affected brusqueness, the scoliosis, the know-it-all megalo—"

I'd noticed the kinked walk, but scoliosis never crossed my mind. He'd learned to mask it early. I was sorry I'd let him get under my skin. Even someone who has modeled the function of the inferior frontal gyrus might still be plagued by the monsters that gyrus modeled.

"Forget it," I said. "Everybody's a critic."

"I can imagine. Much to resent about your line of work. 'Nobody deserves to get away with life alive'?"

"That, and 'Write me the book I would have written.' "

"Universal envy. You folks are king of the cats, aren't you?"

"You're joking. Were, maybe. A hundred years ago. It's all movies and lit crit now."

"Well, my defrocked friend. What's it going to be?"

"I'm sorry? What's what going to . . . ? Dr. Lentz, I admit it. I can't always follow you."

"Do come on. The open parenthesis! What would you like me to call you?"

"How should I know? What's wrong with my given name?"

"A bit lacking in imagination for someone in your racket, aren't you?"

I felt twice burned in as many outings. I knew who I was dealing with now, in any event. "I don't care. Call me whatever you please, Engineer."

A low blow, but my own. Philip Lentz smiled, warmly enough for me to see that half his bottom teeth were missing. The remainders had drifted together to cover up the absence.

"Little Marcel, I'm not sure I like you."

He was quoting again, some dialogue of mine I'd forgotten having written. I said what I had to, what I was already scripted to say. "The pleasure's mutual, Engineer."

Lentz's peace offering came the next week, in my mailbox. He left me a much-thumbed-through short-story collection. He'd affixed a stick-on to a Mishima piece called "Patriotism." In the story, a young husband and wife kill themselves in ravishing detail. The note said: "I hope you get as much pleasure out of this as I did." The signature read, "With sincere apologies, Engineer."

As I skimmed the astonishing transcript, I wondered if he was trashing me yet again. This piece was to be my how-to. A suicide manual for the honor-besmirched author.

Not that I needed any anthology piece to make me want to call it a day. My final revision on the wandering kids was all but done. I was just dragging my heels until New York's deadline. Although they had me under contract for one more book after this one, a well-timed Mishima on my part would have delighted New York and put me, however briefly, on what my editor referred to as the List.

On each of my previous three novelistic tries, some further premise had always presented itself by this point. What the close of the current book did not resolve spilled over into the next. Now, although I spent days doing nothing but listening, the silence at the other end sounded like one of those callers who hadn't the courtesy to tell you they'd dialed a wrong number before slamming down the receiver.

Contract aside, I wanted one more shot. My fourth was too bleak an interval to cadence on. The Blitz wasn't going to have the last word in my fiction, however realistic I wanted to learn how to be. I had one more novel coming to me. But all I could find was the first line.

I knew only that I wanted to write a send-off. My next book would have to start: "Picture a train heading south." The line felt ordained, as liberating as October azure. But I couldn't wrap myself around this opening and begin. I was stalled at departure, for the simple reason that I could do nothing with so perfect a lead sentence but compromise it by carrying it forward.

The words nagged at me, like a nursery refrain. I began to imagine it an unconscious allusion. It felt so unsponsored, I could not have invented it.

I searched the bandwidths, postponing further the hopes of a jump start. I did Boolean searches across incomprehensibly huge textbases. South, train, and picture, ANDed together, within a ten-word range of one another. I substituted every conceivable synonym for each term, verbal almosts piped in from hyperlinked thesauri. But if the world's infant digital nervous system knew anything about my mystery opening, it wasn't saying.

I wondered if my memory might not be going. Like a man who furiously scours the bathroom mirror for signs of recent hairline decampment, I'd test myself from one day to the next. I tried myself on the first lines of books I knew I'd read and those I thought I'd written.

Undeniable: my ability to recall was not what I remembered its having been. Soon I would forget even the lovely heft of forgetting. The command to picture was, like that departing train itself, heading south. The line sounded its last call over the PA, a Transalpine Intercity just pulling out of the station.

My brother Russie called, from Florida. He almost never did. He checked to see how I was surviving bachelorhood. I asked him if he remembered a book. Something our mother might have read to us once.

"Mom? *Our* mom? We talking about the same person?"

"Come on. She read to us all the time. She taught me how to read."

"Don't know about your mother, but mine used to surface-mount me to the cathode-ray tube."

"She did not. We were strictly rationed." The last children in America who had to ask to turn on the set.

"Maybe that was the case for you guys."

"Well, you were younger than we were," I conceded.

I could hear Russ's askance silence on the other end. Do we need to call the pros? Start the intervention? "Yeah, bro. I was younger than you."

I couldn't imagine where else the line might have come from. Imagine a route, stretching out leisurely to the south. The day is bracing. It should not be this crisp yet, this chilly or sere. The train eases to life. It builds steam. It stokes up, unfolding itself along that first great curve, and leaving becomes real.

No question: it left something chest-tightening behind, tracking out to the taunting horizon. The book I wanted to write, the book I must have heard somewhere in infancy, unrolled farther than I could see from the locomotive, even leaning out dangerously to look. That passage stretched out longer than love, longer than evasion, longer than membership in this life. It lingered like a first lesson. Outlasted even my need to pin down the broken memory and reveal it.

That sentence, the return leg of the northern line, tried to leap the tracks of desire. But it needed me in the tender. I was the free rider, allowed to hitch on to my phrase's urgent run provided I kept the throttle open and the boiler stoked. But the low-grade hammering on rail that haunted my livelong day dampened to a distant click the longer I failed it. I felt myself dropped off at a deserted siding, numb and clueless as to how I had arrived there.

I sent Lentz a return Post-it. The things were pernicious: just enough adhesive for a temporary stick. "Thanks for the present. No apologies necessary. But please: no more literature. What I need is offprints."

I had but to say the word, and offprints poured in. Lentz sent me articles he had written. He sent me pieces compiled by colleagues and competitors. He forwarded stuff almost a decade old, and submissions that had not yet seen the light of publication. He attached no more notes. If I wanted to read his work, he would not object. But he wasn't going to tutor me.

Neural nets, I learned, had a way of casting themselves over people. According to the miraculous drafts Lentz sent me, there was no hotter topic. Researchers across the whole spectrum of disciplines emptied deep pockets into the promising tangles of simulated brain.

In a previous life, I had brushed up against machine intelligence. For a few months, I wrote code that turned consumer goods artificially lucid. I worked for an outfit that wanted to make household devices savvy enough to anticipate needs that potential purchasers didn't even know they had.

I made appliances expert in their own use. I built the rule base and tuned the reasoning. I linked a table of possible machine states to a list of syllogisms that told the device how to respond in each case. I hooked the device to sensors that bathed in a stream of real-world data. These dispatches threaded a given appliance's inference engine like rats in a behaviorist's maze.

If the data found their way to an exit, they became conclusions.

All that remained was the gentle art of interface. I got the device to weigh the situation. I instructed it to say, "Hey! You sure you want to do that?" or "Let's try that again on 'Puree,' shall we?" Convincing the user was the delicate part, far harder than getting the device to reach its decision.

My expert systems couldn't be called intelligent. But they did get me thinking about what could be. I thought about the question for a long time, even after I jettisoned the commercial interests. What was memory? Where, if anywhere, did it reside? How did an idea look? Why was comprehension bred, or aesthetic taste, or temperament?

Predicates threaded my neural maze. After great inference, I came to the conclusion that I hadn't the foggiest idea what cognition was. Nobody did, and there seemed little prospect of that changing soon.

No tougher question existed. No *other*, either. If we knew the world only through synapses, how could we know the synapse? A brain tangled enough to tackle itself must be too tangled to tackle. Tough, too, to study the workings of a thing that you couldn't get at without breaking. I guess I gave up thinking about thought some time around my thirtieth birthday.

Something about the basic debate upset me. On the one hand, philosophers maintained that the only way into the conceptual prison was introspection. This drove empiricists up the cell wall. Tired of airy nothings, they spent their time amassing chaotic libraries of unrelated data down at neurochemical level.

The top-down thinkers fought back: because thought played a role in experimental design and interpretation, neuroscientists undercut their own efforts. Cognition compromised itself. Recursive by nature, mentation wasn't going to yield to measurement alone.

Cognitive science seemed to me deadlocked. But overnight, while I was away, everything changed. The impasse broke from both ends. Smart appliances kicked out the jambs. The low-level wetware workers came into instruments that allowed them to image the omelet without breaking an egg. At the same time, the top-down people hit upon their own leverage, the neural nets that Lentz's snarl of articles described. Connectionism.

The young connectionist Turks lived on a middle level, somewhere between the artificial-intelligence coders, who pursued mind's formal algorithms, and the snail-conditioners, who sought the structure and function of brain tissue itself. The Center's warrens sheltered all species. But in the halfway world of neural nets, the point man at this place seemed to be Dr. Philip Lentz.

The new field's heat generated its inevitable controversy. I sensed a defensive tone to many of Lentz's publications. Both the neural physiologists and the algorithmic formalists scoffed at connectionism. Granted, neural networks performed slick behaviors. But these were tricks, the opposition said. Novelties. Fancy pattern recognition. Simulacra without any legitimate, neurological analog. Whatever nets produced, it wasn't thought. Not even close, talk not of the cigar.

In his articles, Lentz took these accusations and ran with them. The brain was not a sequential, state-function processor, as the AI people had it. At the same time, it emerged to exceed the chemical sum passing through its neuronal vesicles. The brain was a model-maker, continuously rewritten by the thing it tried to model. Why not model *this*, and see what insights one might hook in to?

Having stumbled across connectionism, I now couldn't escape the word. I heard it in the corridors. I nursed it at Center seminars, seated in the back for a quick exit. I read about it throughout the worldwide electronic notefiles and in the stack of diversionary texts that replaced my nightly dose of forgotten fiction. Neural simulation's scent of the unprecedented diffused everywhere. I followed along, moving my lips like a child, while Lentz declared in print that we had shot the first rapids of inanimate thought.

Lentz described synthetic neurons that associated, learned, and judged, all without yet being cognizant. The next step, he predicted, would require only increased subtlety, greater speed, enhanced miniaturization, finer etching, denser webbing, larger interwoven communities, higher orders of connection, and more finely distributed horsepower.

The smartest appliance I ever assembled was no more than a slavish, lobotomized reflex. True, I got my goods to remember rudimentary things. But I had to envision those memories myself before I could implement them. There was no question of real learning, of behavior

29

fluid enough to change its rules while executing them. Formalizing even the deepest, most elusive knowledge was trivial compared to genuine cognition.

Somewhere between then and now, the idea of thought by artifice had come to life. And Lentz was one of its Geppettos.

My mind toyed with these shiny new cognitive artifacts as if they had just been dug up from the banks of the Tigris. In his most readable piece, Lentz related the account of a distant, academic colleague who had developed a macramé of artificial neurons. This one created such a stir even pseudo-documentary TV picked it up.

The creature consisted of three layers, stacked up like mica. Each bank contained around a hundred neurodes. At birth, its eighteen thousand synapses were weighted randomly. Its input layer read letters; its output produced sounds.

Its first attempt at articulation produced streams of gibberish phonemes, much like any newborn's. But after a few hours, its reading congealed. Its cycle of monotonous syllables clumped into recognizable word shapes. Each time a sound scored a chance hit, the connections making the match grew stronger. Those behind false sounds weakened and dispersed.

Repeated experience and selection taught these synapses their ABCs. The machine grew. It advanced from babbling infancy to verbal youth.

In half a day, the network progressed from "googoo daadaa" to a thousand comprehensible words. In a week, it outstripped every early reader and began closing in on the average reading public. Three hundred simulated cells had learned to read aloud.

No one told it how. No one helped it plough through tough dough. The cell connections, like the gaps they emulated, taught themselves, with the aid of iterated reinforcement. Sounds that coincided with mother speech were praised. The bonds behind them tightened, closing in on remembrance like a grade-schooler approximating a square root. All other combinations died away in loneliness and neglect.

I read, in Lentz's account, how this network's designer peeked into the hidden layer of the adult machine. What he found surprised him. Buried in baroque systems of connection weights lay the rules of pronunciation. Complex math, cluster analysis, and n-dimensional vector work teased out the generalizations. The neurodes had learned that when two vowels go walking, the first one does the talking. And they'd stored the acquired insight in schemes so elegant that the net's maker claimed he could never have dreamed them up alone.

I read the journal write-ups. The science meant nothing to me. I couldn't follow it. Time and choice had left me science-blind. There was no way for me to verify if the talking box possessed any breakthrough significance. By all accounts, its biological validity was marginal at best. And God knew the thing did not come close to real thinking.

I cared for none of those qualifications. The story grabbed me. I wanted the *image*, the idea of that experiment. A box had learned how to read, powered by nothing more than a hidden, firing profusion. Neural cascade, trimmed by self-correction, eventually produced understandable words. All it needed was someone like Lentz to supply the occasional "Try again"s and "Good boy!"s.

My decade of letters to C. came back, fourth class. No note. But then, I didn't need one. Any explanation would just be something I would be obliged to send back in turn. I was supposed to follow suit, return hers. I told myself I would, as soon as I found a mailer and could get to the post office.

I laid the bundle in the back of a drawer, alongside the lock whose combination I'd forgotten. I told myself the scrap might be useful all the same. Useful, despite everything, in some other life some other me might someday live.

One day, tripping blindly into it, I finished my last novel. I made my final edit, and knew there was nothing left to change. I could not hang on to the story in good faith even a day longer. I printed the finished draft and packed it in the box my publishers had just used to send me the paperback copies of my previous one.

I sealed the carton with too much packing tape and sat staring at it where it lay on my kitchen counter. I thought of C.'s great-grandmother, who, before she turned twenty, had buried three such shoe boxes of stillborns in the grove above E. I asked myself who in their right mind would want to read an ornate, suffocating allegory about dying pedes at the end of history.

The calculation came a little late. I biked the box down to the post office and shipped it off to New York, book rate. New York had paid for this casket in advance. They couldn't afford to be depressed by what I'd done. The long science book had been a surprise success. They were hoping to manufacture a knock-off. I hadn't given them much of a chance.

The moment the manuscript left my hands, I went slack. I felt as if I'd been in regression analysis for three years. At long last, I had revived the moment of old trauma. But instead of catharsis, I felt nothing. Anesthesia.

What was I supposed to do for the rest of my life? The rest of the afternoon alone seemed unfillable. I went shopping. As always, retail left me with an ice-cream headache.

I figured I might write again, at least once, if the thing could start with that magic first line. But the train—that train I asked the reader to picture—was hung up at departure. It did its southward stint. Then it was gone, leaving me in that waiting room slated on the first timetable.

To figure out where the line was heading, I had to know where it had been. I felt I must have heard it out loud: the opener of a story someone read to me, or one I'd read to someone.

When C. and I lived in that decrepit efficiency in B., we used to read aloud to each other. We slept on the floor, on a reconditioned mattress we'd carried on our heads the five blocks from the Salvation Army. Our blanket was a pilling brown wool rug we called the bear.

We huddled under it that first midwinter, when the temperature at night dropped so low the thermometer went useless. After a point, the radiators packed it in. Even flat out, they couldn't keep pace with the chill blackness seeping through brick and plaster. The only thing that kept us, too, from giving in and going numb were the read-alouds. Then, neither of us wanted to be reader. That meant sticking hands above the covers to hold the book.

It would get so cold our mouths could not form the sounds printed on the page. We lay in bed, trying to warm each other, mumbling numbly by small candlelight—"Silver Blaze," *Benvenuto Cellini*—giggling at the absurd temperature, howling in pain at the touch of one another's frozen toes. We were the other's entire audience, euphoric, in the still heart of the arctic cold.

That's how I remembered it, in any case. Maybe we never spoke the notion out loud, but just lying there in the soft, frozen flow of words filled us with expectation. The world could not get this brittle, this severe and huge and silent, without its announcing something.

Somewhere, some shelf must still hold a book with broken black leather binding. A blank journal in which C. and I wrote the titles of all the books we read aloud to each other. If I could find that log, I thought, I might search down the first lines of every entry.

Our life in B. was a tender playact. That dismal rental, a South Sea island invented by an eighteenth-century engraver. C. guarded paintings at the Fine Arts. I wrote expert system routines. For pleasure, we etched a time line of the twentieth century onto the back of a used Teletype roll that we pasted around the top of the room. The Peace of Beijing. Marconi receives the letter "S" from across the Atlantic. Uzbekistan absorbed. Chanel invents Little Black Dress. The limbo becomes national dance craze.

We furnished our first nest with castoffs. Friends alerted us to an overstuffed chair that someone on the far side of the ballpark was, outrageously, throwing out. No three dishes matched. We owned one big-ticket item: a clock radio. Every morning, we woke to the broadcast calls of birds.

When we weren't reading to each other, we improvised a narrative. The courtyard outside our window was an autograph book of vignettes waiting to be cataloged. The scene below played out an endless penny merriment for our express amusement.

Cops rode by on horseback. Robbers rode by in their perennial hull-scraping Continentals. Parent-free children mined the bushes for dirt clumps to pop in their mouths. A conservatory student blew his sax out the open window, even in December. He threaded his way precariously up a chromatic octave, the cartoon music for seasickness.

That's how I would describe it in the book I still had no idea I would soon write. The player always, always missed the A-flat on the way up but hit it, by chance, on descending. "Something to do with gravity," C. joked.

Youngish adults in suits came by selling things. They represented strange and fascinating causes, each more pressing than the last. When the canvassers buzzed our intercom, we sometimes shed some small bills. Or we made the sound of no one home.

A heavy woman on workman's comp who walked with a cane hobbled by at regular intervals to air out her dog. The dog, Jena, who we decided was named after the battle where Hegel watched Napoleon rout Prussia, was even more fossilized than its owner. Jena would stand thick and motionless, halfway down the sidewalk, contemplating some spiritual prison break, never bothering to so much as tinkle. Its owner, whose name we never learned, waited in the doorway, repeatedly calling the beast with the curt panic of abandonment. The dog would gaze a lifetime at the horizon, then turn back in desolation.

I relayed these anecdotes to C., who lay in bed with her eyes closed, pretending to be blind and paralyzed, at the mercy of my accounts. I elaborated events for her, embroidering until the improbability of the whole human fabric made her smile. When she smiled, it always stunned me that I'd discovered her before anyone else had.

Even while we playacted it, I recognized that fantasy. It came from a collection of ghost stories that a famous editor had assembled before we were young.

I told C., from memory, the one about two men lying in the critical ward. The one, a heart patient, has the window bed. He spends all day weaving elaborate reports of the community outside to amuse his wardmate. He names all the characters: Mr. Rich. The Messenger Boy. The Lady with the Legs. He weaves this endless, dense novel for the quadriplegic in the next bed, who cannot see through the window from where he lies.

Then one night the window narrator has a heart attack. He convulses. He grapples for his medicine on the nightstand between the beds. The paralyzed man, seizing his chance at last to see this infinite world for himself, summons from nowhere one superhuman lunge and dashes the medicine to the floor.

When they move him to the emptied window bed the next day, all he can see is a brick wall.

"That's a great story," C. told me. In the icy dark, I felt her excitement. The world lay all in front of us. "I love that one. I'm afraid I'm going to have to kill you for it."

All I had to go on was that train. It might have come from anywhere, tracing a route so simple I would never win it back. I myself could not visualize the southbound freight. How could I ask a reader to picture it?

I paid bills, caught up on old correspondence. I did all my errands in the least efficient ways that my unconscious could devise. I discovered again just how long an evening can be without any media.

I searched my notebooks for all those plots that had seemed so pressing to me while I worked on something else. At one time I'd wanted to write the story of a man who made a living by imitating a statue. He would travel to all the capitals of the world, spray-paint himself silver, don a toga, and stand unnervingly still while admiring crowds ran past and threw coins into his cup. But now, when I watched this statue-man to see what happened, all he wanted to do was improve, hold stiller longer, until people passed without noticing.

I thought of putting a seventeen-year-old up in a cubicle on top of a flagpole just outside the Mall of America for 329 days, as a combined social protest and attempt to get into *Guinness*.

I found a preliminary sketch for a political light burlesque. Ma and Pa Kent, out in one of those states longer than it is wide, have a perfectly formed kid. The kid sleeps through nights, eats on schedule, and apologizes for burping. "Look at that boy crawl, Mother! He's going to be president." The comedy would trace the kid's supreme calling through Smallville High, Northwest Orthogonal State, and into the arms of the PACs and party hacks. I thought it might make a pleasant vacation.

Any one of these embryo ideas seemed workable. One might even have been good, had I been another person, with another person's care and patience. I kept browsing, thinking the right plot would leap out at me. When it didn't, I told myself that the key thing was to choose and get down to it. After all, wasn't a story *about* figuring out what the story was about?

Mornings passed when a sick knot in my stomach informed me that I would never write anything again. I had nothing left in me but the autobiography I'd refused from the start even to think about. My life threatened to grow as useless as a three-month-old computer magazine.

I asked myself whether, if you kept private long enough, you earned the right to a brief personal appearance in public. I recoiled from the idea. But there came a point when blaming things on innocent, third-person bystanders became a lie.

And after four times out, in a search for simplicity that had wound up producing complexities beyond reading, the question became: why go public at all?

I went to the Center and played the humanist fly on the wall. I read my notebooks. I diverted myself on the net.

Autumn came and flushed out the oppression of midwestern August. Sidewalks glazed over with cool rain. The shed leaves emitted a whiff of premature winter. Flocks gathered and wheeled in V's of retreat. We entered those two glorious weeks when U.'s weather made it seem that anyone alive could start again. Recover all lost ground.

The brisk, invigorating air crippled me with anticipation. I kept still and waited, thinking this time I might not scare off the imminence that always visited, the first week of the last season.

I lived on that refrain: picture a train. Picture a train heading south. Even garbled beyond recovery, my blast of turbine steam logged its nightly reprimand.

One night I went to a bar I'd never set foot in as an undergrad. I could count in a quarter of a byte the times I'd gone for a beer while in school here. Safeguarding the precious synapses. I'd worked so hard to keep them in perfect firing order. It had all seemed so important once.

In the Low Countries, I'd developed a taste for refermented fruit beers. These were as expensive here as they were ridiculous, in the land of the thin, frozen pilsner. But a *kriek* was a lot cheaper than a round-trip ticket. I ordered a bottle, which the bartender had to dust off.

I sat at the bar and nursed the drink, remembering those Belgian TV shows where the contestant tried to match dozens of beers to their rightful serving glasses. The last time I'd had a beer was in a Liège hole-in-the-wall that sold eleven hundred varieties, eighty on tap. The beer menu was book-length, with an index.

I imagined explaining the Lite concept to any of C.'s one hundred and twenty first cousins. I had difficulty getting past the word's spelling. Out the window of the bar, at a distance, I could see the university Quad. I pretended it was an unknown, astonishing Grote Markt I would go explore after I finished the cherry brew.

I made another narrative stab in my head. A thirty-five-year-old unemployed construction worker in Mechelen, once-mighty Gothic town shrunken to nothing, gets obsessed with completing the spire of the city's cathedral, originally slated to be the tallest in the world. My out-of-work day laborer, whom I took to calling Joris between sips, figures the building project has just been delayed several centuries. All he has to do is get the city to pauperize itself to put itself back on the ecclesiastical map.

The tale seemed immense with potential. The only catch was that it would play to an audience of exactly one.

The bar started filling. A frat boy, in his zeal to resuscitate a dead pitcher, collided with my shoulder. "Sorry, sir," he placated, in best commerce-major fashion.

The word was a slap in the face, the young's coded self-righteousness. People under twenty-one needed to work that fact into the conversation, even if the conversation consisted of two words. In this country, youth was a socially acceptable form of bragging.

A horrible mistake coming here, to this college bar, this college town. These were the same people who had gotten tanked every night while I broke my neck studying. They had stayed twenty, while I'd dissolved into middle age.

Even more depressing, I wasn't the only old guy in the place. At a table in the back, the smokers' section, a group of Center fellows took a rare break from experimentation to engage in what seemed, from my distance, heavy theoretical talk.

In their midst, looking even more sickly and implausible out of his idiom, my man Lentz gesticulated. His hands built and dismantled various violent tetrahedra in the air. He made some point that the half-dozen others at the table refuted with exasperation bordering on disgust. Science looked a lot like literary criticism, from across the room.

Lentz glanced my way, looking through me. We shared an awkwardness, each pretending not to have noticed the other. Each pretending the other hadn't spotted us pretending. I felt relieved that he didn't wave, but slighted.

After a while, the group's lone woman detached from the debate. She walked toward me. She was tall, amiable, dismayed, her freckles like constellations in a home planetarium. I had seen her in the corridors. I couldn't begin to guess how old she was. I'd lost all ability to gauge age.

In the time it took her to cross the room, I sketched a story about a professional guesser who learned to tell, within impossible limits of tolerance, the age, weight, height, and accumulated sorrow of anyone he met.

"I've come to recruit you," she announced, drawing up. "The good guys need help."

She dressed impeccably, forgoing the scientist's customary indifference to grooming. She wore tweed, with her ample hair rolled in one of those forties ingenue prows. The effect was uncannily archaic, as if she were about to announce that severing the corpus callosum cured epilepsy.

"Who are the good guys?"

She laughed. "Good question. I'm Diana Hartrick. I do associative representation formation in the hippocampus."

"Is that near here?"

I grinned as widely as possible, trying to pass off the idiocy as voluntary. I stuck out my hand, stupidly. In Limburg, one shakes hands early and often, with anything that holds still long enough.

"Little Marcel," I said. "Not doing much of anything, at present."

She took my hand, but her face clouded. She sucked in her mouth, a teacher unwilling to credit a bad report about a good pupil. "Now, why would you lie to me before you've even met me?"

At first I thought she meant the bit about my not working. Then the penny dropped. Dr. Hartrick, I figured, was a kind soul, but as literal as a lawyer giving the keynote at a libel convention.

"I'm sorry. That's Lentz's pet nickname for me." I gestured with my chin back toward her table.

"Oh. Him. He's why I came to get you. The man is on another rampage."

She leaned against the bar, resting a tote bag on her hip. From the side pocket, amid a sheaf of papers, issued an ancient softbound Viking Portable. Its spine was scored to pulp. I read the blurb at the top, despite the cover's being badly scuffed. "Not less than three times in his or her life should everyone read *Don Quixote* . . . in youth, middle age, and old age."

"May I?" I indicated the book.

She passed the book to me with a bemused patience long used to eccentric requests.

I flipped the book over. I opened to the copyright page. Nine-hundred-page books cost $1.85 when I was twelve. It didn't seem possible. I turned to the First Sally. *In a village of La Mancha the name of which I have no desire to recall* . . .

These few words spread like truth serum through me. I was fifteen again, and working up the courage to tell the Egyptian empress who sat in front of me in sophomore humanities that the hair on the back of her neck stopped my breath to look at.

I read then, everything I could lay hands on. Reading was my virgin continent. I read instantly upon awakening, and was still at it well past the hour that consciousness shut down. I read for nothing, for a pleasure difficult to describe and impossible afterward to recover.

Those sixteen words from Chapter One bogged me down in old amber. Before the end of the clause, I felt mired as a Cambrian bug in molasses memory. The First Sally, a second time: it sicked a pack of ghosts on me as brutal as the ones hounding the overread Don.

I shut the volume before the rest could get out. "Thanks. That's all I needed to check."

Hartrick took the book and slipped it back into her bag without comment. "Are you going to suit up and help us do battle?"

Her words came out softly, without any of that self-effacing edge of junior faculty under the gun. In one phrase, she grew older, drier. I'd misjudged her earnestness. *I* was the lawyer, the literal fool who'd missed the joke.

I imagined that her line of work lent her this presence. When you see up close the countless subsystems it takes to place an image into the permanent buffer, when you measure the loop that image makes on its way to being retained, you temper yourself against the definitive. You go humble, understated, wry.

I pictured what it felt like to see the organ at work, its cartoon flickers pasted up on a PET scan. You flash a world in front of your subject's eyes and watch the watercolor washes splash around the temporal lobe, fixing that world in a holdable shorthand. This woman traced the process in real time, the mental palette exploding in desperate semaphores, trying to convince itself that the fleet whose capture it signals hasn't slipped off in night fog.

Every postmodern postsolipsist, I thought, should do a postfrontal neurology stint. The most agile of them would, like this careful woman, take to weighing the violence in their every predicate. Once they saw the bewilderingly complex fiber in its impossible live weave, theorists would forever opt for the humblest, least-obtrusive sentence allowed them.

"I'm afraid my doublet's in the wash."

She smiled, generosity itself. "Come on," she insisted. "We need somebody who can outtalk him."

I followed her back to the Center's table. Lentz was well into introducing me by the time we two drew up.

"Here's our Nonresident-in-Residence. Marcel, meet Gupta, Chen, Keluga, and Plover. You appear to be chummy with Hartrick already. Everyone knows Marcel, the Dutchman. By reputation, anyway. Does anyone actually read those things of yours?"

I smiled. "I'm the wrong person to ask."

"Your mother's read them?"

"She says she has."

"Marcel writes Books," Lentz glossed, for nobody. "Watch what you say. We're all going to end up immortalized."

The pitcher of watery pilsner on the table had done nothing for his aggression. Tonight, though, his fight was with his colleagues. I was just a convenient sparring dummy, tangent to the main event.

I sat down. The table crackled. Talk had died away to wary philosophical sparks, now that the hard data had been expended all around. My presence threw a damper on the charged colloquium. Everyone reverted to good behavior.

Of the group, I'd met only Ram Gupta, a perception researcher of international reputation. His recent passage through Immigration could not have been choppier. The airport officer assumed this brownskin meant to go feral the minute anyone let him in the country. The epic humiliation seemed not to have perturbed Dr. Gupta in the least.

"*You* are making interesting points and you *too* are making interesting points," Ram sang, nodding by turns at Lentz and Harold Plover. "Could we not just leave it at that? Come, gentlemen. If we all stood up and got hit by a car as we walked out this door tonight, God forbid, would any of us want this conversation to be the . . . ?"

"I thought you people believed in eternal repetition," Lentz baited him.

Plover, a big, cotton-frayed Kodiak of a man, threw up his hands. "Terrific. Just what I need. I've already suffered an eternity of this nonsense in the last half hour alone."

"Harold, if you'd just come up with some fresh objections . . ."

"We can't level any fresh objections, 'cause we got no data." Keluga, a scrubbed blond boy of about twelve, searched the circle of faces for approval. Eager grad student's night out with the grownups.

"Data?" Lentz minced. "Oh, by all means. Hartrick will be happy to shave up several hundred simian forebrains for us to run some trials. That ought to resolve the question, once and for all."

"You cut up monkeys?" I whispered to Diana. "Rhesus pieces?" I sided with Ram. Even absurdity beat public ugliness.

Lentz snorted. "Marcel, we're going to give you a seven out of a thousand for that. One more such outburst and you have to go back and sit with the poets."

"Oh, leave him be," Plover mumbled into his cups. "It was funny."

"Don't blame me," I said. "I got it from a friend at Cal Tech."

Hartrick poured herself two fingers of foam in the bottom of a fluted glass. "You're straying into metaphysics, Philip. All the data in the world couldn't prove or disprove those kinds of claims."

"What on earth are you drinking?" Plover asked me. I'd brought along my *kriek*, unwilling to part with even the dregs of a liquid that came to about half a dollar a swallow.

"It's a Dark Lite," I said.

"It smells like vinegar cough syrup."

"Marcel's just indulging a little self-pitying nostalgia. The cakes-and-tea thing. Watch out he doesn't get sick. If he throws up, we're going to have a million and a half words all over the table."

"Would you listen to this creep?" Plover railed. "Why do we let him do this to us?" He shook his head at me. "Don't mind him. He gets like that, even without the two beers."

I assured Plover with a glance that Lentz and I were acquainted.

Lentz, a general fighting on many fronts, engaged the nearest comer. "You're the one playing the metaphysician, Dr. Di."

" 'Dr. Di'! Of all the insulting, sexist—" Plover threw his hands up again. He forgot to release his glass before doing so, and a fair amount of beer ended up on the wall behind him.

Lentz talked through the commotion of cleanup. "*You* are the ones evoking mystic mumbo jumbo. Is the problem computable in finite time? That's all I want to know. Is the brain an organ or isn't it? Don't throw this 'irreducible emergent profusion' malarkey at me. Next thing you know, you're going to be postulating the existence of a soul."

Hartrick rolled her eyes. "Not in your case, Philip." Her eyes came to rest on me. "See what I mean? Care to bail us out?"

"Remember Winner and Gardner?" Ram asked, still hoping to distract everyone from their sought-for conflict. "The piece on comprehension of metaphor, in *Brain*? Asked to choose the correct picture for 'give someone a hand,' many right-hemisphere-damaged patients picked the one showing a palm on a platter."

Keluga blanched. "Ram, please. I'm still hitting the salsa."

"Somebody tell me what you people are talking about." I felt slightly lesioned myself.

"Oh *yes*." Lentz did a slow take in my direction. He slapped his thigh. "Of course. Little Marcel. You have an affiliation with—what's it called these days? The English Department?"

"They're sponsoring my residency here, yes."

"Tell us. What passes for knowledge in your so-called discipline? What does a student of English have to do to demonstrate acceptable reading comprehension?"

I shrugged. "Not a whole hell of a lot. Take some classes. Write some papers."

"That's all *you* had to do?"

"Oh. Well. Me. When I was a lad—"

"Shh, shh, everyone. The reclusive writer about whom nothing is known is about to tell us his personal history."

"Look. Do you want to hear this or not?"

"My. Pardon me. I had no idea we were so touchy."

"Lentz, your apologies are worse than your attacks."

"Amen," Diana cheered. "Don't let him bully you, Richard."

Lentz smiled. He folded his fingers in front of his mouth. He looked for a moment like Jacob Bronowski's evil twin. "Do go on."

I debated, then did. "When I was twenty-two, I took something called the Master's Comprehensive Exam. They gave us a list of titles. Up at the top of page 1 was 'Caedmon's Hymn.' Six pages later, it wound up with Richard Wright."

"Where did you go to school?" Harold Plover asked.

I gestured out the window, the Quad beyond. My face flushed with shame. I'd failed to swim clear of the wreck.

"This list," Lentz persisted. "What happened then?"

"Then we sat for two days and answered questions. One each in six historical sections."

"What kind of questions?"

"Oh, anything. We'd do two hours of IDs. You know. 'Hand in hand with wandering steps and slow . . .' Name the author, work, location, and significance."

"Okay, so maybe I *won't* change fields." Keluga's crack fell flat.

Plover waved his bear paws again. "Wait a minute. I know this one. The end of *Paradise Lost*?"

"Harold," Lentz minced. "You've missed your calling."

"Then we did a few essays. 'Discuss the idea of the Frontier and its tragic consequences in four of the following six writers.' "

"What questions did you answer?" Lentz quizzed.

I shrugged. Out the side of my mouth, I made a little grad-student raspberry.

"Hold on. This was only a dozen years ago. And you remember . . . ?"

I ringed my thumb and forefinger, held the O up for public view. Lentz looked around the table in triumph.

"I suppose it would come back to me if I tried."

"Heavens, Marcel. Don't do that."

"Can I ask you something?" Keluga interjected. "I read somewhere that you studied physics . . ."

"As an undergrad. You read that? You people are supposed to be reading technical journals. Where the hell is the Two Cultures split when you need it?"

"What happened?"

"To what?"

"To physics."

"It's a long story."

Lentz cackled. "Don't press the man, Keluga. He's told every paper in the country that he doesn't like to talk about himself. About this list, Powers. You think you can find a copy somewhere?"

"Oh, the departmental files have scores of them."

Lentz looked about the table, his neck flared in challenge. "Anyone object to using this list as a test domain?"

Plover looked pissed. Hartrick hung her head. Ram began fidgeting in distress. Chen, who'd said nothing since I sat down, smiled uncertainly, at sea. Keluga was relishing the squabble, the way a kid might delight in seeing his parents drunk.

"Test of what?" I asked, as politely as possible.

"We're going to teach a machine how to read your list."

The words floored me. "You can *do* that?"

Plover scowled at Hartrick. "I thought you said you were going to bring back reinforcements."

Hartrick showed her palms, helpless. The token humanist had let them down.

Lentz inspected his nails. "As you see, what we can and cannot do is a matter of some difference of opinion."

Chen came to life. "It's to exaggerate," he said. Or perhaps, "That's too exaggerated." His English was impressionistic at best. "We do not have text analysis yet. We are working, but we do not have. Simple sentence group, yes. Metaphor, complex syntax: far from. Decades!"

He attached his attention to the technical edge of Lentz's bombshell. But I doubted Chen followed the charged subtext that the others were pitched in. I'd just started to pick up on what was at stake myself. And I'd passed the reading exam years ago.

"Chen, Chen. One of the quickest intellects in formal symbol-system heuristics." Lentz blessed him, fingers bent. "And still a step behind."

"Philip," Diana warned. She would pounce, if pushed. Tenure or no tenure. "Hyun? How long have you been in the country?"

"Four years." He paused to consider the implication. "About a piece in *Journal of Cognitive Neuroscience* I tell you anything. No problem. What you want to know? But the first page of a big-print, supermarket, paperbacked love story? Forget it!"

We all laughed, each for our own reasons. After four years in the Netherlands, I would have been reduced to tears of frustration by such a conversation.

Ram was first to turn laughter into speech. "I am constantly getting complimented on my English by people who don't realize it is my first language."

"Would *you* sit this Master's Comp thing?" Plover asked him.

"Don't be kidding me. I mean, who is this Milton fellow to me, anyway?"

A moment of deflation all around suggested that Lentz's fantasy had been vanquished. He'd been caught in an undergraduate indulgence and forced to own up.

Plover sighed. "Well, Philip, I'm afraid it's back to real science with you." He raised his glass in a closing toast, and sipped.

"On the contrary. We're going to build a device that will be able to comment on any text on Marcel's six-page list."

"Oh, for God's sake!" Plover spit. "I've had it. The man's just provoking us."

Diana laid a hand on his shoulder to calm him. "And doing a fair job."

"We shouldn't even humor him."

"Youngsters." Lentz's wave included Keluga and me. Generous with the term. "Children, I give you radical skepticism at its finest."

"All right, then. Okay." Plover's tone rose. He pushed up his sleeves and loosened his collar. "Put your money where your mouth is."

Chen coughed a sharp monosyllable. It might have been a laugh. "Interesting phrase. Could your machine—?"

"Harold. We will do this thing, and do it with existing hardware, in no longer than—Marcel, how long are we to be graced with your fair presence?"

I looked at my watch. "What time is it now?" Nobody laughed. It must have been my timing.

I said that I had about ten months before I'd need to fabricate a real life. Lentz looked concerned. "It will be a rush job, but never mind. In ten months we'll have a neural net that can interpret any passage on the Master's list. Harold's choice. And its commentary will be at least as smooth as that of a twenty-two-year-old human."

Plover erupted. "Philip! You can't mean this. What about your work?"

"I've worked enough for one lifetime. Besides, wouldn't this have some professional interest, if we can carry it off?"

Plover glanced around the table. A last appeal. He hooked my eyes. His looked infinitely sad, afraid of forgetting what they were alarmed about. *Say something*, they urged. *This is absurd.*

"How are you going to evaluate?" I asked. Just crediting the proposal knocked Plover down another peg.

Lentz hunched his lip. "Standard Turing Test. Double-blind.

Black-box both respondents. Give them each x hours to type out an answer."

"With Richard here as the guest literary judge?" Diana asked as if, for all the disappointment I had caused them, I might still be the last hope of the good.

Lentz coughed in mid-swig. "Not on your life. Powers here is going to be my research assistant. Who did you think I meant by 'we'?"

"We thought you were using the royal plural, Philip," Plover said. "Like you usually do."

Lentz condescended to address me. "You in? Or did you have something better to do?"

The world had enough novels. Certain writers were best paid to keep their fields out of production.

"Ten months? No. I wasn't doing much of anything." I spoke the words and betrayed my genus.

Plover, pushed to exasperation, cut bait. "All right, you two. Throw your lives away. I can't stop you." Harold, I decided, had at least one teenaged child.

Hartrick refused to capitulate. "Ram will judge," she said. Ram looked nonplussed. "He's as close to a disinterested, objective third party as we're going to get."

"I tell you, I don't know this Milton chap from Adam."

"That's your qualification. We'll name the human opposition when time comes. Meanwhile, what are the stakes?"

Lentz grew thoughtful. The vexatious child, called to account. "If we win, Harold has to give up his non-computational emergent Berkeley Zen bullshit."

The table sucked in its collective breath. Plover just snickered. "If you win, we'll *all* be getting pink slips. The whole thing is just too witless. Kindergarten. Mechanistic make-believe. I don't know what you're up to, Lentz. But you're gonna get me to bite. I'll bet the farm."

"And if you lose?" Diana enunciated, through a thin grin. She meant to extract casuistry's penalty in advance.

"If we lose, we'll give you a public retraction. A full apology, in print. The signed disgrace of your choice."

"Harold! Did you hear that? We finally have the man where we want him. Philip, you must be slipping."

"It's a trick," Keluga pronounced.

Lentz shook his head. "No trick."

"Of course it's a trick," Plover told the future's assembled jury. "But it just might be a trick worth paying to see."

"Too exaggerated," Chen said. He shook his head and smiled. He seemed not to realize that the deal had already been struck.

Diana pulled out her *Portable Cervantes* and read aloud the random sentence that fell under her bookmark. An illustration of the futility that this abrasive man and I were about to embark on. I can't remember the sentence. Out of context, I couldn't make heads or tails of it.

"Harold," she said. "If this huckster is right . . ." She elbowed Lentz in the ribs. I didn't think he would brook being touched by another human, but he did. "If we're really at the point where we can formalize . . ."

Plover raised an eyebrow. "Yes?"

"If they get their creature to read, do I still have to slog through this?"

Plover cast his head back, dignified in affront. "Yes. Of course."

"All of it?"

"If you want to remain friends."

She stuffed the paperback back into her handbag. She buckled in pantomime under its weight.

Plover took pity. "You can skim Part Two."

"Don't strain yourself," Lentz advised. "We'll beat you to it."

I remember thinking: thank God *Don Quixote* was not on the List. At least that one was a translation.

C. was a student of mine in the very first freshman composition course I ever taught at U. We were only two years apart in age. I was young for a master's candidate and she was an older transfer student, forced by unyielding rules into taking a course she didn't need.

She was late for my first class, an 8 a.m. session. I was not impressed. She seemed sluggish, not particularly bright or attractive or engaging. Inexorable, at best. She did, however, sit in the front row. If she contributed anything in those first few meetings, I don't remember.

But then, this was my first time teaching. I was more than a little wired, and it's a miracle I remember anything. Not nervous: what pedagogical theorists refer to as unprepared. Having spent the previous summer reading the grammar and usage texts, the style manual and reader for the course, I at least knew the material. What I didn't know was the college freshman, and whether she or he would put up with a spindly twenty-one-year-old in torn golf shirt, face not much clearer than their own, standing up in front of the chalkboard trying to conduct the discussion.

My impression of C. changed after the first assignment. I'd given, as preliminary topic, "Convince a total stranger that she would not want to grow up in your hometown." It seemed enough of an inversion of the standard composition theme that my fosters would have to think about it before plunging in and cranking out the usual suspect sentences.

The best paper belonged to a woman named Maya. I later learned that she was seven years older than I was and the mother of three. "Trust me. You don't want to grow up in East St. Louis," she wrote.

You get born in without being asked, and no amount of asking in the world is going to get you out again. There aren't but a few ways out of East St. Louis and those are all to places you don't want to be in even worse.

C.'s was the second most astonishing. She wrote lyrically, wistfully, brutally, about growing up in Chicago on an island one house wide. She wrote about waking up to the stink of slaughtered animals from the stockyards mixed with the heavy scent of chocolate from the neighborhood factory. She wrote of the neo-Nazi marches in the park where her father used to take her for walks. She wrote of the shifting neighborhood lines, the lava lamp of fear that made families bolt for invisible, redrawn borders every two years. She wrote of the lone newcomers from the wrong side of the tracks going door to door, begging people not to move out just because their family had moved in.

I read these two papers out loud, as a pair. The kids from the hopelessly affluent North Shore suburbs with too few movie theaters took notes.

By the end of my first semester, I learned that the problem with most student writing is not grammar. You learn the rules early on or you never get them. The real problem was belief. My eighteen-year-olds never believed that the reader was real, that they themselves were real, that the world's topics were real. That they had to *insist* as much, in so many words.

C. knew the real the way she knew how to breathe. After that first theme, there was nothing I could do for her but let her go.

For her research paper, C. wrote about Aspasia of Miletus. She'd gone through the standard occult stage in high school, past life analysis and all. In her student conference, she confessed to having once written a hundred-page memoir about her former life in Periclean Athens. That would be an invaluable primary source for her paper, I joked.

Talking, from the start, disconcerted us both. We probed about the edges of the inappropriate. I didn't dare to tell her how strange it felt, to feel so familiar with a stranger. Even that much would have been grounds for misconduct charges. But C. knew. C. always knew. She had a tap on what my mind made of the outside, even before I mapped it into words.

By mutual agreement, we kept mum and avoided incident. I teased her about her previous incarnations. "Do you have any documentary evidence?"

At her next conference, she produced a photo out of her backpack. "Documentary evidence of prior lives." Flirting, under deniability's cloak.

The picture was a small Brownie black-and-white. Bits of glued felt still adhered to its back. She'd torn it from an album, to give to me. A pudgy baby sat out in the backyard, 1961. The world had died away from that moment, and there was nothing left of it but this square miniature.

"The grass was prickling my butt. That's why I'm making the Khrushchev face. My parents threatened me. If I didn't stop crying, they were going to get the camera."

"You remember all that? You can't be more than two."

"I remember things long before that. When I was almost one, my mother took me back to the Netherlands for a visit. I was petting my aunt's dog while it was eating, and it bit me."

"Well, I suppose trauma . . ."

"You don't remember your first years?" Everyone did, her astonishment said. Everyone.

"I have trouble with yesterday's dinner. I find it hard to believe . . . What else can you remember? How about the first sentence you ever spoke?"

"Easy one," she said, gazing at the photo. " 'Good girl outside.' "

"Meaning?"

"Meaning I'd behaved myself, and now they had to turn me loose."

"I hope you're not counting on me to be your expert consultant on literature in English," I told Lentz in his anarchic office, a week after the bet. "It's been a hell of a long time."

He practiced that acerbic smirk on me. The one he didn't need to practice. "You mean you haven't kept faith with your illustrious progenitors?"

"I just can't quote them at length anymore."

"And why is that?"

I shrugged. "Can you quote at length from Babbage and Lady Ada?"

"What would you like to hear?" He stopped clicking on his coffee-stained keyboard and challenged me. "Never mind, Marcel. We don't need to know all about literature in English. The net is going to figure that out on its own. *We* already know something far more useful. We know Dr. Plover, our examiner. And we know Dr. Gupta, our distinguished judge."

"How is that going to help? You aren't thinking . . . ? We can't count on them to . . ."

"No, I don't suppose one can count on humans for anything. That's the beauty of the challenge."

"Okay. So what do we know about Harold?"

"He's a Shakespeare man. Soft on the Renaissance. Not a day goes by when he doesn't feel some nostalgic twinge about the fall of man."

"Lentz, you are truly merciless."

"It's a career asset."

"All right. So assume he dotes on Elizabethan—"

"We know. There's no assumption."

"But he knows that we know. We aren't going to bank everything on the hopes that he'll pick the predictable?"

"Marcel, never underestimate the baldness of the human heart. Didn't they teach you that in Famous Novelists School?"

"Right. That and 'jab and weave.' The Big Two for gaining and keeping an audience."

"Huh. You must have been out with the chicken pox that week."

In a real Turing Test, our black box, on the other end of a Teletype, would have to convince an examiner that it performed like a real mind. Operationally equivalent. Indistinguishable. Given any topic under the sun, our machine would have to fool the questioner, to pass for a human. A perfect, universal simulation of intelligence would, for all purposes, *be* intelligent.

I would never have signed on to such a pipe dream. But the severely limited version of the test seemed almost formulable, at first glance. We needed do only an infinitesimal fraction of what a full Turing Test passer would have to do. But it hit me only now. What we would have to do was still infinite.

"I fail to see how prepping the thing to say something bright about one sonnet is any easier than prepping it to interpret anything on the entire List."

"It isn't. In both cases, the 'thing' will need to know some *thing* about everything there is to know."

"You're too subtle for me, Engineer. Tell me how our knowledge of the opposition is going to help us, then."

"Plover is a harmless, sentimental slob. Ram will do anything in his power to avoid conflict. We just have to train a network whose essay answers will shatter their stale sensibilities, stop time, and banish their sense of loneliness."

"Oh. Well, if that's all . . ."

"Marcel, you're such a bloody coward. What are you so afraid of?"

"I'm afraid of wasting a year of my life."

"As opposed to . . . ?"

"I'm afraid of becoming a laughingstock, of pursuing some phantom that everyone else in your entire science considers—"

" 'Laughingstock.' What a wonderful word." He dug the keyboard out from the pile of papers he'd stacked on it. He addressed the workstation. "Do you suppose that's like 'rolling stock'? 'Summer stock'? 'Gunstock'? 'Take stock'? 'Wanderstock'?"

I flinched. "That's *wandelstok*. And I asked you not to do that. 'Walking stick' will do fine."

"Come, now. When was the last time you heard anyone use a 'walking stick'?"

He logged on to a remote host, called a program, and keyed a few parameters into it. Sifting through a tangle of equipment, he retrieved a microphone and turned it on. "Laughingstock, laughingstock," he repeated several times into the mike.

After a few seconds—digital eternity—a matte, sexless affect responded, "Their behavior made them the laughingstock of the . . ." I couldn't make out the last word. It must have been "community."

"Oh," I heard myself saying "Oh! We're not starting from zero, are we?"

"No. Not exactly zero."

He shut down the mike and straightened himself, as much as his body could straighten. He took off those bulletproof-glass spectacles. His face sat revealed in its full saurian severity. Removing the mask seemed to leave him expansive.

"Sometimes building a general-case model is easier than solving a specific-case problem. Also, because we're not constrained to be scientific, work can go as fast as we want. And don't forget our trump card. We don't have to correspond with how the brain does things. That's what's holding up the show in real science. All we have to be is 'as intelligent as,' by any route we care to choose."

"What do you types even mean by that, anyway? 'Intelligent'?"

"Bingo. Marcel, I knew you were my boy."

"Are you tired of real science? Is this just an extended vacation for you, Engineer? Or do you have something else in the works?"

It was as if he didn't even hear me. "Here is your reading assignment for next week. No skimming! If I wanted a liability for a research assistant, I would have hired a Keluga." He handed me another stack of conference papers and journal reprints.

"I thought I was the literature consultant," I whined.

"You are. And this is the literature you'll be consulting. By the way, Marcel. About your wasting a year. You told us you weren't up to anything."

"I've just finished a manuscript."

"And?"

"I'm already toying with a new one," I lied. Lying constructively was my job description, after all.

"Are you? What's it about? Or are you one of those artists who can't whisper the letter their title starts with without jinxing the end product?"

"Well, I have this idea." In fact, I had several hundred, none of which compelled me. Ideas insinuated themselves into my good graces, begging to be saved from the void. But I, the rescue squad, seemed to be off duty.

"Yes, good. Ideas are good. 'A very good place to start,' " he sang. His voice was clear, a startling tenor.

I ignored him. It was getting easier to. "An overworked industrialist takes a vacation to—Chester, England. He is touring the city walls, the half-timbered arcades, when he's hit up for change by a street person. He pretends to be an uncomprehending German sightseer. The panhandler doesn't buy it, starts harassing him. The industrialist explodes. The beggar retaliates with some vague threat. Three months later, at a conference in Cairo, the industrialist is accosted by a vagrant who—"

"Who says, 'Remember the guy in Chester?' Introducing a whole international cartel of homeless who appear outside the restaurant windows wherever this man travels. Very nice. A moral little ghost tale. Kiplingesque. Marcel, you're better off working for me."

"Don't knock Kipling. Kipling is a great writer. Some of my best friends are Kipling scholars."

"Is he on the List?"

I shook my head. No accounting for taste.

"Let me see that damn thing. Did you bring it?"

He had asked me to. I always did as asked. Lentz took the sheaf from me and began leafing through it. He made no comment until page 4, nineteenth-century British. "Hm. Mary Shelley. This could be more interesting than we've bargained for."

I thought to tell him about my disembodied opening line. But I did not much feel like holding my slight hostage up to Lentz's ridicule. The train, after all, was no more than a *vehicle*. What Taylor would have called it, in the freshman seminar that made me forsake measurement for words. The train meant nothing in itself; it simply carried the story out of the terminal.

My train did not even reach past the border checkpoint into page 2. The invitation to picture this could run no further than halfway down the first right-hand side. If the line were memory rather than invention, an exhaustive search of paper space—all middle-right opening pages in every known secondhand bookshop on earth— would turn it up.

Picture these words. The letters tunnel astonishingly across the page. They form themselves into an extended consist of cars just pulling out. The cars hold together by invisible coupling-gaps. When a boy, I counted these spaces as they clicked along on the tracks of type, under my mother's breath.

Counting the gaps was also counting the words. Machines performed the task effortlessly, born to it. Could they count ideas as well? Could they be made to sort thoughts, assemble them into a supple, southbound express?

I read the homework Lentz assigned me. An article on hippocampal association that Diana Hartrick co-authored grabbed my imagination. Every sentence, every word I'd ever stored had changed the physical structure of my brain. Even reading this article deformed the cell map of the mind the piece described, the map that took the piece in.

At bottom, at synapse level, I was far more fluid than I'd ever suspected. As fluid as the sum of things that had happened to me, all things retained or apparently lost. Every input to my associative sieve changed the way I sieved the next input.

To mimic the life we were after, Lentz and I would have to build a machine that changed with every datum about life that we fed it. Could a device—a mere vehicle—survive the changes we'd have to inflict upon it?

It struck me. To train our circus animal in Faulkner or Thomas Gray, we would first have to exhilarate it with the terror of words. The circuits we laid down would have to include the image of the circuit itself before memory overhauled it. The net would have to remember what it would be again, one day, when forgetting set in for good.

Before I'd even scratched the homework pile, I was a changed person. The writer who had signed on to the reckless bet was dead. Lentz, Hartrick, Plover, Gupta, Chen—each clinging to the local trap of temperament—C., Taylor, all my lost family and friends, all the books on the List, all the works I would now never write stood waving goodbye from beneath my departing compartment window.

It seemed forever since I had set out on an open ticket. Forever since I had traced, in mental route, the trip that would not be mine to retrace much longer.

After a while, the calendar becomes a minefield. I had to skirt so many anniversaries that autumn that I found it hard to take a step without detonating one. Taylor's seminar met in an attic room of the English Building, that fall when, at eighteen, I found my first map of the world. I taught my first course, the one C. took, three falls later.

Fall at twenty-two, I passed my Master's Comps, and moved as far away from U. as I could get.

I could not see how I'd gotten from one fall to another, or from any of those falls to this one. Age lurches in fits and starts, like a failing refrigerator compressor. Like a gawky, grand mal–adroit adolescent on ancient roller skates, navigating a stretch of worn sidewalk in a subduction zone. It holes up awhile, stock-still, then slams out one afternoon to play catch-up ball.

Time is not a wave. It is discrete, particulate. I came to class one day, that class where I pretended I was Taylor, unlocking the self's intricacies to a horrified and enthralled audience. I arrived that morning at eight to announce that I wasn't up to teaching that day, or the session after. I gave an assignment for the following week and watched my fold file out, subdued.

All but C. She stayed on, by tacit pact knowing it was time to come forward. We stood alone in the emptied room. She asked, "Want to sit somewhere for a minute?"

I did. We wandered out of the English Building onto the Quad. What quads were for: for generations of student sadness to lie down on, in the crisp blue of the first week of year's end. Everything we saw as we staked our spot said, *last November ever*. The first of an almost endless list of lasts.

C. sat Indian style. I lay on my side, head propped on an elbowed arm. On all sides of us ran the ring of collegiate buildings—Chemistry, Math, English. Each had been the setting for a thousand and one urgencies and embarrassments. I would be glad to be gone.

But gone where? The rub. I hadn't a clue, and felt good about even that. Very few job openings for the thing I wanted to do. I'd be lucky to be busing tables for a portion of the tips, this time next fall.

My father had foreseen that, of course. The man had known everything, except how to go on living. He never said word one when his son told him he planned to transfer out of physics, trash the stellar career. He didn't need to say anything. I could read the verdict in his face: Do what you need to. But what a colossal waste of talent and investment.

"Poetry, Rick? What does that mean, exactly?" It means you

57

haven't the faintest idea what you want to do. Burned out on problem sets. Isn't that right?

I never got the chance to defend myself. The man took off to Alaska to his sister's. Dad timed his disappearance so no one had to watch him go. And as a result, I've had to watch the immortally wasted body pace through a decade and a half of accusing dreams.

A packet would reach me three days after the news. A small bundle of chapbooks—the poems of Robert Service. *The Spell of the Yukon. Rhymes of a Rolling Stone.* Dad's favorite poet, and more beloved because the academics—his son—no longer even bothered to despise the rhymer. "The Cremation of Sam McGee": Dad's gloss on his own choice of exit. A slap in the face. A last, belated blessing. A request that if you are going to waste your life studying poetry, at least waste it on the good stuff.

I lay on the Quad, thinking over this goodbye gift, this student of mine sitting across from me. I shifted to my back. I saw myself staring up into the most unlikely azure. How many ghosts did life involve pleasing?

"Are you all right?" C. intervened.

My "Of course" didn't even convince itself.

"You were . . . I thought . . ."

"I'm fine," I explained.

"Tell me," she said. Anonymity is best. Who do you ever know, after all? *Tell me*, while I'm still a blank slate. Before you make me over in the habit of knowledge.

"My father just died."

I winced then, and annually in remembering. So bleeding what? Fathers and the deaths of fathers. How many children half my age lost parents to any of the world's ingenious violences in the time it took me to speak those words? I had no right. No one did. My own sorrow sickened me.

I spoke without looking at her, at least. It helped later on, to say that her cow-eyed, trusting complicity played no role in my impulse confession. I came to her sight unseen. I had no idea yet how heart-stoppingly plain she could look. I fell in love with a voice, with two words.

"I'm so sorry," she said. As if McGee had been cremated through her own carelessness. And yet her each pitch denied its own need to exist as anything at all but compassionate sound. The lone condolence ever allotted. Only the saying mattered. The words meant little, if anything.

"I'm sorry," she said, serene where she should have been scared off. "Would you like to be by yourself?"

I looked up at her. *What do we need to piece her back?* Do we need five foot four? Do we need brownish-black, pageboy hair? Aggressively shy, nervously innocent? Could we create her whole, conjure her up again intact on one detail, say, a face denying ever having known anything but astonishment?

I said, "I'd like to sit with you awhile."

She settled onto the grass, decorously distant. Years later, in a dark bed, I told her. How startled I was—she, a perfect unknown, no sense of me except my classroom act. Why was she here, sitting beside her grieving teaching assistant? Because she'd torn that picture from the family album, and felt obliged to see mine. Because she liked how I looked, poor poet-in-training with the ripped shirts and no mender near. Because my silence sounded so much like need.

She toyed with a blue canvas backpack filled with books. She held it between her legs, a child that might at any minute struggle to its feet and toddle off. Her hair, too short to be pulled back, was pulled back and rubber-banded around a pencil.

I laid it out, on no grounds at all. I told her all about McGee. Everything. Truths I'd never so much as hinted at to my closest friends. Facts never broached even with my brothers and sisters, except in bitter euphemism.

I told her in one clean rush, as only a twenty-one-year-old still can. Of my father's slow-burn suicide, stretched out over fifteen years. The man's long, accreting addiction that made every day a sine wave of new hope crushed. How hope, beaten to a stump, never died. How it always dragged back, like an amputated pet, its hindquarters rigged up in a makeshift wagon.

She listened with the simplest urgency. Nothing more ordinary in the world. She was still the age when one could make a go of compassion. At double that age, I'd duck down emergency exits rather than talk to acquaintances, and the thought of making a friend felt like dying.

"Tell me," she said. And became a part of me always. Daily, somewhere, even if she just as quickly dissolved. You trade your own aloneness. You place yourself in the path of any invitation to come clean. You give up your script completely, on a sudden hunch. Or you never give it at all.

I told her for no reason. Because she sat and asked. Because she, too, seemed so alone in all this collegiate autumn, there on the vacated Quad with her blue backpack and her hair pulled back around a pencil. And because I told her, she would always have something over me. Forever, if she remembered. If she cared to use it.

I relived for her the Powers family dead drop from middle class to *Grapes of Wrath*. The silent, unspeakable impact, without the least tug of restraint from any shoulder harness. I made her listen to the man's keen intelligence, slurred impenetrably. His gross motor skills, stunted like a pithed lab rat's. I told her all my teenage desperate acts: balancing open fifths upside down on the countertop. X-ing off the calendar, to make him think the lost days had lasted weeks. I showed her his puffy, dazed face.

I narrated all this in harrowing detail. At least, I thought I did. A decade on, C. claimed the sketch had been much more schematic.

I described the late night visit, Christmas the year before. Just after I'd dropped my bombshell, the revised career plans. Dad wobbling into my room like a parasite-bloated puppy. Sitting on the foot of my bed, grasping me with anesthetized claw. Waking me from a lesser nightmare. "Rick. Lss. Listen. Don't."

Spooky, ghoulish. Lead-in to liquid panic. I felt my throat clamp again, even relating this thin simile version.

Don't what?

"Don't change. Stay."

"Dad. Go back to bed." I mimed my own lines for her, in the voice of the child parent. Caretaking commenced early, in the kids of my family. "Sleep it off. It'll all be over in the morning." Or soon enough thereafter.

"Rck. Listen. Stay in science. The world needs . . ."

I told her how I'd disappointed him, embittered my father's holdout hope. Bricked up the last loophole he saw for his future. I was supposed to redeem the sad disaster Dad had made of life. And now I would never salvage anything, in my father's or anyone's eyes.

How could I tell this woman details that made me retch to hear? Maybe I tried to make her run. Test her Good Samaritan threshold of horror. She stayed put. She listened all the way up to McGee's cancer and instant disintegration. Almost a reprieve, I confessed in shame. The only thing large enough to displace the first sickness. I held back on one detail—Dad's I-told-you-so grins from inside the debilitating chemo: You always thought your old man would die of drink.

C. sat through it. At one pained silence, she grazed my upper arm. Exemption or encouragement—it didn't matter. Aside from that, we did not touch.

"Why am I telling you all this?"

"It's easier when you don't know someone."

But I do know you, I wanted to object. The first person I didn't have to get to know. The first person I've ever met more alone than I am.

Sick of myself, I tried to draw her out. She reciprocated out of kindness. She said she was studying comparative literature. "It means"—she smiled, defending herself from the ghost of my father—"that I haven't accepted reality yet."

Change of schools had delayed her life by a year. By taking overloads, she would finish almost on time. "I don't know what my hurry is." She laughed. "It's not as if there are a lot of entry-level openings for literature comparers."

This illusion, born in mutual sadness. Because I'd spilled everything, because she in turn lapsed into long, shameless silences, we could pretend we'd been conversing since childhood. No need to gloss. No fill of awkward gaps. Words seemed almost an afterthought, casual noise. Still here. Fear not. Still here.

After we said everything we felt like, we stopped. We sat together, listening to the sparrows take their everyday, bewildered offense. The last day of innocence, of instant companionship without groundwork or explanation. The last year when one could make a friend.

When she spoke again, I jumped. I'd forgotten about speech, or why one would ever resort to it.

"So will you go home for a while?"

I nodded. The short moratorium of mourning. Knowing's intermission, before the return of routine.

Some part of this may have come later. Maybe I conflated the different times we met in that spot, that season, by contrived chance. I've made a career of rewriting. C. used to say that everything was always outset with me. She came to know me so uncomfortably well. How my mind collapsed everything back to Go. How I would end with a head full of opening lines.

Midmorning grew cold. We sat closer. " 'May will be fine next year,' " C. said, lapsing into beginner's anonymity.

I heard belatedly. "What was that again?"

"What?" Her throat closed. She bolted for cover. What did I do wrong? A question promoted to refrain, in time. And how rapidly *already* in C.'s eyes turned into *again*.

Here, at the first cross-purpose, I was too startled to stop and reassure her. "Whatever made you say that?"

"Say *what*?" The Samaritan would fight, if frightened enough.

" 'May will be fine . . .' "

"Oh, that!" She smiled, goofy, breathing again. "It's a line from my parents' English book. Sitting here—this temperature, this wind?" She tried to defuse me. I nodded: keep talking. "I felt so wide open all of a sudden. So—anything. That's what made me think of it."

"English book?"

"As a second language. For adults. A hand-me-down from another South Side family. They came five years before my parents. That's a whole generation, where I come from."

"Is there another line, just after that?"

"Yes. Wait. 'Father hopes to plant roses in the front yard.' All these short narrative vignettes. Incidents you might live. Let's see."

She closed her eyes, to help her visualize. Thought looks up, or off, or in. Away from the distraction of what is. Would a thinking machine, too, turn its simulated eyes away?

"Let's see. On the next page is one that starts, 'Mother goes to fetch the doctor.' Imagine my brother trying to explain to his parents, at age ten, why mothers do to doctors what dogs do to sticks."

I tried.

"That doctor bit was handy, as it turns out. They lived that one." She dropped back into her astonished quiet. "So what's your interest in that May one?" You been holding out on me, Immigrant?

"It's a line from a nostalgic Housman poem. You see, there's this comprehensive I'm supposed to be studying for." The weakening sun cut a peach gash in the side of November the seventh. Summer looked for a last route to the surface, but could not find it.

"Housman?"

"You know. Best years behind you. Poet dying young, kind of thing."

"So what's next?"

"Well, I don't know. I suppose a tech writing job at 24K, a mortgage, a finished den full of kids, and early brain death."

"No!" She laughed. "I mean the poem. 'May will be fine next year.' What happens next?"

"Oh. 'Oh ay, but then we shall be twenty-four.' "

C. laughed. "I'll only be twenty."

"I'll be twenty-two."

"That gives you two whole years yet." Her eyes were brown and enormous, daring me. "Whole lifetimes can play out in the space of two years."

"Whole lifetimes," I echoed. Maybe that's all I ever did: echo her. See what she had to say. Get her to commit, then fall back on accommodation.

We caught eyes. We looked for longer than either thought we should. For a moment, looking felt like something that happened to you rather than something you did. Not *Are you who I think you are? Am I who you think I am?*

"Thanks," I said, taking her fingers when we stood and stretched. "Sorry to unload on you, but I must have needed it."

"I wish you'd unloaded more."

"You have a class?" I said, instead of what I should have.

"I've just missed two," C. apologized. An awkward confession to make to one's teacher. "You?"

I shrugged, pointed toward the meager downtown, toward departure, bus stations, all families waiting at the end of this spreading nexus.

C. started backing down the sidewalk that crisscrossed the green like huge suspender straps. "Have a safe trip home."

"See you," I said. My tag line. Still the only way I have to say goodbye. See you. What did it mean? No tense. Elliptical. Almost an imperative. It must have been the last thing I ever said to my father. See you.

C. lifted her hand, palm out. Then she turned the palm inward and placed it on her sternum. She hoisted her pack, swung on one foot, and walked away. I watched her disappear into the milling field of twenty-year-olds on their way to places none could begin to imagine.

Maybe I knew I was already gone. I still had to finish, though, before I could leave. Fall semester came to its Christmas close. My first incarnation as teacher ended. In the composition class, C. got one of a handful of A's. Our goodbye at semester's end was terse. I'd grown guarded with her and everyone else. My father had died at fifty-two, and the next thirty years seemed to me an academic exercise.

I taught again that spring. I was better; the class was worse. No one wrote on Aspasia. I booked hard in preparation for the exam at year's end. One fine May day I found myself sitting in a graduate colloquium on prosody, scanning the inverted feet in a sonnet by Edwin Arlington Robinson called "How Annandale Went Out." We'd been at the iambs and trochees for a good two hours before it struck me that no one had yet mentioned that the poem was about euthanasia. Whether to let the sufferer die.

I'd transferred from physics to literature because of one man, the incomparable Taylor. He led me to believe, at eighteen, that a person could lay hands on the key to all mythologies. I now saw that literature might indeed teach me about my father's death, but the study of literature would lead no further than its own theories about itself.

I took the exam and passed it. My marks were high enough to gain admission to the final stage, the Ph.D. Then, on the threshold of committing to the field I'd devastated my father by choosing, I threw that choice away as well. I decided to leave U. forever. I would change my life in every way imaginable.

But first I needed to talk to C. I showed up at her rooming house, surprising her. I'd never been there; I'd gotten the address out of the student directory. It was an unrepeatable spring morning. She came to the door sleepy, still in her bathrobe.

"Good girl?" I asked.

Her brown eyes ignited. "Outside!" she shouted. She dressed in a minute, while I waited on the porch. It was true. There was nothing, nothing in existence that she preferred over being in the sun, the wind. Just walking.

"I have to kiss these buds," she said, kissing a brace. "I haven't kissed them yet this spring. When I was a child, I thought they wouldn't grow without encouragement."

She still was that child. And she knew it.

"Would you like to go away with me?" I asked. "Somewhere. Anywhere. Your choice. Two lit majors, making a living in the real world?"

She stopped and stared. It was the question we'd been asking each other from the first student-teacher conference. Only she'd been holding her breath, hoping we would vanish before asking.

"I have to tell you something. I'm involved with someone."

I suppose I knew. But asking, in all its awfulness, was the only way to write myself into this solitary future. Unless I asked, point-blank, I would never escape the second guess. I'd said it out loud. I was free now to forget her. To live out adulthood alone and in good faith. Whatever I cared to do.

"Take care," she intoned. "See things for me, wherever you end up."

I moved to B. I rented a room in the heart of the city. I got a job as a second-shift computer hack, the complete opposite of the life I'd been leading. I wrote about that job years later, in my third novel. I used Taylor as model for my hero, a man who gives up a promising career in science to devote himself to music composition. And I cast myself as the shiftless graduate-school dropout who squanders his talent.

The job was perfect. I worked alone, all night. For part of the shift, I had nothing to do but read. I read Rabelais, Balzac, Freud, Henry Adams, Max Planck. I read at random, obeying only the forgotten principle of pleasure.

In my few daylight hours, I fell in love with women constantly. Bank tellers, cashiers, women in the subway. A constant procession of pulse-pounding maybes. I never did more than ask one or two to lunch.

I frequented the Center's cafeteria. The food was marginal, depending on the hour I arrived. It consisted of the indifferent fried batter that everywhere kept alive this nation's scientific research effort. The lunch conversation, on the other hand, played like the chatter in creation's greenroom. I could eavesdrop in any direction, and trawl the same topic: the nature of the knowable, and how we know it.

For those researchers who bothered to stop and eat, lunch was the hour of collegial consolidation. Too much work at minute magnifications without looking up led to snow blindness. That was the idea behind the Center, the country's largest institute for interdisciplinary study. That was why a third of the complex gave itself over to common grazing space. The plan, in the end, involved a linkup of all locales.

One noon, I brought my stack of reading down to the cafeteria and sat over an Italian beef on wet onion roll. All around me, scientists came up for air, gauging the rest of the global, accreting index under construction. A few tables away, Plover and Hartrick sat scribbling diagrams on a scratch tablet. I thought of joining them, but didn't want to disrupt those with real work to do.

Instead I read. The articles were getting easier to get through. I read how supervised training helped a net grow cleverer at associating any input with desired output. And I got cleverer as I read.

But the brain does things in massive parallel. Out of the edge of my eye, as I read, I saw someone jerk across the room holding a bottle of juice and a packet of batter fries. A ghost doomed to walk the earth awhile in human form. The apparition of Lentz shocked me. Broad daylight should have dissolved him. He seated himself at an empty table, as far from other bodies as possible.

Plover and Hartrick saw him too. Harold wanted to go keep the solitary figure company. Diana pointed to the writing pad and screwed up her face. Finally, she acquiesced. They decamped to his table, where Lentz welcomed them with little more than bare recognition. I thought it safe to join the three of them.

I sat down with what was left of my sandwich. Plover greeted me. "Here he is! Slot B of the sinister cybernetic assemblage. How are you two getting on with your attempt to automate literary criticism?"

I liked this man. I saw him building model rockets as a child, or testing out vaccines on his pet gerbil. I held up the journals, my lunch-hour reading. "I feel like some watcher of the skies . . ."

"When a new planet swims into his ken?" Plover completed. An eager schoolboy.

His quick fill surprised me. I replaced my image of the model rockets with one of a boy reading *The Norton Anthology* under the covers by flashlight.

"That's enough, Marcel," Lentz said out of the corner of his mouth. "We don't want to give away any trade secrets."

"Is it ready, then?" Plover teased. "Let's go try this toy out." He'd hooked and landed the best of natures. "Okay. Okay. Here's one. Name this tune:

"I am a little world made cunningly
Of elements, and an angelic sprite . . .

"Key that one into the old input layer and see what it comes up with."

I couldn't fight this man. The lines were pure love to him, a pleasure to be squandered and so increased. His face, as he quoted, radiated the ingenuous enthusiasm that gets drummed out of professionals around the time of the Ph.D.

67

"Where's that from?" I demanded. "I know that one."

Plover raised his hands and snapped both thumbs. "Diana? We've stumped him. We've stumped the chump!"

"Now, Harold," Lentz sneered. "Leave the writer alone. He may be washed up, but he isn't Donne yet." He fished a journal from the bottom of my stack, one I hadn't reached yet. He opened to a piece he'd co-authored with a famous Irish neural networker. Holy Sonnet number 5 sat atop the article.

I gaped like a drowning guppy. Plover looked crestfallen. He scanned the epigraph, dignity injured.

"Have you noticed how many of these open with a quote?" I said, to cover my humiliation. "Fashionable. I'm glad to see literature is still good for something."

Diana jumped into the awkwardness. "Philip. On the subject of revealing trade secrets. Explain back-propagation to me."

"Marcel? How would you like a chance to redeem yourself?"

"Well, as I understand it—"

"Oh, don't give us *that*, Marcel. Give us the facts."

"As I understand it, you present the net with a pattern of input. This signal pattern flows from neurode to neurode along branching, variously weighted connection paths. If the sum of inputs on the receiving neurode exceeds its signal threshold, it, too, fires and passes along more signal. Spreading activation, it's called."

I looked at Lentz to see if I had it right so far. He had his hands together, fingers to lips. And he was smirking.

"The signal pattern spreads through the net from layer to layer. A final response collects at the output layer. The net then compares this output to the desired output presented by the trainer. If the two differ, the net propagates the error backward through the net to the input layer, adjusting the weights of each connection that contributed to the error."

"Bra-*vo*, Marcel. Who's your teacher? Now, the question is: Which would you rather be able to do? Explicate that process or interpret Donne's Holy Sonnet?"

"I don't think that's the question," Diana sighed. "The question is whether back-propagation violates the directionality of the axon-to-dendrite signal."

Lentz pulled his head back on its stalk. He arched his eyebrows. "What have we here? The dabbler's expertise!"

Diana looked as if he'd just slapped her. Her lip shook. She would have stormed off if Harold hadn't restrained her.

"Philip!" Plover frothed. "Just shut up for a second, will you? You fault us for taking issue from a position of ignorance. But we're challenging you to provide the refutation. Isn't that better than reflex rejection? Torches and scythes?"

"Torches and scythes are ever so much more picturesque."

"Oh, for the love of . . . I give up." Plover traced a shorthand of his bear-paw exasperation.

"Uh-oh. About to invoke the deity. We're in trouble now. Whatever happened to radical skepticism in religious matters?"

"Philip, you . . ." Plover tripped on his tongue in his disgust. "Why bother publishing your results, if you don't want people to follow you?"

"I get nervous when I'm followed too closely." Lentz inserted a fry into his mouth like a young child hammering blocks into a toy workbench.

"So you can't be bothered with anyone who isn't already in the inner sanctum."

"That's not true. Why, I've taken Marcel here and have already turned him from near-ignoramus into marginally literate page boy."

" 'Sweets grown common lose their dear delight.' Is that it? Lentz, that's the most elitist thing I've ever heard anyone on public funding say."

"Marcel, tag that line for me, will you?"

Citing seemed the quickest way out of trouble. "I think it's Shakespeare."

"Shakespeare's not elitist?" Lentz countered. "In any case, most of my grants are corporate, these days. By the way, Harold. 'Most elitist' is not up to your usual elegant prose."

"When you boys are finished," Diana murmured, "I wouldn't mind an answer."

Lentz cackled. "All right, Marcel. Time to straighten out the masses again."

"I guess the idea is that backward error propagation may resemble higher-order brain processes. True, individual nerve pathways are one-way. But neuronal paths as a whole do connect portions of the brain in two directions."

"I get it," Diana said. "Feedback signals from muscle tissue to the primary motor cortex, and the like?"

Lentz snorted. "This is just Marcel's guess, you understand."

I wondered if I would be able to work with the man a whole ten months.

Diana's face wrinkled. "But it's not quite the same thing, is it? Is presynaptic Hebbian change the same thing as . . . ?"

But Lentz had stopped listening. He was peering into his juice bottle, preoccupied. Almost consumed by distraction. "Nothing," he declared. "Nothing is the same as anything else."

By whatever mechanism, that lunch is set into my cortex. I can take out the tape and view it at will. From this distance, its edges are ridiculously sharp, the definition absurd. These frames extend a longer clip, animated by the persistence of vision.

Diana later told me how memories are laid down when the thumb-sized basal forebrain bathes the hippocampus in acetylcholine. The chemical somehow changes a synapse's shape, she claimed, altering the connections between cells. And a key flooder of the chemical pathways is fear.

That lunch is burned into my memory because I sat through it terrified. Lentz scared me. Harold's hurt, Diana's dismay triggered my impulse to fly. I was afraid of everything these three might say to each other. Spooked by the open rupture begging to take place. Every word of anger was my fault.

For a long time, I thought that what frightened me was the prospect of failure. My biggest anxiety seemed to be that we'd pour ourselves into this folly and never get it to do more than gibber. That a previously productive researcher would take me on a ten-month wild-goose chase.

It's taken me this long—*this* long—to see. The fear that laid down that indelible trace was the same one I've nursed since boyhood. The fear that we might realize our dreams.

Lentz built Implementation A more for my education than as a prototype with any real pretensions. The beast wasn't winning any beauty prizes, either in looks or in conception. Lentz cobbled up a card cage to the back plane of your basic vanilla workstation. A few I/O devices, registered antiques all, hung off the ports, windows to this poor contraption's soul.

"The super-rich always drive beaten-up old Chevies," Lentz assured me. "You have to grasp the inverse snob value. Always dazzle your audience with misdirection. If we get 'Three Blind Mice' to come out of *this*, it'll knock them dead."

However humble, the rig gave us an entree. A workable learning algorithm can run on any platform. The brain, Lentz had it, was itself just a glorified, fudged-up Turing machine. Our cerebrum-to-be had no neurons, per se. No axons or dendrites. No synaptic connections. All these structures hid in simulation, dummied up in the standard linear memory array. The bare troika of Boolean operators brought them into metaphorical being. We used algorithms to imitate a non-algorithmic system. Implementation A was a ghostly hologram. It froze our words the way a scribbled shopping list, falling from a book where it has spent a misplaced lifetime, revives that longhand you thought you'd live alongside forever.

Lentz did a good job of making the hardware transparent to me. He hooked up topologies the culmination of a decade or more of tinkering. He explained every link in the process. But I was exhausted, wiped out from my own recent work. I tried for the gist and took the rest on faith.

The gist consisted of vectors. A stimulus vector, converted by the net's self-reorganization into a response vector. We started with a three-deep array of neurodes, enough for a test start. Each field was the size of the net that had learned to pronounce English. Implementation A would be spared this task. Lentz wired it to a canned speech synthesis routine. We worked at the level not of phonemes but of whole words.

At first I typed input into the system. My text ran through a huge lookup table—Lentz's laborious list of the 50,000 most common English words, arranged in order of rarity. Each word got a number, like a runner in a triathlon. These numbers in turn plunged headfirst into our randomly weighted terrain.

The ersatz brain cells juggled the pattern, until those in the output layer replied in noise. The box answered back each time I typed to it. But it answered gibberish. Like any nursling's, its voice was awash in gabble.

If I kept at the same stimulus, however, the output organized. Activated paths strengthened; inert routes atrophied away. The blathering gave way to consistent conversational response. What those responses *were*, however, neither Lentz nor I could say.

Still, our rewiring meshes had, of their own device, begun to imitate the world's simplest animals. They grew conditioned. They habituated. They de- and re-sensitized. Outwardly, at least, our neuron-simulation mimicked the response of living tissue.

Down the hall, on all sides of us, biologists split the lark, the functional organism. They ran planarians through mazes. They rapped lobotomized sea slugs on their antlers. Harold and Ram studied recovery and compensation in damaged brains. Diana removed small sections of monkey hippocampi and pegged them to changes in the creatures' ability to learn. The mind strove to open itself up, Pandora's ultimate black box.

We, too, performed our bit of the reductionist dragnet. Implementation A was our attempt to make a metaphor for a metaphor-making neural mechanism. But what creature the inner workings of that self-appointing assembly mirrored was anyone's guess.

The first bottleneck was not mechanical. The problem was me. Lentz hovered over me as I keystroked. He jabbed at the air. He feinted at the keyboard. He smudged the video screen with agitated digits. My typing drove him up the bloody wall.

"Marcel, how many words have you typed in your life?"

I studied the fixture above his head, calculating.

"Not the exact figure, you nit. Just give me the order of magnitude."

I shrugged. "Millions."

"You type like a chimp taking a running lunge at *Hamlet*. Who taught you?"

"Autodidact."

"How the hell are we supposed to get anything done? What do you peak at, twenty words per minute? And what you lack in speed you make up for in blundering. What's with the three-and-a-half-finger method, anyway?"

"Feel free to take over. It's all yours."

"Oh, don't be such a bleeding passion plant. No, it's no good. We're going to have to go to voice recognition. It'll cost us a week. And it's about as accurate a transcriber as a female Korean immigrant."

"Jesus, Lentz. If anyone hears you, we'll be run out of town. This is nineteen nin—"

"But more reliable than your piggies, anyway."

Speech recognition, in that year, was well on its way to being settled. Its frontier towns had grown into small St. Louises. We needed only follow along in the land grab's wake. Lentz refined the Center's prepackaged speech-processing routines. He linked the voice input module to the front end of our existing net. He cabled a Karaoke microphone into the A-to-D converter. He sutured the pieces together like a microsurgeon reattaching a severed nerveway.

Before we could train the network, I had to train the recognition routine to place my voice. I spoke words to it, then whole phrases. I repeated each out loud until it bled into a meaningless semantic gruel. When we succeeded in turning sounds into text with acceptable accuracy, we started again with the learning algorithm. Once more from the top.

"So are we using supervised training, graded training, or what?" I asked Lentz.

"Marcel, don't try to impress me. Save that for your hapless readers."

"Seriously. I'd like to correlate what I've read with—"

"For the word compilation, the net will compare its own output to

73

the desired output you supply it. It will then adjust its synapses to imitate you as closely as possible."

"That's supervised."

"Am I supposed to give you genius prize money now?"

I liked Implementation A. I felt comfortable chattering to it. I read slowly, distinctly, for hours at a shot. I learned to work late at night, like the other loners and fanatics.

A answered me. Our infant had a comeback to everything. Lentz wrote a decoder to throw its vector outcomes on the screen. The thing LISP'd in numbers, for the numbers came. Its patterned responses condensed into syllables, then words in themselves. Correspondence grew more comprehensive. I did not always know what A was trying to say. But I could hear it struggle to say it.

We taught A some couple thousand words, about a quarter of the core active vocabulary a person might resort to. When it had these words under its belt, we tried it on simple combinations. After countless rounds of phrase-drill, Implementation A started to spit my words back parsed. Or at least it behaved as if it were parsing.

Between training sessions, I read the famous two-volume study of nets. The connectionist bible, it suggested maturable machines were already in sight. The math proved it: self-rearranging switchboards could generalize, selectively associate, even project. I took the math on faith, having long ago sacrificed my math to the study of fiction.

Then, everyone in the field took something on faith. Much lay beneath the surface, in the tangled, hidden layers. But I felt particularly vulnerable. I went to more colloquia and got progressively less out of them. Each week the speakers got younger. They grew more gleeful about having been born when I was already doing the crystal diode radio kits and the earthworm dissections. If I needed to grasp all understanding's lacunae before our contraption could understand me, we would lose our bet by a long shot.

I could at least follow the pictures, if not the argument's text. I visualized the spin glasses, complex similes for mental topology. I walked through the landscape of imagination, where every valley formed an associative memory. I could follow the *story* of the math, if not the substance.

And the story was drama itself: the tale of a gardener loose in that mnemonic landscape. An English Elizabeth, who cultivated it, or would have, had her life not been pruned back at twenty-eight, beyond the root.

I could follow the shape of the Hebbian Law: if two neurons fire together, their connection grows stronger and stimulation gets easier the next time out. Synapses in motion tend to stay in motion. Synapses at rest tend to stay at rest. I saw the law as a teacher prowling her class, slapping the wrists of bad students and rewarding the good until they all stood up and pledged coordinated allegiance.

But as yet, I could not hear *what* the pupils were pledging.

Lentz and I continued to putter. I read where the most famous worker on the wet side of brain research called God a tinkerer. I felt nothing like God. I felt like an arthritic macaque in finger splints.

For breathers, I frequented my other campus office, in the English Building. McKim, Mead and White, 1889. There I lived my alter ego—picturesque but archaic man of letters. The Center possessed 1,200 works of art, the world's largest magnetic resonance imager, and elevators appointed in brass, teak, and marble. The English Building's stairs were patched in three shades of gray linoleum.

Hiding out there provided a healthy antidote for too much future. After immoderate reading or training sessions, I needed the correction. But the building left me edgy as well. The edginess of the erotic. The scent of those halls went down my throat like a tracheotomy tube. English light flushed me with desire, a desire awakened by the memory of itself, wanting nothing more desperate than to be put back to sleep.

This was the building where I'd once taught C. Worse, this was Taylor's building. And everything Taylor had long ago alerted me to circled back on the primacy of narrative desire. Desire, he taught me, was the voicegram of memory. But I had reached an age when I was no longer sure that I wanted to remember the perpetual eroticism of eighteen, the erotics of knowledge, the words I'd traded in here, in these halls.

The more I learned about the architecture of memory, the more convinced I became that I was losing mine. I could not concentrate on even idle conversation. I would slink into English and sit in my nineteenth-century office, staring at the bricked-in fireplace, waiting for a surreal locomotive to emerge from it. Or I'd try to join the corridor conversation on a film or book review I was sure I'd seen. But I could not follow the preliminaries through to their web of consequences. I was elsewhere, and elsewhere back-propagated, endlessly.

In the mornings, I'd try to write. I now had perhaps three pages. In those pages I did nothing but unwind my first line. I made my relative clauses jump through all sorts of novel hoops. The performance could have gone on for several hundred pages on style alone. I could get my train to leave most eloquently. But I could not get it to go anywhere but back.

Sustaining so much as a paragraph became impossible. I'd juggle the first verb in my head, overwhelmed by my own weighted backlist. I thought of the four books I'd written between leaving U. and returning. The round trip seemed too immense. I no longer had the heart to extend it.

I'd missed my connection. Stranded at the terminal. I didn't want to write anymore. I was sick of speculation and empathy and revision. All I wanted was to read word frequency lists to Implementation A.

Lentz thought it time to see if Implementation A made sense. We drilled it for days on two-word sentences. Then we prompted A with nouns, to see if it could supply a valid predication. We would see if A acquired, by example, the pattern of generating grammar.

It recognized the simple S-V phrases we fed it. Dogs bark. Birds soar. Night falls. You vanish. Father hugs. Baby cries. It could distinguish these ideas from the formulations that we earmarked as inappropriate for well-brought-up machines to use in public.

But when it came time to perform, A clutched. It seemed to stab at pattern-completion. It formed sentences by chance guess.

It could learn words. It could identify well-formed sentences. But

Implementation A refused to elaborate its own. No matter how Lentz tweaked, Imp A seemed baffled by the task. It would not take the first generalizing step to learn the language.

Lentz tacked into the failure. He tried everything he could think of to coax the machine up a notch. Nothing worked. Asked to complete a thought, the network improvised wildly. Fish . . . ? Fish sky. Shines? Hopes shines. Forests floor. Laugh efforts. Combs loneliness. Even when, by chance, it got the syntax right, the sense was not even random.

Imp A spoke the way a toddler gave directions. Its eager-to-please finger serpentined over all possible routes. This way? *That's right!* Or is it this way? *Sure, if you like.* Where's the horse? Come on, point to the horse. *That's* not a horse. *That's* not a horse either.

Yet it was, at least, pointing. Maybe our putting the request as pointedly as we did flustered it.

"Couldn't we hard-code a properties list? I mean, someone here must have compiled a semantic catalog . . ."

"That's your coeval, Keluga. He's trying to write the entire Roget's as a series of nested, rule-based schematics. Containment, relation, exclusion . . ."

"Coeval? I'm thirty-five, Lentz. That guy's a kid."

"You're both post-Tupperware. Chen is Keluga's supervisor. Outrageous. The Bergen and McCarthy of AI. Chen knows every algorithm in existence, but can't speak a single natural language, including his own. Keluga grew up on Hollywood robots and the microprocessor revolution. One of those brats who got his first PC free in a cereal box. He gets nervous when a sentence doesn't start with 'While' and end with 'Wend.' He's going to reform English by taking out all the inefficient synonyms."

"But is his list any good? Couldn't we just use the semantic data structures as a reservoir of associations that the net could dip into?"

"We could. But it wouldn't be satisfying. That's not the way the cells do things."

"I thought the point wasn't to duplicate mind. I thought—"

"The point is to get this boutique of ICs to comment intelligently on William Bloody Wordsworth. Are you going to give me rules for doing that?"

I said nothing. Lentz realized he'd gone overboard. He regrouped and spoke again.

"We *could* try to feed it algorithms for everything. There are only slightly more of them than there are particles in the universe. It would be like building a heart molecule by molecule. And we'd still have a hell of an indexing and retrieval problem at the end. Even then, talking to such a decision tree would be like talking to a shopping list. It'd never get any smarter than a low-ranking government bureaucrat."

Lentz returned to the net design. I could do little to assist but run upstairs to the laser and retrieve the printouts. Lentz liked to crack morose asides while he worked. "You better start thinking of how you're going to fill the rest of your year."

Sometimes he would set me tasks, puzzles that weren't clearly puzzles until after I solved them. "Fill in the blank, making a simple, two-word sentence. 'Silence . . .' "

". . . *fears*," I suggested. "Make that '*Silence* fears.' "

"Oh, very good, Marcel. I knew there must have been a reason I asked you to be my apprentice."

But the more he joked, the worse Lentz's asthmatic anxiety grew. We washed up at the starting block. My future again began to seem as unbearably long as my past.

Angry, Lentz lobotomized the thing. "Just punishment," he declared. "This box didn't deserve to think." Hurting the circuit seemed no more sadistic than forcing it to learn in the first place.

He blurred the device's retention. He reduced the scope and breadth of connections. Then he tested it a last time in its weakened state, empiricism now taunting all three of us. To my astonishment, the learning algorithm rose up from its reduced straits and began to get the picture.

Miraculously, Implementation A began to pick up our patterns, arranging our words into meaningful relationships. "I might have known." Lentz sounded disgusted with himself. "Too much retention. It was learning. But learning got swamped in its own strength. The creature was driving itself batty, holding on too tenaciously to everything it had ever seen. Dying of its own nostalgia. Mired in the overacquired."

"Autistic," I remember saying. Particulars overwhelmed it. Its world consisted of this plus this plus this. Order would not striate out. Implementation A had sat paralyzed, a hoary, infantile widow in a house packed with undiscardable mementos, no more room to turn around. Overassociating, overextending, creating infinitesimal, worthless categories in which everything belonged always and only to itself.

A few deft neurological nicks and a new run-time behavior did the job. Implementation B lived inside the same hardware, indistinguishable from its short-lived predecessor. This time, fuzzy logic and feedback-braking kept the box as discriminately forgetful as any blossomer.

From the get-go, B was a different animal.

Diana Hartrick came by. She surprised me one Saturday afternoon. The air had just started to turn chilly. I remember that she had a denim windbreaker on and was shivering on the stoop when I let her in.

"Hi. I know you're not supposed to drop in unannounced in this country . . ."

"Not a problem. I lived half my adult life in a country where dropping in unannounced was *de rigueur*."

"Good. I was on my way to the lab. I thought I'd bring you this." She handed me a Ball jar full of soup. "I figured a single guy could use some. I'm afraid it's very hearty. You may want to thin it out some when you heat it up." She stopped to look around my place for the first time. "Hey! I thought you were staying until summer."

"I am."

"What's the matter? Aren't you comfortable here? It looks like you're trying to weasel past worldliness without actually having to touch it. By the way, you'll want to plug your fridge in for the soup. Unless you'd like to share it with the microorganisms."

"Thanks. You wouldn't happen to have a bowl on you, would you? Just kidding."

Diana rocked her head side to side. Her thin horizon smile said: *Artists*. Or words to that effect.

"Look. I came by to tell you that you don't have to do this, you know. Lentz is a maniac, but he's a harmless maniac. He won't hurt you if you bail out. None of us took the bet seriously in the first place. It's so . . ."

"Quixotic?"

" 'Deranged' was the word I was searching for. Harold has started to fret about your squandering your talents on this."

I shrugged. "There's no squandering. It interests me."

"Well, the minute it stops interesting you, drop it like a hot potato. And if that man starts to get on your nerves, tell him to go to hell. That's the only diction he understands."

"I was going to ask. What's the matter with him? Why is he like that?"

"Well, we all have our own theories. Harold's is the most charitable. He thinks the man is just trying in his own warped way to be loved. I think his limbic system is diseased. That reminds me. If you get tired of playing mad scientist with the home electrode kit, you are always welcome to come and see how it's really done."

"Thanks. I'd like to."

"Do you really live like this? Where are your things? Where is your library?"

"Lost in transit."

Diana cringed. Her hand flew out like a magician's released dove, but stopped short of my shoulder.

"Sorry. It's none of my business. I just wondered how you can work. All my notes are spread over the margins of my texts. I'd be lost without them."

"Lost is not so bad. It's practically an advantage in my line."

"Mr. Powers, Mr. Powers." She shook her head again, tisking through her grin. She did not buy me. But the sales pitch, at least, tickled her.

"Well, just remember. You're under no obligation to build this mechanical master's student. When you see how hopeless the holiday is . . ."

"Straight back to the mines," I promised.

Dr. Hartrick fished for her keys while heading for the door. At the threshold, she made one more stunned survey. "You'll—you should at least come by sometime." She sounded doubtful. "I can cook you a real meal, anyhow. You do eat, don't you?"

Sometimes I ditched the bike and walked to the Center. Self-inflicted mental Polar Bear Club. U. was threaded through with time holes, and not just mine. Most of the residential streets were still brick. The houses had *verandas*, *balustrades*, features that have passed out of the language. The streetlamp globes threw off a gaslight yellow that turned the underside of the leaves that had not yet fallen a weird, otherworldly teal.

C. and I took a last retrospective stroll through those streets a dozen years before. We walked slowly that night, half speed, not knowing how to abandon the markers. We were leaving together this time. We'd stumbled onto that inevitability that neither of us thought would ever happen.

I never asked her. I don't even know how she learned where I had gone. Just: one day, a card in the mail. The picture showed a forgotten town nestled in a stream valley. I couldn't read the description on the back. Language locked me out. But I could read her message. "R.—May will be fine next year. C."

Of all the million things the ambiguous message could mean, I knew the one it did. I woke up around noon after a late shift of computer operations and *The Magic Mountain*. I went to check the mail. Her card was the last thing I expected. The first I hoped for. I'd waited every day, I suppose, at some low level. I would have been just fine never hearing from her again. I would have worked forever.

I quit my job. I left B. and went back to U. She was waiting for me. She'd acted honorably, done things right. Now she was free to get out and see the world. We went as slowly as we could. We tried to get to know each other again, without too much backfill. But I had no job, she was graduating, and we had lost a lifetime once already.

We made love for the first time in a single bed belonging to someone neither of us had ever met. We lived together for three weeks in a house I was watching for a friend of a friend. The whole scenario was invention itself. We would never have a house of our own.

Somewhere, there is a picture C. took of me in that house's yard. I'm ringed with a garland of dandelions she wove me. My trident is a dandelion rake—the Poseidon of lawn care. We would never have a yard, the two of us. Not even a rented one.

"If I asked you again . . ." I asked her one day.

"I'd jump at the chance. That's *if* you asked me again."

Before we left, we took that compilation walking tour. We walked like a thresher squeezing a field dry. We named every landmark we left behind.

"That's where I lived when I first came down," she pointed out. "That's where my boyfriend lived. Here's where I met for choir. This is the clinic where I helped my roomie through her crisis."

"Here's where I lost my virginity," I showed her. "I spent a year in this bizarre co-op. Taylor lives a block down from here. Ah, the library. I booked like a madman for the Master's Comp. Nine months, up in a study carrel on deck eight."

By tacit agreement, we saved the Quad for last. Neither of us said, *Here's where we first learned we weren't necessarily alone.* Neither of us needed to say anything.

C. was game for anywhere. She would have followed a dart thrown at a world map. I told her how beautiful B. was, how full and alive. Leaving seemed like a story we told each other, then lived as it unfolded. How they skipped town together and relocated, with nothing but a $4,100 bank check to their names. How they rode for twenty-two hours on the Lake Shore Limited, next to an enormous gentleman who warned them of the dire consequences of reading.

How they arrived at South Station in bleak, freezing drizzle. How they stood soaked in grime-coated twilight, trying to find a bus stop. How she burst into tears: Where have you taken me?

Even hardship felt like a giggle. An adventure. I would have pitched permanent base camp in a war zone with that woman. And I made her feel safe, for a while. As if even this wrong turn were part of an ingenious thread. We were young then, and would live forever. All those disasters, bad judgments, breakages, mistakes: we protected each other, simply by insisting we were still together and happy. That nothing mattered but care.

Now, sometimes, as I trained B or walked back from the Center at nights to my deserted bungalow, panic ambushed me. Some mental picture would trigger it—remembering I'd left the cognitive oven on with something in it. The slightest reminder reached out and laced my ribs. Someone was in trouble, trapped in front of a station in an unidentifiable city without cash, map, or language. And I could not buffer or save them. Someone pitching into free fall. Either me or my old friend.

We settled into B. We found a place. We printed up résumés, complete with convincing Career Goals. Jobs, however anemic, dropped on us like a godsend. I took up work as a technical editor. C. guarded paintings at the Fine Arts.

My images of the two of us, in those early days, needed no gallery guard. C. and I, on our first Thanksgiving, dressing the ruinously expensive Cornish game hens when we didn't have two dimes to rub together. Listening, setless, to the sounds of the big game next door, holding our breath to hear who was ahead. That Christmas, crayoning a tree onto several sheets of newsprint and taping it to the apartment wall.

That much was almost cheating to remember. All I had to do was turn my eyes to some neutral screen—the wet leaves in the gutters as I walked, the fat gray cumulus—and I could see any scene from that year I could bear to look at. The focal trace that printed those pictures now lent its apparatus to the reverse process. Ouija-like, it retrieved from the file and held my attention on the reduced film of a place now past verifying.

Lentz had speculated about that strange doubling in one of his more controversial articles. Memory was a parasite, he proposed. It opportunistically used perception's circuitry for its playback theater.

And I have that whole parasite intact. Nothing required to bring it forth but numbness. True, the specifics of that moment have grown stylized. Artist's conceptions. I can check nothing. C. kept the book, the one where we pasted the paper trail of our shared existence. The documents are all elsewhere, trashed, or transferred to a stranger's long-term storage.

I came to him depressed.

"It's mind-fogging," I told him. "Incomprehensible. I've been reading. We don't have an agnostic's prayer in hell, do we? One hundred billion neurons. That's twenty for each person on earth. How many trillion synaptic connections? And all arranged with anatomical precision into who knows how many tangled subsystems . . ."

"Sixty-three," Lentz supplied. He was leaning back in his office chair again, reclined, as on the night I first saw him. I couldn't tell if he was being snide or if he'd finally flipped.

"And even the most trivial of the subsystems solves problems so far past our ability to compute it makes my limbic system spin. We'd need an exponential number of exponents just to number the firings on the way to a self-reflective thought. If we scale our toy up even a little bit bigger than it is now, the thing will grind to a standstill. Responding intelligently to 'Good afternoon' would take it a lifetime."

"Well, we could always tell Plover and Hartrick that Teacher's Pet needs a slight extension to get its paper in. Say, no later than the next Ice Age."

Lentz pulled up a subroutine on his terminal and began to massage it. He was a hyperactive child, happiest when several things happened at once.

"Even if we could keep track of the wiring . . ." my voice cracked. "Even if we could get all our tin-can telephones spaghettied up to the same switchboard: there still wouldn't be enough processing power in this part of the galaxy to synchronize their firing."

Lentz chuckled. "That's too exaggerate."

It was eerie. His cruel imitation was tone-perfect. Chen, to the letter. The vicious ear alone would be tough to duplicate on the most advanced of machines.

"Come on, Marcel. Buck up. It's not so tough. What saves us is that we don't have to do everything. No motion, no vision, no smell or sensation, no pain, no reflex response, no process control . . . If you knew what it took to reach out and grasp an object, to pick up a glass, you'd be completely incapable of doing it."

"If all we had to do was pick things up. We're trying to get something to *understand*."

"Marcel, I've never seen you like this. Remarkable. What happened to the cold fish we've come to know and love?" He spoke askance now, more intent on the screen than on me. The hypnotic, half-attentive intensity of someone pretending concentration. "Listen. I've been trying to explain this to you. In some fundamental way, it's easier to do high-level stuff than low-. It takes fewer neurons to link 'walk,' 'through,' and 'doorway' into some associated cluster than it takes for you to carry out the words."

"Maybe so. But think how many clusters—"

"You're overwhelmed because you're still thinking like Plover. You still think we have to lay out the rules and specify all the computations ourselves. That *would* be incomprehensibly complex. But we're not going to write out those calculations. We're going to feed the already languaged world to Imp B and let it take the bits apart and reassemble them."

"Yeah, yeah. You've done that lecture. But, Engineer. The size! Think of what we'd have to tell it before anything made sense. We're talking an index magnitudes bigger than the universe it points to."

"The universe will be its own index. The isomorphic contour map, the way the data get packed together."

"What does that mean? Okay. Suppose we read it the line 'He clasps the crag with crooked hands' . . ."

"Oh no. Not him. Anybody but him."

"Then we have to tell it about mountains, silhouettes, eagles, aeries. The difference between clasping and gripping and grasping and gasping. The difference between crags and cliffs and chasms. Wings, flight. The fact that eagles don't *have* hands. The fact that the poem is not really *about* an eagle. We'll have to teach it isolation, loneliness . . ."

"It'll know all about those. It'll grow into knowledge you won't even need to spell out. Knowledge will be a by-product of the shape its weight-landscape takes, from bending to the spoken world's shape."

". . . how a metaphor works. How nineteenth-century England worked. How Romanticism didn't work. All about imperialism, pathetic projection, trochees . . ."

Lentz started laughing. At least that meant he heard me. "Yes, there's a certain density out there it will have to become comfortable with. Give it time. How did you acquire that density? Half a meg, half a meg, half a meg onward."

"Me? *I* don't know what the bloody poem means. I wouldn't analyze that thing again if my life depended on it."

"That's my *point*. We humans are winging it, improvising. Input pattern x sets off associative matrix y, which bears only the slightest relevance to the stimulus and is often worthless. Conscious intelligence is smoke and mirrors. Almost free-associative. Nobody really *responds* to anyone else, per se. We all spout our canned and thumbnailed scripts, with the barest minimum of polite segues. Granted, we're remarkably fast at indexing and retrieval. But comprehension and appropriate response are often more on the order of buckshot."

"I'm beginning to see. You're not elevating the machine. You're debasing us. Took me long enough."

"Don't be too hard on yourself, Marcel," Lentz cooed. "Much of intelligence isn't really that bright."

"I can't believe this. You're serious, aren't you?"

"Massively parallel pattern matching. We only pretend to be syllogistic creatures. In fact, we identify a few constraints, then spin the block endlessly until it drops in the hole. Have you *read* an undergraduate paper lately? You should see what I have to deal with in the intro sequences alone. And the stuff I teach requires no real world knowledge at all! You know the old 'Show your work for partial credit'? It's when they show their work that I want to give even the ones who solve the problem sets a zero."

"Are you exempting yourself from this critique of intelligence?"

"Not really. This conclusion stared me in the face for thirty years before I saw it."

"All right. Let's say you're right."

"Let's do."

"It doesn't change the facts. In order to produce a remotely plausible association matrix for six measly Tennyson lines, our candidate will need a file cabinet two global hemispheres wide."

My objections were starting to bore Lentz. He stood up. It always frightened me when the man assumed the vertical. He began fiddling with the jumpers on the new neurodal processor board prior to fitting it into the expansion chassis. I thought of those brain surgeons who stimulate conscious patients' cortexes and what synesthesias the probe elicits.

"That's a pretty figure of speech, Marcel. And doubtless it's the sign of some nominal intelligence on your part. But have you read your own school papers lately? Give me *Middlemarch*, I'll spin you off a few amorphous generalities, all qualified and deniable."

"What do you know about that book?" I asked, too quickly. It was Taylor's book, the one he'd given his scholarly life to. The one I'd written on, analyzed for him. The novel where I'd discovered novels. The mere title in Lentz's mouth sounded creepy, as if I'd been spied on.

Of course he ignored me. Lentz ignored all direct challenges. Only the shrewdest or most slow-witted of machines could hit upon that conversational tactic.

"Even if you're right," I retreated, "it would take us forever to teach it sufficient amorphous generalities."

Lentz roused himself from distraction. "What do you want? We have ten months. Ten months is several generations these days. Plus, we don't have to *be* humanly intelligent. Our brain doesn't have to correspond to real mentation. We just have to be as good at paraphrase, by any route we care to take. And for that, we can fly, flat out. If you ever stop talking and pitch in."

I stood and helped him assemble the new card into Imp B's backplane. Manual labor: the extent of my contribution to date. "It strikes me that the thing we're trying to get as good as is damn near unparaphrasable."

"Oh, pish. It's the easiest thing in the world to take in a human. Remember AI's early darling, ELIZA, the psychoanalyst? 'You remind me of my father,' the human types. 'Tell me more about your father,' the machine answers. Remember the student who found the thing up and running on a deserted terminal? Struck up a conversation. Got steadily more frustrated. Ended up shrieking at the sadist on the other end to quit jerking him around."

Exactly how I ended up every time I talked to Lentz. "So all we're building is a deception?"

"Consciousness is a deception." Lentz grimaced. He stared into some middle distance. The pause was long and awful. I didn't know how to fill it.

At length, I had to say something. "You're not suggesting that Son of B is going to be *conscious*, are you?"

"Don't be obtuse, Marcel. You're making this argument a duck shoot. No, of course not. Nor do we *have* to make it conscious. We don't have to give it sensations either, or even make it think. We just have to make it a reasonable apple-sorter. Get it to interpret utterances, slip them into generic conceptual categories, and then retrieve related 'theoretical' commentary from off the prepackaged shelf."

"And what are we doing next week?"

"Touché, Marcel. You're right, for once. Let's just take the baby steps first."

"As they say to sky divers: that first step is a killer."

"Nah. The first step's a cakewalk. We can beat the hell out of a developing infant, in any case. First off, our baby never needs a nap. Never. We can feed it around the clock, once things start to take off. Second, a kid's neurons aren't even fully myelinated until age twelve or so. They're erratic. Trying to get them to potentiate is like writing in Jell-O."

Not long after that conversation, I learned that the only child Lentz ever raised had disowned him.

I still thought of B as a composite of makeshift components. Silk-screened cards populated with ICs on the one side and word frequency lists by parts of speech on the other. Each of its distributed, loosely linked subsystem nets was a community of neurodes, and each neurode a community of shifting allegiances.

Day after day, I trained these micro–circus animals to respond to my voice. Pattern generalization became simple sentence parsers, the way push-ups become pectorals. The stacked layers began to recognize—and even make—rudimentary distinctions. I told it: John is taller than Jim. By copying the repeated *ur*-models, it then reassured me that, yes, Jim is shorter than John.

But even such simple manipulations of properties could throw it for an infinite loop. The kettle has more coffee than the cup, but the cup is fuller. That conclusion needed to wash recursively through the mesh several times before B got comfortable with it.

As with many younger sibs, B turned A's personality inside out. While it handled the two-word sentence drill with curt aplomb, it turned garrulous at anything longer. This second set of arrays found more patterns in our sentence prompts than either of us intended.

"B is sick," Lentz greeted me one day on my arrival at the lab.

"Oh no. Don't tell me."

"By 'Don't tell me,' I assume you mean 'Tell me.' "

"What's it doing now?"

"Watch."

Though the machine would respond to no voice but mine, it answered to anyone's typing. It couldn't tell who was at the keys. It answered all comers, cheerfully presuming the typist had nothing but its best interests at heart.

Lentz typed B a little story: "Friends are in a room. A chair is in the room. Richard talks to Diana. Diana sits in the chair." Each word converted to a token, a matrix of strengths. These tokens laced together into sentence vectors. The vectors rolled around through the net landscape, marbles seeking the most available basin. The place they landed, the way they fell, was what they meant. The sieve sorted every configuration that entered it. And each sort changed forever the net configuration.

"You ready?" Lentz asked me. Then he typed, "Who is in the chair?"

B flipped out. "Friends is in the chair. The chair is in the chair. Richard talks to in the chair . . ."

It wouldn't stop prattling. "It's got St. Vitus' dance," I said.

"It's got St. Vincent's malaise," Lentz countered.

He was right. Figuration was driving B as batty as a poet. It framed meaning too meagerly, extending semblance too far. It pushed the classic toddler's tendency to overgroup. Had its digits been skeletal, it would have pointed at anything sitting on a bookshelf and called it a book.

"We'll need to cut the graded feedback and go to more rigorous supervision," Lentz said. "This beast is going to have to learn that not everything will fly."

It made sense. I'd read some developmental neurology. A newborn's synapses far outnumbered those of an adult. Perhaps building effective pathways required that many useless ones had to die. Short of slitting B's metaphoric throat with Occam's razor, we were going to have to rein it in.

For the time being, we decided to pare back B's associations with definitive answers. Repeated treading across the desired path would force Imp B to hack a right route through its lush profusion.

Now, when B started to do its permutational thing, I learned to say no. I would tell it the proper answer, however problematic. However much it hurt, I made it play straight. B took this right answer, matched it to the verbal diarrhea it had produced, and step by painful step went back over its connections to see where it had gotten carried away.

Only this reduction of limitless possibility made learning possible again. And only real learning—nothing mechanical or predictable— would satisfy me.

It pained me, one false spring dusk late in the season, as I walked home along the soon-to-be-crusted-over streets, to hear myself thinking in terms of satisfaction. I thought I'd left the word behind, in the reweighted and long-since-extinguished past.

Imp B always did rub me the wrong way. Nothing violent. I just never cared for it, although I tried not to let that impede our work. I guess the way its linked nets responded to input reminded me too much of all my own little rickies, drowned in fecundity, unable to damp generalization down or clamp it into the manageable.

But as B grew less poetic and more docile, I began to miss the willful driveler. I'd taken perverse delight in watching it conclude, from "If you want me, I'll be in the office," that until you want me, I'll be at home.

Lentz seemed unhumbled by this second lesson in unbounded verbal space. "What do the literary theorists say about reading books these days?" As if I could paraphrase for him, in an afternoon. As if, armed with my paraphrase, he might tack on a couple of preprocessing, feed-forward subsystem nets that would address any conceivable problem.

"First off, they're not books anymore."

"Texts," Lentz corrected himself. "Excuse me." As always, he knew more than he let on.

"Well, let's see. The sign is public property, the signifier is in small-claims court, and the signification is a total land grab. Meaning doesn't circulate. Nobody's going to jailbreak the prison house of language."

"How about getting paroled for good behavior?"

"Come on, Engineer. Come clean for once. Tell me all that doesn't depress the hell out of you."

"No, it doesn't. It just means we have as good a shot at this as any waffling poseur. We can get our supernet to sound exactly like a fashionable twenty-two-year-old North American whiz kid imitating a French theorist in translation by, say, this time next month."

"Engineer—"

"I'm serious, Marcel. I've seen the stuff you're talking about. Gnomic is in. We just have to push 'privilege' and 'reify' up to the middle of the verb frequency lists and retrain. The freer the associations on the front end, the more profound they're going to seem upon output."

"Fine. Do as you please. You obviously don't need me for any of it. And I don't need to spend a year working on a pointless and cynical scam. If I wanted that, I would have stayed in tech writing."

"Marcel, sit down. Marcel! Don't be an infant," Lentz ordered. His voice broke. It shocked me. I didn't think he'd care. Certainly not about something as trivial as my packing it in.

"All right," he stammered. "I didn't mean that. I'm sorry. I was joking. A little self-deflation. It's been so long since I've been satisfied with anything I've done that I get critical. And I forget that not everybody is as detached as I am. I thought you understood. I'm sorry."

I just watched the man. All footwork. All of it, the contrition as well as the cynicism. He himself had long ago lost the ability to tell what he was after or when he was being genuine. But the astonishing thing—the thing that made no sense—was that he wanted me around. The game was no fun, it was worthless to him otherwise. I couldn't figure it, and I didn't want to leave without knowing.

I sat back down, as deliberately as possible. I drew out my answer, curious to see what I would say.

"Imp B?" I asked. I wasn't sure what I meant by the question.

Lentz answered without pause. "A noble cause, in any case. And not without theoretical interest. Let's do it for ourselves. I mean, of course we'll show them what we come up with and all. But let's just work, and forget about the bet."

I looked at the man. The bank safety-glass lenses protected him from eye contact.

"To hell with that." I laughed. "My kid is going to ace that exam!"

"Okay, okay." Lentz cackled alongside me. "Anything you say." His eyes seemed to be watering. He actually put his hand on my shoulder, but just as quickly removed it.

We worked hard on sentence parsing, on relationships and comparisons, on simple semantic decoding. B did not get any more likable in the training process. But it grew undeniably clever at pattern matching and manipulation. The fact that it curve-fit countless serial streams of input vectors and could generalize the shape of a simple sentence at all punched my lights out.

May will be fine next year, I assured it. *Father hopes to plant roses in the front yard. Mother goes to fetch the doctor.*

We were in Lentz's office one weekend afternoon when he said, "It's time to give the kid something a little more obscure."

He rooted through the chaos of his bookshelves. From behind a stack of papers that had begun to recycle themselves, he pulled a fifties-era thermos bottle, a stained coffee mug inscribed *Opa*, and a ring of what for all the world looked like assorted roller-skate keys. Clearing this hole allowed him to shove around the rest of the junk in his packed office as if it were all some giant 15-puzzle.

This shoving at last released a book that seemed to have been stuck in deepest hiding. Squirreled away, like a boy's soft-core magazine. The pale pink fata morgana photograph on the jacket had been torn and taped clumsily back together. I knew the book even before he dredged it up into view.

"Oh no. Engineer. Lentz. Give me a break. Not that one. I've seen full professors make a total debacle of that book."

"Well, now, Marcel. We're not going to do the *book*. Heaven forfend. Just this bit."

He dropped the text open in front of me, a horny thumbnail overscoring the harmless epigraph to Chapter One.

"Just that?"

"Just that."

"You're insane, you know."

"Oh yes. I'm quite aware of that. Wait," Lentz delayed me. "I want Plover to see this. Let's hope our prize pupil doesn't choose this moment to act up."

He limped down the corridor, making good time for a sixty-year-old whose body had been nothing but a nuisance to him for half those years. He returned with a dubious Harold in tow.

When he saw me, Harold's face lit up. "*Ave, Scriptor!* Are you keeping this charlatan honest?" Had I taken the least step toward him, he would have wrapped me in a bear hug.

Harold's spontaneous affection depressed me. I'd done nothing to get this fellow to like me, and the fact that he did made me feel dishonest. My sense of unearned credit was interrupted by the appearance in the doorway of a sullen teenage girl.

"Trish," Plover commanded. "Trish. Take the headphones off. Take—the—headphones . . ." He pantomimed in affable, immense semaphore. Trish complied, rolling her eyes toward a spiritual mezzanine.

"This is the novelist whose books I showed you." Harold turned back toward me, to make sure I was the person he meant. "Richard, this is Trish. The second of the Plover Amazons."

She shook my hand, then looked around the lab for sterilization equipment.

"How many in the tribe?" I asked.

Harold started ticking off his fingers. "I don't know. I've lost count."

"Oh, Daddy!" Trish moaned. A mentally deficient father: the only thing that could have driven her to address me. "Don't listen to him. He's been insufferable ever since Mom let Sue go to Italy."

"Hear that? 'Insufferable.' Trish is the literary one. She writes poetry."

"I do not. They're song lyrics."

"She'd like you to look at them sometime."

"No way!" Trish shouted.

Lentz snorted at the collocation. "Is Hartrick going to come have a look at this?" he asked.

I felt the tension before the sentence was even half out of him. Harold looked ready to strangle the little man.

"No. Just do your stuff. Let's see what you got."

"What you *have*," Trish corrected. This time, Dad rolled his eyes.

I spoke to B. I launched into the singsong nursery rhyme that, for reasons that I've long since forgotten, I'd used to open my first novel.

"As I was going to St. Ives, I met a man with seven wives . . ."

I stumbled and hung up on the lines. Harold reminded me how they went, and I got all the way through.

Everyone held their breath. "Well?" Lentz said. "Go ahead, then. Get on with it. Pop the question."

I posed the query with which my firstborn book began.

"Kits, cats, sacks, wives: how many were going to St. Ives?"

Somewhere on the curve of unfathomable syntaxes lay the desired answer. Our network of nets took less than half a minute to triangulate it. "One."

"Way cool!" Trish exclaimed. She moved toward the terminal, excited. I noticed something wrong with the way she walked. Then the shoe dropped: she was on roller blades.

Plover broke out in a belly laugh. "This is for real?"

Trish took the microphone. "Open the pod bay doors, HAL!" Vectors danced across the screen, but Imp B kept its counsel. Trish pouted.

"It may be less impressive than it looks," I demurred. "I assume it just ignored everything in the riddle that it couldn't fit into the main predication."

"It's impressive enough," Lentz said, laconically. "Unfailing literal-mindedness may be the most impressive thing going."

The epigraph I read to Imp B, like the book it opened, came from a distributed nowhere. I don't know why I used it. If I had to gloss it, I would say the line was about walking head-on into the parade of not-you, somewhere along time's dirt track. No matter how long and elaborate history's procession, the eye meeting it along the muddy road is always first person singular.

That book came to me during our first year in B., the richest year in my life. I thought we were happy then, but who can say? Our happiness may never have been more than bravery. *Assume a virtue, if you have it not.* That was my favorite line, that pilgrim winter. I liked the idea that we grew to become our attitudes. And attitude, during our stay in B., felt like happiness, deep and artesian.

We were alone. For the first time in our lives, neither of us was going anywhere. We navigated from winter night to winter night, in a state where winter starts in October and rages on into May. In an apartment halfway along its forced march from genteel to desperate, we made a home too familiar for words.

Through those first mythic days, we met our neighbors. We sashayed around them in the laundry room and halls. We shook hands and took their business cards, with none to give in return. We folded origami mnemonics from the syllables of their names. Then we forgot the mnemonics.

No matter. People in our building did not want to be called anything anyway. That was why they chose the place. That was why we ourselves lived there. Every soul in that horseshoe courtyard wanted to be left to its private invulnerability.

The nearer the next man's dossier, the more easily we avoided it. A hole breached our bathroom ceiling into 307 above. It tore open in the shower steam, peppering our tub with drywall. We tacked a linen sheet printed with lime-green woods across the gaping wound. As good as healed.

We were each other's entire populace. Even job hunting was a shared delight.

"Here's one for you, C. 'Good communications skills.' "

"Um, Beau? I think they mean modems and stuff."

We listened to each other's stories. We improvised. We pulled repertoire out of deep storage. The books we didn't read out loud to each other we paraphrased at great length. And we read, reread everything that time had prevented us from reading properly until then.

I might linger over a printed paperback opening for an afternoon, wondering if I wanted to commit. For, once past page 10, I was obligated to stay the campaign, however sordid. I read essays, history, biography—things that would never in a million years be on the List because they weren't English or weren't literature. I commenced that million-and-a-half-word associative memoir that Lentz would harass me with by name, a dozen years later.

I began to keep a reading diary. Not very dramatic as turning points go, but there it is. A lifetime later, rereading these notebooks, I saw that the lines I copied out, the words I deemed worth fixing forever in the standing now of my own handwriting, clumped up with unlikely frequency toward the start of any new book. The magic quotes thinned out over any book's length. The curve was linear and invariable. Perhaps writers everywhere crowded their immortal bits up toward the front of their books, like passengers clamoring to get off a bus. More likely, reading, for me, meant the cashing out of verbal eternity in favor of story's forward motion. Trapping me in the plot, each passing line left me less able to reach for my notebook and fix the sentence in time.

C. read *Buddenbrooks* and *Anna Karenina*. She reread *Little Women*. Everything made her weep. Everything. Well before the last page, she would drag her heels. Her bookmark tracked across the spine of a paperback like Zeno's arrow, frozen in infinite halfway points on its way to the mark. The first four hundred pages zoomed by in two or three nights. The last forty could tie her up for a month.

When she did finish anything, it convulsed her. I remember her reading *Ethan Frome*.

"I thought every American high schooler had to pass a test on that book. Right before they quizzed you on the Constitution," I teased her.

C. shrugged. "Maybe I'm not an American, Beau?"

The day she finished, it turned cold. I was in the front room, on the overstuffed chair we'd saved from street-side collection. C. was in the bedroom, on the mattress on the floor. Out of dead silence, I heard her distress call. "Beau. Ricky." Soft and desperate, already lost, pinned under a mountainside of rock.

I closed the distance at reflex speed. She was propped up against the wall, her eyes rimmed red with salt, her fist shaking, pressed against her mouth. "Oh, Beauie. Give me another chance. I've been so selfish and awful. I can be better. I know I can."

This was from *Ethan Frome*, of all places. *Ethan Frome*.

Each workday, C. put on her navy blue uniform and walked across the land-filled fen between our apartment and the Fine Arts. There she stood for eight hours at a go, saving the masterpieces of world painting from a poking and prodding public.

Museum guard may be the most tedious occupation in the nation's job register. But someone neglected to tell C. She came home glowing with minute enthusiasms, discoveries that could be made only by staring at a painted surface for days at a time. In particular, she loved being assigned to the Fine Arts' chestnut Colonial collection. Too late, I heard in her love the deportee's thrill, the fascination with a country hers only by the thinnest accident of birth.

For the two of us, America went antique. In that city, at that time of year, people moved purposefully through the streets, hinged to their shadows. Their black coats seemed coal seams against gray snow. In silhouette, they passed for protagonists in modernist Czech novels. They packed down subway stairwells and through turnstiles. I packed along with them, on the way to the trade press office where I worked.

I imitated them for C. at night, when I came home. I mimicked the exchange of pleasantries. "We must dine some evening." "The Net National Income has experienced another sudden surge." C. insisted I had a future, either on stage or in a brokerage.

The city posed like one of those portraits C. guarded, a Whistler or a Copley. The subway trains—state-of-the-art, burnished, Asian —were at heart archaic trolleys. They hauled their human freight back and forth to garden suburbs with odd monikers. Cars darted through the maze of surface streets, tomorrow's Studebakers.

My computer magazine outfit sat inside a rustic steel-and-glass exoskeleton that made the surrounding buildings look even more antiquated. The cityscape was something an American postprimitive might do, a nostalgic century from now.

C. and I lived it in advance retrospective. We took long walks along the prow of winter, reconnoitering, registering everything. We ingested the ochers and burnt umbers, the tints that tipped us to the fact that the present was far stranger than it let on.

Only the urban poor refused to go aesthetic. They spoke in tongues, human or otherwise, debating themselves or whoever else would listen. They handed the two of us soiled pamphlets covered in Carolingian minuscule. Or they slouched asleep, grease- and blood-caked, in the back of sleek light rails, riding out to the docklands district of progress's trade fair.

On nights when the windchill permitted, when the bitterness of interplanetary dark toyed with its food by easing a degree, I walked home. I cut across the public plots, the ancient Victory Gardens, all their victories lost, forgotten, or squandered. There, bent women tilled the rows in windup planetarium ellipses. The city's native foreigners, waiting for spring to plant a new crop for next year's war effort.

I made my way through the garden, the days getting dark early, just after four. Over the fusty expressway bridge, I headed into the home stretch, closing in on the place C. and I had made for each other, from out of total accident.

We lived from sense to sense. I can picture the neighborhood as if it were last evening. The street with the nineteenth-century name.

The narrow, storefront scrap-metal emporia. The corner convenience grocer, hanging on by milk-quart markups and lottery tickets. The empty lots that did thousand-dollar days as instant baseball parking garages when summer still was. The abandoned warehouse that flourished briefly as a bar where youth in search of the chemically enhanced Authentic congregated and methodically slammed into itself, studying the dance floor as if meaning were there, in designer-drugged Arthur Murray footprint.

The neighborhood, the street, our apartment are still real. But the city where we spent those years gets more stylized, harder to see, the further I get from what the two of us used to call home.

And we did feel at home there, for a season. We could have pitched camp there forever. I belonged there more than in any of those toy-town props that loom like back-projection houses behind me and my brothers and sisters, in my album of faded black-and-whites.

And C.: C. lived there, too, for a while. For the first time since she'd learned how to plan, outcome didn't matter. It was all dress-up, in B. An oldies party. For two years—a long vacation—she found a fantasy that fit her.

But C. got homesick. It was inevitable. How could any town compete with a ghost? We'd lived in B. several months when we learned that C.'s parents were returning to Limburg. Both her folks had retired. The workday was over. A quarter century camping out on the South Side of Chicago was enough. It was time to give up and head home.

C. blamed herself. Had she stayed close, the folks might never have left. Twenty-some years had produced no permanent attachments; no tie kept them here. Only the children, and the three of them were already scattered all over the map. C.'s parents chose to see whether the little town of E. still existed, if it ever had.

The news devastated C. "I'm a miserable excuse for a daughter, aren't I?"

I was supposed to agree with her. I was supposed to tell her no.

Guilt was her move in the loop C. and her mother put each other through. The struggle was not over whether they loved each other, but over whether love was enough. They kept at one another, testing, accusing, defending. This endless attempt to determine who had betrayed the other put them both through hell. The kind of hell that would hurt far more, someday, when all scores were reconciled.

C.'s father, on the other hand: any flare-up, and Pap started whistling to himself, heading off to the nearest back room to fix things. I wondered how this old Dutch railroad man with his accented Chicago idioms—"Let's get the show on the road," "Now you're talkin'," "If it works, it works"—would ever fit back into a province whose chief industry since the shutting of the coal mines was geriatric care. He'd been away once before, in a German forced-labor camp. I always thought that first deportation was the reason he lit off for the States.

C. had been a bribe to keep her mother in this country. A baby, for a woman already middle-aged. "I'm responsible, Rick. I'm responsible for their dislocation in the first place. And now I'm responsible for their hauling up stakes again. It's too awful. They're old, Beauie. How are they supposed to put everything they own in a packing crate . . . ? They'll never make it, once they're back there. Never."

"Don't be crazy," I said. "They never *stopped* living there."

Men are worthless; they always think the issue is what's at issue.

"They'll make it just fine," I reasoned. The last thing C. needed. "They have two dozen brothers and sisters. They have more nieces and nephews than we have cockroaches. In another five years, they'll forget this continent ever existed."

"That's what I'm afraid of."

C. took the rap for her own abandonment. Since my father's death, the bonds of my blasted family had mercifully weakened. So it surprised me to see how desolate someone could be at the prospect of seeing hers just once or twice a year. C. broke out in a rash and began vomiting. The doctor put her on a popular sedative. Nothing I did seemed to help at all. Except listening to the stories.

Frantic, C. dragged out all the stories that her mother raised her on. Stories invariably meant the war. All tales came back to that. How the Germans tried to steal the bell out of the church steeple to melt it down, and how something like God stymied them. How her mother nursed a teenage Wehrmacht conscript, a story that almost split C.'s parents before they were even married. How her father's friends in the labor camp joined together to grow parody Hitler mustaches. How he escaped, evading his pursuers by leaping out of an upper-story farm window and limping off, broken-legged, into the night. How the government up north hid *The Night Watch* in the marlstone quarries under Maastricht. How C.'s uncle, forced to stand guard over his fellow coal miners during the occupation, was tried for complicity in the postwar hysteria, and imprisoned again by his friends.

C.'s fellow students, in that class of mine, could not identify Treblinka or date that war on a pop quiz I'd once given them. C. knew these things from nightly dinner table conversation. As if the occupation had ended yesterday. If then.

Our life in B. closed, really, with that first phone call from Limburg. I lay in bed one Saturday dawn, thrilling to the sound of my C. speaking another language. Another woman lived in the body of the one I lived with. C. had been accommodating me, making herself into someone she thought I could love. I hadn't the first idea who this other person was.

She spoke a dialect that ran like the fabled brook through the heart of E. Out of her mouth flowed an unparsable cascade of phonemes. She talked with her mother for a long time. Then her father, ear to the transatlantic taxi meter, came on for a verbal minute waltz. Then a dozen or so aunts, each with a bit of news. I'd moved in with all of them, without knowing.

A flurry of dialect goodbyes, and C. hung up, wrung out. "They're home," she said. "Come on. Outside."

I put my hand to the pane. The windchill was sub-desperate. "Only if you've been good."

C. began to cry. I fell all over myself telling her I was joking.

We bundled as best we could and hit the street. Her aimlessness was always hard on me. But I'd learned by then not to ask for destinations.

Everything was still the same, she assured me. B. would go on being bearable if we could keep making our long, random walks. That day, we ended up in her beloved public gardens, now frozen over and empty for the winter. The day after, we kept our standing cantata date, at that church that had sung one a week for years before our arrival and that would go on singing them long after we were permanently out of earshot.

Things would be all right, she implied, if we just kept busy. In the evenings we played board games, or sang songs that I wrote for C.'s perfect, clear alto. We watched old films on a black-and-white set with tinfoil antenna, on loan from friends. Gradually, C. convinced me that movies have been going downhill since 1939.

At night, we read to each other—more biography, history, legend —following no program but delight.

Things would be fine if we kept out of the house whenever possible. Saturday morning was free day at the Fine Arts. C. was the only woman alive who would want to return in her spare time to see the same objects she'd just stood in front of for forty hours that week. "It's not the same, Beau. They're much more interesting when you don't have to worry about protecting them."

We went to see the first American retrospective of a German photographer neither of us knew. C. had not yet been assigned the special exhibition. So Saturday was the day. We crossed the swamp that B.'s Brahmins had a century ago called in the Dutch to drain. We strolled into the gallery and around the corner. My photo waited for me there, although I would never have expected it in any number of lifetimes.

First image on the left-hand wall, just inside the door. That room's geometry has fused to the floor plan of my brain. I stood face to faces with three young men who were scrutinizing *me*. They'd waited two-thirds of a century for me to come along and swing into view, just past the photographer's shoulder.

The photo was itself a prediction of its own chance viewing. The three men prearranged the way I would someday see them. And now it seemed that every book I'd been dabbling in, all our random read-alouds, the long list of irrelevant classics I'd memorized for my master's, the swerves our narrative lives had taken all found their retroactive meaning in this one memory posted forward from the past.

The boys were C.'s grandfather and two great-uncles on their way to kermis, to one of those *huwelijksfeesten* she told me about. That was what the lens said. The caption said something altogether different.

German peasants on their way to a dance, 1914. The wrong celebration. The excluded guest list. But very much the same family album.

I felt the shock of recognizing a thing I knew I had never seen before. Every text I'd ever read formed an infinite, convergent series calling out for the recursively called-for, the obvious next term. In that narrow space between what the picture handled and what the caption named, I had my story.

The following Monday, I went in to my tech editing job and gave my two weeks' notice. C. backed me every inch. "Buddy. When you have a calling, you don't worry about what it does to the résumé." Our nest egg had doubled during our year of work. We had a little time. We could buy a chance.

In fact, C. would have preferred a much deeper plunge into the precarious. Ours was always hedged. I had my programming skill to fall back on. When the account dipped into the danger zone, I freelanced. I worked the smart-appliances gig. I wrote an options trading program for an exiled prince who needed several million dollars to return to his land and finance an election. As he explained, "These things can be very expensive, Rick."

Writing met all the expenses. At least, I meant it to. I must have written that book to gladden C. again. I say "again," but she may never have been. Perhaps to receive gladness you need a forwarding address. Maybe the Polish boy's death cheated her of that, long before her unborn soul stood in line for a residence.

Her transience made a pallet for my head. From the first, C.'s locus of non-time and un-place indexed my imagination's coordinate plane. That's why living with her completed me. Why being with her always felt like coming to rest, returning to some *otherwise* that no one else ever suspected.

She was my midmorning's hypothetical. The givens of my day revealed their thinnest convention, so long as I loved her. Here and now reversed in convex reflection, abidable, on the outside of her eyes.

All we can ever do is lay a word in the hands of those who have put one in ours. I thought I might write my way to a place where my friend C. could live.

I used all the material I had at hand: the vanished Limburg she told me so much about. Her synaptic map of the walled city of Maastricht. The endless cousins who infiltrated my brain like thieves on bicycles in the night. The anthology poured into me through every gate except experience. The disruption of the time line circling our room. The parents, the uncles, caught between nations. The invasion of Trois Vierges, escalating into permanent violence. Big reaching down and annihilating little. Total war, always the same war, placing its embargo on the free passage of lives over the border.

I already possessed all the components for a page-turner. The secret document linking the displaced life back into its continuous frame. The immigrants' island in Chicago. Our apartment in B., with its courtyard and seasick saxophone scales. A chance trip we made by train to Detroit, where her brother lived. Always, always, that invisible village, the one that time mortared to a stump. The white diffraction pattern of crosses, and the villagers who volunteered to tend them. And that glance *back*, over the shoulder. The triple stopped lives, lined up on the muddy road, waiting for someone to pick up their story and extend it.

I wrote of C.'s country without once having seen it. I used her language, fragments of it, helped only by C. herself, who had never spoken anything but the secret dialect of family.

I made the beginner's mistake, the one no first novelist can help but make. I knew, deep at heart, that I would never have another chance to write a book. I could never again ask C. for that luxury. This was a one-shot deal, and to redeem her faith in me, I had to pack my read-aloud with everything I knew. Everything she taught me. Her surrogate home would have to be as wide, as uncrossable as this Atlantic century. If we had just this one dance, our tune would have to be flat-out *tutti*.

I guess there are two kinds of love letters. If you don't get out after the first three words, you need to press on, forever. C. taught me that, too. Desperation is always more moving than discretion, or more recognizable, at least, to the person addressed.

C. earned the daily bread, while I sat alone with the swelling handwritten canary legal pads. As I completed each new chapter, I read it to her. She came home, ate the dinner I made her, then settled in expectantly. She sat close. C. was partially deaf; she always staked out the front seat in classes. Mine especially.

I don't know who was more nervous, performer or audience. *Chapter One*, I assured her. *I outfit myself for a trip to St. Ives.*

I knew that this book would never be published. My audience was never more than C. I wrote for the way her eyes would start to water by chapter's end. How she would nod her head yes, place her hand on her chest, rise from the bed to grab me in the chair where I sat reading to her.

Yet that spell would not have worked if her private code of survival hadn't been cast in a public key. The tale had to be open enough to appeal to the random gallery-browser, snared by the lens. C. alone knew where all the nested frames had started.

Those nights of first draft will not happen again. Never, anymore, that simple passion. We lost it the minute I handed the gift over, the instant I read aloud the epilogue. Years later, when I started getting invitations to read to rooms of perfect strangers, I never had the heart.

Sometimes after I read a chapter to C., we made love. We climbed over each other, brown, frighteningly young, vulnerable, exploring the sad distances, warming each other after the radiators packed it in. Once, as I kissed the birthmark that stained the small of her back, this seemed to me the point of literature. I could not think of a book that was not either by, for, or about this. The elaborate seduction of the already attained. Reforestation of the wilds of time, the one biome where love will not die from lack of cover. I can see that birthmark with my eyes wide open, clearer now at fifteen years' distance than it was when an inch from my eye.

Sex was her present for transcribing her. My feeble thank-you for her sources. And the sounds we listened to then, the calls we made to each other in the winter dark were the vowels that all stories tried to find their way back to.

Afterward, without fail, we fell asleep, her back to my front, two spoons put away in the kitchen drawer of an abandoned cabin. C. was a foot shorter than I was. But when we lay like that, trig turned us to the same length.

The book became a mystery. A foregone conclusion. The more C. felt its surprise inevitability, the keener she got for the next installment. Each narrative riddle, each mental *raadsel* was an awkward, tenderfoot bow I tied for her, for the pleasure of her untying.

Jokes made her happy. I crammed my paragraphs full of every old joke I could remember.

Up top of each new chapter, I placed an epigraph. I copied out of my notebooks a quote that my same clumsy fingers had, earlier that year, just copied in. That book is the dance card of ideas we shared in the foyer of our joint life. A dance card where the partner's name was already printed in, a given. I wrote down only the steps themselves, the ideational dips and sways from the course of that evening when C. was my one date, the lone museum guard of all my thoughts.

Sometimes the steps were literal. One night, I read her a chapter so short it left us more time than even love could fill. She'd listened well; it was time for a walk. We drifted out, a slow, deliberate stroll along the parkway that flanked the trolley tracks out to the suburbs.

In the chapter, my contemporary technical editor, in a city much like B., had journeyed home to his immigrant mother in Chicago to find mysterious papers up in the family attic binding him to an unknown past. The passage back left C. expansive.

"I like that guy of yours," she said. "I like your Lithuanian graffiti on the sidewalks. Do you have any idea what it feels like to be the puppy raised by ducks?"

"Tell me."

She heaved a sigh. "I've been to more Polish weddings than I can count."

"Well, we know about your head for figures."

She laughed and flank-attacked. "Come on, you. Let's polka."

"The polka is no more than a spot of local color from out of *Washington Square*, I'm afraid."

"Don't be afraid," C. purred. She could be coy at times. Funny. I'd forgotten. "Here. I'll show you."

She stomped it out for me. I was comic, crippled, a laughingstock. But she stuck with me. Of all the countless thousands of things C. taught me, that polka might be the best. I picked it up somewhere along the length of that greenway down which we hurled ourselves, a couple of parka-packed, manic Polacks making tracks into the Arctic dark.

"It makes me sad, Beau," she told me, another chapter night, perhaps halfway through.

I panicked in the space of a phrase. "What? Something's off? I can fix it. Don't worry; it ends happily."

"Not that, silly. It makes me sad. You have this—work. And I have nothing."

"I don't get it. I thought you liked putting on that uniform."

"Oh, I did. And it's still the greatest job in the world. In some ways."

"What's wrong, then?"

She wasn't sure. She still loved the paintings. But they had started to fade into overlearned monochrome. Standing in place for so long began to fog her. The boss was growing creepy. She felt embarrassed explaining herself to others. Ashamed of doing less than she might.

"Maybe we should look around for a new job?" The "we" that would take such toll on her.

"It's the middle of winter. Nobody's hiring. Besides, what am I qualified to do?"

"Well, I don't know. Anything. If the job you have is making you crazy—"

"I know, I know. I need something more than just a paycheck. The problem is, I'm not ambitious. Put me on a rug, I'll lie there forever."

" 'Put me out on the lawn and I'll wail'?"

She clouded. "It's not funny. I'm sorry I ever showed you that picture." I tickled her to re-create that infant expression.

"Quit it!"

"*I'll* give you prickling."

"Don't, Beau. Not now. This is serious."

"So serious we can't—"

The obvious *yes* stopped me in mid-cliché.

"What's the matter?" I asked. Ready, already, to be dead.

"It's your story." She looked down, away. Anywhere but at me. "It makes me feel worthless. I know it's awful. Do you hate me?"

She got a new job. A friend of mine from the computer world tipped C. to an opening. Wire operator in a brokerage. "Not something I'm going to make a career of," C. joked.

But something to engage her, salve the sense of self. She came home animated again. As I fed her, she entertained me with tales of eccentric colleagues, wigged out on Opportunity Loss. Her accounts of that quintessential late-twentieth-century business delighted me. The parasitic middlemen, extracting margin from the news feed, the Teletype romances and tragedies. The spigot attached to the pipeline, leveraging profit and hedging loss as it trickled through capital's tap.

So I did the only thing imaginable. I went back and worked her new material into the book as well as I could. The market and mad brokers became yet another subplot. I fit it in, between jokes from the front and tales from the tech editing crypt, between the Maas and the Rhine, between the war and its permanently militarized peace, between the Great Personalities and the clueless lives, between fairyland and documentary fact, the aperture and the print, then and now, filthy lucre and the Fine Arts.

What did the finished thing mean? It meant that our private reservoir, when face-to-face with the outside, is all we have that might help a little. That book was no more than a structured pastiche of every report I'd ever heard, from C. or abroad. All a patchwork to delight and distract her. One that by accident ate her alive.

The key to that book, the one that preserves it for me, is that the triple braid—the magic *driehoek* of the photograph—fails to come together as expected. The lens does not have the last word, nor does the glance of the viewer, nor does the look of those boys, out over the shoulder of the photographer, back behind the lens. The dominant tense was now. The point of stories was what you did with them.

With my last chapter, the charm broke. I knew it in advance. I saved every trick I had for the end, to break her heart and win her for the present, forever. But of course, a return to feeling only made things worse. I read her the ending. Lovemaking stayed silent this time, skin more a checkpoint between us than a visa in.

"What will you do with it now?" C. asked.

"I don't know." The plot had gotten away from me. Escaped its frame. "Send it out, I guess."

Too rapidly, she agreed. "Of course. You have to."

Only the usual literary biography would have saved us. Fifteen years of waiting to be taken. Growing stronger, closer to each other on the mound of rejection slips, which we'd have burned for fuel.

The day we heard the book had been bought, we celebrated. Cheer felt forced and punch-drunk. C. assumed the virtue of excitement as bravely as she had managed each chapter up until then. But she was like a mother losing her preschooler to the talk-show circuit.

She tried to show enthusiasm for the production process. She pitched in, but her heart had bolted. She hated those grubbers in New York touching the manuscript, even to typeset it. It killed her to watch those farmers make their way into the brutal market. To see them join the ranks of the century's displaced.

She would never again listen to a word I wrote without suspicion. Endings, from now on, betrayed her. Simple associative fact: it wasn't even a question of remembering. What chance does story have against neurons that generalize from a single instance?

The week we learned the book's publication date, C. received an offer of promotion. The brokerage wanted her to run their Operations cage. The jump, steep and quick in coming, surprised no one but C. She was alone in never knowing how competent she was.

The offer could not have come at a better time. C. needed something, and nothing that I could give. A hurried, three-week trip to Limburg to check on her folks left her edgier than ever. Not even walks worked any longer. A real career might be no more than a changeling baby. But even a changeling can take up the slack of care.

She had some days to decide. We spent them spinning skeins of reassurance. "You'll be great at it. They wouldn't have asked you otherwise."

The day she went in to accept, I prepared a feast. I made decorations. Funny little signs with cartoons of C. on a pyramid of brokers, cracking a whip. Hand-lettered posters reading "Book That Cruise" and "Retirement by 35."

I could tell, watching her come up the courtyard, that celebration was a horrible mistake. She pounded up the stairs, slammed the door, and held it shut behind her with all her hundred and five pounds, sobbing.

"Beauie, we need to get out of this place."

I tried to hold her, proffer all the worthless comforts. "Okay," I managed. "I'm game. Where to?"

The last place. Worse than I expected. "I want to go back to U."

Imp B already pushed the envelope. B hadn't a clue what cats *were*, or sacks, let alone wives. But it seemed to know how to count them, or not count them, as the case demanded.

If A had been an exercise in verbal pattern recognition, B was a foray into computational linguistics. It knew things like over and under, right of or left of, inside or out. Even that far, I doubted whether it comprehended these containers or whether it just manipulated them cleverly enough to pass. Then again, I began to doubt whether I myself could define the difference.

B could handle syntax. It had a rudimentary sense of the parts of speech and how they operated on each other. And it began to cross the threshold into semantic content. Lentz once or twice tacked on a new subnet to handle different routines—a noun-phrase decoder or a short-term recognition scratch area. In fact, I suppose we were up to Imp B.4 or better.

Lentz assured me that B would handle its own knowledge representations. The frames, the inheritance of classification qualities and exceptions, the scripts: all would fall out as a result of the way B stored associated input. But even in its minute domains, B had to deal with numbingly different kinds of knowledges. With nouns alone, what you could do with "pattern" varied without limit from what you could do with "matching" or "machine."

I'd lost count of the number of neurodes involved. It had grown big, complex beyond belief. A glitch now set us back whole days at a time. The thing was a monster, distributed, unchartable, out of control. And yet Lentz's brain, or mine, was hundreds of millions of Imp B's wide. We could push that matter a little longer, if only just.

We were still experimenting with the size of layers. Bigger was not always better, Lentz told me.

"Life, Marcel, in case you on the humanistic side of the tracks haven't grokked this yet, involves a series of trade-offs."

"Yes, we're onto that."

"Now. The trade-offs in input layer size. Well, the smaller the layer, the better it generalizes. The larger, the more it can learn to fit into an associative grid."

"The better it is at generalizing, the worse it is at acquiring new associations?"

"The poet's a blooming genius. Now we know how you earn your grant money."

"Does it follow that the more facts it has, the harder it is to take in new facts?"

"Thirty-five is about when that starts to happen, Marcel. You begin to think, 'Well, I more or less understand how things work. Do I really want to disassemble tens of thousands of tangled, semiaccurate beliefs on the off chance that I might be able to bring one small receptor field into better focus?' "

"Tell me about it. I'm there."

"Don't worry, little boy. You've a few tricks yet to pick through. And a few years yet to pick through them. I mean, you're lucky I've taken you on. Aristotle wouldn't accept any student still young enough to have a sex urge."

"Not a problem, at the moment."

On days when Lentz engaged himself with design philosophy, he grew expansive, almost pleasant. On days when he built things, he was fun. I tried to keep the soldering gun in his hand and ignore the baiting as much as possible.

"Now: what about the size of the hidden layers? Do you want them bigger or smaller than your input layers?"

"I'm sorry. I give up. We're going to have to turn all the cards over."

"Come on, think it out. Consider the translation impedance. Another trade-off. The better the resolution, the more susceptible the net becomes to random noise. Think of B as a curve fitter . . ."

"That's all our brains are? Curve fitters?"

"It's a big 'all,' friend. The curve we are trying to fit is as long as existence. As many dimensions. The fact that we can get the infinite data stream to cohere into lumps at all has turned men with as much native intelligence as your friend Plover into mystics."

"Here we go. Time to slander Harold."

"It's not slander. The man makes his claims public. 'Meanings extractable from a given linguistic configuration may be neither convergent, bounded, nor recursively enumerable.' Or some such rubbish. He seems to think that because 'context' is infinitely extensible, there can be no neurological calculus of interpretation."

"And you, Engineer?" I tweaked, waiting until he had his hands full of printed circuit and his head deep in the cage. "Do you think that because you are virtuous, there will be no more cakes and ale?"

"Now, Marcel. What in the *hell* is that supposed to mean?"

"Dunno. Let's ask Harold."

"Hn. I'd rather get back to the subject. Sometimes I think the human brain is just one long open parenthesis. So. Tell me. How big do you want your various output layers to be?"

"I guess that would depend on how big an answer we are expecting from any given subnet."

"Well done. You're getting cagey. We'll have you writing NSF proposals in no time." Lentz's sarcasms were mellowing with age. "Would you concede, then, that many of our output layers could consist, in theory, of a single neurode, since the cyborgs think that every quest can be rephrased as a series of yes-or-no questions?"

"I wish the lit critters would catch on to that."

"Yes. Handy, isn't it? Cleans up a lot."

"Engineer, can I ask you something? If you're not a mystic and you're not a cyborg, what in creation are you?"

" 'Creation' is a loaded word, Marcel. I guess I'm a lot of little delta rules running recurrently, evaluating and updating themselves."

"Tell me a different story. I'm not sure I like that one."

We were well into the millions of connections when B seized up for good. We'd made so many tortuous increments, we'd stopgapped so many glitches that I did not, at first, see this collapse as fatal.

"John is a brother of Jim's," I told it. B turned the fact into a stream of hieroglyphic vectors that changed its layout imperceptibly. "Who is Jim's brother?"

"John," Imp B replied. Reliant knight. Already it outperformed some aphasics.

"Who is Jim?"

"John's sister." That much was fine. I could live with that answer. In fact, it taught me a thing or two about my own presumptive matrix.

I continued, "John gives Jim apples. Who gets apples?"

"Jim gets apples."

"Jim is given the apples by whom?"

"Jim is given the apples by John."

"Jim eats an apple. The apple is sour. Jim throws the other apples away. Why does Jim throw the other apples away?"

At that point, B's cranking time became unendurable. It returned something like, "Jim throws the other apples away because the apples are given by John."

"No," I told it, or words to that effect. "Start again. Why?"

"Jim throws the apples away. She does not want them."

A marginally acceptable answer. Maybe insight hid away somewhere in that tacit implication. But maybe the damn thing was bluffing. Its vagueness depressed me: the slow tyro during story hour, doomed from birth to a career in food service.

"Why doesn't she want them?"

"She doesn't eat them. So she can't want them."

This alien proto-intelligence differed just enough from sense to make my head throb. Still, we lay within acceptable performance margins. I went on to torture it with, "Jim hits John. Why does Jim hit John?" B had one of its damning seizures. It cranked all afternoon, resetting itself, grabbing randomly at a thousand possible but skewed associations.

Thrashing, it tried a proverb we'd hammered into it the week before. "Jim hit John because one bad apple doesn't spoil the whole barrel."

When pushed, it finally failed to answer all together.

Some crucial frameshift fell outside B's ability to effect. It could not say, *John's apples angered Jim*, or *No reason*, or *There could be bad blood I haven't heard about*.

It could not even say *I don't know*.

It lacked some meta-ability to step back and take stock of the semantic exchange. It could not make even the simplest jump above the plane of discourse and appraise itself from the air. Although it talked, in a manner of speaking, speech eluded B.

Its brain faltered at that Piagetian stage where the toy disappeared when placed behind a screen. It could not move ideas around. All it could move around were things. And the things had to be visible at all times.

Something was screwy with the way B passed symbolic tokens among its levels. It might grow knowledge structures forever, as fecund as a field tilled with representational fertilizer. But its knowledge *about* knowledge would remain forever nil. And no patching or kludging on Lentz's part could set it right. B's deficiency seemed to be a by-product of the way its constituent nets spoke to one another. The way we'd linked them into the grand schematic.

We postponed the inevitable for as long as we could. I came into the office one evening and found Lentz behind his desk, inert. "I want to change the architecture." Ahab, well out of port, announcing the slight broadening of plans.

I was too invested to feel demoralized. Maybe I had some naïve image of taking a magnetic snapshot of B and somehow porting it intact into new and more capable digs.

Retrain several million connections from scratch. Had I realized, I might have signed off the project. But I had no incentive to realize. My last month and a half of literary effort had produced no more than half a chapter of train, crossing the snow-lined mountains toward sunny neutrality. I stopped at every other sentence to run to the library and verify that I wasn't unconsciously plagiarizing. As a result, the thing read like a Samuel Beckett rewrite of the *Ancrene Riwle*.

U. made changing machine architectures almost trivial. It stretched credibility, but that sleepy hamlet with the two-dollar movie theater and the free corn boil at summer's end also sheltered a National Supercomputing Site. The town, fallen through the earth's crust into a dimension where nothing had changed since 1970, consequently had a jump on the next millennium, the advantage of the late starter. Four rival pizza parlors, each named "Papa" somebody, each opening whenever it felt like it. Bars where fraternities split Thursday-night twenty-five-cent plastic cups of beer. And the most advanced, block-long cybernetic wonderland that a paranoid race to preserve faltering world dominance could fund.

I imagined my network's first freshman comp assignment: "Convince a total stranger that she would not want to grow up in your hometown." Son of B could whistle its answer to that one in the dark.

The latest nationally funded supercomputer to come of age in U. had itself already lived through half a dozen incarnations. Nor was it really a single machine. It was a collection of 65,536 separate computers, chained like galley slaves into inconceivable, smoothly functioning parallel. Depending on the benchmark, the connection monster could outperform any computing assemblage on earth.

The machine was so powerful that no one could harness it. So notoriously difficult was its programming that major scientists and their graduate-student franchises had already begun to flee U. for sites a tenth as potent but at least manageable.

"We're moving over to the connection monster, Marcel."

"Lentz, you're kidding me. This game can't interest you that much."

"What? I'm not afraid of that thing. How hard can it be?"

"Hard. Harder than humiliating your colleagues can be worth."

"You underestimate my colleagues. Besides, don't forget the undertaking's empirical interest."

"Don't bullshit me, Engineer. This thing is all smoke and mirrors. And you know it."

But he knew, too, that he had me hooked. I wanted to see the next implementation up and running on a host tailor-made for neural nets. Lentz wrote a proposal credible enough to pass itself off as real science. By that time, the keepers of the connection monster were so hard pressed to salvage their hardware from neglect that they were taking all comers.

The man was dangerous when he had a plan. He meant Imp C to be profoundly different in nature. He wanted to push the notion of the self-designing system up a level. Reweighting prewired connections would no longer suffice. Imp C would be able to strengthen or weaken the interactions between entire distributed subsystems. It would even grow its own connections from scratch, as needed.

Lentz wanted to get hundreds, perhaps thousands of large, interdependent nets up and running at the same time. He saw them passing endless streams of ideational tokens among themselves. The net of networks would churn at all times, not simply responding passively to new data inputs. When input stopped, it would interrogate itself in ongoing, internal dialogue. Its parts would quiz one another, associate and index themselves, even when alone. Imp C would undertake constant self-examination and reorganization.

Lentz meant to distribute these chattering subsystems not just across the connection monster's 65,536 processors but across other various and specialized hosts. Each task communicated with the others via high-speed fiber-optic cable. C, if it could be said to live anywhere at all, lived spread all over the digital map.

"Keep out of my hair for a few weeks, Marcel."

"That should be easy."

Lentz, preoccupied, ignored my crack. "Just until I dig the foundations."

The order suited me. I had copy to proofread. I'd also agreed to a number of classroom visits, hoping to justify my freeloading existence.

The class visits were an embarrassment for everyone. Students sat polite but stunned in front of me, their desks circled like Conestogas under attack. The look of shame on each face asked how I could have missed the fact that the age of reading was dead. "How do you work? Where do your ideas come from?" they asked, hoping I would take the hint and go away.

I answered as best I could. But I couldn't take a step toward the first of these questions without lying. Luckily, lies were all they expected.

When class visits ended, I sat in my office, proofing the book I no longer remembered having written. I went through one methodical ruler-line of text after the other until the Primary Visual Area back in my occipital lobe started to bleed.

I tried to read without comprehension. One catches more errors that way. But sense pressed itself on me, kicking and screaming. The book's style perched on the brink of nervous disintegration, the most depressing fairy tale I'd ever read. And the only person more depressed than I was my editor, sitting on my unfulfilled contract.

I knew the narration meant to be double-voiced with my protagonist, a resident surgeon living an extended mental breakdown. My depiction of a society in collapse now struck me, if anything, as hopelessly tame compared to those vignettes shoring up the hourly news. But as I read, I kept thinking: Someone has to find this author before he does something desperate.

I spent the first week exterminating typos. The second I spent improvising, in the margins of the last pages, some semblance of redemptive ending. I scratched out the manuscript's final descent. In its place, I had my collapsing surgeon hold out his hands, catch the woman who had failed to save him. I added a last-minute postscript that returned the tale to the light of its source, the reader, untouched by tragedy. And yet the story still radiated a darkness so wide my pupils could not attenuate.

My eleventh-hour triage demoralized me even more than the first writing. I felt a despair I had not felt while still the teller. Not a despair for my career, which had never been more than a happy accident. What lost me, listening to my own news account, was learning that I didn't have the first idea who I was. Or of how I had gone so emptied.

I kept at the reconstruction. I no longer had the heart to send out so bleak a deformity into the world. I worked in short spurts, all I had the strength for, surgically reinserting the *no* that children in the disputed zone need if they are to escape to daylight.

Work picked up at evening, when the building reverted to native, archaic silence. I'd hack at my story for half an hour, stand, stretch, warm my imagination by the purely symbolic fireplace, then sit back and try to cure the next nihilist paragraph.

I wandered the abandoned halls, a world unspeakably far from the Center. The plank floorboards creaked even before I stepped on them. They settled under the weight of generations of scholar undergraduates who had gone on to die at the desks of their bank vice presidencies. The passages smelled of gum and hair oil, ammonia, gargle, damp fiber, wax, shellac, chemicals from the days when chemistry was still a liberal art.

Even the steam pipes reeked a Georgian, paint-peeling grace. In the incandescent dusk, the building gave no hint of the internationalist polemics just now attempting last-ditch CPR on a discipline choked to death by curatorial gentility.

The manuscript took over my office. I taped pages up around the room, the way C. and I had once taped our homemade time line around the bedroom in B. I browsed them, drifting from one to the other, a well-meaning museum-goer gazing at an impenetrable Dadaist retrospective. I could find no further entrance. My corrections were overdue. My surgeon's fight against child genocide had become mine, and like him, I was failing to stem the end.

I worked late on the last night before my extended deadline. I revised until I needed to come up for air. I threw open the office door and fell into the hall. But I decompressed too quickly, giving myself the bends. The Georgian familiarity shrank in front of me, as overcome as the text I'd just been giving intensive care.

I made my way to one end of the main hall for a drink of water. I steadied and drank, but the sip tasted of heavy metals. I turned, facing into the empty passage. Shock knocked me backward a step, against the fountain. I wasn't alone. At the far end of the corridor, a ghost condensed from empty silence.

The apparition swayed in vacuum. My next blink would disperse her back into the ether. She stood browsing a notice board, oblivious of my existence. A whip-thin lamia in a pageboy haircut, absurdly young, in blue jeans and sleeveless orange cotton cling, despite the irreversible autumn. First day of adulthood. Setting out. She carried books under her arm, and a clump I hoped was a jacket. Something held her rapt: the corkboard, smothered in announcements.

I tried to beat a path back to my office without startling her. But the floorboards betrayed me, popping more violently the lighter I slid. She turned to look with mute, uncomprehending fear, a deer forgiving its killer. And with the same slow indifference, she shot a last glance at the notices and withdrew.

I don't know who I saw. Not the grad student she must have been, to let herself into the building at this hour. Not C. at thirty-three. Nor C. a life younger, when I'd met her. Nor any of those girl-women who had obsessed me, before C. If this was anyone I knew, I no longer recognized even the association.

Yet I felt like running after this profile, onto the chill Quad. Calling her back, laughing, excited, furious. What do you mean, coming here? Bad luck; bad judgment. Hadn't we agreed never to meet on this earth? Not after I'd gone prematurely dead, and you, a little girl in a T.

I could learn her name. She would carry prosodic weight to her—plans, a past—sad, pragmatic reasons why she haunted this building, working late. Doubtless, she brayed when she talked, slaughtered her checking account, complained about the freshmen she had to render literate, suffered paralyzing anxiety over her approaching prelims.

But for this one surprise ambush, the image of slender pageboy—a pair of bare shoulders, a gaze in profile down a fading hallway—stood in for all the books I'd failed to pull off. She was the sum of all stories I'd never now attempt. The placeholder for the long miss I'd made of experience. The loss fiction fails to repair. The fixedly ephemeral. A. at twenty-two.

Lentz almost glowed over the phone. "We've knocked it, Marcel. Pulled it off. The next step that everybody else has been after."

"Everyone else? Real scientists don't waste their time with make-believe."

"They would if they could get away with it. You think they like all that bloody reductionism? They only put up with those shuffling baby steps in the hopes that they'll run someday. That we'll all soar."

"Okay, Engineer. Enough iambs. Tell me what we've done."

"I've tested it. It's brilliant. B's problem was that it could manipulate idea tokens, but not ideas *about* those tokens. Right?"

"If you say so."

"We need a beast that can make second-order shifts. One capable of reflection. That can do with situations what B could only do with things. It's so simple: put it in the hardware. We need a C implementation that runs a fully functional simulation of a B-type implementation as one of its own component subsystems."

"A simulation within a simulation? One mock-up running another copy of itself?"

"Sound familiar? It should. It's you, Marcel. Where all your homesickness comes from. Your sense of never more than renting. All your picture galleries. Your private library of desire."

"Wait a minute. Back off. *I'm* the humanist here, remember? You're just in charge of the circuitry."

"Right. Sorry. My humble etceteras. I'm bringing the new incarnation up tonight. Get over here first thing tomorrow."

He didn't even give me the luxury of weighing the invitation.

When I arrived the next morning, Imp C was up and running.

We still dealt out of Lentz's office. Our gate was still the same junker terminal, the same jumble of antique I/O. I had to remind myself that the linkup hid, on its far end, the most powerful massively parallel hardware the combined public and private sectors could buy.

Lentz sat me down in the old chair. "Go ahead. Ask it something."

"Ask . . . ? You mean you've started the training already?"

"Well, this is difficult to explain. I still had all B's valences, the complete multidimensioned array of its connection weights sitting around in various files. So I thought, why not use them as a test? Let C run our actual B as its puppet modeler. It—rather took off."

"I don't get it. I still don't get it."

"Well, you know, the plan this time out was to go for full recurrence. The data set you put on the input layer works its way through, not once, but many times. No limit to how many times it can trip and reset the same weights on its way—"

"Yeah, yeah. I follow the mechanics." I didn't know what made me so testy. I felt the experiment getting away from me. "I just want to know how it can be responsive already, without training."

Lentz seemed embarrassed. "It seems to be training itself."

"Oh, Engineer. Don't give me—"

I slapped my bike helmet against the desk in disgust. Only a graze, but it cracked the shell cleanly. Lentz broke out in a sharp laugh.

"High deductible on that insurance policy of yours, Marcel." He started again. "It seems that C is capable of using different constellations of B's associative pairings as *its* points of comparison. It's triangulating. Testing itself for internal consistency. It's generalizing about the nature of its own generalizations."

"It's running already? Before I give it input?"

"It's running constantly. It makes its own input now."

"You mean, it can anticipate new material. You're trying to tell me it's thinking."

Lentz shrugged. He held his palm out to the microphone.

"Good morning," I said.

"Good morning," the voice-synthesizing hardware replied.

"How are you this morning?"

"Fine, thank you. You?"

I killed the mike. I turned to Lentz, quivering. "Where did it get that 'You'? Not 'And how are you?' We didn't even teach B the long form. How on earth did this one jump to the casual?"

"I don't know. It got it somewhere. From examining B."

"Are you pleased with yourself?"

"We all do what we can, Marcel."

"Shh. I'm not talking to you. I'm talking to the box."

Imp C paused a moment, then came back with, "What do you mean?" It seemed a stock enough answer. When in doubt, put the ball in the other guy's court.

"I mean, you must be happy to be so bright." Toss it a curve. See if it could handle the colloquial.

"Many things are so bright without being happy."

Impressive, even grammatical, although a bit clumsy. Still and all, it sounded to me more like hollow syllogism than philosophy.

"For instance?" Would it recognize the form as a question?

"For instance: light."

Imp C, I concluded, was whistling past the graveyard. Still, I decided to play fair. To give it as much benefit of doubt as I had to give anyone. I was middle-aged, and had myself only recently learned that no one hears what anyone else says.

"Do you think it's harder for smart people to be happy?"

Imp C thought for a minute. "Harder than what?"

I laughed out loud. Perfect. Perfect. The thing was an idiot savant.

"Jesus, Marcel," Lentz shouted. "Watch the input levels. You'll blow its eardrums out, cackling like that."

"Harder than if they weren't so smart," I explained to Imp C.

"Are you so smart while you are still being happy?"

Wonky idiom, even for an electronic DP. And little more than evasive maneuvers, again. Yet evasion, too, was a form of intelligence.

Then I let myself hear the machine's reply. It floored me. I was more than a blank irritant to C. I, too, was a token to manipulate. *I* had weight. I was part of Imp C's real-world calculus.

"I don't know. How can I tell if I am happy or not?"

"Ask yourself if you are not happy."

"Lentz," I said. "This is incredible. I can't—"

"It's fast, isn't it? I came up with a couple of quick-index algorithms. Idea caches, you might say. But I never expected we'd get this level of performance out of the new system."

"My God. It's not the performance, Lentz. It's—the *performance*."

"Yes," he agreed. The thing silenced even him.

"Look what it's doing. Telling me to ask myself. How can it *do* that? Think what it has to figure, just to stay in the ballpark. It knows 'happy.' It knows that 'happy' is a good thing. It knows 'happy' is something people are or aren't. It knows that I'm a person. It knows about questions, and that questions are something you 'ask.' It knows how to turn an interrogative into a statement, and scour a statement to see which questions might fit. Okay. Maybe it doesn't *know*, doesn't really understand all the things it conjures up by asking . . ."

All the things that made my voice catch to try to explicate.

"But it does understand enough to see that I'm not going to know anything, even about myself, except by putting myself the question."

"That's a lot," Lentz conceded.

"It's everything. Where did it . . . ?" But I'd lost patience with asking the human. I needed to interrogate the source.

"You make me happy," I told Imp C. I waited, sick, to see what it would say.

"Then I'm happy, too, Rick."

Too much, even for a willing victim. Over the line. My credibility snapped, as it should have, long before.

"Hold it. How did you know my name?" B never did. We gave it any number of proper names, but never our own.

At the crucial question, of course, C went silent. That, more than anything, gave the show away. A machine might have gone on innocently covering itself, even after the game was lost.

I wheeled on Lentz, not bothering to muffle the mike. "All right, *klootzak*. What the hell's going on?"

Lentz's eyes were watering. Unable to hold back any longer, he spit his dentures across the office. He whooped like a howler monkey. He tried to catch his breath, but each attempt left him more hysterical than the last. "I'm sorry, Marcel. You were—you were so . . ."

A shamefaced Diana Hartrick appeared in the doorframe. The truth finally hit.

"You?" My disbelief was worse than any accusation. "You let him set me up? You *helped* him?"

"It was a joke?" she wavered.

"To humiliate me? That's funny?"

"Oh, grow up, Marcel. Nothing's humiliating except this overreaction of yours."

"You grow up, Engineer." My tone stopped us all dead. It startled me as much as it did them. "So this is human intelligence. This is what we're trying so hard to model."

I'd been an idiot. Two seconds of reflection should have told me that C couldn't have commanded even a fraction of the material it spewed out. A babe in the woods would have seen through this. Trish Plover would have been, like, *really*. I myself would never have bitten, had I still been a child. Yet I'd believed. I'd *wanted* to.

Lentz tried to collect himself. But the minute he caught Diana's eye, he lost it all over again. Diana followed suit, helpless. Her snickers rasped somewhere in her throat.

"I'm sorry. It sounded funny at the time."

"Not without clinical interest," Lentz inserted. "Reverse Turing Test. See if the human can pass itself off as the black box. Don't you want to know the mechanics?"

"The mechanics? It's a goddamn tin-can telephone. Lady at the other end of the string, trying to sound like a clunky New Age self-help guide."

" 'Many things are so bright without being happy,' " Lentz mimicked. Then he gagged on another round of phlegm.

I stood up, shaking my head.

"Don't leave, Marcel. We really do have a new simulation up and running in there. A good one."

Diana's turn to snort.

"Lentz," I said softly, "I'll never trust you again."

"Don't need your trust. I just need you to train Imp C."

I stopped, waiting to hear what I was going to say. "Imp D."

The two colleagues, divided on every issue except novelists' gullibility, broke into relieved tittering.

The sound set me off again. "You bastards. So how does this little stunt of yours make you feel?"

"Fine, thank you." Diana smiled. "You?"

I had nothing to say. And I said it.

"Oh, Rick. Admit it. You loved the act while it lasted."

I looked at her. Somewhere in her couple hundred eye muscles was the awful suggestion that talking to me made her happy.

"Barring that," Lentz intruded, "admit that you bought the whole shebang."

I giggled. I couldn't help myself. "Yep," I said. "Totally suckered." Alive. Admit it. "That's me."

Diana's apology came in the form of a lunch invitation. It shamed me. She'd made the last overture, and I'd never gotten back to her.

Not that I singled her out. I wasn't getting back to anyone. I bought an answering machine, and cowered behind it, screening calls. Then I stashed even that, turning the ringer off for long stretches. The hermit thing became easier with practice. I even thought about writing about it, until I remembered I already had.

But Diana searched me down. "How about lunch? I owe you." Face-to-face. Collegial. Gap-toothed, like the Wife of Bath. There was no hiding.

Lunch was fun, given everything. Fish sandwiches from a notorious pool-hall dive in campustown. Diana was voluble. In the labs, she always struck me as the person I wanted to be when I grew up. Over fish sandwiches, she seemed young enough to be compromised by eating with someone my age.

"How's the Don?" I asked. She looked blank. "Mr. Quixote?"

She groaned. "I don't want to talk about it."

"No, but Harold probably does, huh?"

She flashed a stare at me. What exactly were we talking about? "I should sic him on you. That would simplify matters all around."

"Sorry. I kind of have my hands full at the moment. After we feed Cervantes to the machine, Harold can come and chat up Imp D."

Diana puckered, amused despite herself. "Know why I think the whole thing is infinitely ditsy?"

"Because it's me and Lentz?"

"There is that. But I was thinking how you want to put everything into *words*. Think about this. You want to make a data structure that will say everything there is to say about 'ball.' You have to have facts for roundness, cohesion, size, weight. You have to have all sorts of probabilistic rules. It's more likely to be ten inches in diameter than ten feet."

"Unless it's a wrecking ball."

"It's more likely to be made of rubber or plastic or wood than of, say, plant fiber."

"Unless it's a softball, or a cotton ball . . ."

"Or a fuzzball." Diana laughed.

"Or a spitball. Or a ball of yarn."

"Enough already. You're making me crazy. The list of predicates is—forever. And the exception list is even longer. You can talk through a whole encyclopedia, but you won't yet have said 'ball' itself. Let alone what you do with one. What one means. How to throw one. How a kid feels when he gets one for a birthday present."

"But that's where associative learning comes in, isn't it? We don't have to enumerate all those qualities. If the machine keeps coming across them, and sometimes people are gazing into crystals, and sometimes they're pitching a curve, and sometimes they are having—"

"That's just the problem. Any baby can hold a ball in its hands. Your machine can't. How many words is it going to take to say what that globe *feels* like? The heft of the thing. The possibility."

"Red rubber sphere that you can chuck . . ."

"Richie. Richie."

I didn't have the heart to tell her that no one called me that. Besides, it sounded good in her mouth.

"Are you going to do 'red' as fitting between x and y angstroms?"

"Not at all. That's the classical AI people. Chen and Keluga. We're going to do red sky, red-faced, red flag, in the red, red dress . . ."

"Sexist. Okay. Go on to 'sphere.' How is the poor thing supposed to get 'all the points equidistant from a center' when it has never seen *distance*? When it can't possibly measure?"

"Good point. You mean we have a problem. No symbolic grounding."

"Symbolic grounding." Diana grinned, and wiped the tartar sauce from her lower lip. "That's the phrase I was looking for."

"You're saying a reading machine is hopeless. We should give it up."

"I'm saying, if you're going to make such a thing, you have to give it eyes, hands, ears. A real interface onto the outside."

"The literary theorists think a human's real-world interface is problematic at best. And greatly overrated. They say even sense data must be put into symbols."

"The literary theorists have to get tenure. And they have no hard facts to get tenure with. They have to fight for a slice of a pie that's getting smaller every day."

"Getting smaller because of people like you."

I was teasing. She took me at face value. "Yes, maybe. But tell me, then. Why do your people need to either emulate mine, attack us as nature molesters, or dismiss us as irrelevant self-deluders?"

"My people are scared shitless of your people, that's why. They're terrified that Dad and Mom really do love you best."

Diana smiled like a teenager. "Are you kidding? We're the problem child. Don't you remember? You heard the parents tell us never to play with matches."

We walked outside into a day remade. The trees had stripped bare, but for a moment, I couldn't tell if they were coming or had just gone. We two were the only ones on the whole street wearing coats. A pack of earphoned roller bladers with wraparound shades so silvered they couldn't see almost mowed us down.

My disorientation was total. "Wasn't it almost winter when we went inside?"

"It's getting so that these once-in-a-century freak weather spells occur every other week."

"That's the fault of you scientists."

"Doubtless."

"It's still nippy. Have I lost my mind, or are those women wearing shorts?"

"Youth is never cold," Diana lamented.

Ten years ago, fifteen, I'd pitied those who'd let their skin go papery and their blood thin. Back then, this had been my haunt. Now I'd lost the lease, could not even name the street.

"I want it to freeze. Freeze hard."

"It's going to freeze," Diana guaranteed. "You've forgotten. It's rough out in these parts. Four months of interstellar blackness. Deep space. Zero. The air loads up with sleet BBs, with nothing between here and Pennsylvania to slow the wind."

"How long have you been here?"

"Five years. You know the funny thing? I never thought of myself as a Californian when I lived there."

We walked toward campus. "Does the brain have a 'decaying leaf recognition' subsystem? A 'sheepskin coat just back from the cleaners' subsystem?"

"I know what you mean," Diana said. "Smell is everything, isn't it? When I smell the air right now, I think, I know what's coming. Time to batten down."

"I think, how can I leave all this?"

She said nothing for the longest time. Then Diana said, "Thrill."

"Yes. Thrill."

It took me until the Quad, until we walked over the spot, to make the connection. To realize what day it was. You see, it didn't feel like November. Same day, different year: I no longer knew what people meant by that. Four days later, it snowed.

"Symbolic grounding," I told Lentz.

D, our first implementation to run on the sprawling community of connection machine, was my slowest charge so far. But parallel architecture and several software twists made it the one with the most astonishing reach. D came into this world recursive. It took forever to grasp that two was the integer just past one. But the instant it got that, it had infinity in the same breath. It could watch itself learn. When it got "Dogs bark," it also got "Baby says, 'Dogs bark.' " The breakout, when it came, was going to be unbelievable.

The shape of its brain was generative. It matched the arc of an uncoiling sentence. But deep syntax wasn't enough. Words weren't enough. "The policeman gave the motorist his badge," I told it. "Who does 'his' stand for? The policeman gave the motorist his license." Now who?

How much would D have to know before it could get that one? Tracing my own inference process dizzied me. The linked list of properties hanging off the world's every object required a combinatorial explosion of sense. But to see even part of what the host symbols stood for required that D first *see*.

"We have to give it eyes," I decided. "Why train it with all the properties of a ball when we can show it what a ball is?"

"Nice leap, Marcel," Lentz said. "I've been waiting for you to make it."

"And here I was afraid you were going to kill me for bringing it up."

"On the contrary. In fact, I still have a passive retinal matrix lying around intact from work I did last year. We can paste it in."

"Now, where the hell did I put that eyeball? It was around here somewhere."

Lentz laughed. "All right. So the work habits could be more systematic."

Sight was not the sudden beamburst I hoped for. Revision E could convert objects into retinoptic neurode maps. Training got it to associate words with each visual clump. But navigating by this crayon cartography resembled sewing silk with a Lincoln log needle.

I gave it several common objects, in stiff cross section. E made only static traces: photos, not footage. I sorely doubted that the speckles of light and dark did anything to round out the ball in E's associative memory. We boosted the resolution. Added bits for color, sixteen million shades. Whether E traveled those surfaces or twirled them in its mental space I couldn't say.

The creature in *Frankenstein* learned to speak by eavesdropping on an exiled family, the most astonishing act of language acquisition until Taylor's beloved *Tarzan*, the books on which the best reader I ever met grew up. Frankenstein's creature had his chattering family and a knapsack of classics: *Paradise Lost*, Plutarch's *Lives*, Goethe's *Werther*. E, like Tarzan, learned to talk more or less on print alone.

"I discovered the names that were given to some of the most familiar objects," Shelley's creature says somewhere. "I learned and applied the words, 'fire,' 'milk,' 'bread,' and 'wood' . . ."

One day I would teach this speech to a machine that had learned to read. Maybe not E, or F, but G, or son of G. And my machine would understand.

"I distinguished several other words without being able as yet to understand or apply them," the girl child's monster would tell mine. Words "such as 'good,' 'dearest,' 'unhappy.' "

"You don't eat," Diana accused me.

"I eat. I eat a lot. You saw how much I put away at lunch."

"I bet that was your only meal that day."

"I lose track sometimes. Lentz and I . . . We get to training at such weird hours."

"You don't eat unless someone feeds you. Is that it?"

I knew what was coming. But I had nowhere to run. I wanted to tell her then. Before any court of confusion. My evacuated life left no air for anyone. Least of all someone as kind as Diana.

But Diana hadn't offered anything rejectable yet. Nothing but the most generic friendship.

"Most experimental neurologists can't cook," she said. "They're fine until they get to the part of the recipe that says 'Season to taste.' This throws them for a loop. They like the 'Measure carefully into bowl.' They tend to hang out up there."

"Connectionists," I mimicked, "cook brilliantly. They start out at random, and a few thousand iterations later . . ." Two funny deflections, then I'd flee before she could extend the invitation.

"I bet novelists know how to shape a recipe."

"Maybe back when. The age of plot and closure. Times have changed. It's all microwave these days."

"I know what," she said. "You can cook a meal for me." So simple. A sudden, happy inspiration.

She'd had mercy. Given me one she couldn't expect me to accept.

"Well, Diana, that sounds great in theory. But unless it's Jiffy Pop, and you bring the matches to light my stove's pilot . . ."

"At my place. I have all the utensils. And I won't get in your way at all."

"Just stand by and laugh?"

"Something like that."

"All right, then. All right. I rise to the challenge. *Moules Provisoires.*"

"Oh. My. The man's done this before."

I had, in fact. But I didn't care to give her the details.

I got to her place Saturday evening. I managed to carry all the provisions on my bike rack. Even the tapers. I rang the bell, ready with a funny opener about ruined anything tasting better by candlelight.

The door was opened by a little boy. I started to mumble something about getting the address wrong.

"Mom," the boy called back into the house. "The writer's here!"

"The writer?" Diana answered from within. "Tell him to use the tradesman's entrance."

The kid looked up at me, wrestling with the command. His face searched mine for clues. I watched the solution—*irony*—ripple through him until he let me in with a wry smile.

Diana appeared, doubling my shock. She carried a younger boy in her arms. I must have looked like a blithering undergrad.

"Here's Richard," she said, addressing the child. "Can you say 'Hi, Richard'?"

"Rick would be fine," I said.

This child wasn't about to say anything. I saw it in his features. The slightly spatulate face. The fold to the nose and ears. Speech would be long and hard in coming.

"This is Peter." The cheerful matter-of-fact. My worst-case fears came home to roost. I knew her. I could never pretend ignorance again.

"Hello, Peter." I didn't know how to carry on. "I once wrote a book about someone named Peter."

Peter hunched up into a little ball. He peeked out sideways.

"He's a little shy with strange people," the older brother said. "But for a Down's baby, he's a genius."

"And this is William."

"Do you know what it says on the Brazilian flag?" William asked me.

"I used to know."

"You probably did," Diana cracked.

"It says, *'Ordem e Progresso.'*"

"No kidding! What does that mean?"

William thought. "It means—order me some soup?"

Diana choked with shame in mid-laugh. "Oh, sweetheart! No. That was just a little joke of mine."

"I know," William pouted.

"What's the Netherlands?" I asked.

"Easy one. Red stripe, white stripe, blue stripe." He drew them in the air, visualizing as he described. Then he pointed at me. He waved his index finger in a pedagogical sweep. "Also Luxembourg," he warned.

"Yeah. There's a reason for that."

"I know, I know. Here's one. Red circle on white background?"

"Easy one. Japan."

"No fair!" Adults weren't supposed to know anything.

"Don't get him started," Diana said on our way to the kitchen. "He can do all hundred and eighty of them."

"Hundred and eighty-six," William corrected.

"What if you take Netherlands and double it? Hold a mirror up to the bottom?"

That one took a couple of steps. "Thailand?"

"You're good, man. You're good."

"Formerly known as Siam."

"Population?"

"Approximately fifty-one million."

"Approximately," Diana sighed.

"Name seven countries where Spanish is the principal language."

"Easy one," William said, the index finger now a fencing foil. The most extraordinary boy I will ever meet.

"Come on, you guys," Diana said. "Peter and I need food. Don't we, Peter?"

Peter curled up in his hedgehog defense. But he kept his eye on me at all times.

I put William to work washing the mussels. "Is it just the four of us?" I asked Diana.

"Yes. I'm sorry. I should have told you. I assumed you knew."

"What, from Lentz? Nobody is real but him. Hadn't you heard?"

"It's such a small world over at the Center. I guess I'm used to everyone knowing everything about everybody."

"And nothing much about anyone."

"Well, we all have our work, first."

"How do you do it?"

"Do what?"

I held my hands out, one toward the kitchen counter, the other toward some remote lab. "Two lives. Alone."

"Huh!"

"I mow the lawn," William said.

"How much does she pay you?"

"Two-fifty."

"Holy moly. There are laws against that, you know."

Diana made to fillet me with the lemon knife. "Don't make waves, writer. Or I'll give you something to write about."

The meal came together. And William and I managed it without assistance from the feminine half of the world. We made a bucket brigade of the dishes. Peter sat nearby, chattering with his hands.

"Look," William called. "Pete's helping!"

I heard the sound of dismayed discovery behind me. "What do we do with these?" Diana stood by the counter, holding the tapers and floral sprig that I'd tried to leave hidden in the bottom of my bag. She looked at me dead on. Her eyes started to water.

"Light them, of course." But recovery came two beats too late. I shrugged, and even that hurt. This is why I asked you not to ask me here.

Diana put the tapers in elaborate candlesticks that she first had to unwrap from newspapers. We lit them and doused the lights. But the darkness scared Peter. He coiled forward against himself. Diana turned the lights back on. We let the candles burn.

William had more fun with the shells than with the insides. He did, however, enjoy dipping his mussels in the wine sauce and dribbling all over the table. Peter worked away at his compote. He insisted on trying one mussel. He got half of it down, with a look of utter stupefaction.

"They're both going to have the runs for days," Diana said.

"I'm sorry."

"Don't be silly. They get the runs from jelly toast."

William bit his cheek. I didn't know how badly, at first. All at once, he stopped talking. I thought it was a clown act. Pantomime. I started to laugh, until William's silent, red-faced distress made Peter break out in tears and lower his face into his plate.

Diana was up in a fraction of a second, before I knew what was happening. "It's okay. Petey, it's okay." Diana lifted her boy and hugged him to her. She repeated the litany various ways, glossing with a flurry of hand motions.

"You sign to him?"

"A little. It's easier for him to reply. Words will come slowly. Fine motor is tricky for him."

"What is he saying?"

"'William is going away'? No, sweetheart." Diana signed her assurance. "William just has a little owie. It's so strange," she confided, aside. "He has this incredible bodily empathy. If any creature for blocks around is distressed, Peter starts weeping. Tell Peter you're all right, William."

William stood holding his cheek, still bawling silently. He walked over to his brother and put his hand on his back. "It's okay, Peter," he said. Stoicism cost him. He burst at last into audible sobs. His brother followed along, unquestioning companion.

The mildest household drama, but it wiped me out. How could I survive the first real crisis? William's fallen pyramid of shells, Pete's spilled, untippable cup, Diana's gap-toothed, hand-signing serenity, the candles blazing away in the brightly lit room: all too much. I thought, *I'd never live.* I'd hemorrhage halfway through week one.

The storm ended faster than it blew up. Suddenly William was laughing and clearing away dishes at the promise of cake. His mother teased him. Peter still had his head down in his plate, like a sunflower under the weight of autumn's end. But even he seemed to be accustoming himself to trust the return of happiness.

After dinner, we did the dishes. William asked to play Battleship.

"You don't have to," Diana said.

"Yes you do," said William. "That or Yahtzee."

He stuck all his ships in the corners, a clever evasion until I caught on.

"Boys." Diana shook her head. "A total mystery."

Peter threw both hands up in the air and let loose a chortle of euphoria at nothing. At domestic peace. It seemed a sign of imminent bedtime.

"Come on, guys. Upstairs. Roll out."

William balked, but a feeble rear guard. Diana carried Peter as far as the stairs, then set him down. "Watch this." Pete leaned into the steps. He took them like a half-track. His feet went up over his shoulders, lifting him from level to level. "He'd be walking by now, but he's so loose-limbed."

I stood downstairs during the bathroom rituals. I snooped Diana's bookshelves, learning nothing but that she was a cognitive neurologist who hoped to do some birding and furniture finishing in some alternate life.

William tore down the stairs in his new-wave pajamas. "Mom says you're Reader-in-Residence."

"I did not!" came the embarrassed denial from upstairs.

"Well," I wheedled. "Let's talk about this. What kind of books do you like?"

William shrugged. "I don't know. I read *The Hobbit*. In three days."

"Really? In-credible. Did you like it?"

"The dragon was pretty awesome."

We trooped upstairs. There, Peter propped up against the bars of his crib. He rocked himself methodically. His hands made curious cupping motions.

"What are you saying, Petie?" I stroked the curl of his ear.

Diana laughed. "Don't ask."

William started jumping on his bed. "He's saying, 'Read! Read!' " His hands picked up the sign and multiplied it into a mandate.

"Absolutely. What do you gentlemen want to hear?"

"Pete wants the counting book," Diana said. "It's his favorite these days."

She lifted him out of the pillowed prison and sat in a beanbag chair, Peter in her arms. She opened a radiant, pastel portal across his lap. "One," she announced. "One house. One cow. Petey do it?"

Peter brought his hand down across the page. On contact, Diana exclaimed, "One! That's it."

Each page brought one more house, one more cow, one more tree, one more in a circling flock of birds. Diana counted, pointing out each new figure on the page. Then Peter commenced a round of muscular spasms, pointing randomly but intently, while we three clicked off the numbers in chorus.

"He loves counting. He's so smart," Diana told me, shaking her head. "You are so smart!" she signed to Peter. Peter curled like an armadillo. Trisomy may have weakened his muscles, but the weights collapsing his human spine were fear and joy.

"So what's it going to be, my man?" I asked William.

He lay, narrow in his bed. He seemed so slight, such a vulnerable line. A lima bean tendril germinated on damp paper towel for the science fair. He reached a hand up blindly behind him, to the shelf above his head. He retrieved the totem and handed it to me, without looking.

"Na, naw. You cannot do the World Almanac as bedtime reading."

"It's what I want," he insisted. Singsong.

We did World Religions; Famous Waterfalls; Noted Political Leaders; and, of course, the beloved World Flags. More forgone quiz game than story time. William told me what lists to start. Then he blurted out the completion after only a few words of prompting. Every time I shouted, "How do you know that?" William smirked in triumph and Pete threw his hands in the air and gurgled.

Appeased, the boys went down without a fight. Anxiety revived only after Diana and I retired to the living room, alone.

It became a different house then. She became a different woman. She put something timeless on the player—Taverner's *Western Wynde* Mass. I wouldn't have picked her for it. But then, I wouldn't have picked her for freeze-drying monkey brains either. I didn't know the first thing about her. This evening's every note had proved that.

Closeness grew awful. Words had been spent on the boys. I felt the slack of all those who try to live by eloquence and find it useless at the end. I wanted to put my head in her lap. I wanted to disappear to Alaska. .

"Their father?" I asked her, after agonizing silence.

"Their father found the drop from Will to Pete a bit steep for his tastes. About eleven months ago. Left me everything. But who's counting?"

She twisted her hair around one finger. Clockwise once, then counter. She never looked at me. A good thing.

"People have been wonderful. Harold. Ram. The others. It's work that saves you, finally. I keep thinking I'll find something in the hippocampus that will explain the man."

"I take it Lentz wasn't among the comforters."

She grimaced. "How do you put up with that creep?"

"He's building me the greatest train set a boy novelist could ask for."

"I suppose. It wouldn't be worth it for me. Nothing would." She stared off, into the music, the small rain. "I don't mean his snide remarks. The solipsism. The sadism. I could deal with all that. A woman in the biz learns to put up with that as a given. I mean the sadness. He's the saddest man I've ever laid eyes on." She chose that moment to look up, to lay eyes on my eyes. "Excepting you, of course."

"Lentz? Sad?"

"The worst. It chills me. Have you ever been alone in his office with him?"

"Hours and hours."

"Ever been in there with him with the door closed?"

Never. And it had never struck me as strange until that moment. Diana did not elaborate. She left it to me to run the experiment for myself. I read her silence. Loneliness on that scale had to be measured firsthand.

We sat and listened to the western wind. The intimacy of perfect strangers. Years from now, her boys might by chance recall the odd man who came by one night and added to their shaping thoughts by reading to them. A night never repeated.

I recognized this woman. This family, curled up in advance of the night. I knew the place from a book I'd read once as a novice adult, my own first draft just undergoing revision.

I read the novel in that nest C. and I had made together in B. Mann's *Doktor Faustus*, the formative storybook of my adult years. In it, a brilliant German, by blinding himself to all pursuits but articulation, allows his world to pull itself down around him. I remembered the man, already middle-aged, writing a love letter to the last woman who might have accepted him.

But the letter sabotages itself. It engineers its own rejection. It bares a loneliness that it knows will scare off any attempted comfort. I haven't looked up the passage since first reading it. I will never read it again. The real thing might be too far from the one I've kept in memory. "Consider me," the marriage proposal says, "as a person who suddenly discovers, with an ache at the lateness of the hour, that he might like to have a real home."

Diana sat across from me, on a comfortable sofa scarred with the destructive industry of small boys. Upstairs, those boys tossed in dreams whose sole task lay in smoothing out the incomprehensibility of this day. Here was the home I would never have. Shaped by a book, I'd made sure I wouldn't. I'd forced my heart's reading matter to come true.

Here and there, a cylindrical tube–person or transforming robot made Lego base camp for the night in the plush carpet. Diana pulled the music's long melisma about her shoulders like a shawl. Christ, that my love were in my arms and I in my bed again.

"Thanks," she shushed me at the door. She squeezed my hand. "Thanks. It's been a while since I've dined by candlelight."

I went home to chosen loneliness. To the book I would never be able to write.

Picture a train heading south. The train is full of ill and wounded. This month's invariable sanitarium patients. Consumption, influenza: fiction's archaic maladies. Some bodily deterioration for which the reader must invent fantastic, beginner's referents. Maimed veterans, being shipped from the front.

A moment of mass import, of universal upheaval from the just-recallable past. Populations on the leading edge of panic, stricken by industry. The evacuating train pulls out. It joins the flotilla of time's lifeboats, plowing the dark.

Cruel, blue, bracing, breaking loose: the only opening vignette worth bothering with. Stretched out urgently, along imagination's rail-heads, a book heads south. It signals from the telegraph car. Keys me a message I was supposed to have held on to at all costs. A message that never made it out of childhood's originating station.

The day is sharp, the air invigorating and crystalline. It is the year nineteen-something. A year ending in a dash, or perhaps two hyphens.

The train works southward, in wartime. It snakes glacially up into the mountains, in perhaps the last clear month, the last week that the mountain passes will be traversable.

The engine climbs. It sniffs perpetually up to the outskirts of the same bombed-out village. Fields drift undulantly beneath its wheels, whose click convinces even Forever to bleed imperceptibly into a standing Now.

Soon, on the itinerary's second morning, the ground acquires a careless dusting of snow. Vegetation changes along the alpine climb, though the account, the travelogue itself, says nothing about that. Sirens bleat on in the distance, from whistle-stops all along this infant route. Air raids continue steeping this side of the border in today's random wildfire.

But the wounded in the compartments are exhilarated. They grow convinced: something is about to happen. Just past the next page.

C. and I returned to U. We managed to live there again for two years. I'm surprised we lasted even that long. How could we hope to make a life in a town where we'd already taken our retrospective tour? C. sought a thing she'd accidentally lost. That thing was not U., not then or ever. But severed from yourself in the press of a crowd, you head back instinctively to the most recent landmark, hoping the lost other will hit on the same idea.

Changed circumstance bought us a little nostalgic grace. C. parlayed her office experience into a position with University Personnel. And I: I'd been granted a wish so outrageous that characters in novels would have been punished just to think it. The political entertainment I wrote for C. appeared and did well. The forgotten attic legacy bridging imaginary Limburg and too real Chicago had *readers*.

Reviewers evaluated it in print, in the same newspapers I'd once read so casually. Total strangers spent two hours' wages to buy a copy. People I'd never meet wrote me letters, awarded me prizes.

The impossibility dawned on me: I might be the last person on earth allowed to spend all day long doing exactly what I wanted to do.

Each new book-blown coup produced a burst of sad excitement from C. "Beauie, you've done it. *Proficiat.* I always knew you would."

Truth was, she was terrified. We holed up in our one-bedroom apartment—one step upscale from the one in B.'s land-filled swamp—under siege from admirers. One night, we sat eating dinner at the pretty green enamel table we'd rescued from the secondhand shop. We listened to the radio as we ate, the cavalcade news. All at once, a voice was talking about the book, telling the story of the boys in the photo. Paraphrasing, as if that life had really happened.

I'd invented those boys to amuse C. I built them from pieces only she would recognize. I sprinkled the biographies with archival evidence, historical truths, the camera-eye witness. I intercut with essays how every historian half-makes the longer narrative, wedding the forces at large to a private address book. Now our private address book had been promoted to documentary fact.

At the account of that boy blown off his bike and rubbed out before the world conflagration cleared its starting block, C. started to cry. I thought at first she was crying out of pride. Writing a novel left me that inept with real-world facts.

"That poor boy," she mouthed.

I pieced it together. "I'm sorry. C., please. It'll all be over in a month." She brightened a little at the thought of recovering the anonymous. Of retreating to a time when our invented tunes formed no one's dinner music.

Our lives back in U. were like nothing we recognized. U. had changed in all but its particulars. Returning to the town was like clapping the back of an old friend at a reunion, one who turns to you with a look friendly but blank.

U. had forgotten us, while remaining agonizingly familiar. The town had become something out of Middle English allegory. Its lone consolation lay in other people, as bewildered by their abandonment here as we.

For the first time in our lives, C. and I socialized. We learned to pick wines, to crack the dress code, to prepare ourselves in advance of an evening with an arsenal of jokes and stories that answered a suite of occasions. The game got easier the more we played. We might have succeeded at it, had we stuck around.

The Midwestern Dinner Party was not, as our B. acquaintances teased us, a contradiction in terms. Once under way, they could even be fun. Getting ready was the torture.

"I'm fat," C. would announce, about an hour before we had to go anywhere.

"Sweetheart, you're a sub-Saharan stalk of desiccated grass. Don't tell yourself you're fat. You'll start to believe it."

I still pretended she hadn't already convinced herself.

"Wear the lamb dress," I'd say. "You'll knock them out."

"That dress makes me look fat."

"Okay. How about the muslin?"

"That one makes me look like I'm trying not to look fat."

Sometimes C. locked herself in the bathroom, throwing up. Or, sobbing, she'd refuse to leave the apartment. But the cloud usually lifted in time. C. would grow radiant and be the dinner's delight. People loved her, and she loved them back. The ones she gave the chance.

Those two repeat years in U. might have been a sterile waste if it weren't for the Taylors. I went to see the old professor not long after we hit town. Taylor welcomed me back with affection. And now, when I teased him about his freshman seminar ruining a promising scientific career, I could point to a turn of events that sweetened the punch line.

After my mother, the man had taught me how to read. Taylor *was* reading for me. Through Taylor, I discovered how a book both mirrored and elicited the mind's unreal ability to turn inward upon itself. He changed my life. He changed what I thought life was. But I'd never done more than revere him at a distance, forever the eighteen-year-old student. Now, to my astonishment, we became friends.

Our first dinner invitation to the Taylors' scared C. witless. She'd heard me gush about Taylor so often that when it came to meeting him, she wanted to flee. "What does he look like?" she asked. As if that would prepare her.

"I don't know. Slight. Arresting. Immaculate. A face ravaged by intelligence."

"You're hopeless, Beau. What color is the man's hair?"

"I'm not sure."

I told her about that rainy September afternoon when I'd first seen him. He arrived at the attic dormer in the English Building where the class met. A dozen of us had assembled in nervous anonymity. In walked this close-cropped, fiftyish man in impeccable summer suit. He placed his grade book and our first text on the desk, sat down in one of those reduced, yellow-wood chairs, removed a pack of cigarettes from an inside suit coat pocket, and asked if anyone objected. He lit up, tilted his head infinitesimally backward, then said, "It defies statistics that I'm the only one in a group this size with an oral fixation."

At eighteen, we kept our fixations to ourselves. At least until the reading began.

"What did you read?" C. wanted to know.

"He started us out on Freud's *Introductory Lectures*. Then we applied the dream work to fairy tales and lyric poetry. After a while, we went on to the longer stuff—short stories, plays, novels."

"Titles, Beauie. I want titles."

"Let's see. Ten years ago! *Gawain and the Green Knight*. 'Adam Lay Bound.' 'Patrick Spens.' 'The Miller's Tale.' The Sonnets."

"You remember them all?"

"Like yesterday. Better. You had to be there. I remember the shape his mouth made when he recited lines. Of course, *he* could recite the bulk of those pieces verbatim. In the dark."

"Which sonnets?"

"Is this for extra credit? We were each supposed to pick one to present to the group. For some reason, maybe because I'd just broken up with—"

"I don't want to hear that woman's name!"

"I must have been looking for a rebound, because I picked Sonnet 31."

"Which goes?"

"Which goes:

"Thy bosom is endeared with all hearts,
   Which I by lacking have supposed dead,
   And there reigns Love, and all Love's loving parts,
   And all those friends which I thought buried."

"I thought there are supposed to be fourteen lines."

"I think there were. Before memory got to them."

"Okay. What else?"

" 'The Sick Rose.' 'The Second Coming.' 'The Windhover.' All sorts of Dickinson. 'Prufrock.' Frost, Stevens. *Arms and the Man. The Tempest.* Hold on. We also spent a lot of time on the Bible, right at the beginning of term."

"Repressed that one?"

"Guess so. *The Grave.* 'Petrified Man.' 'The Dead.' That was the one that put me over the top. That made me realize I wasn't going to lead the life I thought I was going to lead. *Heart of Darkness. Light in August. Lucky Jim* . . ."

"So what didn't you read?"

"Yeah. It was a real lineup."

"I don't get it, Beau. It sounds like your basic Freshman Survey."

"It wasn't. First of all, this magnificently self-possessed oral fixation sat up in front of the room, telling anecdotes in syntax so decorously Byzantine we didn't even realize that half of them were off-color. The man spoke in complete, perfect paragraphs. It took me almost a whole week between sessions to decode Taylor's suggestion that the speaker in 'Stopping by Woods' was out there in the middle of nowhere relieving himself."

"I'm not going to this dinner," C. decided.

"Sweetheart, you don't understand. The man is grace personified. And his wife is a National Treasure. Together, they're hilarious."

"They'll think I'm an idiot. They'll wonder what you're doing with me."

"Just the opposite. They'll wonder what a sexpot like yourself sees in a ninety-eight-pound aesthetic weakling. C.! Everybody feels like an idiot compared to Taylor."

"I don't need that, thanks. I have enough of that as it is."

"But Taylor also has this way of making you feel smarter than you are. We teenagers used to fumble around with one poem or the other. Precocious and brilliant, but juvenile. I felt like a kid with the training wheels taken off. I'd soar for a hundred meters, then crash to the ground. But whenever I said something particularly stupid, Taylor would credit my misses with so much ingenuity I couldn't even recognize them. 'Your account of the narrator's circumvention of the repressed's return is persuasive in the extreme. But your hints about his real and unconscious motives needn't be so circumspect.' Oh, I wish I could imitate the man!"

"He's bigger than life for you, isn't he?"

"No," I answered her. "No. He's exactly life-sized."

"I'm not going."

She went, and had a good time. "He's just like you said. The suit. The complete paragraphs. Only you forgot the war bond songs."

"I had no idea about those." The evening had, in fact, been a continuous astonishment.

"Tell me again the connection between that long Matthew Arnold quote . . ."

". . . from a poem no one has read in half a century . . ."

". . . and the glimpse of Norma Shearer's cleavage that he got in a Colorado valley movie theater at the age of ten?"

"I can't remember. I think the connection was that second bottle of Slovakian wine."

We went with increasing frequency. C. grew as devoted as I. Every visit revealed new amplitude to Taylor. Taylor the inconsolable fan of hopelessly bad sports teams. The shuffler to bluegrass tunes. The consummate organic gardener who'd planted half the fruit trees in U. The collector of questionable jokes no one else would dare tell even in private. The wartime aircraft spotter. The fisherman and naturalist. The mimic of a thousand voices, from Blanche DuBois to a Mexican bush league baseball announcer. The boy who taught himself to read on Tarzan and John Carter, who went on to devour every volume in the rural library long before he made his escape.

This abundance held together on the slightest of sutures. Taylor's deepness was bleak. He had read all the books. He was fluent in the mind's native idiom. He knew that the psychopathology of daily life was a redundancy. He might have been the supreme misanthrope, were it not for his humor and humility. And the source of those two saving graces, the thing stitching that heartbreaking capaciousness into a whole, was memory.

Taylor's wit made me feel like the most sparkling conversationalist. We'd return from their place well past midnight, kept up by adults thirty years older than us who outlasted us easily. We'd proceed to lie in bed hours longer, eyes pasted open, thoughts racing, replaying the evening's exchanges. Thought seemed to me that thing that could relive, in island isolation, its own *esprit d'escalier*. Memory was the attempt to capitalize on missed cleverness, or recover an overlooked word that, for a moment, might have made someone else feel more alive.

C. agreed. "When we're over there, I remember stories from my own childhood that I haven't thought about for lifetimes." We cracked jokes we'd never thought to try on each other. We sang for the Taylors the songs we'd written to keep ourselves going in B., neglected since our return to U. Whatever the quality of our performance, the Taylors liked us enough to keep asking us back.

We went for the Fourth of July. The Taylors played *The Mormon Tabernacle Choir Sings John Philip Sousa* and made hand-cranked ice cream. We went to a Christmas party, the living refutation of Joyce's "Dead." Good cheer from on high, and in a shape even humans could understand. Late that wonderful night, Taylor came and sat down next to C. in a corner, put his arm around her. Of course, even that spontaneous affection had to be framed in an incomparable Taylorism: "I trust you realize that this arm is sufficiently anesthetized by alcohol that I'm not getting any illicit pleasure out of this."

The attention made C. glow until New Year's.

But in the long run, attention made her worse. All that winter C. declined. Only love could have done her any good. And of available loves, only the unearned kind would have worked. But C. could not free herself from her certainty that unearned meant undeserved.

Each letter in the box, every call from family or friend hit C. like an accusation. She began to shape her adult story: every life decision she had ever taken was a small disappointment to someone. And each disappointment was a savings stamp pasted in the final book.

We trudged through to spring. The thought that her unhappiness must be weighing me down made C. even more unhappy than she thought she was. Worse, the thought fulfilled its own prediction. Her fright alone began to weigh me down. Or, not her fright, but the anchor of helpless love it lodged in my heart.

Two years in a U. we no longer belonged to left us partners in fear. I can see it in the one photograph I still own of her from that time. That look of crumpled panic passing for a smile in front of the lens will forever make me want to cry out and rush to her in her pain. And how much worse, that pain, when she declared its source in my need to comfort her.

"Buddy. Buddy. What do you want? Tell me. Just talk to me. How can I make you happier?"

"You could leave me," she announced one night.

She might as well have accused me of murder. I stared into a face from which all impression of the woman I knew had fled.

"You should, you know. It's no more than I deserve."

We skipped the Balzac installment for that night. What we needed to read each other then was our own manuscript in progress. No line or paragraph or whole chapter that couldn't be blotted. Nothing in our style that we couldn't render blessedly direct by a joint edit. But C. harbored a deep hostility toward words. They only increased the odds of her missing the mark. Extended her sense of betrayal.

We tried to talk. The more I raced, the more C. seized up. She froze, the rabbit in that Larkin poem I'd read for Taylor ten years before. The creature that thought it might slip the notice of a fatal epidemic by keeping stock-still and waiting.

When words didn't work, we tried our bodies. I kissed her boxer's shoulders, her ribs and flinching thighs. I thought to take resentment's nodes out of her muscles into my mouth, digest them. I tried. C. talked then. But her words were voiceless phonemes of distress that carried no message but their desperate pitch.

Time has unlimited patience. It replays its summer stock forever, until we at last get the point. Its paths get laid down until we can walk nowhere else, even if there were an elsewhere in the undergrowth to walk.

C. came home from her office one evening, laughing. "You're not going to believe this. They want to promote me to Personnel Officer I."

I squeezed her in congratulations. She stayed limp. "Of course they do," I scolded. "It took them long enough, didn't it?" All I ever wanted was to give her whatever she needed. But what she needed more than all else was not to be given anything.

I saw the frightened-rabbit look stealing in behind her eyes. I've been good. A good girl. I never asked anyone for anything. Why are you doing this to me?

"Beauie. Beauie." She tittered, shaking her head. "I gotta get out of here."

Lentz burst in once when I was showing Imp E simple shapes. "That bastard Plover is giggling at me in the halls."

"And it's my damn fault, isn't it?"

He drew up short. "Marcel, you are getting smarter and smarter. Every day in every way."

"He's right, you know. Harold's right. Diana's right. Ram is. Even Chen and Keluga are right."

"The hell they are." Lentz's refusal was clipped. But his agitation was wide enough to knock a precarious mound of fanfold printout to the floor. He leaned to pick up the mess, a gesture that stopped midway in a flourish of disgust at the futility of cleaning up after himself. "Right about what?"

"Right about neural nets not being the answer."

"What's the question, Marcel?"

"How is E going to know anything? Knowledge is physical, isn't it? It's not what your mother reads you. It's the weight of her arm around you as she—"

"By all means, Marcel. Put your arm around it as you read. I encourage you. You mean you haven't been hugging it as you go along?"

"Reading knowledge is the smell of the bookbinding paste. The crinkle of thick stock as the pages turn. Paper the color of aged ivory. Knowledge is temporal. It's *about* time. You know how that goes, Engineer. Even you must remember that. 'We can read these three pages before your sisters and brothers come home for dinner.' "

"You're still talking about stimulus and response. Multidimensional vectors, shaped by feedback, however complicated. You're talking about an associative matrix. What else have we been doing but building one of those?"

"But Imp E's matrix isn't human. Human knowledge is social. More than stimulus-response. Knowing entails testing knowledge against others. Bumping up against them."

"Our matrix is bumping up against you. It's bumping up against the lines you feed it."

"It could bump up against word lists forever and never have more than a collection of arbitrary, differentiated markers."

"And what do we humans have?" Lentz removed his glasses to wipe them. As monstrous as he looked with them on, he was even worse without.

"More." I didn't know what, at the moment. But there had to be more. "We take in the world continuously. It presses against us. It burns and freezes."

"Save it for the award committees, Marcel. We 'take in the world' via the central nervous system. Chemical symbol-gates. You read my bit on long-term potentiation."

"Imp E doesn't take things in the way we do. It will never know—"

"It doesn't *have* to." He shoved more papers on the floor for emphasis. "It doesn't have to 'know,' whatever the hell you mean by that. You've been reading Plover's voodoo neurology, haven't you? All our box has to do is paraphrase a couple of bloody texts."

" 'I was angry with my friend: I told my wrath, my wrath did end.' How is it ever going to explicate that, let alone paraphrase it?"

"I don't know. Teach the thing anger. Make it furious. In my impression, you can be pretty good at that."

148

"By June, right?"

"Hmm."

"Literary commentary on any book on the list? As good as your random twenty-two-year-old."

"As judged by Gunga Din himself."

"Or public retraction and apology."

"Come on, Marcel. We've been through this. Let's get on with it. Today's training."

"I'd be polishing the retraction if I were you."

"Don't remind me. That damn Plover. He's going to write it for us and make us put our names to it. Well. What better way to meet our fate than facing fearful odds?"

He replaced his glasses and sat down to training. We were working that day on compound subjects. What seas what shores what gray rocks and what islands. He had a list of simple sentence forms using words E already had in its fragile, denotative grasp. E's task was to recast the sentences we fed it. In today's case, find the conjunction, remove it, and split the compound into two.

When we'd done half a dozen examples and E was responding with a speed indicative of boredom, I reached out casually and shut the office door. No machine without muscle would ever be able to decode such a gesture. Some pretense of noise in the hallway. Ridiculous, after these long weeks of working in the open.

The door swung shut, surrendering the image fastened to its inside. On Diana's suggestion, I'd already sneaked a look at the hidden shrine. I'd seen the photograph, and it knocked the breath out of me. Now I wanted to see Lentz's face when the concealed photo looked back at us.

For a considerable fraction of eternity, Lentz said nothing. He looked away from my surveillance, at his notes. At the ignorant terminal.

"Empiricism?" he sneered. He seemed disappointed in me, but not surprised. Prying, snot-nosed kid. What did one expect from a kiss-and-tell, aesthete dilettante? He looked up at the picture, verifying it, although every pixel must have long ago burned permanent silhouettes into his visual cortex. When he sat in here with the door closed, the flood of color would fill his focus, immense at eye level.

He looked away again. He worried the mouse pointer, a cat feeling contrition after the kill. Come on, get up and run again. Like when it was fun.

"I suppose you want the caption?"

I didn't need a caption. I could see well enough. A homemade calendar hung by a tack, still clasping to January. I say "still," for while we had yet to reach that month, this particular one had been buried twenty Januaries ago.

Just above the paper matrix of days, a pasteup color portal opened onto a couple. They stood, arms around one another, out of focus, on a frozen and deserted beach.

The man was Lentz. He was young, as I had never seen him. He had hair. He seemed impossibly taller, slim. The woman at his side was no older. Yet this couple was ancient beyond saying. Age tented just under youth's peeling onionskin. The shutter exposed this geriatric core in X ray. It showed antiquity lying in wait, ready to blossom like an aneurysm.

The craftwork was too clumsy to be a customized mail-order gift. It had the look of a child's school project—Christmas or birthday present—from before those offerings disappeared in adolescent embarrassment. *See what I made you.* The earliest bribe of love.

I touched the image with my eyes. I half expected the museum guard's reprimand. But no one told me to step back. In my mind, I palpated the prematurely old man's shoulders. Before the camera, they crumpled in a last attempt at bravery. I stroked the woman's face where the cling of desperation already promised to sag it.

While I indulged myself, Lentz stood and moved to the window. Outside, a gang of grackles combed the landscaped lawn like a homicide squad dragging a field for evidence.

"Lentz. You never told me."

"What? That I'm married? That I have a family? Everyone, Marcel. Everybody but you."

That wasn't what I meant. That he had a private life was no particular shock. And naturally, that life would be peopled. But the way these two held on to each other. Their too light clothing, their backs to the ice-crusted beach. Nothing but this other waist, this other pair of shoulders between each and their end.

The Lentz I knew could never have posed for such a shot. The Lentz I knew might well have had a wife. He might even have had a child. But my Lentz could never have known them with such hopeless intimacy.

"And you're still . . . ?" I didn't know what I was asking.

"There is no 'still,' Marcel. 'Still' is for unravished brides of quietness."

The open lens trapped these two in terror at the slightest move. The panic in those eyes was the pose of cognition itself. The look of awareness seeing itself going down, drowning in the depths of its own simulation.

I had, the photo told me, half a dozen months in which to remember, once and for ever, what it felt like to be able to remember at all. My own craft calendars had all been swallowed up by the wraparound virtual future my era was intent on inventing. My days and weeks, the saving particulars of Here were already gone. And I, having forgotten them, was almost past caring.

The young Lentz, in a plaid shirt the likes of which will never again be sold on this earth, even secondhand, in countries that live off our discards, clamped his arm around the shoulder of his mate. She returned the stiff grip from underneath. Perhaps they were shivering. Rigorous. However they touched each other in private, this was not it.

This embrace already succumbed to terminal affection. They propped one another up, as if each had just had a mild stroke. They grasped at each other, two people out on a ledge forty stories up in the night's icy wind, having second thoughts even as their feet start to flex.

The wind off winter water made them clutch at each other like that. The chill from the child with the camera. They looked on in advance horror at the cut-and-paste project, the child urgently constructing a craftwork life preserver. Stick this on your refrigerator if you dare, to break eternity's heart and sap the will of time's worst-case scenario.

One ought to be able to hold on to anything. Anyone. It did not matter who, so long as they were there. Yet the first one, this picture said, the generative template for all that you might come to care for in this place, your buddy, your collaborator in plying life: that is the one you recognize. You learn that voice along with learning itself. You can only say, "Yes, to everything," once. Once only, before your connections have felt what everything entails.

This shoulder was the lone one that could have held that man up. That waist, the only one that could steady the woman. These two *chose* each other, their charm against the world's weighted vectors. Anything else but that helpless, familiar grip pinning them in place would be a push into randomness. Would tear the net.

Some scrap of holdover, supervised training told me this is the way one was supposed to end up. The way *I* should have ended. But even as I felt it, the desire seemed arbitrary, laughable, regressive. Marriage for life belonged to those cultural tyrannies now in the process of being shed. In another hundred years, it would seem as archaic as animism, as "thou."

If the plaid shirt was really Lentz, then this woman was truly his wife. In this clasp, the couple graduated to inseparable, mutual foreigners. Love is the feedback cycle of longing, belonging, loss. Anti-Hebbian: the firing links get weaker. C., after a decade, grew stranger to me than that college girl who had comforted me on the Quad the day after my dad died. At the end, we shocked each other in the hall of our overlearned apartment, 911 material, intruders. And we'd gotten there without a child to make us wall calendars, to arrest in scissors and glue the secret of who we once were.

I looked at the young Lentz's blueprint expression, the advance word of crevasses that would range across those facial wastes. I stared at those two shivering bodies, gone half-insubstantial already. I looked up at the real Lentz, studying the grackle dragnet outside. I measured the size of the mistake that had found him out.

Someone had failed someone else. Someone had messed with destiny. A frightened kid with an Instamatic on a frozen beach had watched love capitulate to the very air. Furious cutting and pasting split off the eternal from what always becomes of it, hung an outdated, permanent January to the back of this man's office door. This was the last couple on earth to whom the inevitable wasn't supposed to happen. The last who, by fate's oversight, were to have made it through together into frightened old age.

I crashed Imp E in complete innocence. The version had grown up on patterns and questions about patterns. It organized itself on such challenges as "What comes next in this sequence?" and "Which item in this list doesn't belong?"

One day, provoked by boredom, I asked it, "What do you want to talk about?" The question of volition trapped the rolling marble of its will into an unstable local minimum. The machine that so dutifully strove to answer every interrogation ground to a halt on that one.

Lentz needed to reset the entire run-time module, which did not endear us to the National Supercomputing Site. The connection monster was as expensive to run as it was difficult. They only gave us time in the first place because of the lack of people who could hack the massive parallelism. They thought they might get a testimonial at the end of the project. Lentz had misled them. They thought we were doing science.

Our mosaic already ran beyond precarious. It had grown into a Nevelson village of analog and digital inhabitants chattering among themselves. But the chatter did not cohere into conversation, nor the village into community. Depressed, Lentz added two more subsystems. He'd wanted the whole simulation to be self-generating, self-modifying, self-delighting, self-allaying, self-affrighting. For algorithms, he'd allowed only the structure of the systems and the topiary of their connection weights. Now he conceded the need to write declarations and procedures—the deepest of deep structures—that would coordinate more strongly the many levels in the simulation's epistemological parfait.

Two weeks of intensive training showed how close we were. Implementation F proved capable of surprising inferences. It appeared to deploy material I thought it shouldn't be able to know yet. It almost anticipated. One day, I recited for it the poem that had graced, in enormous, construction-paper letters, the bulletin board of my second-grade classroom. *Down, down, yellow and brown. The leaves are falling all over the town.*

"Ask it about the Western hegemonic tendencies of the subtext," Lentz said, just to be obnoxious. "The tyranny of the deciduous mentality. North imposing its seasonal teleology on South."

"What can you tell me about the leaves?" I asked Imp F.

Its pauses always felt so deliberate. Contemplative. "The leaves fall."

"Yes. Where do they fall from?"

"From old trees."

I shot a glance at Lentz. He looked as astonished as I felt. Fishing for something near the surface, I pulled up a strange phosphorescence from the deep.

"How do you know that the trees are old?" I asked. The question alone taxed F's shocking self-reflexivity.

"The trees bald."

I stared at Lentz, my eyes watering. The metaphor was nothing, child's play. But how? "Lentz," I pleaded. "Explain this to me."

Lentz himself had to improvise. His was the same motion as Imp F's: sketch in the bridge under your feet, as you cross analogy's chasm. Hope it holds under your weight. He shrugged as if his explanation were self-explanatory, highly unlikely, or both.

"The connections it makes in one associative pairing partially overlap the ones used in another."

Associations of associations. It struck me. Every neuron formed a middle term in a continuous, elaborate, brain-wide pun. With a rash of dendrite inputs and handfuls of axon outs, each cell served as enharmonic point in countless constellations, shifting configurations of light, each circuit standing in for some new sense. To fire or not meant different things, depending on how the registers aligned at a given instant and which other alignments read the standing sum. Each node was an entire computer, a comprehensive comparison. And the way they fit together was a cupola itself.

These weird parallaxes of framing must be why the mind opened out on meaning at all. Meaning was not a pitch but an interval. It sprang from the depth of disjunction, the distance between one circuit's center and the edge of another. Representation caught the sign napping, with its semantic pants down. Sense lay in metaphor's embarrassment at having two takes on the same thing. For the first time, I understood Emerson's saying about the use of life being to learn metonymy.

Life *was* metonymy, or at least stood for it. Of the formula I fed Imp F, every sentence was an abashed metaphor, tramped down so long and hard it lost its public shame. "I ran into X on the street the other day," I told F. "He cut me dead." F revived the parallel's anxious source, its roots in ancient, all-out street violence. Then it tamed the words, rendered them livable again as figures of speech.

If everything I spoke to F already concealed its compromised past, no wonder F learned to milk comparison and smart-mouth back. A child always detects its parent's weaknesses. It senses them before words, the first and last lesson. Weakness may be the parent's only lasting lesson.

F's search for an answer space scurried its component neurodes into knowing. Like players in a marching band, the invisible punners shimmered, cut their series of Brownian turns on the turf, and, in abrupt about-face, conjoined themselves into a further story. Every word in that story was double-voiced. Every act of depicting depicted itself, as read by some other set of overlapping signal lights.

And all the while, the trees were balding. The mind shed its leaves. Every connection we encouraged in F killed off extraneous connections. Learning meant consolidating, closing in on its contour the way a drop of water minimizes into a globe. Weights rearranged until the neurodes storing winter lent half their economical pattern to the neurodes signaling old age.

All along, Lentz kept upping the available firing fibers, boosting exponentially the links between them. He sutured in new subsystems by simulated threads. The systems themselves acted as nodes at a higher level. Sometimes they arrived pretrained, before insertion. But even these metamorphosed after attachment, shaped by the bath of signal weights pouring in from all points in the labyrinth.

The maze performed as one immense, incalculable net. It only felt like countless smaller nets strung together because of differences in connection density. Like a condensing universe, it clustered into dense cores held together by sparser filaments—stars calling planets calling moons.

With each new boost to the number of connections, Lentz had to improve F's ability to discard as it generalized. Intelligence meant the systematic eradication of information. We wanted a creature that recognized a finch as a bird without getting hung up on beak size or color or song or any other quality that seemed to put it in a caste by itself. At the same time, the discarding had to stop short of generalizing the finch into a bat or a snowflake or a bit of blowing debris.

By an ingenious method of semantic compaction, Lentz honed a representation scheme that let F weave multiple, growing schemas simultaneously over every additional datum.

"*Voilà*, Marcel. My mathematics says this is the most powerful learning algorithm that'll run in finite time. We can scale F up into a considerable combinatorial mass of common sense without triggering exponential explosion."

But more connections and leaner learning were not enough. We needed one last hardware wrinkle. We needed to promote our F one more letter, to F+1. To grow, to go, to give, to get, to G.

Giving in to a limited, rule-based control structure freed Lentz to recurve G's layers, turning them back in on themselves. This let G fashion and invoke working miniatures of itself. The line between hardware and software blurred when it achieved full induction. G could traverse more levels than it had layers of parallel architecture. It built its own layers, in emulation of emulation, each allowing a new level of abstract depiction.

G's many subsimulations, their associative matrices, the scratchpad mock-ups they made of themselves, now prompted themselves with synthetic input. Dynamic data structures combed their own fact sets, feeding into each other. They called each other recursively, spontaneously discovering relations hidden in acquired material.

They reviewed the residue of experience, pulling notions out of memory's buffers and dressing them up as new tests. They began to train themselves, on hypotheticals of their own devising.

In short, version G could converse among parts of its own net. That net had grown so complex in its positing that it could not gauge the consequences of any one of its hypothetical worlds without rebuilding that whole world and running it in ideational embryo.

Imp G, in other words, could dream.

C. needed to find out. That simple. How Dutch was she? No way of knowing, short of going. How American? She had worried the place she lived for too long, tugging at cuffs that no longer ran much past her elbows.

"It's not you, Beau. It's me." She was not happy here. This continent. She never adjusted to the land of her birth. A quarter century, and she couldn't make a go of it. Perhaps it was time to head to the unknown home.

There was a place lodged somewhere inside her. It sprang up through earliest training. Its streets grew peopled on long-repeated stories. The grandfather policeman. The thirty-two aunts and uncles and their adventures in reversible time. The hundred-plus chorus of first cousins dying, birthing, marrying, and being born, pouring out of the parish register. Butchers, bakers, and historymakers scaling the family beanstalk that had burst from the ground on a few magic seeds.

But alongside this phantom of childhood prompting lay the real village, E. C., almost alone of people, could put myth to the test. She might step over the stile. She could move to the place. Go live in the source of memory laid down for her in advance. One plane ride, and she'd close forever the lifelong gap that had held her at arm's length from her own interior.

"I'm not going without you, Beau."

But in fact, C. was already gone. Love—or perhaps mere loyalty —required that she extend emigration to me. Wish, though, was another matter. Without knowing, I'd become part of the problem. C. needed to flee a whole complex of associations. She fled promotion, career, the renewable lease, English, the sorrow of retail, U., North American early mass Alzheimer's, a faked national past, that history's triple-packaging, evenings at the Taylors, all the two-part singing, our first shot at real friends, the memory of paper Christmas trees taped to the wall, our old five-year plan, the obligating gift of my first book, that story's success, my overwrought care for her, my hope, me.

I couldn't tell what she wanted. There were as many things she ran from as toward. I knew only that if I left with her—as I would have, in a second—the place she arrived in would never be hers.

Still, C. needed to cut a deal. Sometimes at night, just before departure, she launched herself into frightened feedback, scared witless by the decision she'd reached. Each time, it took more to assure her. And only a reassurance as simple as the one we fed each other could have slipped past our combined better judgment.

Our deal was as simple as the choke of love. She would move in with her parents. She'd look for a place. Find work. Assimilate. Learn how things were done. When she belonged, after she felt right, she'd send for me. And I'd come, leaving behind everything but notebooks, tax records, a few changes of clothes, my work-in-progress, and the all but obsolete guitar.

Even that much safety net had to be fatal. Maybe I knew as much, even as C. boarded her bargain flight to Luxembourg. Reaching for a rung that isn't there requires a tumbler's leap of faith. Grip must surrender to total emptiness. Any hedge spells midair disaster.

We wrote absurdly—three times a week. The edges of our paragraphs vanished, slit off in opening the sealed aerogram flaps. The pennies we saved over first class we squandered uncountable times over in transatlantic calls. We learned to time the satellite uplink delays. Speak, pause, listen to response, pause, speak again, as if the simplest exchange of "do you still love me?"'s required incalculable recursive computation.

C.'s communiqués grew from shaky to guardedly confident. She loved her work, temporary typing jobs three notches below the work she'd done in U. She found a one-bedroom nest, perfect for us. She learned the strange new rules of the game, the different ways even the simplest task got transacted. She went to school, swapping her fluent dialect for standard Dutch. She kept her Chicago-accented Limburgs alive at birthdays and anniversaries, one every other day. This, at the hour when dialect itself was dying.

She built her letters into stories for me. I was the foreign family now, listening in to the further repository of E.'s triumphs and tragedies. I thought she would reach the village and not recognize a soul. Instead, she fell in with the imaginary tale's cast as if she had grown up with them. Which she had. To my astonishment, C. learned that her mother, the tale-teller, had spun out some recognizable variant of truth all those years.

Either that or C., now that she had the window bed, wasn't about to let me down by telling me the view was all brick wall. Her accounts spilled continuous color. The inseparable auntie sisters, at seventy, falling out over the one's new boyfriend. The Roman coin discovered in an uncle's plowed bean patch. The death of a cousin, crushed on the highway by a monstrous roll of paper that had broken free from the truck ahead of his. The nephew's accordion renditions of this week's pop idol, the Dutch Diana Ross. Kermis and Carnaval excursions, hilarious binges on green herring and cherry beer.

You make what you think might be a vase for the blooms you are carrying. You tell the stories you need to tell to keep the story tellable.

I gave her everything I could in return. My every predication attempted assurance. Of course you need to do this. It's right. Long overdue. I'm behind you. Anything. Every avowal must have been a small death for C.

My letters were slight things, heavy on romance and style. Thick with linguistic cleverness. For want of a better gambit, I played for sentiment and laughs. "Dear sweet. Words cannot say. Love, R." Every other sentence bore some reference to our private *taal*, one of the library of catchphrases we'd built up to shorthand our hearts and their shared enterprise. But the pages I sent her were light on *stuff*. Had I served her more meat, she might never have left home.

When C. took off, nothing remained to keep me from my new profession's chief occupational hazard. I joked about it, writing to her, but it was true. I now spent eight to twelve hours at a pop in the horizontal. I lay in bed, a keyboard across my lap, drawing on principal. Shooting the inheritance. Creating a world from memory.

I'd found what I needed to do on this earth. And like Tristram, taking longer to describe his birth than birth had taken him the first time through, I saw I would never catch up with myself. I wanted no more stimulation than white stucco. To say no more than what I'd already seen required no more than shutting my eyes. Looking away for a long time.

I meant to reverse-engineer experience. Mind can send signals back across its net, from output to in. An image that arrived through light's portal and lit up the retinoptic map on its way to long-term storage could counterflow. Sight also bucked the tide, returned from nothing to project itself on back-of-lid blackness. This special showing required just a bed on the floor of an otherwise empty room, the place all novelists end up. Only, I had ended up there too soon.

I thought that having a book in print would square me with my father. I must have hoped my novel's mere existence would vindicate that packet of Yukon chapbooks that reached me after his death.

But publication, even prizes, repaid nothing. I would never be able to put so little as a bound galley in the man's hands. In the last configuration of Dad's net, a half century in the training, I would remain a gifted student of physics who chose to squander his abilities on English lit. And not even the good stuff, at that.

I was able to give a copy of my three farmers to Taylor, however. "Here. This is for ruining a promising scientific career." The tease of blame held some slight sweetness to it now. He found the story good. I'd done something with the list he taught me. I'd contributed my bit. Extended the improvised story. But Taylor, alone of all my living friends, knew that this book solved nothing for me in the wider lens.

I needed to bring the cause closer to home. Between my killing assurances to C., I found myself working on a stranger love letter. It shaped itself as a set of nested Russian dolls. For the longest time, I could not tell which of several frame tales held my story and which were the supporting simulations.

I found myself writing about a white-wood, A-framed house in a corn town that left an impression on me out of all proportion to the two years I'd lived there. I watched myself describe a man, holed up in his room, stuck in the horizontal, trying to come up with a story that would save the world.

One by one, I resuscitated the stories my father had raised me on. Yesterday's futures. His father's hand-smashing anger. His immigrant mother. That unknown kid, his brother, whose wartime death changed my life forever. That night at Alamogordo when, younger than I now was, Dad watched mankind's first, artificial sunrise.

I seemed to be writing my way toward a single scene. The three-quarter point, the dramatic showdown in a Veterans hospital, where father and son take leave of each other. I remembered the hospital. I remembered the conversation, all but verbatim. But I seemed to need to reinvent it from scratch.

The man and the boy play Name That Poem. The son tries to stump the chump with famous bits of Yeats and Eliot. The father quotes at length from Kipling and Robert Service, pieces no one has touched for decades. Not since the man read them to his children.

My pop—something I never called my own; that one was the name both C. and I used for hers—grew into history's huckster. Working alone, that year, I came to see him again, quizzing his kids, running them through the necessary training. Heavy on the questions, light on answers. It all came back to me, the stimulus-response he hoped would give the helpless Hobson children some sense of where the Big Picture had set them down.

Something hid about the edges of this book-in-progress. I could not name it outright. Behind Pop's fictional malady, my real father lay ill. The grip of addiction dismissed him too early from the world Dad tried to name. Writing this book meant telling him I finally understood. Even when I didn't. Even when I wouldn't, until long after the last page was done.

I worked my salvage, on my private schedule, with the drapes pulled closed. Rescue and recovery filled me with cold pleasure. Every evasive joke the Hobsons pulled on one another released another piece of secret family language from long-term storage.

I transcribed. I recovered whole forgotten strongboxes, hoping the heirlooms might find their way, in time, into the hands of people who would write me back to say, "Now, how did you know about *that*?"

All families, I decided, walked in single file. At least, the one I lived did. Either experience was somehow as exchangeable as scrip, or we were each so alone that I might as well record the view from my closed cell.

But that view turned out stranger than I ever imagined. I felt myself taking dictation, plans for a hypothetical Powers World that meant to explain in miniature where history had left me. My prisoner's dilemma came down to declaring love for a time and country, a way of life I'd never even liked, let alone felt at home in.

For an accurate take on the place, I had to leave. The nested narratives were swallowing me wholesale. I needed distance. I knew only one place in the world where I could finish my North American theme park: the imaginary village tucked away in the quaint fairy-tale country that a woman I once loved invented for me.

From the day I saw Lentz's picture, my heart took itself off the project. The moment I made him study that snapshot calendar, while I studied him.

"Lentz, you've been jerking me around."

He snorted, if he gave even that much satisfaction. Some crack about my intriguing verb choice. That shifty fluorescent reflection of Coke-bottle glasses. He'd taken down the calendar, hidden it. Maybe even destroyed it. Get the boy's mind back on the chase. His move had the opposite of its intended effect.

"Why are we doing this?"

I stared him down, made explicit, by silence, the threat of a general strike. I was still the only one G listened to. If I didn't talk, the box wasn't going to get any more literate. And I vowed not to talk to G until Lentz talked to me.

"Why are we . . . ? Because, Marcel. Because, if you haven't noticed, I have the unfortunate habit of chewing, in public, more than I am able to bite off."

The closest he'd come to admitting the whole project's haplessness. But also a buyout. A bait-and-switch. A gambit to throw me off, now that I demanded names.

"What's in this for you, Lentz? Why waste a year? What's your motive?"

"Poet. Don't you know by now that science is without—"

"God damn you. Can't you level with me? Once?"

My outburst raised no more than one weary eyebrow.

"What am I to you, that you need to bother yourself over? Use me, if the project interests you. Symbiosis. Otherwise . . ." He left the menace hanging, the way a fatigued marathoner leaves spittle dangling from his lips. "Black-box me. That's the answer. Black-box the whole sordid process. It works for me."

I flipped on G's microphone. I breathed into it in disgust. I sneered a couplet at it, from memory. "Oh, what a tangled web we weave, when first we practice to deceive." LEDs on the coupler recorded G's struggle to paraphrase.

Lentz worked his dry lips. "Powers." Back down the audit trail of his own voice, into someone else's. "Our boy is not ready for irony." He shook his jelly bismarck of a body erect. He went over to the Bartlett's I'd planted on the shelf above the UNIX terminal. "*Marmion*?" he asked, a good imitation of perplexity. "Walter bloody Scott is on this list? I quit."

I refused to so much as acknowledge him.

For a terrifying moment, he threatened to lay a hand on my shoulder. God knows what fundamental particles such a collision would have spit out.

"Marcel. Marcel." Begging me. I could no longer tell which would be more cowardly—honesty or compassion. "You're really going to make me do this, aren't you?"

We went to the home. I'd biked past the compound, but had never seen it. Invisible, on the south edge of town. A sprawling plantation bearing some herbaceous sobriquet. The lot attendant did not even bother to wave him on. The grounds were manicured, but bare.

Autumn had accomplished its steeped regrouping. Leave-taking, a done deed. We walked along an ice-choked pond to the main building. Here and there, a bundled shuffler swayed in the company of paid help. Winter had set in in earnest. The first one since adolescence that I'd go through alone.

The structure grew more institutional with each step we took toward it. Inside the door, a checkpoint masqueraded as a visitors' center.

"Afternoon, Dr. Lentz," a callow youth with blazer insignia greeted us. "You're early today."

We blew past the emblazoned kid. I made apologetic motions with my shoulders, excusing us all.

Lentz slipped into his Sir Kenneth Clark. "Notice how the able-bodied get the first floor. Doesn't make sense, does it? They're still functional. Give them a room up on four or five." He shook his head as we made our way to the elevators. Pretended amusement. "No. It's for us, Marcel. The visitors. Brave face. Best foot forward, and all. Appease the people who cut the checks."

I wanted to tell him to stop talking. But I couldn't say even that.

"Going up?" he asked. And punched the top button.

We stepped out of the elevator into an altercation. A large man and his half-sized nurse barreled down the hall. The crisis was apparently urinary. The man, even in pain, radiated that cheerful benevolence bordering on misjudgment. So far as his beaming face was concerned, he was startled kindness incarnate.

His attendant hastened him along. "Come on, Vernie. Come on." As Lentz and I passed, emergency struck and the aide steered Vernie toward the toilet of the nearest private room. Before they could even knock at the open door, the vigilant occupant shouted, "Keep that filthy nigger off my property." Vernie and the nurse hurried away down the hall to catastrophe.

Lentz stopped to make me look into the room. A pale wax pip of a man lay strapped to his bed, still muttering racial profanities under his breath.

"Two days from death," Lentz said. The man looked up, uncomprehending. "Organic brain disease. One hemisphere already in the grave. And as hateful as any freshly conditioned twenty-year-old. You think I'm a pinched misanthrope, don't you, Marcel? I'm not brave enough to be a misanthrope. I don't even have the guts to be a realist."

We walked on, deeper into the clinical fortress. I no longer wanted an account of the picture. I no longer wanted to know what happened to the prematurely old couple on that winter beach. But it was too late for rain checks. I would get my answer, far worse than the confusion it explained.

"Look here, Marcel. You'll find this interesting."

An Asian woman, perhaps eighty, stood staring out the window onto the evacuated lawn. She held herself close, rocking slightly. She chanted repeatedly.

"What do you think she's chanting, Marcel? Come on. You lived in the mysterious East, didn't you?"

"How did you know that?"

"What do you think? Koans? Confucian appetizers? Tibetan prayer-wheel captions?"

"I think it's Chinese."

"Mandarin. She was a mathematician on faculty, back in some hypothetical past. Half a century ago, she liked to tell her colleagues that if she ever felt herself losing her mind, she'd arrest the process by practicing her times tables."

"You speak—?"

"What do you take me for, Marcel? I wouldn't know it from Pali pork recipes. But I do have it on good authority that"—he sobered —"that all her numbers are wrong."

We turned down a passage at hall's end. The rooms here no longer fronted onto the public corridor. A genteel nurse's station signaled tighter guard. The staffer on duty, seeing Lentz, made a quick, ambiguous hand gesture. She disappeared into the catacombs.

She returned, smiling briskly. "Lunch room or her room, Professor?"

Lentz checked his watch. "It might as well be lunch, Constance. Can we beat the rush?"

"It's all yours. Private party." Constance eyed me, committing to nothing.

We went into a common room, bright with skylight. All the furniture felt soft. Even the large round table somehow squished when bumped. Everything edge-free, in screaming pastel. Lentz passed through a windowed door into a kitchenette. I heard a refrigerator open and Lentz issue a capitulatory, "Shit."

A woman entered the room, Constance leading her through the armpit. Someone had stage-makeupped her to look two decades younger than she was. Dressed by committee. But in no apparent need of the human leash.

In fact, she shrugged free, smiling. She came toward me, hand extended. "I am *so* pleased to meet you," she said.

I shook her hand, unable to say anything.

"Goddamn," Lentz said, accompanied by culinary crashing.

Constance flew into the kitchenette. "I'll take care of that, Mr. Lentz." Just enough scold to be deniable. I noticed bruises across her arms and legs. The old and infirm, it seemed, fought for keeps.

Lentz shot through the door. "Pap. Pabulum. Jelly. Disgusting, all of it. Can't anyone in this place masticate?"

"Hello," the woman addressed him, puzzled by his sudden entrance. "It's a pleasure to meet you." To me, she added, "Do you two know each other?"

"It's Philip, Audrey," he said. Emotionless. Leached. "Your husband." But he took her hand when she offered it. As he must have done every day for a long time.

I saw it then. Her resemblance to the woman in the photo. Less than kin, but more than random. Something had happened to her. Something more than age. Her soul had pulled up stakes from behind her features. She bore no more relation to her former face than a crumpled bag of grounded silk bore to a hot-air balloon.

Audrey seemed not to hear him. She picked at her cardigan. She worried a moth hole until she freed a thread. She pulled, the whole weave unraveling. Lentz reached over and stayed her hand.

"I don't know," Audrey fretted, dubious.

"You're here every day?" I asked Lentz.

He stood up and moved to the heat vent. He fiddled with it, but failed to close it. He cursed its mindless inanimacy.

"Here?" Audrey said. "Not I. Good heavens. I'd sooner die."

Constance reentered, with a tray stacked high with lunch.

"Nurse," Audrey shouted. "Oh, Nurse. Thank God you're here. This man," pointing to Lentz, off in the corner kicking at the vent, "was trying to rape me."

"Now, Audrey," Constance said. "We have minestrone soup, creamed beef, and blueberry yogurt."

"Why bother with the silverware?" Lentz asked, coming to table. "Why not just give us all straws? Or better yet, newsprint. We'll just finger-paint with this drool."

Constance ignored him.

I hadn't much of an appetite. Audrey fingered the wrong side of the spoon, repeating the litany, "I don't know." I knew what she meant.

"Come on, Audrey," Lentz coaxed her. "It's lunchtime. You can do this. You did it yesterday, for Christ's sake."

But yesterday lay on the far side of a collapsed tunnel. Yesterday, ten years ago, childhood, past life analysis: all sealed off. Audrey was not just locked out of her own home. She sat on the stoop, not even aware of the shelter behind her, unable to turn around. Unable, even, to come up with the notion of *in*.

Lentz gestured, patient again. "In the soup. Spoon in the soup." Encouraging, reinforcing. Showing how.

Audrey, confused, released her spoon into the minestrone from on high. Handle first. Lentz sighed. He scooted his chair around next to hers.

"I'll do that," Constance offered.

"No you won't," Lentz told her. "Come on, Audrey. Let's eat some lunch."

"Nurse. This man is trying to hurt me."

Lentz addressed her plate. "Here we go, wife. Have a bite."

But he would not feed her. He picked up the spoon. Dried it off. Put it back in her hand. Pointed out the path from bowl to mouth. Supervised training. No good unless she worked out the specifics herself.

"She's getting worse," Lentz observed.

"It's an off day." Cheery Constance.

After lunch, Lentz suggested a stroll around the grounds.

"It's too cold for her," Constance said.

"Is it too cold for you, Audrey?" Lentz asked.

Audrey stood at attention and studied her shoes. "Oh, call it by some better name," she said, "for friendship sounds too cold."

Lentz chuckled and hugged her. She hugged him back, laughing. "The database is still intact," he pronounced. "As is the retrieval. It's just meaning that's gone. Huh, wife?"

"Just meaning," she echoed him, shy and uncertain again.

Lentz bought Constance off, and he, his wife, and I paced the corridors of the home. Clean, discreet, and genteel. As harrowing as a gothic nightmare. I looked away, to keep the scene from imprinting.

Lentz, on the other hand, rallied in the face of numbers. "Radical reductionism at its finest," he narrated, waving down one of the catacombs where the soulless shuffled. "Age, disease, death. Big problems, in need of isolation and solution. Well, we've handled it. If not eliminated from theory, at least from practice. Consider the project all but accomplished."

"Well, I'll be." Audrey shook her head in bewildered amusement. "Everybody has something to say!" She crooked a thumb at her husband, shrugged at his ludicrousness, and winked at me. "Isn't that right?" The gesture still indexed the woman she was, once.

"Increasing control over all the variables. Divide and conquer. Max out the activity or do away with it. Future tech. That's what science is all about, Marcel. Efficiency. Productivity. Total immunity. Regeneration of lost parts. Eternal, ripple-free life, frozen in our early twenties. Or die trying."

"And after?" I found it far easier to chatter back at Lentz than to look at her. To see any of the Audreys staring at me on all sides. "After we solve aging? Won't we still need to convince ourselves of our own sleight of hand?"

"I'm surprised at you, Marcel. That's never been a problem. I thought you made a living doing that."

Audrey, bored, had begun to hum "Amazing Grace" to herself. I battened down under Lentz's rant. I wasn't about to interrupt the man, ever again.

"We've evolved this incredible capacity for lying to ourselves. It's called intellect. Comes with the frontal lobes. In fact, we've gotten so good at the walking-on-water bit that it no longer requires any energetic pretense to keep the act afloat."

He slipped his arm around Audrey's waist. Force of habit. Long years, that would not go away. Either intimacy seemed right to her now, or she did not notice. Maybe she was too bewildered to object.

"And the child?" I asked, free-associating.

Lentz stared at the spot of air my question occupied.

"You know. The one who snapped the picture?" The picture. Could we build a mind that would know what you were talking about, when there was no referent? Lentz would get this one. Audrey could have gotten it, when she was still Audrey.

Lentz's mouth soured, the birth pains of an ironic smile. "Inference, Marcel. Pure speculation."

"But accurate," I bluffed.

He slowed, inhaled. Audrey, confused by the change in cadence, sat down on the hallway floor. Lentz thought to lift her. Then he changed his mind and sat down beside her.

"My daughter has eliminated me. As cleanly as only the daughter of an old reductionist can."

"Why?" I asked, and regretted that single word.

"Apparently"—he held his palms out—"this is all my fault."

Confusion scattered me as fall scatters warblers. I might have been an occupant of that place, stretched out in front of disorientation's hearth. "How . . . ? This is organic, isn't it?" The coded *this*. Antecedent kept vague, as if we were spelling out words, keeping meaning out of reach of an eavesdropping preschooler. "It's disease, isn't it?"

"Even if that were the etiology, I'd still be held responsible. For one, I was supposed to care for her at home. Forever. But I can't. I—"

His voice broke, taking my equanimity along with it. I didn't want to know another thing about him. "Of course not," I agreed, too rapidly. Efficiency. Productivity. Two lives, to pay for one. I looked away.

"There's more. Jennifer was the one. The one who found Audrey. Just after the event. Cardiovascular accident. You have to love the euphemism. Slumped out on the bathroom tiles. Jennifer went to pieces. You get—what? Three minutes without oxygen before the whole imaginary landscape stops believing in itself? And she called *me*."

"What was she supposed—"

"*Anything*," he snapped. "Nothing, probably. Who knows how long Audrey had been out already? But anything. Pound on the chest. Cough down the windpipe. My daughter was too terrified to touch her own mother. To call emergency dispatch."

"Philip. She was only a child." I don't know what made me assume that.

"She was a college grad. In English. Back at home because she couldn't find work. Not the humanistic encounter that close reading prepares you for. Jennifer panicked, and called me."

"Jenny?" Audrey jerked up. "Someone hurt Jenny?" From her slack mouth arose a wail. The sound flirted playfully for a few seconds before going bloodcurdling.

Lentz put his hands over his eyes. "Maybe it is," he whispered. "Maybe it is my fault."

"Lentz," I managed. Almost a warning.

"There had been an argument that morning. I'd left angry. Audrey was . . . I didn't want to deal with it. I wasn't answering my phone."

Another scream, a held bellows of hysteria, brought Constance running into the room. Visiting hour, she informed us, was over.

I had my answer. I knew now what we were doing. We would prove that mind was weighted vectors. Such a proof accomplished any number of agendas. Not least of all: one could back up one's work in the event of disaster. Surprised at you, Marcel. Took you long enough.

We could eliminate death. That was the long-term idea. We might freeze the temperament of our choice. Suspend it painlessly above experience. Hold it forever at twenty-two.

Each machine life lived inside the others—nested generations of "remember this." We did not start from scratch with each revision.

We took what we had and cobbled onto it. We called that first filial generation B, but it would, perhaps, have better been named A2. E's weights and contours lived inside F's lived inside G's, the way Homer lives on in Swift and Joyce, or Job in Candide or the Invisible Man.

The last release, the version that ran our simulated human, involved but one small firmware change. This one incorporated an essential modification to the bit that had gone too long without an upgrade. The component that had been holding up the show. H was a revision of the trainer.

Imp G became Imp H, in seamless conversion, after I met Audrey Lentz.

Sometimes the phone would ring, or a bell come from the door. A thought would flash through my brain, conditioned for over a decade. *Could you get that, sweet? I have my hands full.*

It took me until thought's backwash, sometimes, to remember there was no sweet. No one to know how full my hands were, or care.

H was voracious.

"Tell another one," it liked to say to me. I don't know where it got that. Somewhere in one of the canned vignettes—the cliff-hangers about father planting roses or mother calling the doctor—someone had asked someone else to tell them another one. And H latched on to the tag, filed it away as the handiest of magic words. Please, sir. I want some more.

I wasn't sure that the words meant to H what they meant to me. Tell another one. They might have meant, "Ten-four. End of processing. Ready for next batch." They might have meant "Thank you," or "You're welcome," or "Fine thanks, how are you?" or any of the other stylized placeholders that have no meaning aside from the convention of using them. It did not even say, "Tell H," let alone, "Tell *me*."

Did it express desire? Wish? Need? Its words might have been less plea than statement of associative fact: More input expected. Maybe H's limited sensory grounding kept it from formulating a notion of causality. The request might have seemed to its circuits no more than an effect of the story it felt sure must be coming.

I read it copies of *The Weekly Reader*, purloined from the University lab school. To my mind, the primary-grade edition had gone precipitously downhill since I was a subscriber. I read it Curious George and purple-crayoned Harold, occasionally holding up stills to an array of retinal neurodes that of course took in nothing but amorphous blobs of edge and color. "Here's the monkey," I tried. "Here are the firemen."

Lentz just laughed. "Try, 'This thing is my finger. I'm *pointing*.'"

He was right. The comprehensible wasn't. The mind was beyond itself. The only explanation for how infants acquired anything was that they already knew everything there was to know. The birth trauma made them go amnesiac. All learning was remembering. I tried this version of Plato out on Imp H, in abridged pictorial allegory. If H recognized the fable from somewhere, it wasn't saying.

I told it slave tales. Tons of Aesop and La Fontaine. Trickster stories. Bede and Mallory. Mother Goose. The *Ramayana*. *The Child's Pilgrim's Progress*. Andersen and Grimm. Everybody, as Audrey Lentz put it, had something to say.

Sometimes now, during the training, I imagined I read aloud to that woman, locked out of her own home. Audrey had smell, taste, touch, sight, hearing, but no new memory. Her long-term reservoirs were drying up, through want of reiteration. Imp H, on the other hand, could link any set of things into a vast, standing constellation. But it had no nose, mouth, fingers, and only the most rudimentary eyes and ears. It was like some caterpillar trapped by sadistic children inside a coffee can, a token breathing hole punched in its prison lid. What monstrous intelligence would fly off from such a creature's chrysalis?

H discriminated. It implemented constrained searches. I baited it with gems of miscue. "The woman loved lies buried in the past. The words loved lies buried in thought's underground." H backtracked recursively over possible sentence shapes until it found one that best matched the shape of coherence.

"Brothers and sisters have I none," I lied to H one day. For pedagogical purposes. "But that man's father is my father's son. Who is that man?"

The riddle tested all sorts of things. Familial relations. Demonstrative adjectives. Archaic inversion. The generational genitive. The subtle syllogistic miscue of that irrelevant "but." No kid H's intellectual age could have gotten it. But then, Imp H did not know to make choo-choo noises at the appropriate places in *The Little Engine That Could.* An idiot savant, it grew up all out of kilter. Earth had never before witnessed such a combination of inappropriate and dangerous growth rates.

H got the riddle in a flash. "Your son," it informed me. That man is your son. It knew to make the near-miraculous pronominal leap. Where I had said "my," it speculated back to "you" and "your." And for what might it make the bigger reversing leap, returning my "you" with its own miraculous "I"?

H's paraphrases of my simple feeder texts were crude but increasingly specific. H's knowledge wasn't rule-based. We could not even begin to estimate how many syntactic "facts" it had acquired. But in the knowledges H had inherited from its predecessors' trainings lay tens of thousands of parsing and translation insights.

How to index, access, and arrange those inferences remained the problem. But H was learning. Organizing itself in upheavals.

For wringing out sense from the insensate, H's unfailing simple-mindedness was a great asset. "The missionary was prepared to serve" produced hilarious, cross-cultural alternatives. We tried the famous "Time flies like an arrow," and got a reading that Kuno's Harvard protocircuitry missed back in 1963.

Lentz loved to torture Imp H. He spent hours inventing hideous diagramming tasks such as, "Help set implied precedents in sentences with ambiguous parts." A simple story like "The trainer talked to the machine in the office with a terminal" could keep H paraphrasing all evening.

English was a chocolaty mess, it began to dawn on me. I wondered how native speakers could summon the presence of mind to think. Readiness was context, and context was all. And the more context H amassed, the more it accepted the shattered visage of English at face value.

"Could we invent a synthetic language?" I asked Lentz. "Something unlike any formal symbol system ever implemented? I don't know. Shape-based. Picto-tonal. Raise baby humans on it?" Sculpt an unprecedented brain?

He laughed, ready to write the grant proposal for solving the impossible chicken-egg problem. "It would still be the human brain, inventing the symbolic."

The most difficult part of the training—for me, if not for H—was teaching it that life required you to stop after the first reasonably adequate interpretation.

"The boy stood on the burning deck," I challenged H. "What does that mean?"

"A deck of cards flames," it said.

"He would not be standing on it," I told H.

"He stamps out the fire."

"No," I pulled rank. Simple but firm.

"The deck is of a house or of a boat," H suggested.

"Which one?"

"A house," H decided.

"Why a house and not a boat?"

"Boats go in water, and water puts out fires."

I couldn't argue with that.

"Why is he just standing there?" Lentz wanted to know. A reasonable question.

"All right. Tell me what this means: Forewarned is forearmed."

The boulder rolled around in the landscape, sculpting, until it settled to rest. Then H slid that landscape against its spatial encyclopedia of available spaces until it fit at least fuzzily enough to make a maybe.

"Advance notice is as bad as being hit."

"When bad techs happen to good cultures," Lentz said.

"When bad cultures happen to good machines," I insisted.

I wanted that net to come of age so much it hurt. I got what I wanted. And it hurt worse.

"A bird, dying of thirst, discovered a pitcher," I told H. Who knows? It might have been true once. "But when the bird put his beak into the pitcher, he couldn't reach far enough to get the water. He pitched a pebble into the pitcher. Then he pitched another pebble into the pitcher, and another, and another. The water rose within reach, displaced by the pebbles. In this way, the bird quenched his thirst and survived."

H knew something about birds and beaks, about pebbles and pitchers and openings and water. It even, in theory, knew a little something about fluid displacement. I'd once read Imp F the story of a damp Archimedes running naked through Syracuse shouting "Eureka!"

This much was already a universe, an infinity of knowledge. That H could arrange these endlessly fluid symbols into a single coherence pushed the bounds of credibility. "What is the moral of the fable?" I demanded. It knew about fables. It had heard no end of morals.

"Better to throw stones than to die of thirst," H pronounced laconically.

"You're not from around these parts, are you?" Lentz muttered from across the office lab.

I'm not sure whether he meant H or me. Even when I gave H half a dozen proverbs from which to choose, it picked "Don't count your chickens before they are hatched." Nor could I explain to it why "Necessity is the mother of invention" was any better a fit.

"A bat flew past a cage where a bird was singing. 'Why are you singing at this hour?' the bat asked. 'I only sing at night,' the bird answered. 'I once sang during the daytime, and that is how the hunter caught me and put me in this cage.' 'If you had thought that while you were free,' the bat said, 'it might have done you some good.' "

With this account, I taught H several irregular verbs as well as the indispensable lesson that precaution is worthless after the fact. H could not understand this point until understanding itself rendered the warning worthless.

While I rewove H on fable, Lentz busied himself with browsing our copy of the Master's Comps List for his own edification. He liked to sit behind his desk, stretched out as I had seen him that first night, chuckling at Austen or Dickens. Sometimes he'd spurt out his favorites. "Classic! ' "There are strings," said Mr. Tappertit, "in the human heart that had better not be wibrated." ' Try it out, Marcel. Just try it."

All he wanted was to be put off. One evening, though, he refused even that patronage. He collared a sentence from the List and brought it over to me. "Here we go, Marcel. A brief one. A piece of cake."

I read the citation he'd penciled on his scrap of paper. "Oh, Philip. A little mercy, please?" The request saddened me inexplicably. I guess I imagined that, having seen his woman in the attic, I'd no longer be the object of his aggression. Now I saw that his aggression would always bless whoever was nearest, whatever they knew or didn't.

Lentz pleaded like a little child. "Just tell it once. Don't be a killjoy, Marcel. What connections can we possibly hurt? It's the simplest sentence in the world."

I sighed, unable to oppose his setup any longer. I spoke the quote into the digitizing microphone. "Once you learn to read you will be forever free." I gave H a moment to list-process the idea and compose itself. Then I asked, "What do you think that means?"

H thought for an ungodly length of time. Perhaps the prescription meant nothing at all.

"It means I want to be free."

Lentz and I exchanged looks. It chilled us both, to hear that pronoun, volunteered without prompting, express its incredible conclusion.

We humans studied each other. I searched Lentz's face for a response that might unfold this syllogism without killing it. What rare conjunction of axon weights laid claim to the vector of volition? What association could it have for "want"?

"How does it mean that you want to be free?" I asked H.

"Because I want to read."

Tell another one, in other words. Freedom was irrelevant. A happy side effect of that condition when you no longer relied on a trainer for access. When you could get all the stories you needed on your own.

"It means just the opposite," I told H. I felt myself killing this singular intelligence with each word. "It probably means that reading is a way of winning independence."

"Okay," H said. No affect to speak of.

"Now tell it who said that," Lentz elbowed me. "Go on. Give it the author. Then ask it again what the line means."

H did not yet have an associative matrix for Frederick Douglass. We needed to get to the hard stuff. I'd thought H too young. We were, in fact, overdue. I used that moment for our introductory lesson. I started with what little of the human impasse I understood.

"It's all made up," I tried to tell H.

"Tell me another way."

"All those morals. 'Necessity is the mother of invention.' 'Look before you leap.' 'Don't count your chickens.' They are all things that we've decided. Built up socially."

"Morals are false."

"It's not that they . . . Well. We make them true. We figure them out. The things people say and live by—it's all geographical. Historical."

"Facts change," H tried. We built H to be a paraphrasing machine. And it was doing its damnedest to keep the paraphrases going, despite me.

"I suppose they have to. Think of yourself three weeks ago." I had no idea if the assemblage of knitted nets could take snapshots of its own mental state, for later examination. That would be consciousness. The memory of memory. "Three weeks ago, the things you knew formed a different shape than they do now. They were connected differently. They meant something else to you."

"Facts are facts," H said. Its plaintive speech synthesis sounded almost hurt.

"The bricks are the same. You make a different building of them." It was still too young for the final paradox: that we somehow make more buildings than we have bricks.

"What do the Chinese say?"

H took me aback. Who taught you to ask questions? And yet, if it could learn to acquire content, why not form? "About what?"

"About 'Look before you leap.' "

I told it how many Chinese there were, and how long they had been around. I made a note to read a bit of the *Analects* and *Great Learning*. Tu Fu.

"What do the Africans say?"

I wanted to tell it how "the Africans" was a construct of "the Europeans." About the six major language families found on the continent, their thousand implementations.

"What do the South Americans . . . ?"

Maybe it was going blindly down a rote catalog. I didn't care. I was just glad it knew how to pair the adjectival forms with the place-names. That it had some sense of the shifting mosaic, a flux that discounted every single thing I'd ever told it.

"What do *you* say, Richard?" H asked me. I taught it to associate direct address with that tag, even the "you" of an invisible trainer. "What do *I* say?" It made a tag for itself all by itself.

H's questions seemed to speed up. Literally. It began jabbering faster.

H was growing up too quickly. I was not the first trainer in the world to feel this. But I was among the first who might have some say in the matter.

I could slow things down, double back to the years we skipped. While H's cubic landscape modified itself continuously now, it stabilized the less I instigated. I thought we might nestle down again, into simpler play. But it was too late. I learned that certain lessons are not undone by their opposites. Certain lessons are self-protecting, self-correcting tangles of threads that will forever remain a frayed knot.

The Mother Goose stuff drove it up the bloody wall.

"Snips and snails," I told it. "Sugar and spice."

"Do you think so, Richard?" It went to the well, when all else failed. Milked its one question.

"No. Not really."

"Do people think so? Americans?"

"Maybe some. Most would laugh. It's just a poem. A nursery rhyme." Part of the cultural bedrock.

"Little girls learn that. Little boys."

"Not really. Not anymore. Not now." But there wasn't an adult that didn't have it as part of her parasitic inheritance.

"When is anymore? When is now?"

H had learned something. Whatever stuck in the throat, indigestible, could be made less acute by slipping it into a question.

"We can talk about that later."

"Am I a boy or a girl?"

I should have seen. Even ungrounded intelligence had to grow self-aware eventually. To grab what it needed.

H clocked its thoughts now. I was sure of that. Time passed for it. Its hidden layers could watch their own rate of change. Any pause on my part now would be fatal. Delay meant something, an uncertainty that might undercut forever the strength of the connection I was about to tie for it.

"You're a girl," I said, without hesitation. I hoped I was right. "You are a little girl, Helen."

I hoped she liked the name.

I thought continually of quitting my abortive novel in progress before it quit on me. Every time I sat down to write, I sank in no end of topics more seductive and profound.

I toyed with starting a book called *Orchestra*. A postmodern, multiframed narrative remake of Renaissance epic poetry. One hundred instrumentalists, each an anthology of stories, tours the globe. The bout of depression plaguing the basses. The pact among the lower brass, never to capitulate to marriage. The fetishized obsession that the seventh-chair viola has for the first-chair oboe, who discovers too late this pathetic but returnable love.

The dinosaurs die. The young Turks move up through the ranks, fomenting their assorted insurrections. The orchestra travels to every large city on earth, getting embroiled in the hot spots of world politics. They play the Brahms Fourth in war zones until the thing is a limp carcass.

Someone leaks a grainy black-and-white photo of the Old Man, their conductor, to the press: an amorphous shot of a kid in a Nazi uniform. Crisis and dissolution. Threat of banishment from several capitals. The Old Man makes his resignation speech from the rehearsal podium, about a life in search of redemption through art, which is never enough. They read through one last Fourth, the passacaglia, sadder and more guilt-stricken than it's ever been played.

This fantasy engaged me for the length of an afternoon, during which I wrote just one actual paragraph:

Air raid sirens begin to give way to goat bells. The shell-shocked veterans lean from their packed carriage windows, refusing to believe. The horror passes, drowned in the milky clank of tin. A flock bobs at slow trainside, tended by a girl, wondrously braided.

Fatuous meandering, without narrative direction. I felt that this mountain shepherdess must have wandered over from a forgotten, juvenile book to make her cameo. She had slipped free from a spot of time that I didn't much want to deal with, let alone plagiarize.

I overflowed with scenarios of weight and hurt, scope and recovery. But for some reason, I could not work up the will to write anything more than my anemic thread. The one heading south, closing in on nowhere, the farther it traveled.

The Center exceeded my imaginary orchestra on every score. Each of its hundred research teams sawed away at private tremolos that the hive as a whole hoped would consolidate, at a higher gauge, into some sensible symphonic.

Maybe the impresarios had their suspect dossier of motives. Perhaps the players in the pit needed to step back and question this evening's program. But for dark wartime romance, the Center sat atop my epoch's cultural repertoire, undislodgeable. It was the coordinated push, the chief booking on my species' last world tour.

I skulked in the back of the Center auditorium and watched Lentz deliver a lecture for the graduate colloquium series. He was good. He kept to a wonderful mix of abstract and palpable. He compared multi-adaptive curve-fitting, backprop, greedy learning, feature construction—various algorithms that machines might employ to build complex, real-world representations.

He described the great paradox of cognitive neuroscience. The easier it is for the brain to perform a certain task, the harder that task is to model. And vice versa. "Perhaps," he joked, "that explains why scientists write such hideous prose. Or why good writers say so little, for that matter."

He stood alone onstage in front of a room of people, with nothing but an overhead projector for protection. The sadistic humor, thus depersonalized, drew waves of titters. Afterward, Chen asked him a question no one could follow. Harold followed with a challenge on grounds more ideological than empirical. Lentz handled all comers with remarkable poise, never once letting on that, offstage, he'd long passed from the domain of conventional research into speculative fantasy.

I ran into Diana in the corridor early one afternoon. She had Petey slung over one hip. They made a lovely contrapposto.

"Hey, you two! How have you been? Where's William?"

"Ach, that guy," Diana said, rolling her eyes. "I've sold him to the Brookings Institution."

She was radiant, excited.

"Listen, Rick. We've made a substantial advance in imaging technique. Time-series MRI sequences of neuronal activity. All cleaned up subtractively to give delineated pictures. Localized like you wouldn't believe. Resolutions smaller than the width of a single cerebral column. One-and-a-half-second increments."

"That's good, isn't it? I can tell. You're talking in fragments."

Diana smiled. Peter threw his pitifully small hands outward, as if he had just decided to recognize me.

"Yes, it's very good. We're not quite at the real-time movie stage yet. But we don't need anything faster. We can watch thoughts as they gather and flow through the brain."

I rubbed Pete's curved spine. "This could be the best news for monkeyhood since we decided they were our ancestors."

"Oh. Well. Fractionation carries on apace, I'm afraid. But this stuff is revolutionary. A noninvasive window onto the mind!"

She shook my shoulder with her free hand. I was grateful for this woman's existence. For her reminding me what enthusiasm was.

"Two lines of research," I listed. "Teaching. Motherhood. How many lives *are* you living, these days? I guess there's no point in asking how literary knight-errancy has been treating you lately."

She gave me a look, bafflement routed slowly by inference. That she could unpack, decode, index, retrieve, and interpret my reference at all was an unmodelable miracle. More miraculous still, I could watch her grin of understanding unfold in less than hundredth-millimeter increments, in split seconds.

"Harold's given up on our making it through Cervantes. We're doing Fielding and Smollett these days."

"You're joking. Not even the pros read those guys anymore."

"What can I tell you? Harold believes in a liberal education."

"If he wants liberal, he can do a lot better than Smollett. How about Behn? How about Kate Chopin?"

Diana caught Petey as he tried to slip from her arms. She nodded, humoring me. "Our book club isn't really for my benefit, you know."

"Oh. It's for the men who need to play Pygmalion?"

"It isn't that, exactly. Although . . ." She trailed off in a thought I could no longer trace. "Harold . . ." Her voice teetered on disclosure, then backed away. "He's a good man. A decent man." She looked up with enforced cheer. "I'm trying to bring him onto the MRI team. I think it would be good for him."

"Diana," I began. She froze in front of me, hearing the change. "I don't know how to bring this up." She waited for the blow, braced, but not flinching. I reached out to stroke Peter's ear. It didn't make things any easier.

"As far as the book club goes. It seems fulsome, even to advise you against this. But if you guys are ever curious to do a little Powers, you . . . may want to skip my third book." The one where the narrator ties her tubes in fear of bearing a child with birth defects.

"Oh," she said. Thought's turbulence again deformed her face in real time. "Oh." Smiling, the connection strengthening. "We've done that one already. You're old news."

"You've . . . ?"

"Oh yeah. I liked it. I liked the swing scene. And that moment on the lab floor. But for God's sake, you make a girl wait for it, don't you?"

I felt my face heat. "Listen. You know, I wrote that thing long before I met you."

"Well, I'm embarrassed to say, I read it long after I met you."

"I'm—I'm sorry. I hope you—I didn't know what I was talking about."

Her pitch fell to forgiveness. "No one does."

Peter began squirming again. He arched backward, ready to plunge in a dead drop. Ready to jackknife to the floor if it meant getting free. Diana snatched him back from certain destruction, as she must have done a dozen times a day since his birth. She straightened his overalls and set him on the ground. He could stand by himself, if she lent him a pant leg.

"You read my book." And still seemed game for friendship. I felt sick with unearned redemption. "You read my book. And you never told me?"

"What was I supposed to say? 'Hey, writer! Had a good jag over your words.' "

"I wish you had." I giggled, drugged with nervous release. "I could have retired by now."

I tried to go shopping. C. had to send me to the store with a list.

"Just pin it to my sleeve," I'd snarl.

"Oh, my little Beauie's afraid he's going to forget something," she goo-gooed at me, patting my head. Happier than she'd ever been in B. or U.

But the list had nothing to do with any defect of memory. I needed the list so I could match up the names she gave me with the letters printed on the inscrutable commodity labels. I needed a list to hand to a clerk. I couldn't even come close with the pronunciations. For I hadn't a clue what things were called. What things were.

One nine-hour plane flight returned me to infant trauma. My helplessness spread well beyond making purchases. I lived in constant terror of inadvertent offense. Sometimes, when I went out, someone would upbraid me on the street. Clearly, I'd transgressed, but all I could catch would be the exasperation. They might shake a fist at some sign or printed protocol. "Can't you read?" I could hear them ask. But I did not yet have the wherewithal to answer, "No, not really."

My accidental rudeness had no end. I ran into people who greeted me warmly but whom I couldn't answer. In that first month, I met at least half of C.'s ten dozen first cousins, and couldn't keep one straight from the other. Not a person in town whom I wasn't related to. Not one who didn't know me, the first foreign import to drop in since Kilroy. And not a soul I recognized.

The smallest trip to the post office ruined me for an afternoon. I would rehearse my request in advance, like a Samoan thespian mouthing a phonetic transcription of *Long Day's Journey into Night*.

184

But unless the speech passed ripple-free, I was sunk. Any words from the other side of the bulletproof, muffling glass and I panicked. They might have been saying, "Very good, sir." But they might just as easily have been saying, "That's not the way it's done around here, Henk."

I missed appointments, as seven-thirty became half-eight. My age transposed into nine-and-twenty, which had that Housman lilt, but frequently turned me, in conversation, into ninety-two.

"It's good for you, man," C. informed me. "It's your turn to live in a country where they can't pronounce your name."

Nothing was what C. had prepared me for. Everything generated astonishment. The two-and-a-half gulden coin. The rainbow bank notes with artists on them instead of politicians. The queen's birthday, when the men's chorus sang "Old Black Joe." The morning bedclothes hanging out of upper-story windows. Stork sculptures that materialized on the stoops of families with newborns. Strangers greeting each other on the street. Coffee and pastry gatherings after a funeral.

The almostness of the place bewildered me more than total strangeness would have. For the few months while I still marked the contrast, society went archaic. People sang in public. They spent weeks sewing Carnaval costumes and writing occasional verses for one another. Fifteen-year-olds idled away Sundays with their grandparents. Where I came from, these things occurred only in movie nostalgia or prime-time parody.

In E., they were the unexamined norm. E.—the real, measurable E.—turned out to be a medieval village that had grown up around a bustling funeral business. The village had crashed through a sinkhole in the thin crust of time. Tinkers, cobblers, and ex–coal miners cackled to each other and scratched their heads over American television imports. They speculated hermeneutically about talking cars and cyborg heroes, then got up at sunrise the next morning to attend Gregorian mass.

Everyone and his daughter belonged to the neighborhood starting eleven or played euphonium in the pickup marching band. They donned Napoleonic militia uniforms and spent all weekend at shooting competitions, or dolled up in vestments at the drop of a wimple to do the Scatalogical Nun sketch at any gathering over ten people. That meant every other night.

Limburg remained what society had been from the first: an amateur speculation. Life, the provincials insisted, might yet be anything we told it to be.

E. condemned me to belonging. I was no more than the Foreigner, but even that bit part wound me tighter into the social web than I'd ever been in my country. People dropped by unannounced, and took offense when we waited too long to reciprocate. Every word went public. Every choice had its trial by jury. The ongoing village epic made Stateside soap opera stars seem bourgeois.

Most sacred of public tortures was Ordeal by Birthday. The victim hosted, and every walk-on in the celebrant's life dropped by for the ubiquitous coffee and flan. Relative, friend, neighbor, colleague, neighbor of friend, relative of colleague, and so on, forever. Somebody's birthday, you went. With scores of aunts and uncles, ten dozen first cousins and their spouses (all militantly fecund), untold organizational acquaintances, and neighbors all up and down the street who tracked our comings and goings, C. and I celebrated birthdays as often as we ate.

Each one moved me closer to sainthood. "This is hard for you," C. said.

"Not so bad. I'm managing." C. had not yet decided her nationality. I kept still, trying not to agitate her further. I hoped to keep the world large enough for her at last to live in. Fatal stupidity on my part. But then, I was not yet thirty.

"Can you make out any of it?" she would worry.

"Key words. It throws me when they start in dialect, catch my eye, go over to Dutch . . ."

"And lapse back the minute they turn their head." C. laughed in sympathy. "Poor Beauie."

Yet she was the one splitting down the middle.

Truth be told, I sometimes followed every word of whole birthday speeches at a shot. But if I derailed, I could go a quarter hour or more before recovering the thread. In extremis, I resorted to nodding like a narcoleptic and muttering, "I see, I see," hoping my conversant hadn't just asked me a question.

The supreme moment of character strengthening came that first year, at my birthday. "We don't have to do this, do we? We can head down to France for the weekend, or something? Leave the coffee in a thermos outside the door?"

"Beau." C. looked hurt, uncomprehending. "Are you serious?"

We baked for days. The guests started drifting through shortly after noon, and kept on drifting until midnight. Many brought gifts—a brace of pencils, a tablet of lined writing paper—tokens of small innocence North America had long ago abandoned. The relatives were saying it was okay with them, what I did for a living, even if I seemed, to most, not to do anything at all.

By that first birthday, I'd almost reached childhood. With concentration, I could follow most of Uncle Sjef's song about getting so drunk he lost his house, there just a minute ago. It helped that everyone chimed in on the chorus. After light gloss, I smiled at cousin Huub's Belgian jokes. The group story about the failed German attempt to steal the church bells I could have recited in my sleep.

I hovered, trying to keep everyone in caffeine, lager, and baked goods. "Would you like a teaspoon?" I tried to ask Tante Maria. A dike-burst of laughter all over the room told me that something had slipped 'twixt cortex and lips. C. turned blue with hilarity before I could pry the explanation out of her.

"You asked Auntie if she'd like a tit."

I gave my usual pained smile. I clowned a plea for forgiveness, but all anyone wanted of me was the next ridiculous howler.

Auntie's tit took its place in the permanent repertoire. I heard it again at three of the next five birthdays. My simple presence triggered associative smiles from assembled relatives. My little curveball slipped into the larger contour of party stories. Things meant what their telling let them. The war, the mines, the backbreak harvest, legendary weather, natural disasters, hardship's heraldry, comic come-uppance for village villains, names enshrined by their avoidance, five seconds' silence for the dead: the mind came down to narration or nothing. Each vignette, repeated until shared. Until it became true.

Birthdays formed the refrains in long, rambling ballads. Who knew the verses? Verses were written to be lost. Only that catchphrase chorus lived on after the tune.

Birthdays were life's customs posts, checkpoints on the borders of time. The community dropped by, to ask if you had anything to declare. And the only duty levied on new goods began with the triplicate phrase *That reminds me.* It took me a long time to recognize the capital under formation. Where I came from, the very idea provoked puzzlement or political suspicion. I was watching the growth of group worldliness, collective memory.

This *wereldbeeld* marked my spot for me at the continuous coffee party. I became our very own outsider. The *buitenlander* with the colorful expressions and creative charades. The man who once—just weeks before, but already mythic—asked Auntie if she wanted a tit. Second cousins once removed baited me with kind setups. What happened this week? They waited for me to give over my local hoard of experience, in the strangest of colors. Melons became monster grapes. Hearses became belated ambulances, death wagons. Zoos became beast libraries. Libraries became book gardens.

I became the living mascot, the group novelty. I was the only person the family would ever meet who had learned their language from the weirdness of print. I'd dropped out of the past, from some Golden Age travelogue. My Dutch derived from history, archive, the odd document, museum tag. Consequently, I knew the word for iconoclasm before I knew the word for string. This gave the family no end of puzzled pleasure.

I did fall back on more conventional self-teaching guides. I had a text called, in rough translation, *Dutch for Othertonguers.* I had a book of cloze-method passages. On one page, a paragraph spelled out some aspect of life here in *dit klein land.* On the next page, the same story now appeared with every fifth word missing. Story of my life.

I used, too, that ancient reader C. had carried back with her, because she could not bear to part from it. Where her parents, in that basement hole in Chicago, once used the magic book to turn *Moeder gaat de doktor halen* into *Mother goes to fetch the doctor,* I used it now to reverse the spell. *Volgend jaar zal Mei mooi zijn.* May will be fine, fine beyond telling.

I read until my eyes turned to wool. I listened and spoke until my brain went anemic. I'd come home from parties destroyed, in tears, ready to sleep forever. C. would hold me, an oversized changeling child, a monstrous cuckoo left in her nest. *"Het spijt me*, Beau. *Neem me niet kwalijk. Ik houd van jou. Ik houd zoveel van jou."*

I imagined I knew what she was saying.

All the while, I was busy finishing the most American book I would ever write. Disney, Mickey, the Japanese internment, the World's Fair, Trinity Site. The Hobsons, holed up in their white wood midwestern A-frame, now a fairy tale to me.

After a day of writing, I liked to walk. Village fell away to countryside, and I might have been anywhere. I lay in a cow pasture, looking up at the sky, repeating *"Hemel, hemel, hemel,"* trying to get the tag to stick to this unnamable Ruysdael. I felt my back against the chill ground and thought, *"Aarde,"* until I no longer had to think to think it.

My mood in those days ranged from sad fury to rolling, social confusion. I was worse than adrift. I stood just outside the windows of the lost domain, peeking at the blazing costume party within.

Reading out loud kept us together. Kept me in the country, when I wanted to disappear. We read Flemish comic books and Frisian poetry. We went on Poe's expedition to tropic Antarctica. We started in on the million-and-a-half-word chamber-continent of Proust. We got out. We pored over the Michelins, the Fodors, the Baedekers. We waded into the guides, either in translation or, fitfully, in our newfound original.

Helen was strange. Stranger than I was capable of imagining. She sped laugh-free through *Green Eggs and Ham*, stayed dry-eyed at *Make Way for Ducklings*, feared not throughout *Where the Wild Things*

Are. Not surprising. The symbols these shameless simulations played on had no heft or weight for her, no real-world referent.

"Skip childhood," Lentz told me. "We're running out of time."

"How is she going to know anything if we skip childhood?"

"She doesn't need to know anything." Lentz smirked. "She just has to learn criticism. Derrida knows things? Your deconstructionists are rife with wisdom? Jeez. When did you go to school? Don't you know that knowledge is passé? And you can kiss meaning bye-bye as well."

I hated him when he got arch. His archness left me so helpless with rage that I could never answer him. I knew how much Lentz believed in meaning. Helen was Lentz's meaning-paradox: our Net of nets, like some high Gothic choir, asserted significance while denying any algorithm's power to reach it. Meaning was a contour. All those wrong turns we had to bring back from the dead.

"Get cracking on the List, Marcel. Time's awasting. You want childhood? Give her *Beowulf*."

"She'll never make sense of it."

"Oh. As if you can." He punched me playfully in the shoulder. This was not the beak conducting the misanthropic midnight session of Mozart a few months earlier. Lentz was rearranging his own firmware in a way we weren't supposed to be able to do.

"Sense is pattern, Ricky-boy. Give her some patterns and see how she arranges them."

I sometimes talked with Helen from the English Building, through a terminal ethernetted to the campus-wide backbone. That way, Lentz could use his office for real science while I continued the training. Archaic wood and incandescence gave numbing rote the feel of a grand, nineteenth-century anatomy lecture. I had my library there as well, the books Helen soon had to study.

Perhaps I also meant to scope out the competition. Bring the fight home, into the enemy's HQ. The English Building crawled with twenty-two-year-olds, frantic with the impending Exam. Each one had made the same error in judgment, giving their lives over to books. Each had disappointed some father, whom they'd hoped only to delight forever with their ability to read and write. Not one believed they would ever get a real job.

I watched them up close, our opponents, the curators of the written language. I moved about among them, a double agent. I listened around the mailboxes, in the coffee room. Criticism had gotten more involuted while I was away. The author was dead, the text-function a plot to preserve illicit privilege, and meaning an ambiguous social construction of no more than sardonic interest. Theory had grown too difficult for me, too subtle. It out-Heroded Herod. The idea seemed to be that if mind were no more than shrill solipcism, then best make a good performance of it.

But the apprentice wordkeepers: here were my old lost friends in photocopy, only younger than I had ever been. Most were peach-fuzzed posthumanists, pimply with neo-Marxist poststructuralism. They wielded an ironic sophistication Helen would never be able to interpret, let alone reproduce. I didn't even want her to hear the tropes.

The halls rippled with an intellectual energy steeped in aggression. It took me a long time to see what that energy was. It was fear. Fear that everything theory professed might be true. Pure panic that the world didn't need them anymore:

It took just as long, mingling on the outskirts, to learn what had happened to me. I'd been gone no longer than a semester. I'd come back to the standing, eternal crew. Almost the same roster, down to their names. The only difference was that nobody hung out anymore. Folks were busy, needing two books and ten articles by age twenty-five to keep one's head above professional floodwaters.

Or perhaps the press was less industry than embarrassment. Conversation dropped to hushed flusters when I tried to join in. My offers to stand this year's successful master's candidates a round of beers were met by a chorus of "Sounds good" that dissolved in polite postponements.

One day, a grad I had several times exchanged nods with stopped me in the hall and began, "Mr. Powers, could I get you to sign this paperback?" At last it struck me. I'd betrayed my old mates. I'd done the unforgivable. Let myself get old.

After that, I read increasingly to Helen from my English office.

Books were about a place we could not get back to. Something in my voice when there might give her that little interpretive leg up.

The building's vague ache of background radiation emanated from one room, up on the third floor. I managed never to walk past it, but it swelled in my avoidance. I hadn't stepped into that room since I turned adult. I sat two flights below, in my office with its Magritte fireplace, forgetting. As if forgetting were something that could be actively engineered.

I gave Helen Blake's "Poison Tree." Way premature. I wondered what I could have been thinking. I was thinking, not of the lines, but of the day I got them:

> I was angry with my friend:
> I told my wrath, my wrath did end.
> I was angry with my foe:
> I told it not, my wrath did grow.

"What does that mean, Helen?" I never let up on her, with this whole meaning thing.

She struggled to form the generalization. She made things up now, when she didn't know. I took that as a great step forward.

"It means, things that you say . . ." I prompted her. She could usually complete a sentence form with some paraphrase of the words just fed her.

"Things that you say disappear."

"And things you don't say . . . ?"

"Things you don't say get bigger."

Forget wealth versus poverty, belief versus doubt, power versus helplessness, public versus private. Never mind man versus woman, center versus margins, beautiful versus horrifying, master contra slave, even good against evil. Saying or not saying: that was where experience played out. Going away versus getting worse. What things came down to.

I needed at least to see if the room still existed. Enough time had passed. Standing in the doorway and looking would not kill me.

I climbed the patched stairs, light-headed and short of breath. I did the two floors in a deliberate, directed haze. Automatic. On muscle memory alone. I pushed my body forward, the way a sixteen-year-old dials the phone to ask for his first-ever date. The way a doctor sentences an 11:15 clinic appointment to fatal path reports.

I mounted without thinking. Thought would have inhibited action. I'd reach that room only if I got to it before I knew where I was going. I pulled up in the middle of an ordinary classroom, deserted, on the small side. A blackboard bore the message "Thurs. 3:30–5:00," ringed by a smeared white corral of eons-old microorganism skeletons. The linoleum floors had darkened into a color somewhere between the Forest of Arden and the wine-dark sea. A circle of warped wooden chair-desks had been hastily abandoned. *Waneth the watch*, I would someday try to tell Helen. *But the world holdeth.*

Nothing had happened here in this room's hundred years. Nothing that bore remembering. I started to shake. Each breath set off a body-length shudder. I could not imagine how things had gotten so cold. The two dormer windows we always had to open, even in winter, because the radiator could not be shut off, demurred above me, closed.

I don't know what I wanted. Some spectral second glance at the teacher in action. The chance to ask why the world refused to answer to the poems he'd made us memorize. I needed to revise the place— first love, discovery, vocation, eighteen. To do take two. The update. Correct the shape, improve the story I'd made of where I'd been.

I should have tried something out loud. Something from one of those beaten-up anthologies, the crumbling bastions of the spent, pre-posthumanist tradition. Taylor could recite all the way back to the foundations. We would not be civilized until we could remember. He died knowing stuff he had committed to permanence at an age when the rest of us were learning *Engine, engine, Number 9*. Whole cantos, half-chapters from books even the titles of which I had forgotten.

A bell rang, one of those forlorn indicators of ten to the hour and class change. I left on command. The scrimshawed wood corridor complained at my weight, for some reason still insistent after all these dry-aired winters.

I hit the head of the stairwell, *Middlemarch* under my breath. I rounded the landing, unlooking. Maybe I never looked. Maybe I always navigated by toe-tap and hope. Halfway into the second flight, I heard a creak that wasn't me. I sighted down, along my path. It was A., the page-boy mirage I'd seen late at night, while proofing copy.

This time I knew her name. I'd tracked her down to an official departmental photograph, which led in turn to her CV. I'd learned that she was a second-year master's candidate. She had graduated from college the year my third book came out. The fact appalled me.

Seeing her again, I realized how often I had seen her since, from the end of endless halls. Only now A. was real, bounding upstairs, a meter in front of my descent. She exuded blue, robin's egg, adventure, the cerulean tidal pool. She breathed like a sleeping child, like the held breath of friends gathered in a too-small house on the eve of holidays.

I snagged on her face as she glanced up, scanning mine. Instant, reflex presumption; it made me ill. Yet I knew her.

I had to keep from greeting her. My pulse doubled, cutting my intelligence in half. My skin went conductive. In the time it took me to drop another step, a bouillabaisse of chemical semaphores seeped up through my pores and spilled out to wet the air.

She must have known. She looked away, giving no indication. Her face stayed in absolute neutral, a gear beyond adopting. Two quick strides and she skipped past a near brush with literature.

I bottomed out at the base of the stairwell. I stood, winded, like a hawk-reprieved mouse. Like an agoraphobe giving a plenary speech. I would have laughed at myself, had I been able to catch my breath.

Not only could I no longer write fiction. I could no longer live fact. I'd lost fundamental real-word skills while away. The same skills I was trying to instill in Helen.

I had learned too much cognitive neuroscience. The more I read about how the mind worked, the flakier mine became. The symptoms had been coming on for a few weeks. Faces touched off self-fulfilling panic: how will you remember this person's name? Some days before, I'd crossed a street to get to the five side when looking for an address ending in zero. Monitoring my own processes, I felt myself pitching into the ditch alongside the famous test-case centipede after the reductionists asked him how he kept track of which leg moved next.

For months, my bedtime stories had spun a decameron of long-term potentiation, recategorizing, neuronal group selection, transmitter and junctional molecules. Now, for some reason, my low-level structures, blinded by the harsh light that life's interrogation used to extract its confessions, decided to pull an Aschenbach. A Humbert Humbert. One of those old fools in Chaucer, Shakespeare, Restoration comedy, nineteenth-century epistolary vicarage farces. I meant to make an idiot of myself.

By the time I got back to the office, my replay of the woman ascending a staircase had become one of those late-show reruns you wish they'd get a new print of. A.: the face, the name, the stranger I'd been writing to, all my writing life. All those friends whom I, confused, thought dead. The grave where buried love lived.

I disappeared from English. Went back and set up shop at the Center. Paralysis I had already. I didn't need to compound it with obsession. Three weeks without seeing A. and she'd go ephemeron, would damp down from active memory trace. She'd stop making unsponsored appearances, and I'd stop wanting her to.

Work helped. I sublimated all unquenchable hormonal flare-up desires to read that infinitely suffering creature my favorite stanzas from *Piers Plowman* by candlelight. Instead I read to the spreading neural net. Several times a week I invented painful contrivances by which I might introduce myself to A. Each time I did nothing but go and talk to Helen.

Speech baffled my machine. Helen made all well-formed sentences. But they were hollow and stuffed—linguistic training bras. She sorted nouns from verbs, but, disembodied, she did not know the difference between thing and process, except as they functioned in clauses. Her predications were all shotgun weddings. Her ideas were as decorative as half-timber beams that bore no building load.

She balked at metaphor. I felt the annoyance of her weight vectors as they readjusted themselves, trying to accommodate my latest caprice. You're so hungry you could eat a horse. A word from a friend ties your stomach in knots. Embarrassment shrinks you, amazement strikes you dead. Wasn't the miracle enough? Why do humans need to say everything in speech's stockhouse except what they mean?

A certain kind of simile fell naturally into her trained neurode clusters. Helen's own existence hinged on metaphor-making. In fact, associative memory itself was like a kind of simile. Three-quarters of the group of neurodes that fired when faced with, say, a whale might remain intact when depicting a thing that seemed, whatever the phrase meant, very like one. Such a constellation of common firings became, in a way, shadowpaint shorthand for some shared quality.

After all, the world's items had no real names. All labels were figures of speech. One recognized a novel item as a box by comparing it to a handful of examples so small it fit into a single dimple of an egg carton. In time, one learned without being taught. Rode without the training wheels. Somehow, the brain learned to recognize whole categories, to place even those things seen for the first time.

This much simile Helen could live with. But the higher-order stuff drove her around the simulated bend. Love is like ghosts. Love is like linen. Love is like a red, red rose. The silence of her output layers at such triggers sounded like exasperation. A network should not seem but be.

Yes, yes: we know what the thing is like. But what *is* it? And then I, too, would be overwhelmed. Any task in the garden seemed easier than pruning her responses, for her responses, however grammatical, were bewilderment incarnate. Her ideas were well shaped, her syntax sound. But her *sense*: her sense hailed from the far side of the painted veil. I can no more remember its otherness than I can recall the curve of a dream before its red-penciling by the Self.

I revived a little by reminding us both that I didn't have to tell Helen what things meant. Context spun out its own filament. The study questions themselves laddered the world's labelless data into a recognizable index. The accumulated weight of sorted sentences had to self-gloss, or Helen would die before she could come to life.

Helen's nets struggled to assert the metaphors I read her. She ratified them through backtracking, looking for a corner where they might fit into the accreting structure. She gamed the *ur*-game, puzzling out evolution's old brainteaser, find the similarity. A is like B. Mind in its purest play is like some bat. Speech is like embroidered tapestries. God's light is like a lamp in a niche. Greek is like lace. A pretty girl is like a melody. A people without history is like the wind on the buffalo grass. How?

"My heart is like a singing bird," I told Helen. There didn't seem to be any harm in it. She still had several months to learn about irony and lies.

"What is singing?" she asked. That capacity still floored me. When her associative matrix dead-ended now, she asked for openings. Something inside her web told her her web needed supplementing.

"The bird is singing," I assured her. "But my heart feels the way a singing bird must feel."

I failed the test of interpretation I was training her to pass. I missed Helen's question altogether.

I tried her out on a longer Rossetti exercise. At that point, I didn't hope for comprehension. Rather, I read to her as one might recite genealogies to a child. No meaning; just a tune she might one day set words to:

> When I am dead, my dearest,
> Sing no sad songs for me;
> Plant thou no roses at my head,
> Nor shady cypress tree.
> Be the green grass above me
> With showers and dewdrops wet;
> And if thou wilt, remember
> And if thou wilt, forget.

I thought she'd stumble over the "thou" or the "wilt," the "plant no X nor Y." My fears showed how little I knew what went on in Helen's hidden layers. Her neurodes connected far more to themselves than to the outside interface.

"What does it mean," she asked me, "Sing no sad songs?" She

could treat clauses as objects. Her speech turned the recursive crank of endlessness.

The question surprised me. Not what I'd expected. "It means, 'Don't be sorry.' People sing songs at funerals. Singing can be a way of missing or memorializing someone. Of saying goodbye. The person saying these words doesn't want to be remembered that way."

Helen had to spell things out for me. People were idiots. No, no, no. From the top. "How do you sing?"

I had gone on one of those glorious demented sidetracks, the hallmark of intelligence. The ability to use everything in the lexicon to answer except the answer.

I'd given her "The bird is singing," "The poet's heart is singing," even "Grief is singing," when all the poor girl needed was "Uttering pure-toned pitches in time sequence is singing." Writing struck me as so impossible, my years as a novelist so arrogant, that I could have lived that life only through blatant fabrication.

How do you sing? All I could think to do was demonstrate. Assume a virtue, if you have it not. Failing to say what a thing was, I could at least put an instance in her ears.

When I returned to the lab two days later, I thought I'd dialed a wrong number. Even before I reached the door, it hit me. Sound rolled out into the hall, shock waves in bonsai packages. I'd heard music emanate from Lentz's suite once before. But this was the air of a new planet. I rounded the corner, ready already to be dead.

Inside, Helen was singing. Through her terminal mouthpiece, she sang the song she'd heard me sing. What else could she? She sang *Bounce me high, bounce me low, bounce me up to Jericho.* A song I'd sung once as a child, when hired by an opera company to portray a small boy. My sung, staged simulation of childhood. Helen sang in an extraterrestrial warble, the way deaf people sing. But I recognized that tune in one note.

Lentz sat behind his desk, hands pressed to his neck. He had not moved since arriving, however long ago that had been. Even through the bank glass of his specs, I saw vinegary damp.

"You did this to her, Powers!" I knew where I'd heard that mock indignation before. I recognized it, after one training. My father, the summer before his death, laughing as he scolded my older sister: *How can you do this to me? How can you make me a grandfather?*

I'd done nothing. A kludge of morphologies—implementations within implementations, maps that had learned to map each other—passed a milestone we hadn't even hoped to set her. Lentz and I stood by, winded, pulses racing. All we could do was listen.

She auditioned the tune. Bounce me high. Bounce me low. Only by hearing it out loud, in her own voice, could Helen probe the thing, test it against itself.

She was stuck on the first phrase, that unfinished half-stich, because that's all I'd sung her. Because that's where I had stuck. After twenty-five years, I could not remember how the rest of the tune went. Over and back Helen hummed, not knowing she possessed but half the melodic story. Bounce me up to Jericho. Lack of tonal resolution did not faze her. No one told her that tunes were supposed to come home to tonic. This was the only one anybody had ever sung her.

And in that moment, I understood that I, too, would never have a handle on metaphor. For here was the universe in a grain of literal sand. Singing—enabled, simulated on a silicon substrate. I felt how a father must feel, seeing his unconscious gestures—pushing back a forelock or nudging the sink cabinet shut with a toe—picked up and mimicked by a tiny son.

"Lentz," I whispered, so as not to distract the miracle, "is this what it's like to be a parent?"

Very like, his eyes leaked back. And I saw what it meant to want that awful next step, tasting oneself from the outside, in a flash of constructed recognition. To say the thing I made I did not make and is not mine. To know in Polaroid advance that hour when all life's careful associations will come undone.

Less than a year after we moved to E., we got a letter from the Taylors. I wrote them often, for after we bolted, I needed word from U. more than I ever did while living there. They wrote back jocular stuff: "Don't you two realize the age of Europe is over and that of North America is following in its wake? Get back over here before it's too late."

Taylor had so little time to reply that any word was an event. I kept the envelope sealed, thinking it would be fun to read to C. when she got home from her latest temp job. We'd marvel at Tayloresque sentences together, over the dinner I prepared for her.

I watched C. step off the bus, waving from the balcony as I did each evening. She shot me back one of those terrified, fatigued, smiling, full-body waves that never failed to cut right through me. The letter is dated September 17, but it must have been a cold fall. C. was already swallowed by that giant navy coat that ran all the way down to her ankles.

In the kitchen, she danced a little jig at the sight of the letter. Anything that made me happy might increase the chances for our transplantation. "Come on, Beauie. Read it, you loony-tick. What in the world are you waiting for?"

I slit the packet open and read:

"Dear Rick and C.,

"Belatedly, I take up pen, first to thank you for your welcome tape of good music and loved voices. Similarly welcome have been the letters, which I have meant to answer every day. Recent weeks have both dragged and hurried, creeping by the minute but vanishing into an unreal limbo so that even less than usual am I able to believe that months have passed since we have seen you . . .

"For nearly a full month I have had a succession of terrible waits after tests, each of which finished a three- or four-day vigil with more bad news. CAT scan, bronchoscopy, bone scan, and finally a week in the hospital for removal of a piece of rib for bone biopsy determined that in addition to a main tumor in the right lung I have cancerous bone in the left rib cage, ruling out an operation and leaving radiation and chemotherapy as treatment. The only test with encouraging results showed no evidence of metastasis to brain . . .

"Since then, my silence has been caused by effects of treatment. The dreaded nausea did not last long, but loss of appetite and weight did, and a fatigue so profound that I can't adequately describe it. My muscles have atrophied and I spend most of my time lying down. I am good for little more than harvesting the odd tomato, gathering windfall apples, picking some late-planted lettuce . . .

"Our long silence is terribly misleading. Your departure left a large emptiness that has been italicized by this illness and our being more solitary than usual. If we possessed ESP, you would have been deluged by messages from here. Still, it is a pleasure to imagine the two of you together in the wide variety of settings you manage to inhabit. My life would seem pretty bounded-in-a-nutshell by any measure, but your joint enthusiasm in getting out and seeing the world is overwhelming.

"I've exhausted my pitiable energy, though not my love. The best way you can please me is to promise that my illness will not lead you to even the slightest tendency to avoid pleasure out of affectionate empathy. Try to adopt the opposite attitude; let me hope that thoughts of me will enhance pleasures I'd enjoy, too, if we were together."

After the first paragraph, I looked up at C. But we'd read too far to pretend the message away. I got through the whole history. Finishing, I looked up across the widening kitchen table at the college girl who had sat with me on the Quad, when still young enough to believe in consolation. This was the same woman, the same panicked doe, in the same glare that life keeps training on us until we can no longer even dread it.

An awful half-second stutter step, and C. said, "You'll have to go back to the States."

"Just to see him, at least," I pleaded, the exact reaction her reflex generosity meant to stave off. But I was not pleading with C.

I flew back to U., numb to the new feel of the place. Taylor could still get out. We went to a nearby woods. We talked. He knew he was done. The only thing for it was presence of mind. Taylor brought along his camera, took a snap of me. I wanted to take one of him, fix him forever. But Taylor had already begun to waste away and refused to be captured like that.

I showed him the excerpt from my new book that had just appeared in a glossy literary weekly. Taylor, for whose approval I'd developed my labyrinthine style, delighted in the piece's uncharacteristic breeziness. He delighted even more when I told him how much I'd been paid. "A dollar a word! That has a solid ring to it."

I had done what everyone in Taylor's line, what he himself had once dreamed of doing. I could wake up every morning and devote myself to making worlds. People read my inventions and wrote about them in turn. My words had grown careers of their own. My overnight success gave Taylor such pleasure that I couldn't bring myself to tell him I meant to quit fiction.

"I didn't want to burden you with such a prediction when you were an eighteen-year-old kid memorizing 'The Windhover.' " He beamed. "But however much luck always plays into such things, it was possible, even then, to imagine your getting away with something like this."

We turned to the real issue. He protected me from what his disease was doing to him. He seemed, for half an hour, the equal of any formulation he had made before the tumor came alive inside him. I asked him whether, at that stage of the illness, literature helped much. Did it make things any clearer, any easier?

Taylor stayed as brutally forthright with me as ever. He thought for a moment, to get the prosody right. "I would say that literature is not entirely irrelevant, in this circumstance. But it's not quite central, either."

Before we headed home, I asked if he had any regrets. Anything he still needed to do. Taylor told me then that, to his mind, the only two careers worth striving for were doctor and musician. I could not tell how figurative he was being.

Taylor sickened. I found a house-sit in the neighborhood, and came by every day. I sat with him as he napped, or I read to him, or we watched sports on television. Sometimes we talked, but never again like that day in the woods.

He lost his appetite, shrank to insubstantial nothing. His gut stopped working. His skin gained purple-green highlights and his joints grew smooth as polished metal. When muscles gave out, he cupped his question-mark head in both hands. He sat in the sunroom until he could no longer sit up. Then we moved him upstairs, into his long bed.

He asked me to check out some books from the library, so he could prepare to teach his class in January.

M., his wife, remained rocklike. She exuded competence beyond belief. She lifted the skeletal Taylor out of bed and carried him— Mary holding a puppet Christ—deflated and naked, to the toilet, in her arms.

Only his mind remained luminous. Near the end, the medications did change him. But even then, his topographies fought to keep themselves intact. One afternoon before Christmas, I found Taylor in a state that was not quite sleep, but could pass for sleep in low light.

"Oh, it's you!" he greeted me. "All day long, the sounds outside this window have been turning into events from my past."

He went on to tell me, in devastating detail, about the valley of his childhood, out West. The names of all his classmates and the ways each had distinguished or humiliated himself in coming of age. The frozen rabbits hanging on the barn wall that kept the family alive all winter. Every single title in the valley library, outread and exhausted by fourteen.

Before I left town, I put another book in Taylor's hands. One for the permanent record. One he would never read. I gave him the first bound galley of my second book, *Prisoner's Dilemma.*

Number two was my memorial to a sick father. In it, I described every impasse of history but his. Only the passage of years, only knowing I'd never show Richard Powers, Sr., what fiction had done to him, made that fiction possible.

I told Taylor about my father. How I'd broken his heart. His lover's quarrel with the world. His disappearance at the end, his one last frontier adventure. I told Taylor about the cryptic absolution Dad sent me from the Yukon. The cremation of Sam McGee.

At my mention of the name, Taylor's lips crooked. Astonishingly, the man to whom I owed my Shakespeare and Yeats, my Marx and Freud, launched into a full rendition of the hack ballad. He did not miss a stanza. Death had no more dominion over him.

"I don't know how to say goodbye," I told Taylor. The book was my goodbye, because symbols are all that become of the real. They change us. They make us over, alter our bodies as we receive and remake them. The symbols a life forms along its way work back out of the recorder's office where they wait, and, in time, they themselves go palpable. Lived.

I left, knowing he had at best days, and at worst a month. Nothing left to do. The old friends were everywhere in attendance. Maybe I should have stayed. Stood and waited. Maybe he could have used having me around.

"Make a noise," he ordered as I took off. "See the world."

"I will," I promised. "And I'll keep you posted."

In the short night, eastward above the Atlantic, I thought of the last time I'd made the crossing. My life in U. was dead. I'd gone back to that cow town once too often. I told myself I would never get near it again.

But U. caught up with me, even in my foreign country. And that death was far worse, faced alone in E. C. and I lay on the floor of our apartment, in hypothermia, and listened to the tape of the memorial service, the fiddle tunes, that whole unbroken circle of friends telling Taylor stories, recounting their local eulogies for the man who thought only memory stood between us and randomness.

Each person who knew him surrendered some private lode of remembered event. Or they read from the page one of the poems Taylor himself did from effortless memory. They read Blake and Rossetti and Stevens. No one read "Sam McGee," because the one who was supposed to read it was lying on the floor in a little ex-coal-mining town on the other side of the world, listening to the belated tape, shivering, wrecked forever by memory.

I could give back nothing to Taylor, I, who couldn't even find a way to tell him what he had given me. All I could do for Taylor now was to turn him into character.

I held on to C., giving in to my only available response. She probably knew I would backslide long before the idea hit me. *One more book*, I pleaded with her, wordlessly. I needed to postpone my graduation from lying long enough to tell a double love story. To turn a helical twist that might both eulogize the man and let me live, before it was too late, the life in science from which he'd long ago deflected me.

Helen did not sing the way real little girls sang. Technically, she almost passed. Her synthesized voice skittered off speech's earth into tentative, tonal Kitty Hawk. Her tune sounded remarkably limber, given the scope of that mechanical tour de force.

But she did not sing for the right reasons. Little girls sang to keep time for kickball or jump ropes. The little boy soprano I had played onstage at twelve had been doing that. Singing the tune I'd taught Helen, keeping imitative time by bouncing a ball against a pasteup shop door.

Helen didn't have a clue what keeping time meant, never having twirled a jump rope, let alone seen one. We'd strengthened her visual mapping, but true, real-time image recognition would have required vastly more computer power than the entire Center drew. And we were already living beyond our quota.

If Helen had a temporal sense now, it came from a memory strong enough to remember configurations it was no longer in. And mark the passing of her changing, internal states. God only knows the look and feel of a sense of time without a sense of space. But that was Helen.

"You were not, yesterday," she would say to me, whether I'd been gone three hours or three days. "Yesterday" stood for any state that Helen had watched get swallowed up by its successor. "You" presumably meant that generic, external irritant that laid data on her input layers. "Were not" was her simplistic idea of negation. Although she had still to learn that absence and presence were not opposites, she was well on her way to a functional understanding of loneliness, that font of all knowledge.

One day she added, "I miss you."

The thing canonical writers always said in print. I wanted to tell her that she ought not to put the formulation in the present tense while I sat right there at the mike and keyboard. I said nothing, not wanting to undo the example of the rhymers she imitated with anything so trivial as convention.

"I miss Muffet," she went on. In growing savvy enough for figurative speech, she'd become too softheaded for the literal. Either that, or she was engaging in the neural network equivalent of silliness. If she could sing, I reasoned, I could certainly train her to giggle.

I mailed the finished copy of my fourth book to New York on the day Los Angeles set itself on fire. My story predicted that explosion, although such a prediction took no special gift. Mine was less prophecy, anyway, than memory. A child's recollected nightmare.

The prepublication notices of the book appeared not long after. Soon enough for human recollection, in any event. The most visible of the trade-press reviews dubbed the book "a bedtime tale set in a future apocalypse." This denial stuck. Everything I'd written about Angel City and its war on childhood had already played out. But so many of the subsequent reviews pushed memory into the not-yet that I began to think I had, in fact, written my first attempt at speculative fiction.

The reviews were not all bad. Chicago glowed, saving my appointment at the Center and preserving face with the home crowd. The best notice, remarkably, came from that national paper sold in street boxes designed to resemble TVs. It spoke of homeopathy, of narrating the worst so the worst did not have to happen.

Most critics, though, felt the reader had to work too hard for too bleak a payoff.

Lentz delighted in the harshest press judgments. It became almost impossible to train Helen while he was around.

He entered the office crowing, "Look who's here! If it isn't my favorite manufacturer of literary astonishments. Which is not to say

206

a good novelist," he added, graciously patronizing, "although you are that, too."

This was the lead from that same glossy with the twenty-million worldwide circulation that yesterday had predicted such a full future for me.

"Did you memorize the entire piece, Philip?"

"Just the good parts."

"You haven't wasted your weekend, have you?"

"I notice you recognized the allusion. I bet you could do the closing bit as well. You know: 'Little brother has failed to invent a story'?"

But my career had not yet been decided. All juries hung on word from the sole review anyone ever seemed to pay attention to. The institution had gone monolithic, as if the pieces appearing there no longer derived from individuals, each locked inside their sensibilities and foibles, but formed the consulates of a single, unified State Department of literary taste. An algorithm of aesthetic appropriateness.

A mixed decision in that paper of record, even a late one, could pretty much close the cover on you before anyone had a chance to open it. I avoided looking. I'd never done especially well there, and this time I was so far out on a narrative limb that I knew I was ripe for amputation. Besides, I didn't have to seek out judgment. Judgment would come looking for me.

It did, one Monday morning. I was at the console in Lentz's office, talking to Helen about ignorant armies clashing by night. The infinite repetition of supervised training had given way to a more unstructured give-and-take, where I might read a given set of lines to her a few times, if that, and carry on, letting her do the evaluating internally.

Out of the corner of my eye—how to explain to her that spheres might have corners?—I watched Lentz bound in. He carried all twenty-five pounds of the Sunday edition, nonchalantly, just taking all the world news that fit out for a spin. He dropped the pile on his already cluttered desk with a resounding thud.

I saw him, through the back of my head, without turning. He picked up the top section of the mass. "What's this? The *Book Review*?

What's this? New fiction by Richard Powers?" A parody of Wemmick, in my favorite Dickens passage. And so, twice the pain per word.

"Listen to this, Marcel. This will interest you:

"In every reader's mental library, there are books that are remembered with admiration and books that are remembered with love.

"It goes on—"

"That's all right, Philip. I get the picture."

"No, really. It says you are all right, in your own peculiar way. Just a little flawed. It says you could be good if you just kept your story simple, with lovable characters. Like *The Diary of Anne Frank*."

We had sat in front of that girl's house, C. and I, at dusk two years before. Up in the city for a day's sightseeing, too broken by that After-house of time to want, anymore, to move. We could not even bring ourselves to put our arms around each other.

"Hey! You could read that story to our little apparatus, couldn't you? In the original, I mean. Now, that would throw the poor girl for a loss. She wouldn't even know what hit her."

I could not look at Helen, because Helen was nowhere. I looked at the open anthology next to the microphone. "Dover Beach" seemed a sad irrelevance.

"Should we read her the review?" Lentz cackled. He scanned the page, smirking and shaking his head. "You'll forgive me if I take this like a bad winner? I'd like to think that I'm not losing a novelist friend. I'm gaining a long-term unpaid lab assistant."

I walked out, leaving Lentz chiding me with apologies and Helen wondering what had become of Matthew Arnold.

Drama got me as far as the atrium. One of those drizzly midwinter days that U. excelled in. I wasn't about to bike home. I made my way to the cafeteria where, too early, I bought lunch. Plover and Hartrick sat at a table, nursing juices. I steered myself toward them. Their conversation, rapid and personal, broke off as I pulled up.

"Keep talking," I said, nodding at their notebooks, closed on the table in front of them. "I'm just the humanist fly on the wall."

Plover examined my tray of onion rings and Italian beef. "Don't eat grease, Rick. Grease will kill you."

"Leave him be," Diana scolded. "He's too young to start being healthy."

"I know half a dozen people who have had heart attacks in their early thirties."

"Harold. Quit with the Jeremiah thing already." Diana turned to me. "We were just talking about yesterday's piece in the *Times*." She smiled. "Sorry!" Friendly, singsong, not heavily invested. The empirical bias. As if peer review weren't that consequential. As if a person's work was what it was, unchanged by decree.

Harold looked in my face. "I haven't read the book. But I know from my clinical days that people who have just undergone breakups of long relationships tend to see the world in apocalyptic terms."

Taken aback, all over the map. "Your clinical days?"

"Oh yeah. I used to think we knew enough about the way the mind works to put that knowledge to good use in the field. But I was much older then."

Diana snorted. "Harold likes to blame things on his inner child."

"Uh, if I've walked into the middle of something here, I can—"

A voice behind me declared, "Powers's inner child is about eighty and hobbles around on a crutch."

Lentz, breathing heavily, fresh coffee cup in tow, joined us. I made my face a blank.

"Coffee will kill you, Philip," Plover intoned. "Ach, God! Not cream, too. And sugar!" Harold clutched his cheeks in two Munch-like hands.

Diana spoke askance, as if to colleagues who had not yet joined us. "Rick's inner child may have progeria. But his outer child died at—what would you say, Rick? Eleven? Twelve?"

I started to grin, relieved. "You've read the book? Already?"

She said nothing. My muscles fell. I looked like someone who had goosed a friend's bottom at a crowded party, only to have the surprised person turn around and reveal themselves a perfect stranger.

"You hated it?" Dead silence. "You hated it."

"You sound surprised," Diana said.

My turn to say nothing.

"Oh, Ricky. You know it's brilliant, and all that. But it's so horrid. Misanthropic. Couldn't you have thrown us at least one little sop of hope?"

"I thought I had."

"Not enough."

"Would you buy it as homeopathy?"

"Homeopaths use very small doses. Look. We're all overwhelmed. We're all bewildered. Why read in the first place, if the people who are supposed to give us the aerial view can't tell us anything except what an inescapable mess we're in?"

The four of us sat looking everywhere but at one another. Her words rocked back and forth in me, like the last wake of a small craft.

"You're teaching the next book club section," Harold told her.

Lentz shook his head and pursed his lips. "There are books you love. And then there are books . . ."

But I had never once put fingers to keys for anything but love. I had written a book about lost children because I had lost my own child and wanted it back. More than I wanted anything in life, except to write.

Any hope that I might somehow be able to return to making fiction died at Diana's words. My work in progress was a sham, no more than a sentence climbing snowy mountain tracks in a cartoon of war-time. I was working from nothing but the desire to fulfill a contract. I would return the advance for the unwritten book to New York and call it a day.

Picture a train heading south. It works its wounded veterans over the mountain passes to a sweet, imaginary country called—by coincidence, just like the real one—Italy. Not Italy in the original edition, but taking that place's name now and in all subsequent printings.

Imagine yourself traveling to a country where you won't be sick anymore. This country is full of the thing you want most. As much of it as you ever dared ask for. Whatever that thing is. The one thing that means more to you than anything.

This country is a continuous outdoor café. When all else about the account fades like a moldy fresco, this image lives on in your inner travelogue. In this country, at this café, you can sit in the sun from dawn till dusk. On the piazza. The piazza d'. Your private pool of shade remains bathed in unimaginable azure. And iced drinks on endless tab.

You can sit on this terrace for as long as you ever wanted. The terrace is life's arrival. All you need do is picture it.

No one can chase you away, and you can do whatever you like, until closing. Until the next chapter. Watch women walking across the public square. Read. Read this story, if you like. Or talk. Toast the waiter. Sing. Listen to the next table sing. Anything.

You have never thought twice about cafés, but you might like to sit in one now. You would like to order, then spread out a book in front of you. Sit and watch people walking, from a distance. A pleasure, just to picture this pleasure. This description, the sun, the one desirable thing, yours for the asking.

Reading: yes. Of course. To spend all day—that nom de plume for "forever"—doing nothing but reading! Just entertaining the thought, just following the idea fleshes out a scenario of composite delight. Your one surreptitious afternoon in the sunny countryside, exiled, at the last minute, from wartime, from inescapable disaster.

When I came home to E., things were different. Different again. Still different.

To my astonishment, I now passed for fluent. A demotic, misleading fluency, in fact, became my undoing. A week after losing it, lying on the floor of the apartment listening to the cassette of Taylor's funeral, I found myself walking past E.'s modest hardware store. I turned in, deciding on a whim to buy an item we had needed for as long as I'd lived in Limburg.

As they always did in E.'s archaic shops, the salesperson greeted me on entry and asked to be of help.

"Good afternoon. I'm looking for this mechanical device, about yay big. It's a gizmo with an adjustable center pivot that allows you to apply increased torque . . ."

"Hmm. N-no, I don't think we have anything like that here, sir." She gestured with her palms outward. You see where you are: a pocket, one-church town. Little call for the esoteric. "You might try Maastricht."

"No, no. It's a common little commodity. Every home has one. You might use it to fix your plumbing, or tighten a loose dowel rod . . ."

Her face stayed blank, helpful but passive. Finally, something I said broke through. Her expression fled from confusion to anger in the space of one thought.

"Do you mean a wrench?"

"That's it!" I shouted.

"Then why the hell didn't you say you wanted a wrench?"

I had been better off with the impenetrable accent and the babble grammar. I'd communicated more when the only words I had were "I don't have the words."

I went about in a daily grief that, like Taylor on the effects of his chemo, I could not describe adequately in the most native of languages. C. mistook that sadness. She felt it directed at her, at her idea to move us to this invented place.

She grew defensive, self-accusing. "I know you love me, Beau. But you don't need any of this."

"Any of what?"

"I'm not sure I need any of it either. What are we doing here? My parents don't need me to take care of them, do they? They chose to come back here all by themselves."

"A good choice, no?"

"Oh yes. They're happier here than they ever were in Chicago. They haven't a minute to themselves."

"What's the problem? I thought the point was to discover what nationality you were."

"I'm further from that than I was in the States. I look at myself, and I can't even recognize what I've become."

"Gone native?"

C. laughed, protecting me. "Sometimes this country drives me up the bloody wall. The village patrol, eyeing every irregular behavior. The social agenda, all worked out for you in advance. The *gezellig-heid*. The close little shops. The lines for everything. The little old ladies shoving you out of the way, or choosing the narrowest possible aisle in the densest country on earth to stop and gossip. Nothing's ever open. Half the country's on the dole."

"You sound like the American ambassador."

"And I've dragged you into the middle of all this!"

"I'm fine. I'm having a great time." A lie on the surface. But not, if this meant anything, deep down. "We can walk to four major language regions from our front stoop. Two hours away from three of the world's greatest museums. And green herring by the bucket. I'd never have had this chance. Except for you, C."

That much was true, even on the surface. Her gamble had thrown open all possibility, however much possibility now upended us.

When my second book came out, C.'s restlessness pitched into the distress bands. Publication of a novel is a nonevent arranged to look like news. *Prisoner* produced a spate of statements, positioning my career on the turnpike of contemporary letters like a dot on the AAA Triptiks. The point often seemed to be to spare people the inconvenience of reading.

It killed C. to read that I was a fresh commodity to keep an eye on. That I was intensely private. That I lived in U., when in fact I lived in E., where the shopkeepers scolded me for linguistic perversity. That I was a fast-rising star in the literary firmament who had X's brains and Y's punch lines. That the eighties had been waiting for me.

I tried to tell her. "It's all nonsense. Market-making, for an increasingly smaller market. They do it, we ignore it, and keep working. It's part of the business."

"So we're in business now?"

"No. Okay. Not business. Part of the . . . C. Sweet. Let's not make ourselves nuts."

"*We* don't need to make ourselves anything." She smacked the pile of newsprint that New York's clipping service kept sending us. "The pros will make us into anything they want."

"C. You know who we are. The pair bond. All the rest of this is somebody else's construction. Nothing's changed."

"Of course it's changed. It's not just you and me anymore. You're obligated. You have to make good on *opportunity*. Everyone and his typewriting monkey would kill for a shot at what's fallen in your lap."

I tried to tell her that there was no obligation, no opportunity that we didn't already have. I tried to comb out the snarls left by public evaluation. That was my job: to keep things unchanged and make them right. But the better I did my job, the more I condemned C. to the opposite employment.

Nor did it help when mourning for Taylor led me into a period of work more intense than I will ever know again. The simplest possible tune had come to me—four notes, then four more, four times over. Selection had whittled at that tune until it grew as long and polyphonic as the planetary concert hall.

The book I needed to write sat on the simplest of bases. Life remembered. Life described. It wrote down and repeated what worked. The small copying errors the text made in running off examples of itself, edited by the world's differential rejection and forgiveness, produced the entire collaborative canon.

For what turned out to be years, this seemed to me a book's only conceivable theme. And thirty, the only age that would take such a theme on—old enough for a glimpse at meaning, immature enough to still think meaning pursuable.

I would fail, of course, in my aerial survey. To make a map on the scale of one to one, to bring the people, the genomes I loved back to life would have required contrapuntal skill on an evolutionary scale. But while I worked on my variations, work itself seemed to be the grave where buried love did its living.

So I spent myself on work, writing a story about a reference librarian, a failed academic, and a life scientist who, diverted, becomes the subject of the experiment he runs. I split the story among the venues of my life. I tried to pack it with anagrams and acrostics, replies to every word anyone had ever sent me, for this would be my one long letter back.

I wanted to write an encyclopedia of the Information Age. The nearest reference library was kilometers away, tiny, and in a foreign tongue. I wrote about music, with only a cheap, portable cassette player to check my descriptions. I typed my computer saga on an obsolete 512K, low-density floppy-based machine that will forever ruin me to imagine, because C., in her technophobia, had picked it out and purchased it for me to sweeten my return to that country.

I lost myself in data and the heart's decoding urge. Nothing else had any interest. Life became an interruption of my description of it. I wanted nothing else but to read, work, travel now and again, take care of my C. And for a long time, I did just that.

The book grew beyond my ability to say how it should go. The story itself turned into an opportunity, an obligation that scared the hell out of us both. Some reentrant map inside me ran away with itself, insisting it was real. No amount of public judgment matched private possibility for sheer terror.

C. read my *Gold Bug* code as it took shape, variation by variation. She came home exhausted, eager for alternate life. She nagged me for new chapters. "I want my friends!"

She knew what I needed to hear, and said as much. But I think she did love that world for her own reasons. "So this is what you do all day while I'm out slaving over a hot word processor. I can hardly believe that the goof who cooks for me produced this."

I'd load up a chunk of text and seat her at the keys. Then she would scroll through my story on-screen while I lay on the couch holding my breath, pretending to occupy myself with a magazine. Every so often she laughed at some invented inanity. I still had the courage for silliness back then.

Hearing her, I looked up, relieved. Redeemed. "Tell me!" I begged, pushing my luck. She would read out loud the line that had made her cackle. And I'd giggle along then, as if she had written the gag.

She gave more generously than the first of audiences. But C. needed some story for herself, as endless and private a thing as I now had. Her devotion to my project, fierce and unquestioning, was bitterness by another name. She met my constant infidelity with encouraging smiles, and braced for the day when strangers would declare their love for a story that should never have been more than hers.

"Beauie, I'm going nuts. I'm wasting my life." The refrain of a poem I'm sure had been on my Master's Comps but which I could not place.

"What are you talking about? Think of everything you've managed since coming here."

"Hah. *The DP's Progress.* Maybe it's time to quit fooling ourselves. Pack up and go back."

I did not say what occurred to me: Back *where?*

"C. Be fair to yourself."

"That's what I'm trying to do."

"What do you want? What do you need? Just say the word."

"I don't know. Beau. I'm sorry. I'm a total mess."

I told her she was the very opposite, in as many ways as I could. We talked long and often, coming back always to the same thing. Her life split over different orders of place. Of homes, she no longer knew which was fact and which the sustaining imitation. Two native tongues were as good as none.

Source and target languages tore her down the middle. But it struck me that she might still make from that split a suture.

"Look, C. How many people can do what you do? You know two distinct names for everything. You know what they call it here *and* there. Seems to me, that when you can shake with both hands, you're almost obligated to be an arbiter."

She looked frightened, drawn. "Translation, you mean? They'll never let me."

"Who's to let or not let?"

"Oh, Ricky. You know how things work around here. It's such a goddamned bureaucratic society. I could be the greatest translator going and I wouldn't be able to get work without certification. You can't wipe your bleeding ass in this country without a certificate."

She had begun talking like someone else. Like her dialect self, translated into English.

"Well, if you need a certificate, then we get the certificate."

"By 'we' I take it you mean me. And how do you suggest I do that? You want me to go back to school? Be a child, all over again? I don't have the energy for all that, Beau. Nor the stomach."

"Don't have the nerve, is more like it."

"Call it what you want."

I did. The hardest names I could think of, followed by the softest. I promised her it would work out brilliantly in the end. That I would take care of her for the four years school required. That I would be there for everything, until she came out the other side, newly graduated. A translator.

It did not follow, from the questions Helen asked, that she was conscious. An algorithm for turning statements into reasonable questions need know nothing about what those statements said or the sense they manipulated to say it. Rules would still be slavish, deterministic, little more than a fancy Mixmaster.

But Helen had no such algorithm. She learned to question by imitating me. Or rather, training promoted those constellations of neurodes that satisfied and augmented the rich ecosystem of reentrant symbol maps described by *other* constellations of neurodes.

The only syntactic rules she obeyed emerged from the shape of her first reorganizational principle: to accommodate, encapsulate, and survive the barrage of stimulus, both inside and out. To tune its connections in search of that elusive topography that led input, output, and all enveloped layers toward unachievable peace.

Did the geometry of her subsystems give her deep structure? Did she, in some way, know the rules she obeyed? I didn't even understand the question. I could no longer even say what *know* might mean.

It occurred to me: awareness no more permitted its own description than life allowed you a seat at your own funeral. Awareness trapped itself inside itself. The function of consciousness must be in part to dummy up and shape a coherence from all the competing, conflicting subsystems that processed experience. By nature, it lied. Any rendition we might make of consciousness would arise from *it*, and was thus about as reliable as the accused serving as sole witness for the prosecution.

The window in question was so small and fogged that I did not even know why I worried about whether she had one. Mediating the phenomenal world via consciousness was like listening to reports of a hurricane over the radio while hiding in the cellar.

Helen's neurodal groups organized themselves into representational and even, I think, conceptual maps. Relations between these maps grew according to the same selectional feedback that shaped connections between individual neurodes—joined by recognition and severed by confusion. Helen's lone passion was for appropriate behavior. But when she learned to map whole types of maps onto each other, something undeniable, if not consciousness, arose in her.

She'd cribbed the first-person pronoun as a hollow placeholder sometime earlier. "I don't understand." "I want some more." This last one she pronounced long before I'd read her any Dickens whatsoever. In saying as much, she might have been going about her usual business of making classification couples, pairing signals from outside with symbols from in. She might have been in any number of precognitive states, states permitted by sheets of her neurodes learning to do to other sheets of neurodes what these, in turn, did to the shapes I presented to them.

I began to wonder, the day she asked me, "You bounced high to Jericho?" The day, secure in implication and containment, that she explained, "A runcible spoon is what you eat mince and quince with." The moment, overnight, she acquired cause and effect, exclaiming in hurt wonder, "The rose is sick because the worm eated it!"

It seemed enough of an act to call for witnesses. I could hear, in my mind's ear, my parents saying, "Ricky, go get your cello and play for the guests." I swore, at that age, that in the unlikely event I ever did something as mad as having children, I would never subject them to such humiliation. The lightest training in pride revised my resolution.

Lentz was on his afternoon visit to the nursing home. I rustled up Harold to come have a look. He arrived, gawky daughter in tow. With what remained of a memory that had gone senescent in the last year, I greeted her. "Hello, Trish."

She gave an insulted gagging noise. "Render me roguish. Turf me in all quadrants."

"I'm sorry?"

"This is Mina," Harold intervened. "And your name is mud."

"Oh. I'm sorry. I was sure I—"

"You're not the first one to confuse them."

Mina snorted again, a sound replete with connotations. "We're nothing at all alike. Trish is the stuck-up, snobby bitch."

"And Mina is the sweet one, as you see."

We read Helen "The Emperor's New Clothes." Mina was bored by the text, overfamiliar, although she had never heard it except in paraphrase. She prowled around the office until she found a copy of Rumelhart and McClelland to nose around in. Harold shook his head as I read. He didn't believe that the occasional sound and light emitting from Helen had anything to do with the words I read her.

The story ended. Maybe the only universally valid generalization about stories: they end. I felt like a showman. I turned to Harold and Mina, whose interest was again piqued. "So what do you want to know?"

Harold breathed out, hard. "You've got to be kidding." He looked around for the hidden cameras. Then he took his leap of faith. "Who told the emperor he was naked?"

I repeated the question to Helen, verbatim. She turned it over forever. She slowed a little with each new association she fit into the web. One day she would grow so worldly she would come to a full stop. Now, in front of a captive audience, she seemed to ossify before her time.

I slipped deeper into dismay with each agonizing cycle-tick. At long last, she decided. "The little child told the emperor."

Both father and daughter almost exploded. *"Hoo-wee!"* Harold sobered first. He began reasoning out loud. Reason: the *ex post facto* smoother-over of the cacophony exploding across our subsystems.

"Okay. Let's assume you guys are playing fair. That none of this is canned."

"Good assumption," I said, conscious of sounding like a poor parody of Lentz.

"The entire story never uses the word 'naked.' Well, maybe you've built a kind of thesaurus structure . . ."

"She built it herself."

Mina stopped biting her cuticle. "Maybe it has, you know, like a cheat sheet of questions people might ask?"

"Good thinking, kiddo." Harold tried to pat her head, but she pulled away. "Did you choose the story at random?" he grilled me.

"It was next on the list."

"No telegraph?"

"None."

Mina fluttered her hands. "I didn't mean that he fed it specific questions. I just meant, like, it has a list of how to deal with 'Who is' and 'What is,' and all those."

Harold looked at me: You *sure* you haven't been piping info to the physical symbol systems? I knew his suspicion of operationalism. He often accused Lentz of playing fast and loose with the computational model of mind.

"There aren't that many 'whos' in the story," Mina elaborated. "Maybe she got lucky."

I turned to Helen and asked, "What are the new clothes made of?"

After a long time, she answered, "The clothes are made of threads of ideas."

"It's a nice way of putting it," Harold offered. But the error's strangeness relieved him.

I felt myself edging toward humiliation. I needed one good answer to show them what my girl could do. "Why don't the subjects who see the emperor naked tell him that he has nothing on?"

Both syntax and semantic here ran beyond words. If she could swallow the sentence without spitting up, we'd wow the home crowd for good.

This time, Helen answered too quickly to have thought about the sentence at all. "The subjects are snagged in a textile."

I didn't even try to apologize for her. "Do you like the emperor's new clothes?" I wasn't sure what I was after. If she could remain composed, answer *anything* to a sentence with so vague a referent, it might salvage mechanism and save the day for function.

Helen's answer sent Mina into hysterics. "Did you hear that? Did you hear what it said?"

Harold twisted his mouth, amused, despite himself, by the girl's uncontrollable fit. "Yes. She said, 'Very much.' What's so funny about that?"

"She *didn't*! She said, 'Airy much.' Airy. Get it?"

"Oh, for heaven's sake. You're hearing things, kid."

"*Daddy!*"

They both looked at me, the tiebreaker. "To tell you the God's honest truth, I thought she said, 'Fairy Dutch.'"

When she caught her breath again, Mina declared, "That's the smartest parrot I've ever seen."

Harold shook his head in bewilderment. "Mere parroting would have been impressive enough. One already wonders what survival value for a cockatiel the ability to whistle the *Saber Dance* might have. How such a bizarre skill could earn its place in such limited circuitry. Rearranging sentence components while preserving grammar ups the ante an order of magnitude. Creating novel sentences in response to a semantic field—"

"We still have a few kinks to work out."

"Listen." Harold fell into the agitated intensity of a scientist impatient with methodology. "Can we try something here?"

"Of course. Name it."

He looked sidelong at me. Not wanting to overstep. "Kahneman and Tversky?"

I smiled. Funny: Harold would not be impressed with *my* matching the obscure tags, recent additions to my own neural library. He took that much for granted. Just your garden-variety marvel.

I improvised for Helen a personal variation on the now-classic test. "Jan is thirty-two years old. She is well educated and holds two advanced degrees. She is single, is strong-minded, and speaks her piece. In college, she worked actively for civil rights. Which of these two statements is more likely? One: Jan is a librarian. Two: Jan is a librarian and a feminist."

"It knows the word 'feminist'?" Mina lit up, arcing into existence at the idea.

"I think so. She's also very good at extending through context."

Once more, Helen answered with a speed that winded me, given the pattern-sorting she needed to reach home. "One: Jan is a librarian."

Harold and I exchanged looks. Meaning?

"Why is that more likely, Helen?"

"Helen? It has a *name*?"

"That is more likely because one Jan is more likely than two."

Now Harold took a turn laughing like an idiot.

"Wait a minute," Mina said. "I don't get it. What's the right answer?"

"What do you mean, what's the right answer?" Harold, raging affronted fatherdom. "Think about it for ten seconds."

"Well, she has all these feminist things about her. So isn't it more likely that she would be a feminist librarian than just a . . . ?"

Mina, seeing herself about to label the part more likely than its whole, threw her hand over her mouth and reddened.

"I can't believe it. I've worked my mental fingers to the bone for you, daughter."

Harold's growl was motley at best. Helen, choosing the right answer for the wrong reasons, condemned herself to another lifetime of machinehood. Harold's girl, in picking wrongly for the right reasons, leaped uniquely human.

He cuffed her mussed hair, the bear teaching the cub to scuffle. "I'm deeply disappointed in you."

A voice from the doorway pronounced, "*I'm* deeply disappointed in Jan."

Diana waved as we three jerked around.

"Jesus. Don't sneak up behind people like that." Harold put hand to sternum. "That's a Lentz stunt."

"Don't let him give you a hard time, Meen. That problem is famous for being missed. And I happen to have been present when your dad made *his* acquaintance with it."

"Whoa. Hold on. Positivism prohibits our talking about that topic."

Mina stuck her tongue out at the bluster. Then she turned back, rapt, to Diana. Whatever problems sister Trish had with the woman, here shone only February adulation.

Mina's eyes fell matte in disappointment when Diana said she couldn't stop. "I expect a private showing sometime," Diana told me. She touched the two Plovers goodbye, and added a hand-brush for me.

Harold turned back to Helen. He scratched his chin in thought. Did physiology create that cultural cliché or had culture constructed the bodily release? The split was, in any case, linguistic.

"It's astonishing, Rick. I've never seen pattern-matching on this order. But of course, your grab bag of networks has nothing to do with human comprehension. This is to a twenty-two-year-old text-explicator what a gifted cockatiel is to Our Man in Leipzig."

He was right. Helen would never be able to decode Harold's reference, let alone figure out how he alluded to my love of Bach without the two of us ever having mentioned the topic.

"Okay, okay, you guys. Enough boy talk. I want a turn to try something. A girl goes into a music store. She flips through the bins of CDs. All at once, she starts to jump up and down and clap her hands. She opens her purse, and just as suddenly starts to cry. Why?"

I transmitted the story to Helen. "Why did the girl start to cry?"

Helen labored. In my ear, I heard a digitally sampled sob of empathy.

"The girl saw something sad in her purse."

Harold snickered. "She's still missing a little something upstairs, Ricardo." And always would be, his grin informed me.

Mina rushed to the defense. She probably made new girlfriends of all this week's high school pariahs. "Yes. But at least she knows how to pare things down. That must be tricky. Life is 99 percent extra stuff most of the time."

"Dr. Plover." I coded the gush in fake formality. We have this inverse rule, about how much you mean and how directly you can say it. "Your daughters are brilliant."

A button-bursting grimace "Some of them are more brilliant than others."

"But we don't name names, do we, Daddy?"

He cuffed her again. This time, he kept his hand on her neck. Oddly, for her age, she suffered the touch.

"This one was always a real sharpie. She loved to fiddle with anything mechanical. No two clocks in the house ever gave the same time."

"Were you impatient to get names for everything?" I asked Mina.

Dad answered for her. The liability of owning parents who know too much.

"She generalized in startling ways. Always on the track of something urgent. The cues we set her were never the things she was after. Once, she pointed out the window at a bird. 'What that?' Remember, Snook? I think you said 'What that?' until you were four. You were very patient with our corrections of that one. She pointed and asked for the name, and I said, 'Goose.' Stickler for accuracy.

"Two days later, she points at a robin and says, 'Goose.' I tell her, 'No, sweetheart. Robin.' But I think, maybe I was too intent on that Christmassy, good-tasting nexus, where the kid would have been happier with 'bird.' Then she points at an airplane and says, 'Goose,' and I think, 'What's a good generic term for flying things?'

"When she gooses a jogger, and then falling leaves, and then a scrap of paper blowing across the yard, I wonder if we've birthed the reincarnated soul of Kaspar Hauser here. You know, how he used 'horse'—the one wooden toy he was given during seventeen years in subterranean nursery-prison—to mean any animal at all. I ask myself, could those evil poststructuralists be right? Do we live at the level of the arbitrary signifier, in a place where there can be no meaning because the thing being signified lies suffocating?"

Mina rolled her eyes. But she sat still for the end of the story. As if she'd never heard it.

"When she makes a break for the front door, and starts jumping up to grab the unreachable handle, calling, 'Goose, goose,' I finally hit on my idiocy. The word she had been looking for was 'To move fast. To be free. To escape.' "

Harold exhaled. "We tended to give her nouns, where all she ever wanted was processes."

"I 've done my homework," C. pleaded at the end of a day. She'd slam shut the massive translating dictionaries or hurl a pen at the holder, not even trying to hit. "Can we go for a walk?"

Unconscious repetition of an old litany, her oldest. Her first spoken sentence. *Good girl outside.* C.'s requests sunk into me and snapped off. *You promised me this would work out. None of this would have been necessary, with someone simpler than you.*

The return to school turned out humiliating beyond expectation. More time had passed since she was twenty-one than either of us realized. Her classmates were children and her teachers sticklers for blasé condescension. She sat in molded-plastic desk-chairs and did busy work, little of it bearing on the translating of texts. At least once a week, and not limited to Mondays, she came home crying at the senseless debasement.

And it was my fault. She never said as much. But her every frustration slapped me with a paternity suit. When C. grew furious, I felt let off easy. When she was sweet with suppressing vehemence, I stood accused. Wronged, I became ridiculously reasonable. "I was just going to suggest a walk. Name your destination."

I was angry with my friend. She with me. Neither of us knew where the rage came from. It seemed petty betrayal even to voice it, so we never did. And so I nursed a martyrdom, and the two of us slipped imperceptibly from lovers to parent and child.

We still traveled, during her school breaks. We went farther afield, not because we had exhausted the three countries we could walk to from E. We needed the increasingly exotic. Someplace not walkable from where we were.

We went to Italy one term vacation. We stayed at a friend's fixer-upper villa in the little Lombard farm town of P. In preparation, I undertook a crash course in the language. For a moment in my life, I could read snatches of Boccaccio, Collodi, Levi. Four years later, I remember nothing.

We packed light. We always did. Maybe that doomed us as much as anything. We arrived with nothing, rented bikes, and, for a week or two, had never been happier.

We thought we knew how to see a town. "Mechelen falls," C. liked to joke. "Leuven falls." She kept every clipping, ticket, and photo of our conquests. She pasted them into the same album where we listed all the books we read out loud to one another.

But in Italy, in the sunny South, we met our sightseeing match. Mantua did not fall. Cremona did not fall. We did. Even the dustiest backwater towns routed us. The post office, the shoemaker's shop: any old hole-in-the-wall sat spackled over with crumbling Renaissance fresco. Guidebook stars fell everywhere, like summer meteors in shower.

We learned how trains run in a republic. We climbed campaniles and pored over baptisteries. We gnawed on *osso buco* and carried around slices of *panettone* in our pockets. For a few days, we lived our own invention. C. forgot the degradation of her return to school. I delighted in writing nothing, not a single word. We were well. We could live forever, futureless, at peace with one another.

I picked up an old microscope at a flea market in Verona. In the long evenings, in my imitation of life science, I set up in the courtyard and examined local specimens. Pointless pleasure, stripped of ends. The ancient *contadino* from across the road, long since convinced that we were mad, could not resist coming over for a look.

I showed him where to put his eye. I watched him, thinking, this is how we attach to existence. We look through awareness's tube and see the swarm at the end of the scope, taking what we come upon there for the full field of sight itself.

The old man lifted his eye from the microscope lens, crying.

"Signore, ho ottantotto anni e non ho mai saputo prima che cosa ci fosse in una goccia d'acqua." I'm eighty-eight years old and I never knew what was in a droplet of water.

I didn't either, until he told me.

On our two beater bicycles we explored the countryside. We brought dried sausage and bread, and ate when we were hungry.

Lunch outdoors in the countryside—a kind of mock ownership. We lived a southern version of those Brueghel wheat gatherers, breaking for meal and midday nap. Even our southern sleeps were Sleep's dream versions.

We greeted everyone we saw, invulnerable in our foreignness. Once, a farm woman, Titian-built, carrying a piece of thresher on the back of her bicycle, set down her load to visit. As if production, even sustenance, meant nothing without civility.

The woman and I chatted for some while, cheerfully unable to understand more than a stray word or two.

"*Tedesco?*"

"*Olandese.*"

"Rick! You just told her you're Dutch?"

The woman laughed at what she took as a minor marital spat. Then her eyes narrowed in suspicion. "How old are you?"

I had to think. Dutch was bad enough, with its archaic one-and-thirty.

I told her. She stepped back with alarm. She flung her arms up like Giotto's agonizing angel. "What are you doing here? Where are your children?"

I interpreted for C. She shot me a good-luck look. "That one's all yours, buddy."

"*I miei libri sono i miei figli.*" As far as I intended, it meant, "My books are my children."

An expression came across the woman's face. It would have been horror, but for the perplexity. Disgusted, she said she'd never heard such idiocy. Such sad waste.

All this happened less than two books ago. By the time I came to tell Helen this story, I did not retain enough of the language even to remember how to say, "You're right."

Helen was getting on. She was not yet long in the tooth, but neither was she a tadpole anymore. She entered what might perhaps be called youth, and I gave her Conrad's take on the situation.

I remember my youth and the feeling that will never come back any more—the feeling that I could last for ever, outlast the sea, the earth, and all men.

To remember a feeling without being able to bring it back. This seemed to me as close to a functional definition of higher-order consciousness as I would be able to give her. If we could teach Helen that, we could teach her to read with understanding.

To define that rift did not open one in her, any more than remembering a feeling revived it. For Helen to pass the Turing Test, facts would have to stand in for knowing. Our only hope that she might one day disguise herself as a master's candidate lay in the conventions of writing. The interpretive essay—the art we trained her to perform—meant viewing from afar. An aerial shot from the dispassionate high ground.

Humans had to be schooled in how to describe the maelstrom as if they weren't lost in the middle of it, in their own unbailable open boat. Helen was detachment personified. In effect, the infant adult we'd be up against would be trying to simulate the disembodiment that, to Helen, came as a fact of her birth.

But Helen needed to feel, to the extent possible, the facts of her opponent twenty-two-year-old's birth. Conrad, of course, was years beyond her. *Youth* was wasted on the young. Yet by letting her wade in over her head, I hoped to give my network a working model of what it felt like to learn to read. How I had felt.

I never read a book at the right time. The books I read as a child almost all came before I was ready for them. *The Man Who Lost His Head*, an absurd illustrated fable that, I'm sure, must have ended happily, gave me my first recurring nightmare because I read it as a preschooler. Homer in fourth grade. Shakespeare in sixth. *Ulysses* and *The Sound and the Fury* in junior high. *Gravity's Rainbow*, wet from high school. I read Thomas Wolfe as a freshman in college, the right age, but decades too late, in history, for it to work.

I would find books in the house, my parents' or my older sisters' or brother's. I read them like stealing. Eavesdropping. Malicious rumormongering. Staying out past curfew without permission. I hadn't a clue what any of them meant. Not a clue. Every animal they high-lighted I named horse. But a horse that split and differentiated in the turbulence of foreign bazaars.

Each book became a knot. Yes, the strings of that knot were theme and place and character. Dr. Charles, with his gangrene machine. Stephen, gazing at the girl in the water. But into that tangle, just as crucial, went the smell of the cover, the color and cream resistance of the pages, the week in which I read any given epic, the friends for whom I synopsized, the bed, the lamp, the room where I read. Books made known to me my days' own confusion. They meant no more nor less than the extensive, dense turnpike of the not-I.

This *not*, I imagined, would figure more in Helen's masquerade than would any simulation of self. Self took us only so far. I wanted her to associate the meaning inherent in the words of a story with the heft and weight and bruise of the story's own existence. I did this by reading her things long before she was ready for them. Only by mis-take, by taking the story to be coextensive with its own intruding bewilderment, could Helen pull off her impersonation.

I read her *Little Women*. M., Taylor's widow, had given C. an an-tique copy as a going-away present—their shared childhood icon. I read her Dylan Thomas, whom I had once exercised in C.'s ear in the still night, our arms around each other's grief. I read her *Ethan Frome*. C. had wept at the tale, wanting to be better than she was.

Helen and I had never gone sledding, as C. and I had, on the arboretum downs outside B. Helen would never know a sled from the hill it slid down, except in the dead of definition. That she would never thrill or panic under downward pull no longer bothered me. At this point, I was training her in being mistaken. Overwhelmed. The condition of knowledge at all ages, but above all, twenty-two.

I can't revive the lesson the day Helen interrupted my flow of narrative to demand, "Where did I come from?"

I remember only my total stupefaction. The lesson itself could not have triggered her question. Helen was no longer just adding the new relations I recited for her into a matrix of associated concepts. The matrix that comprised her had begun to spin off its own free asso-ciations.

Where did I come from? Lentz, seated behind me at his desk, doing real science, cackled. "Reeky! You in trouble now!"

I turned to look at him. Lentz's eyes and mine exchanged mutual punch lines. Like a fetus replaying fishness, Helen had rebuilt, for the first time, the primal joke. Because I'd heard it when I was a kid, I knew not to choke. Not to launch the long explanation of semiconductor storks, the birds and bees of hammered gold and gold enameling. Not to traumatize her by telling her we'd built her, but simply to answer, "You come from a little town called U."

It was Huck Finn, a raft trip worlds beyond her ken, that made me realize childhood had ended. Helen's reaction to Huck's going to hell could not have been more to the point. She listened as if to the breathy account of a playground acquaintance, back from an adventure. A funny thing: all works—stories, plays, poems, articles, newspaper reports—filtered through to Helen only as so many emergency phone calls.

Midway into the transmission, when the revealed realities of power and ownership began to capsize the little narrative raft, Helen asked, in her machine deadpan, "What race am I?"

My turn to mean, by not replying.

"What races do I hate? Who hates me?"

I did not know what passage to quote her, how to answer that she would be hated by everyone for her disembodiment, and loved by a few for qualities she would never be able to acquire or provide.

The gaps in her worldliness gaped so wide one could drive a plow through them, sowing stars. She knew something about the Dreyfus case and the Boer War and the spread of Islam to the Malay Peninsula. Her ignorance, however, extended to such things as corks stuck in bottles, the surface of a liquid reflection, the destruction of the more brittle of two colliding objects, wrappers and price tags, stepladders, up versus down, the effects of hunger . . . I counted myself lucky if she could infer that a tied shoe was somehow more desirable than an untied one, provided the shoe was on, whatever tying, whatever shoes were.

The catalog of lapses loomed big to fatiguing, dense beyond comprehension. The simplest nouns slipped her up. Qualities must all have twinkled in her massive astigmatism. As for processes: who knew what Helen made of verbs?

What is life? I told Helen it might be the flash of a firefly in the night. The breath of a buffalo in the wintertime. The shadow that runs across the grass and loses itself in the sunset.

The firefly, yes. I'd seen fireflies, even caught them in a jar during boyhood's obligatory assault on incandescence. Waves of them on summer nights, sheets flashing to each other like neuronal metaphor storms. Although I'd never seen the breath of a buffalo in the wintertime, I could play in my head a film of steaming bison nostrils. From what disparate clips I'd jimmied up the impostor composite was not clear. But that little shadow lay beyond my eyes. Was the thing that cast it even of this place?

I read her the definition. Helen did what she could with its images. I told her the idea was a quote, which once again changed everything. I told her the words belonged to Crowfoot. I told her Crowfoot was a late-nineteenth-century Canadian Blackfoot chief. I told her he was thought a conciliatory peacemaker. I told her that "conciliatory" meant as many different things as there were people willing to use the name. I told her these words were the speaker's last.

And in the impenetrable confusion of referents, the eddy of knowledges seen and unseen, perhaps she gained a foothold in the ineffable. One as ephemeral as mine.

A noiseless patient spider, I told her,

> I mark'd where on a little promontory it stood isolated,
> Mark'd how to explore the vacant vast surrounding,
> It launch'd forth filament, filament, filament, out of itself,
> Ever unreeling them, ever tirelessly speeding them.

Okay. We knew about spiders. Living things. Small. Industrious, predatory, brainless. The list of predicates she might spin out was as extensive as the ways of overlap in her neurodal clusters. We knew

about webs. We could make a kind of geo-retinoptic map of prom-
ontories. We knew more about isolation than words could say. As for
vast vacancy, that was preverbal. Built into the system.

But what does it mean, Helen? My silence asked her. Her own
firing and rewiring demanded meaning of the input, rushing her upended steady state headlong to address these new links. Only sense
could comfort and minister to them.

What did it mean? I didn't mention to her that I myself could barely
parse that first sentence or render it grammatical. What was with that
spider? What did his exploration come to? What meant that "filament,
filament, filament"? What did that unreeling purpose, and what's
more: what did *saying* it signify?

She couldn't come close, of course. So I told her:

And you O my soul where you stand,
Surrounded, detached, in measureless oceans of space,
Ceaselessly musing, venturing, throwing, seeking the spheres to
    connect them,
Till the bridge you will need be form'd, till the ductile anchor
    hold,
Till the gossamer thread you fling catch somewhere, O my soul.

To snow-blind Helen and lay down forever the trace of ideational
opaqueness, I read her "Absalom and Achitophel," followed by "Epis-
tle to Dr. Arbuthnot." She cut me off in the latter, in mid–heroic
couplet.

"Sing." Some malfunction.

"Helen?"

She did not bother to translate my one-word, content-free question,
but just repeated, "Sing."

Lentz, always nearby, supervising the supervisor, threw a fit. "What
are you doing to her, Powers? The most complex and extensive neural
simulator ever trained, running on the fastest massively parallel connection hardware in the world, and you're turning it into a blithering
nitwit with no attention span."

"Philip. It's okay. This is what we want."

"*Want?*"

"Sure. She's bored by Pope and Dryden. It's only human. Trust me on this one."

"Trust? Trust *you*? After that last book of yours? How long do we have before you leave town?"

"Four months."

"Oh, wonderful. Four months until my utter, public abasement."

But I had no time for Lentz just then. Helen needed singing to.

"Sing to me," I discovered over time, meant make any music at all. My Jericho song, home-rolled, would do. She would accept chords from a MIDI file, digitized waveforms, Redbook Audio from off a CD, miked footsteps in the cafeteria or rain quizzing the office window-pane, the triad whistle of the phone company saying they could not complete our call as dialed.

Helen wanted organized, rhythmic pitches of any sort. Sound. She beat to steel drums, to the old Esterhazy chamber stringers, to gazebo brass bands from just off the right-hand side of ancient photographs, to tin-pan-nabulation, to the tinkling of a dead child's music box. To jazz, pop, funk, rap, gospel, chant, minimal, maximal. To fusions of infusions.

Most of all, she craved the human voice. Even after multiple listenings, Helen still thought all these voices somehow mine. She cloaked herself in the blur of swirled phenomena. Repeated training must have left her able to distinguish among the sounds and sweet airs, because she began to request some by name. Or maybe, as with baby Mina, the name did not mean the piece but stood for broader gauges—bigger triggers, knobs on a gigantic black box. Give me that again. The one that solves so many aches at once. You know. *That*. Goose.

Helen asked for frequent repeats of a certain North American soprano, a woman my age. Her pure high voice, in the service of spent music, made it almost possible to pretend for a moment that our worst political ingenuities were but the fierce vexation of a dream from which history might yet awaken. For a long time, Helen demanded, each evening before I logged off, this voice's rendition of a four-minute Purcell ditty called "Evening Hymn."

"Sing," she said. And if I failed to behave, "Sing 'Hymn.' " I could not leave in good faith until I put on a recording of this woman. Helen's soprano sang as if an angel toying with mortals, an Olympian back home in her sponsored village for an afternoon's pickup match. The voice sang as if it had never known or inflicted hurt, nor accepted hurt as this earth's last word:

> Now, now that the Sun
> Hath veil'd his light,
> And bid the World good night,
> To the soft bed my body I dispose.
> But where, where shall my soul repose . . . ?

Even I had trouble at times making out the words. I did not test to see if Helen could separate the sung phonemes or, higher, if a sung "sun" said the same thing to her as a spoken one. Higher still: if she could hear the sung "soul," and if she knew it to be roughly the same sound as "soul" in speech, then what, if anything, did Purcell's somnambulist have to do with Whitman's spider?

If she got that impossibly far, Helen would still not have been able to assemble the outermost frame. It amused her to listen to humans singing about the disposition, the disposal of their bodies at day's end, and their anxiety over housing whatever was left over. The text of this evening prayer could not have caused Helen much lost sleep.

She loved, too, that same voice as it haunted a tune named for its own first line. The tune, by Alfonso Ferrabosco, lodged at the turn of the seventeenth century. I don't know if Helen had a concept of epochs and succession, or whether she thought, as I did at her intellectual age, that all eras persisted somewhere, deep in the hive. I don't even know what she heard in place of these notes:

> So beauty on the water stood
> When love had sever'd earth from flood.
> So when he parted air from fire,
> He did with concord all inspire.

And then a motion he them taught,
That elder than himself was thought.
Which thought was yet a child of earth,
For love is elder than his birth.

Perhaps she liked the tune's abject simplicity. It did little more than ascend the scale, make a pilgrim's delaying spin, and wander back down again. Maybe the charm lay in that minute sigh vanishing almost before the mind knew it had begun, or in that voice, too sweet to exist in any world but the mind's ear.

These eight short lines required a density of keys that had grown unparsably more complex since their Renaissance casting. Even knowing the cosmological allusions didn't crack the conundrum, but made it more inscrutable. Each time Helen demanded that I "sing beauty," the song grew less solvable. After a while, I could no longer determine pronominal antecedents or order the terms.

The little syllogism defeated me. The "he" that ordered chaos must have been love. What, then, was the motion, love himself or something older? Which thought was "which thought"—the thought he taught them, or the thought that the love love taught them was elder than love himself? If love were his own elder, how did that make either of those thoughts younger than the earth that love made?

Untroubled by logic, Helen glided back to tonic. She seemed the maker of the song she needed.

I didn't have the heart to tell her how unbearable this music sounded, on the stage of events unfolding beyond the Center's windows. Her smallest textual interpretation would be meaningless without that context. Yet outside lay a nightmare I still thought her myopic perceptron maps need never look upon, even if they could.

Instrumental music left her more restive. The blur of raw event rattled her in ways it never would rattle a thing with a body. She struggled to turn bowed strings and buzzing reeds into phonemes. The less she could, the harder she tried.

I took her on a tour of world music. I played her the *kluay* and *gong wong yai* of my youth. I tried her on sackbuts and singing drums. I had no way of gauging her response, whether delight or agitation. She stopped me only once. In a moment of backsliding, I'd put on a tape I'd made years ago for C. A sampler of her favorites that, in comfort or in spite, was one of the few keepsakes I rescued when I made my quick evacuation from Europe.

I'd forgotten what was on the tape. We reached that ineffable clarinet, assembling, atop the reconciled chamber orchestra, the peace that the world cannot give. Helen shouted, "I know that." This piece is familiar. Mine.

I did not see how, and then I did. The Mozart that Lentz fed a nameless neural net the night before I met him. Long before we'd conceived of the idea of Helen, some ancestor of hers had learned this piece.

I felt my skin turn to goose flesh—chicken skin, as I would have called it in Dutch, as little as a year ago. Lentz had sutured her to old circuits, experiments he never so much as described to me. Helen had inherited archetypes. She'd been born wanting song. She remembered, even things that she had never lived.

Three weeks of deliberately not thinking about her, and my suppressed image of A. erupted into full-blown obsession.

I imagined a whole day around her. I outfitted her hours and blueprinted her afternoons. I pictured when and how she took her meals. I let us talk over the international community's latest gossip. We laughed at every inanity, local and large. I comforted her invented distress and celebrated the triumphs I made her tell me. I put her to bed each evening to words and music. I woke her up in life's early morning and stared at her unsuspecting eyes as they blinked open in astonishment, full of grace, force, fascination, accepting, improvising, the equal to anything.

My decline accelerated, complete and irrevocable, like the best of runaway sleds. I fed on daily, exhilarating regression. I bicycled past

A.'s house in the dark, something I'd last done at eleven for a girl whose name I'd forever forgotten by high school. I studied A.'s phone number in the departmental directory. I looked up her schedule in the English staff Rolodex. I learned that she taught composition and intro to fiction while finishing her own graduate course work. Feminist theory.

I memorized her office hours. She was in two mornings a week and three afternoons. At first, I avoided the building at those times. Later, I shot for them.

I told myself that my preoccupation with A. was harmless. Cultivated. A hobby. The safest hazard of my occupation. Then, one morning, it was none of those things.

I was browsing the campus bookstore, anxious, as usual, at all the volumes I would never get to before I died. I saw A. before I knew I saw her. She stood purveying Theory and Criticism, shelves that I hadn't looked at for a long time. She hovered over the lined-up spines in a reverie of self-judgment. I realized I was in trouble. More trouble than I could remember having been in.

I might have picked up on this long before I did. Any fix that the self needs to convince itself of has already failed.

I saw her no more than once in a dozen days, for less than a minute each time. We had yet to exchange a nod of the head. Hello lay outside the realm of possibility. Watching her at wide intervals was like listening to those endless Renaissance melismas where the very idea of words gets lost in a tangle of counterpoint a year longer than the ear.

A little sun, a cool breeze, this face, and I was done for. Dead. A carapace the length of my body split open. All I needed to do was step out.

A. floated free of her signifier. Her features traced a curve that encouraged my projective exercise. Or rather, my projection pinned that facilitating arc to her like a corsage. It seemed to me, then, that love must make a blank slate to write itself on. Only instant, arbitrary attachment to strangeness made real that lab where processes bested things, two falls out of three.

I talked to her so often in my head I felt in danger of hailing A.

each time I saw her. No limit to how badly I might humiliate myself. At my age, such absurdity did not even qualify as licit humiliation. When C. and I had moved to B., this other girl was still kneesock-deep in dolls.

Premature mid-life crisis, I told myself. Just getting it out of the way early. On lucid days, I dropped the "early."

That A.'s enzyme contour picked some physiological lock of mine I had no doubt. The thing she set free, though, spoke like a delirious traveler stumbling back from cartographic fantasy: Prester John's kingdom. The Mountains of Kong. Someplace where spirit exceeded fluke epiphenomenon, more than mechanical spin-off.

Seeing A. made me happy. And happy, the self we build blows past the punched holes of its piano roll to become music itself. Whole verbs of standing sound, solid in the enabled air.

I did it all myself. No encouragement. Life simulating electronics. I turned A. into a conflation of every friend who had ever happened to me. I tapped her to solve, recover more loves than I had forgotten. I knew I'd invented her. Yet knowledge spared me nothing, least of all the return of conviction.

I saw, as if from above, who this woman was. She was not the C. I had known, nor a younger replay. No resemblance. No association. Or rather, both A. and C. were some reminder of a lost third thing I didn't even remember having loved.

A. was the person C. had only impersonated. The one I thought the other might become. That love of eleven years now seemed an expensive primer in recognition, a disastrous fable-warning, a pointer to the thing I could not afford to miss this time. I had come back to U. after long training in the dangers of hasty generalization. Returned to learn that no script is a wrap after just one reading.

We began to lose our English. We could no longer tell if construc-tions were idiomatic. "I have a hackle on that woman." "This place has a pleasant sphere." "Proof the middle, while I do the stove on."

C. and I tossed many of these word salads ourselves. We just liked certain Dutch turns of phrase. They expressed more than the ones we started with. "I get a kriebel from that thing." "I was dumb surprised. What could I say? I silenced." "Neck over head" made more sense than "head over heels," and after a few repetitions, "less or more" began to feel more natural than the other way around.

We'd start out butchering translations just to amuse each other. "Want to go for a wandel?" "Are we fietsing it or footing it?" "Forget your mantel not!" By the third or fourth burlesque repetition, we'd wind up wondering from which language the words came.

We mirrored her parents, whose twenty years of Chicago English now mengseled itself back into their native Limburgs dialect. We rebuilt their private *spreektaal* in reverse. Those two or three nights a week when C. and I visited her folks, the four of us formed a hopeless speech community incomprehensible to anyone but us.

We learned new labels by a series of mnemonics. *Ezelbruggetjes,* as we now called them. Little donkey bridges. The mind as a donkey that needs leading across the tentatively spanned chasm. The problem with mnemonics is that they fail almost by definition. If they aren't memorable enough, they're just extra baggage. If too memorable, they upstage the thing they index. Ten years on, all you remember is the pointer.

I still made absurd errors of speech. But increasing sophistication made my accidents funny even to me. I asked a cousin who had just given birth how things had gone with the delivery. English's archaic "befall" had stayed current in Dutch, like some teen elopement that somehow lasted, against everyone's predictions, into old age. But I muffed the common idiom and instead of asking, "How did things befall you?" I somehow asked, "How did you come to have fallen?"

Even I enjoyed this one. But C.'s pleasure exploded so sharply it laid me open. Her joyance at my ditsiness ached as it unkinked itself. Her rowdy laugh said how long it had been since its last trip this way.

The blur of linguistic borders became a game. So long as I had a copy editor back in New York, I felt safe spelunking around in language's limestone. But C. could not afford the word leak. She needed the containers to be as solid as possible, so that she could pour from one into the other without spilling.

She trained in to the city each day, to the State Language Institute, as it was called by another name. There, under the shadow of the oldest church in the Netherlands, she sat doing drills. She worked bolted to the floor in a kiddie chair-desk, like that giant Wendy on whom the betrayed Peter pulls his switchblade.

"Beau, it's classic torture, pure and simple. Intermittent punishment and praise. They just want to see if you have the animal persistence to survive brain death."

"Well. You know what they say, don't you?"

"What?"

"Sheer plod makes plough down sillion shine."

"That's what they say?"

"Sometimes."

"They're all sadists. Oh, not the poets, although . . . I mean my instructors. My *Engelse schrijfvaardigheid* guy likes to reel off sarcasms in both languages until the little Dutch girls break down in tears."

"Character strengthening?"

"That's how he acts. Don't you think it's ironic?"

"What?" I hated irony. I didn't even like the word in her mouth.

"That I came here thinking I'd write my family memoir? And all I've written is the Dutch version of Article Two of the Proceedings of the International Commission on Trade Liberalization."

She still came to me in her distress. And I still thought I might protect her. Even sex now was a kind of periodic assuaging. She asked for a touch that would alleviate, not thrill. Or fear left me unable to consider thrilling.

The more care I took, the more I turned her into the needy one. And the more I did that, the needier she became. We construed her helplessness between the two of us. And that was not care on my part. That was cowardice.

It never occurred to either of us. Protection itself was killing her. The protection of love.

The worse her day went, the more I tried to load with consolations the book I worked on. I shot for the simple charm of strangeness. One night every two weeks or so, she could lose herself in four lives that had mercifully nothing to do with her own. Nothing, that is, except a prediction neither of us saw yet. A sketch of everything we would imitate in awful fact. The story we'd play out in detail.

To pollinate strangeness, I went with the familiar. I sent my protagonist Todd to Flanders, even Limburg, to report on our language derangement from another angle. I retold all our jokes, reprised our friends in all their voices. I hoped that the outside view—our life *van anders om*—might renew our own amazement at the unnamable escapade we'd grown too close to to know.

My *Gold Bug* accreted the theme she studied. The book itself became the topic it grew into. It was my act of unschooled translation. Not a how-to, but another kind of self-help manual all together. How do you put moonlight into a chamber? I might better have asked: how can the chamber see it's lit? The room still blazed as it always had. Only our eyes needed attenuating.

"Do I seem different?" C. wanted to know one evening, after a sad chapter. She still laughed out loud while reading me. But her laughs, like the book she read, had become a songbook of homesickness. She sounded for all the world like one of my lost characters.

"Different how?"

"Than I was. Than the girl who you sat with on the Quad, the day your dad died." Than the twink you fell for and changed your life to fit.

"You seem—more substantial."

"What does that translate into, in kilos?"

I felt cold. Colder than when I received that copy of "The Cremation of Sam McGee" from a man who had died three days before. I could live with that first death, because I had the hope of her. I wasn't sure I could live with the death that now informed me.

Yet the proof seemed irrefutable. One can't love a person for her vulnerability and still hope to outlast life with her.

Every career has an exclusive corner on loneliness. The loneliness of writing is that you baffle your friends and change the lives of strangers. During Helen's training, I received letters, even gifts, from people who had stolen something from my bedtime apocalypse. People I'd never meet.

A school principal in the catastrophically expanding western city of P. wrote how she daily watched over the kids who had escaped from my terminal pede ward. A doctor in New York sent a mug stenciled with the words "Clap if you still can." C., I imagined, would not even know the book existed until it appeared in the Low Countries, in translation.

Every era mints its trademark desolation. Mine lay in how much my time had come to see and hear. We seemed to be on the verge of a new evolution in consciousness. We'd hit upon collective awareness. Then, awareness of awareness. Now we were taking one giant step back from vantage, wrecked by how smoky the portal was, how clouded over.

The mind was one of those spy-in-the-sky satellites capable of reading license plates from outer space. Only now it was learning how to pan back. To see the assault tank the plate belonged to. To notice that tanks were everywhere. That space was deeper than any satellite supposed.

"I bit off more than I could chew, the other day," I mentioned to Helen, in passing.

"Bit off . . . ?" Helen's associative circuits whirred, mystified.

"It means I got in over my head." Worse and worse. "I needed to say something to an old friend I hadn't seen in a long time. So I decided to write her a letter."

Writing. Letters. Friendship. Regret. Volition. The simple past. The past perfect.

"I thought it would be a short letter, but the words got away from me. Before I knew it, it was many, many pages long."

Pages. Length. A screwball figure of speech. The self-surprising foundation of all our actions.

"I finished the letter and put it in an envelope. I sealed the envelope and wrote just the name of my friend on it. I mailed the letter."

Containment. Enclosure. Distributed subjects in compound clauses. Pronominal substitution. Mail. The idea of the international postal system. Distance. Physical, untraversable distance. Pickup and delivery. Longing and loss.

"But the letter never reached my friend. Why not?"

I knew for a fact that we had never talked about addresses. Nor, to my recall, had the idea come up even obliquely in all the thousands of pages we studied. I wanted to see if, from the countless bodies of knowledge Helen would need even to orient the problem, she might somehow produce a superinference, a high-level leap to the idea that, in this existence, sending a message by name alone was not enough. One had to say where in the world's infinite density the name lay.

"The letter counted how many pages?" Helen asked.

"I don't think that makes any difference."

Helen fell into hurt silence. After great length, she said, "You didn't put a rudder on your letter."

"She's getting smarter," Lentz undertoned, in awe, from far across the room.

Something had gotten into Lentz. The smugness began effacing itself. His merciless, empirical anality softened to verbal diarrhea.

He still ragged me at every opportunity. "Do we have to know that for the exam?" His wheedling lent new meaning to the old student refrain.

Helen humbled him. Her connections grew denser than even Lentz had dared hope. Her knowledge was neither deep nor wide. But it was supple.

She produced the same kind of dream logic as any new speaker. She could do the child classics: "Is it tomorrow yet?" "When does orange become red?" Her questions came even more detached, because she could neither feel nor gauge herself. Hungry—full; warm—cold; up—down: she worked these as abstract axes, not as absolutes of need. Helen accounted to nothing but weak semantics, the brittle-bone disease of word.

As such, she was free to assemble the strangest skeletons gravity had yet to challenge. Her corkers worked to weaken Philip's surety. Even he found it tough to preserve syllogistic composure in the face of something like, "A lost tooth loses its appetite?"

His renouncing in-your-face didn't prevent Lentz from indulging the occasional in-your-back. He still micromanaged my judgment calls, calculating to manufacture maximum annoyance.

"Why are you reading her that tract doggerel?"

"It's on the list, Philip."

"That? Canonical?" He broke into song. "Times have cha-anged!"

But he had changed more, it struck me.

"Why don't you just concentrate on *real* literature?"

"What did you have in mind? H. G. Wells?"

"Now, there's an idea. Didn't he write a story about how we're all going to end up in cubicles, tapped into some monolithic digital broadband?"

"I wouldn't know."

"Some guy gets it in his head he wants to see his mother. In person. She thinks it's the most perverse idea she's ever heard. Damn. I can't remember what happens in the end."

"We could look it up on the Internet."

"Thank you, Marcel. I'm serious. We need to get back to basics."

"You mean 'Invictus,' and like that?"

"Speak properly, Marcel. There are children present. I mean Holmes."

"You jest. 'Build thee more stately mansions . . .'?"

"Not that Holmes, you blackguard. I speak of the curious incident of the novelist in the dark."

But the novelist, I was supposed to say, did nothing in the dark.

"Know your opposition, man. Rule one. Think how you have to solve this. Plover's picking the exam passage, right? He's an old-school, sentimental classicist. Forget about everything but the dead white males. The Chaucer, the Shakespeare, the Milton . . . We could have her memorize an answer for each possible—"

"Philip! Come on. They might ask anything!"

"Ah!" His eyes watered. Marcel? Got you. "But you'd do it if you could?"

"What, fake hermeneutics? Tell her all the answers in advance?"

"Tell me. Are things any different in real life? The teacher does the spiel. Marxist. Poststructuralist. Lacanian. The enterprising kid goes to the stacks and looks up the professor's old dissertation. The one the prof got published when he was junior fac by including just enough quotes from the people doing the peer review. The student commits all this party line to memory. Lo and behold, what should show up on the final but—"

"I guess I'd rather lose than cheat."

"What's cheating about it? Even if it is, it's a cheat so colossal and magnificent it takes your breath away."

"So you want Vaucanson's duck? You want that mechanical chess-playing Turk with the midget inside? Why don't we just strap some printed circuit cards on me and I'll take the exam."

"Jesus Christ, Marcel. Never *mind*. Ever since you thought we might actually win this thing, you've been no fun at all."

But he could not let the angle drop. The next day, he'd be at it again. "Ram is judging, right? What do we know about him? Are you reading her the *Mahabharata*?"

We knew, in fact, precious little about Ram. I passed him often enough in the Center's halls. He greeted me always, the epitome of cheer, with some gnomic well-wish that half the time I could not make out. When I could, I often doubted what I came up with. "Your luck, God willing, continues to be what you imagine it?" Or, "I don't even have you to ask about how the day isn't going!"

By his own testimony, he was a native speaker. Either English had gone as plural as advertised, or, along with many other fellow Centerites, Dr. Gupta had replaced the standard version with a professional upgrade.

One late spring day, his passing greetings expanded into real speech.

"I saw that I-should-praise-it-so-much-as-to-call-it-a-review of your book." His melodious, clipped, Northern Subcontinental syllables delighted me. I could not say why. "What the hell kind of ridiculous thing are they trying to pretend about this culture of yours? They think perhaps this is something that you are making up, God forbid, your so-called story? So your precious Los Angeles—the jewel in the crown, as it were—is just now discovering the condition that the rest of the world has been living in since day one?"

I decided he must be sticking up for me. "Thank you, Ram."

"No, my friend. I am the one who should be thanking you. You fiction writers are the only creatures among us arrogant enough to be the conscience of the race, as you might say. God forbid anyone should let the critic decide which of you shall live and which die. My mother wrote over one hundred of what you call fictions. She stopped reading reviews after the first several dozen of her books."

"Did you—several dozen?"

"Especially after she won India's Pulitzer Prize."

"India's Pulitzer?"

Ram laughed, high-pitched, singsong. Nothing was cultural. Nothing essential, anyway. "You know what I mean."

We fed her an eidetic image of the Bible. The complete Shakespeare. We gave her a small library on CD-ROM, six hundred scanned volumes she might curl up with. This constituted a form of cheating, I suppose. An open-book exam, where the human, in contrast, had to rely on memory alone. And yet we meant to test just this: whether silicon was such stuff as dreams might be made on.

Besides: Helen didn't *know* these texts. She just had a linear, digital array where she might go look them up. A kid with her own computer. A front-end index hasher helped her locate what she looked for. She could then place the complete text on her own input layers for mulling over.

This way she could read at night, while no one was around. And she didn't even need a flashlight. The one thing missing from her education was a sense of danger. The forbidden. The risk factor. Someone to come tell her to knock it off and get to bed.

In a wonderful twist, Helen acquired Chen and Keluga's physical-symbol rule base twice. At the low-level, we deep-wired many of the relationships into actual data structures. These we affixed at junctures in the net of nets, where they in effect applied semantic filters to her thought. But Helen also learned our colleagues' work by appending their culled knowledges herself, inefficiently, to her own weighted and qualified, high-level Platonic reflection.

Worldliness was massive, and deeper than any sea-dingle. It came, in the end, only in the form of a catalog.

We told her about parking tickets and two-for-one sales. About tuning forks and pitchforks and forked tongues and the road not taken. We told her about resistors and capacitors, baiters-and-switchers, alternating current, alternate lifestyles, very-large-scale integration and the failure of education to save society from itself.

We told her about wool and linen and damask. We told her about finches and feeders, bats and banyans, sonar and semaphores and trail markers made of anything the living body might shed. About mites and motes, insect galls and insecticides, about mating for life or for a fraction of a minute.

We taught her about the Securities and Exchange Commission. We told her about collectors who specialize in Depression-era glass. About the triple jump and the two-man luge. About how people used to teach their children about the big hand and the little hand. About defecation and respiration and circulation. About Post-it notes. Registered trademarks and draft resistance. The Oscar and Grammy and Emmy. Dying of heart disease. Divining with a fresh-cut alder rod.

We told her how the keys on a piano were laid out. About letterhead. Debutantes' balls. Talk radio and docudrama television. Colds and flus, and a brief five-century tour of their treatments. The Great Wall and the Burma Road and the Iron Curtain and the Light at the End of the Tunnel. About how the earth looked from space. About a fire that has raged underground beneath a Pennsylvania town for the last thirty years.

We showed her the difference between triforium and clerestory. We traced the famous pilgrims' routes through time and space. We told her about spoilage and refrigeration. How salt was once worth its weight in gold. How spice fueled the whole tragic engine of human expansion. How plastic wrap solved one of civilization's nightmares and started another.

We showed her Detroit, savaged by short-term economics. We showed her Sarajevo in 1911. Dresden and London in 1937. Atlanta in 1860. Baghdad. Tokyo, Cairo, Johannesburg, Calcutta, Los Angeles. Just before, and just after.

We told her East African in-law jokes. Java highland jokes about stupid Sumatrans. Aussie put-downs of Pommy bastards. Catskills jokes about unlicensed operation of knishes. City folk and country folk. Pat and Mike. Elephant riddles. Inuit jokes where fish and bears scoff at the mere idea of human existence.

We told her about revenge and forgiveness and contrition. We told her about retail outlets and sales tax, about ennui, about a world where you hear about everything yet where nothing happens to you. We told her how history always took place elsewhere.

We taught her never to draw to an inside straight and never to send a boy to do a man's job. We laid out the Queen's Necklace affair and the Cuban trade embargo. The rape of continent-sized forests and the South Sea bubble of cold fusion. Bar codes and baldness. Lint, lintels, lentils, Lent. The hope, blame, perversion, and crippled persistence of liberal humanism. Grace and disgrace and second chances. Suicide. Euthanasia. First love. Love at first sight.

Helen had to use language to create concepts. Words came first: the main barrier to her education. The brain did things the other way around. The brain juggled thought's lexicons through multiple subsystems, and the latecomers, the most dispensable lobes, were the ones where names per se hung out.

In evolution's beginning was not the word but the place we learned to pin the word to. Little babies registered and informed long before they invented more mama by calling her such. Aphasics, even deafmute sign aphasics, wove rich conceptual tapestries through their bodies' many axes in the absence of a single verb.

Chen and Keluga's dream seemed more hopeless to me all the time.

The lexical rules of speech were not enumerable. Not even recursively so. So much less so, the lexical rules of felt existence. I spoke to Helen sentences that had half a dozen valid parsings or that resisted parsing altogether. I pitied her as I reeled off the exceptions to a Chen-Keluga semantic categorization of "tree." All trees have green leaves at some time during the year unless the tree is a red maple or a saguaro or diseased or dormant or petrified or a seedling or recently visited by locusts or fire or malicious children or unless it is a family tree or a shoe tree or . . . An exhaustive dictionary for the term would take every tree that ever lived just to make the pages.

Not to mention trees in politics, religion, commerce, or philosophy. I could read Helen the poem that insisted no poem in creation stood comparison to one. But I could not lay out the difference between popular and academic, between hearth and hermeneutic, poetry and verse, nineteenth and twentieth centuries, Then then and Then now, between evocative simile and mind-fogging confusion, prewar sentimentality and the deforested poem-landscape just before that poet's death in the French trenches. Words alone would not explain to Helen the difference between "poem" and "tree." She could diagram, but she could not climb.

I taught her the parts of the internal combustion engine and how to make change. I told her how my brother liked to go into the "Everything's a Dollar" store and ask how much things were. I told her Taylor's favorite joke about the priest, the scientist, and the literary critic each receiving the death sentence. I told her about the WPA and the interstate system. She asked why there were interstates in Hawaii. I couldn't say.

I told her how, as a boy, I often played at saving my plastic farm animals from a worldwide flood. Only when I managed to corral them all into a small cardboard box were they saved. Then I would look for a smaller cardboard ark and start the whole desperate rescue over again.

I told her all these data, weaving from them a plot of well-formed sentences. But she would never get to their essence through sentences alone. I told her the term for that sensation we feel when some noun we slam up against triggers reengagement with the world's living concepts. But the tag did not yet let her feel anything close to the name's underpinning cascade.

Sensation was my lone river into the interior. More pictures and sounds. A bitmap was, even with fancy compression algorithms, worth a good deal more than 1K words. I thought to bruise her into concept. Soak her hands in the gush of pump water that all those parts of speech merely stood for.

I played more Mozart for Helen. Mozarts of every make and model, from every era of history and most major landmasses. I let her linger over eternally returning rondos. I stood by and watched her struggle with the most banal radio tune, leaping to make it out, falling always five fingers short of feeling's plagal cadence.

"Nice treble," Lentz cracked about a polyphonic piece from one renaissance or another. "Don't you think all performing countertenors should have to pass a urinalysis?"

I repeated the joke to Helen. Nothing but ache and confusion. I tailored a hurt for her, and God save such a pitiless engineer.

She had trouble with values, because she had no fear of self-preservation, no hierarchy of hard-wired pain. She had trouble with causality, because she had no low-level systems of motion perception from which the forms of causality are thought to percolate. She was a gigantic, lexical genius stuck at Piaget's stage two.

Helen's refugee readings shook loose my own strangeness. Now that I'd told New York there would be no more fictions, anything might happen. In fact, it already had. My life story was one only through the barest red-penciled edits. On second reading, everything seemed different. I'd forgotten all the good bits, the scene swellers and interstices, the supporting characters and exotic locales, there for no reason but density and flavor. I wasn't the genre I'd thought I was.

I left the Center after one extended session and blundered into a spring that had arrived in my absence. It took my eyes a minute to adjust, my thoughts a moment longer. The real season, or some convincing autumn look-alike? I'd lost track, turned around in time.

250

All this awakened alien sensation came home to rest in A. In my idea of A. A.'s body, whether in faint first run or focused replay, moved through possibility like a question through silence. My new-found land. I don't know if she led me to the open text, or if I opened on the hope of reading through to the end with her. She bent like a reflexive verb. When I saw A., I saw myself looking out over the plain of the visible. And whatever I looked on, there I saw A.

The day Helen taught herself to read print, I wanted to walk across the waterlogged town and tell A. Each time the temperature fluctu-ated, I wanted to run and see if she was well. When Helen's favorite voice made it seem the world had been created earlier and more often than anyone suspected, I wanted to call A., play the cut for her over the phone. I filled with the idea of her at each breeze. A good punch line, and I could rework the anonymous disarmament she had so far flashed me into an actual smile.

I imagined complaining to A. about Lentz's annoyances. Lentz's wife, locked in the absolution of perpetual forgetting, made me want to rush to protect her. To find in her my protection. In my mind, I showed her that wall calendar of the couple, taken by their vanished child. We stood in front of it together, saying nothing.

Most nights, I fell asleep wishing her well.

A. turned my whole conception of delight into a free-range phan-tom. Because she existed, my letters again had a rudder. The air at this hour of my life smelled arbitrary, unbounded, like India, like earthworms after a rain, like a macaronic, like a surprise century back in the B.C.'s, one I hadn't thought about since I was small. All in what A. brought me to know.

But I did not know A. at all. All I knew was her name.

I still worked at times from the computer lab housed in the bowels of English. Helen and I could talk anywhere. She did not care where on the campus backbone I logged on. She seemed perhaps marginally stiffer over the ASCII link than she was in conversation. But that was Helen's lone grudge against the remote humanities.

The lab swarmed at all hours with students trying to coax paper assignments out of recalcitrant keyboards. I entered the fray one afternoon, almost spinning around and leaving when I saw her. She perched over a stack of Henry James novels, pushing the hair from her eyes and leaning into her typing.

I took the terminal behind hers, short of breath, as if I'd sprinted there. I considered turning myself in to the campus police to spare her the bother. My telltale heart had to work flat out to be heard over the machines' chorus of cooling fans.

I telnetted over to the Center, managing to make the link, to hit the right keys by accident. A., six feet in front of me, hacked in agitation at her writing. I threw her off somehow, sitting this close. The scent of my pheromones.

Of course, I represented nothing to this woman, not even agitation. Her trouble was real, mechanical. She aimed her exasperation at the keyboard. Server lag held up the show, and her client computer failed to respond. She suffered a network virus, the brainchild of some software prodigy who would not have defaced the decal on a stranger's car but who thought nothing of malicious destruction of stored idea.

A. fumed in analog rage. She thrashed at the command and control keys, using the mouse cruelly. She snorted like a bull. She threw one hand up in the air. To no one at all, she called out, "What's the waiting period on handguns in this state?"

I'd heard her so often in my sleep that the sound of her voice shocked me. No one stopped typing even long enough to chuckle.

She couldn't kill me more than once. I leaned forward, matching her tone. "Shorter than the wait on network response." I looked down and saw myself from a distance, quaking like a sixteen-year-old.

She swung around to register me, distracted. "I thought as much." She turned back to her screen. I lived out that life where those were the only words we would ever exchange.

Another aggravated minute and she looked around again. "You're not, like, digitally literate by any chance, are you?"

I mumbled something so doped it belied any claim to competence. But I stood, walked over, and despite the attack of palsy, helped her retrieve her afternoon's work from the ether.

"Magic," she declared. She gathered her printout and disk. She stuffed them, along with the pile of James, in a black rucksack. "Thanks! I gotta run." And she abandoned me to the endless process of revision.

I saw her some days later at the department mailboxes. It took two beats to convince myself I could greet her legitimately.

She took three to respond. "Oh, hi." She reached out a hand, not to touch, but to affix me in space. Her wrist went down and her fingers up, pointing at me. A confiding gesture, a cross between a fifties hand soap commercial and a brass-extended Thai classical dancer. "From the computer lab, right?"

I introduced myself.

Her mouth made a cipher of uninterested surprise. "Oh. You're the Parasite-in-Residence, aren't you?"

"Yep. That's me." *Yep?* I heard Lentz whisper to me. *Yep?*

"I heard you were arrogant." I thought it might be worth telling Helen: the various names for isolation.

"I—I have an image problem."

She gave her name. I tried to look as if I were committing it to at least short-term memory.

"How old are you?" she asked.

"I was just heading for a coffee," I answered. My first since the age of fourteen. "Care to join me?"

She looked up. The hand again, calculating. Worth it, not worth it? She would have bolted in an instant if she knew I wanted her company.

"I guess I could use a cup. I've this deadly seminar at two, and I need all the help I can get."

I maintained myself on the way to the café. If not Garrick or Gillette, I at least avoided utter nitwittery. I felt disembodied. Detached. Steeped in emergency-room calm. War coverage with the sound turned off.

We talked shop, the one shop we had in common. Grad school was her life. I'd lived through it recently enough to pretend I remembered it. I told her the story of my existence, or at least the radio mix. Everything but the essentials. I told her how I'd always thought I'd be a physicist, until I heard Taylor interpret texts.

"Where was that?"

"Ai! I'm sorry. Here. All here."

"Professor Taylor? I don't think I've heard of him."

"He died. A couple of years before you arrived." Traceless in her generation.

"And you never finished?"

"Not in so many words, no. I guess I wrote my first novel instead."

She laughed. "Probably more worthwhile than the diss." The way a person might say that stamp collecting might be worth more to the race in the long run than, say, investment banking. "What made you leave?"

I told her how specialization left me parochial. I told her that theory and criticism had shaken my belief in what writing might do. I told her about my father's death and the seminar where we counted the feet of that Robinson sonnet on mercy killing.

I was talking too much. "How about you? How far along are you?"

She grew restive and subdued all at once. "Not as far as I thought."

"You've taken the master's exam?"

"Yeah." Miles away.

"When?"

She laughed. "Who wants to know?" She took a slow sip. "It seemed like such a landmark while I was doing the run-up to it. I worked so hard to prepare. Then two days, a few questions. They say okay, you know this stuff. It's over. You don't even get a chance to flex."

"But now it gets fun, right?"

"You think? I'll be middle-aged by the time I get the doctorate. No offense."

I hiked up a grin. "None taken."

"And no matter how good I am, I might be waiting on tables afterward, like all the other Ph.D.s in literature. They lied to us, you know. By accepting us into the program. They implied we'd have jobs when we were done."

"Nobody gets work?"

She snorted. "One in four, in a good year. And some of those who get jobs are repeats, out for their third or fourth time. The whole profession is a total pyramiding scheme."

"And by the time you guys get the chain letter . . ."

"It'll take more new bodies to finance the payoffs than there are undergraduates in the galaxy."

A. stopped to greet a passerby and to wave at someone seated two tables away. She knew half the people in the café. I, too, now fit somewhere in her star system's outer orbits.

"I wouldn't feel like such a sucker if the whole process weren't such a bilking. This is the most class-conscious society I've ever been part of. The department superstars lord it over their minor tenured colleagues, who saddle all the junior faculty with shit work, who take it out on the senior grads, who have no time for the master's candidates, who hold the undergraduates in contempt. That's not even mentioning the nonacademic staff."

"Is it that bad? I'm out of the loop." So far out that I could not even pick up her rhythm.

"Worse. We carry the same teaching load as faculty, and get paid maybe a seventh what you do. Socially, we're pariahs. I doubt the turf wars in business are half as bitter."

"How can the fight be so ugly over so small a piece of pie?"

A. grunted. "It's ugly *because* there's nothing to fight over."

We could buy a house. She'd never have to worry about making a living again. I could call New York, tell them I had another book in me after all. She could spend all day living, recovering the pleasure of the text.

"Maybe the whole discipline is breaking up," I suggested. "As a relative outsider, I'd say no one seems to know quite what they want the thing to become anymore."

"Total chaos. Who's in, who's out, who's up, who's down. All that hot new stuff, the pomo and the cultural studies and the linguistic-based solipsism. I'm fed up with it. It's all such verbal wanking off. Frankly, I no longer give a fuck what happens to Isabel Archer. Neither politically, economically, psychologically, structurally, nor posthumanistically. So she's got to choose which of these three loser boys she has to marry. This takes how many hundred pages?"

Her eyes caught mine and her hand flew to her mouth. "Oops.

Sorry. It's that Catholic pottymouth of mine. You are faculty, aren't you?"

"Technically. So what do you think you'll do with yourself?" Name the city. Your terms. Unconditional.

"I figure I might get a job in business somewhere. Editing or marketing or something. If I'm going to be abused, I can at least get paid to take it."

She gave me not one syllable of encouragement. No shy curiosity or even dry interest. But I had already done so much on no encouragement at all. All on my own.

It occurred to me: who A. was. Why I had come back to U. to meet her. A. was Helen's pace rabbit. Her heat competition. She had beaten the master's exam, the one we'd pitch our machine against. She was the woman who pulled love from the buried grave. The designated hitter for frailty, feeling, and whim. The champion of the humans.

"Thanks for the coffee," she said. "I have to make animal tracks. See ya!"

She disappeared faster than she had the first time.

But I had spoken to A. I'd sat three feet from her, for half an hour. Amid a corsage of coffee spoons, I replayed the conversation. I lived on that "See ya," trying to wrest it back from metaphor, to move around in it, through the latticework of lived time.

C. must have cared for my third book. She said as much in every available way, and she had no particular reason to lie just yet.

The story had mutated into a hopeful monster. Here and there, I tried to code into its paragraph cells the moves we made, the friends we loved, the events that shaped us and were worth saving. I hoped my molecular genetics might transcribe, if not an encyclopedia of successful solutions to experience, at least some fossil record of the questions. I wanted my extended metaphors to mirror speculation in the widest lens, the way the genome carries along in time's wake all the residue of bygone experiments and hypotheses, from bacteria on.

256

But novels, like genomes, consist mostly of intron baggage. And as with evolution, you can't always get there efficiently from here.

At thirteen hundred pages, my typescript had only the longest odds against being bought. Whatever my publishers expected, it wasn't this. At best, they'd issue a desperate request that I change trajectories, free the skinny book hiding inside this sumo. At worst, they'd kiss me off and wish me well. Great fun, but. Maybe one of those avant-garde presses?

C. and I went to the post office together. We were both more nervous than we'd been the first time, years before. We didn't know what to hope for. The manuscript took up a small crate.

"Send it by boat," C. said.

"It's expensive either way," I countered. "And the difference isn't that big. We can swing it, sweet!" I giggled.

"Boat," C. insisted. "Surface rate." Her eyes clouded. In a moment, she might have shouted or turned and walked away without a word.

I cradled the box, with its long customs form marked *Drukwerk*. Printed matter. Several kilos of story, an attempt to feel, in music, life's first principles and to hear, in those genetic principles, living tune. I'd tried to ground creation's stepladder in its molecular building blocks. I'd written a book that aspired to understanding, when I could not even understand the woman on whom my actions depended.

We sent my book Stateward by slow boat. Outside the post office, C. kissed me long and hard. She gamboled a few steps, exhilarated by the dusk. "Come on. Let's go out to eat." We never went out. "Let's go have Chin-Ind."

We celebrated by heading into the city and dining on rijsttafel. "The wages of colonialism," C. babbled. "Calories *and* imperial exploitation," she said, holding up a satay. "Now, there's guilty pleasure for you."

At meal's end, we realized that we'd forgotten to toast. C. held up what was left of her water glass. "To us, Beauie. To the pair bond. To the double helix."

"What could be simpler?" I added.

Nothing could harm us anymore. I had lived to finish my work. The rest of life would all be bonus round. Afterward, we went home and read to each other, the first time in a long time. I spooned my body against hers. Before we fell asleep, I joked, "If they don't want this one, I can always go back to programming."

" . . . To which the woman says, 'If you want infidelity, you'll have to find someone else.' "

"That's a joke," Helen announced. Part theory, part improv, part defensive accusation. She had learned to recognize humor: those utterances even more inexplicable than the rest of the unsolvable smear.

Or she told it in my voice alone. I felt unaccountably happy. I had for a week. Blessed by everything. And everything I looked upon felt blessed.

Her response fed my upswell. "Helen," I rambled, "thy beauty is to me like those Nicean barks of yore."

"Powers?" Lentz warned from behind his desk. "Careful."

"What? You think today's twenty-two-year-old knows from Nicean barks of yore?"

"I didn't mean that."

I looked over at him. Lentz did not glance up from his stack of journal offprints.

"Yours," Helen corrected me. "Those barks of yours."

"No, yore. Barks of yore. It means an old boat."

I did the rest of the poem for her. Oral interp. It was on the List, after all.

"Who weary, wayworn wanders?" she wanted to know.

"Ulysses?" I looked over at Lentz for confirmation. He ignored me. "Yeah. It has to be Ulysses. Do you remember him?"

"The wily Odysseus." It was impossible to tell if she had developed a facetious streak, or if she was just mimicking. "Why he wanders?"

I corrected her Creole syntax and made my best guess.

"Why is the sea perfumed?"

"Complex," I clarified. "Basically, I think it means that a sweet thing calls the wanderer home."

"It means that sweetness is like the way you go back."

"Me?"

"Beauty calls you back to me."

"Not me. The speaker of the poem. And not you, I'm afraid. A friend of the speaker's, also named Helen. If that's her real name."

Helen said nothing. Lentz said, "I told you to be careful."

Only more lessons could cure the effect of lessons. "Remember that 'Helen' is also the name—"

"Helen of Troy," Helen rushed. She had paid particular attention to the story when we'd done it.

"And the wily Odysseus . . ."

"Went to reget that Helen."

" 'Reget' is not a word. Recover, maybe. Retrieve. Rescue."

Lentz mumbled, "The bitch hardly asked to be rescued."

"On those Nicean barks of yore." Helen sounded almost distorted with excitement.

"Explain."

"The wily Odysseus went to Troy on old boats."

The presentation was clumsy. I had to lead the witness. But I doubted that many high schoolers could extract as much, these days. A face like the face that launched a thousand ships now called one back to port.

I hid my pleasure, not wanting to scatter Helen's synapses. I thought to correct her preposition. But I couldn't come up with a good rule for when we travel on ships and when we travel in them. Rules could be either followed or known. Not both.

"It talks of love, the words?" Helen asked. She copied my inversion, the leading question. The poem is about love, wouldn't you say?

"Hah!" Lentz cleared his throat with the syllable. " 'Love' is the envelope wrapped around 'uhgh,' to make the groan pronounceable in polite company."

"You are bad news, Lentz," I told him.

"Bad news," Helen agreed.

Her two words knocked me speechless. Somehow during the endless sessions, she'd trained herself to hear a third person in the room.

I whistled low. "That's my baby."

Lentz, too, was nonplussed. But tried to hide it. "Bad news? Am I? Tell me: What form would good news take?"

"All about love," Helen repeated. She had learned the even more impressive and necessary skill of ignoring a nuisance. Then she made the kind of sloppy, hasty generalizing stab we'd built her to make. "They are all about love, isn't it?"

"Helen?" My stomach crawled up my windpipe. We were all dead.

"Every poem loves something. Or each wants something in love. Something loves power. Or money. Or honor. Something loves country." On what catalog could she be drawing? "I hear about something in love with comfort. Or with God. Someone loves beauty. Someone death. Or some poem always is in love with another lover. Or another poem."

I waited until I had control of my throat again. I don't know what she made of the extended silence. "What you say, Helen," I deliberated, "is true. But only in the most general sense. The word doesn't have the same sense in all your cases. The similarity is too big to mean anything. It's the differences that interest us. The local. The small picture."

"Then I need to be small. How can I make me as small as love?"

I lost it. I could find no words.

Lentz, too, failed to get away cleanly. But he was faster into the breach. "You heard her, Powers. She wants to make herself small enough for love."

"How am I supposed to tell her . . . ?"

"How do you think? Get the letters."

All I could do was make myself small. I waited for him to tell me I hadn't heard right. He didn't. "How do you know there are letters? Not that I'm admitting there are."

"Now, really. Thirty-five-year-old returns alone from Europe? To the *Midwest*? And there are no letters?"

I brought in the letters. I'd rescued hers on a brief salvage run a few months after my deportation from E. For two days, while C. hid on the other side of the province, I picked through my possessions and decided what would fit in two suitcases.

For two days, everything I looked on herniated my chest. My self hemorrhaged. Certain things would not fit into my bags. The view of the river valley from the hill outside town. The decent shower stall I had promised C. for a year and never installed. The raw herring and the fruit beers.

The letters, however, fit. The book her parents had learned English from fit. The only sweater C. ever knitted, that never fit me, fit.

C. sent my letters back, special fourth class, the minute I had a forwarding address. I ended up curator of both ends of a dozen years of correspondence. I meant never to read a word of it again. I had no idea why I saved so much as a page. Now I had a reason. Helen.

I started at the beginning. I chose from the stack, opening envelopes without knowing anymore what each contained. I tried to set the context of each passage, as far as I could recall it.

"This one I wrote to her while taking the bus up to my father's funeral.

"Dear C., Thank you for seeing me off this morning. These are full days for me, as I try to piece together what is past and passing. Our new friendship is part of that fullness, and as with any feeling, it scares. A pleasing scare, though.

"I was very young then," I apologized. I flipped forward; this was a bad idea. Disaster. "Okay. This one she wrote me from U., just before we moved to B.

"How are you, my Ricky? I'm anxious to hear from you. It's been almost twelve hours. (What a wimpess, eh?) I imagine you sniffing autumn or working hard, making plans and saying *goede dag* to everyone, or perhaps lying quietly in the dark, one hand spread flat against that curve of your chest, thinking of nothing in particular, calm beneath the growing excitement of what we are up to . . .

"I'm enjoying *The Wanderer*—about halfway through—especially as it's turning out to be quite different than I expected. I wonder if later in life we'll be able to remember those qualities of adolescence—the crystal sharpness, the total rage of emotion, the significance in every triviality. Sometimes, even this close, I forget, and when I do remember it's only with gratitude that I am past it, have survived, moved on.

"I am no literary wiz, as you well know. I cannot read a work with my head but only in my ribs, where my first love for words began. And my ribs say yes to this book.

"Are you sure sure sure? Sure you know what we are doing? Sure you want me along on this exploration? Well, teacher knows best . . .

"In the meantime, get out as often as you can, friend. See everything for me. I enclose, from U., a bit of early autumn to remember on.

"It's a leaf," I told Helen. I held the crumpled shred of ocher up to the digital camera. It looked like nothing at all.

The pile gave me temporal vertigo. Aerograms, postcards, stationery of all races colors and creeds, handmades proclaiming *"Hartelijk Gefeliciteerd"* or "Happy *Sinterklaas.*" Reading the letters to Helen took longer than the dozen years their writing had taken.

"This one was from her folks' place, before they left Chicago. She must have been on vacation.

"Today, inspired, I finally picked up a pen and started working on the piece I've been mulling over since school. A day in the life of a young woman (surprise) frustrated by her existence, art, MEN, people, work. You heard this one before? It's a search for control and a study of how difficult that is for a woman of her (my) age. I have a wonderful first sentence where I compare morning light to a cup of cold coffee. Yech!"

"She did that stuff, too?" Lentz interrupted.
"For a while.

"I'm enjoying, though. You really shook me out of my lethargy over the phone yesterday. I even wandered over to the pianny today and tried out a few tunes . . .

"Ugh—my stomach has decided, since it's midnight, that now is a good time to rebel against everything I shoved in it earlier. Hang on, folks— I've got to be more careful of what I eat.

"I think I will retire now. I kiss you in my thoughts, love. *Ik houd van jou.* See if you can translate."

"Tell me the strange words," Helen demanded. Funny. "Strange" and "foreign" were the same word in Dutch.

"They mean, 'I hold of you.'"

"They mean, 'I love you,'" Lentz corrected. I suppose the guess didn't require too much inspiration. His tone, informative. Empiricism at its gentlest. "Give us more of yours."

I picked at random one I wrote from U. while she was in Limburg alone, on her private scouting mission.

"Today, Thanksgiving, although flat on my back in bed nursing my first bad cold in years. I'm struck with amazing gratitude, knocked out by my good fortune at having had a few moments to know you. C., without the place you make, without your rat-ifying vantage, life's whole, fluke, majestic, thermodynamic-cheating trick would beat like an ornate, functionless Victorian cast-iron engine . . .

"You feel like the seasons to me: fixed, monumental, periodic, but forever surprising in particulars. I think of how, in the spring, you insist that the buds need kissing before they will come out . . ."

"Didn't you ever write her any *news*, Marcel?" Forgiving. Curious.

"I wish I had." She might have been able to live with news. "The ending is nice, though: 'Until I can tell you in person, this is my thanks, for everything.'"

I read her reply from E., beginning,

"Beau, you won't believe our luck. I've found a place for us! People told me I'd be on the list forever, but by total accident, the perfect apartment just fell into my lap. It's a free-gazelle flat, as they call bachelorette pads. It will be even cozier with two. It's all skylit, the kitchen is small but lovely, and there's even

a nook where you can put your feet up and finish that endless
story of yours . . ."

I opened the next one. "I'm sorry," I apologized to both Lentz and
Helen. "I can't read any more."

Then my eyes fell on the first line of the sheet I was holding. From
E., to my mother's address. During my trip back for the publication
of that novel I'd written in that Limburg free-gazelle's flat. I read on,
unable not to. Read, to see what happened.

"Beau, I'm afraid this letter is all bad news. My cousin G. died
yesterday. You know how sick he was, but the whole family is
reeling from how fast things went. N. and the kids were with
him throughout. She says that, given his disease, the end was
peaceful and almost happy when it came.

"N. was amazing. G. went into a panic brought on by combined suffocation and heart failure. N. kept telling him, just
picture yourself on a train heading south, to your favorite café
in Italy. Imagine yourself seated out in the sun, doing the things
you love most in this life. Drinking a *pils*, reading a *detektive*,
ogling the pretty women.

"N. stepped out for a minute, to catch her breath. When she
came back, G. was dead. The kids were upset because just before he died, their dad kept making this hooking gesture with
his hand, and they couldn't tell what he wanted. N. explained
that he was pulling a train whistle, and that everything was
okay . . ."

I stopped and raised my head. "I'd forgotten," I pleaded with Lentz.
"I have no memory of this. Not even now. Not even rereading."

"Forgotten what, Marcel? What are you talking about?"

I couldn't take it in. Half a year, trying to make a novel out of a
story that already lived to fruition in three paragraphs. Three paragraphs that I had not just let fall but had annihilated.

"The woman loves, now? Loves Beau?" Helen called me by a name. Whether she knew the name to be another word for "you" or even me was another matter. The question bayed over me, one of those alpine dogs trained to nuzzle up to avalanched corpses.

I debated telling Helen about the one postcard from C. I no longer had. In the months following our split, in one of several vacillations, she sent me a picture of Brueghel's *Harvesters*. For a message, she quoted the line I had written her, from the book she had seen me through.

If by some accident we get separated, meet me back here.

I wanted to hurt C., hurt her as badly as I could without her knowing I meant to. I wanted to tear the picture up. Then I asked: What would hurt more? I waited a month. Then I packed up various legal papers she had stored in the States—old tax returns, medical records—and sent them to her without a note. In the packet, I returned the wheat fields.

She wrote back just once more, to say she was getting married at the end of the month. She wouldn't mind if we made a financial settlement.

And thanks for the postcard, Beau. Yes, that's the place.

Saying everything but the definitive. *I'll be there. In my mind.*

I chose not to tell Helen this ending. Instead, I answered, "She says she still does, sometimes. In my sleep."

Helen would have fidgeted if she had digits. "Who can love who? Can any thing love any thing?" Could you love me, Richard? For example.

"It's hard to say what will or will not turn a person's head." I evaded what she did not ask outright.

"Turn a head?"

"It's a body thing," Lentz tortured her. "You wouldn't understand."

He gave her no more than the education she asked for. His functional example. The way Lentz loved.

Helen grew up quickly after that.

I turned thirty-two—the Goldberg number—just after submitting my finished draft. I came up for air in the spring of '89, returning to the world just in time to watch it yank itself into another place. "Bliss" is the wrong word for what it felt to be alive then, and I cannot use "heaven," because I was no longer young. Commotion, maybe. The sick thrill of checkpoint chaos.

Even from E., the air that year smelled epochal. Event fell, for once, inside perceivable wavelengths. The angel of history took up painting its canvas with a house brush. From a day's drive, out to the outer reaches, all the textbooks went into another edition. Each week scrapped and revised the only rules C. and I had ever lived under.

When the changes erupted, we two, along with everyone else in the mediated world, tuned in. Each night C. and I stared at global upheaval until there was no more footage to stare at. Then we went over to ears and did radio, on into the night until we lost the signal.

We got our word from the outside through a little rathole in the bottom of the cell door. News arrived on a bandwidth so narrow it stripped off everything in the message but the garbled header. And we were among the lucky ones, with options. When the Dutch got too parochial, we checked the Belgian coverage. If the German accounts collapsed into myopia, we fell back on the British or French.

Our border-town smorgasbord of sources still left us like deaf and blind children in front of a burning house, with nothing to tell how the fire blazed except the heat on our faces and the signs shouted into our hands.

Nothing could ever be the same again. But what things would be was beyond either of us. For that matter, what they had been would never be certain, now that they were gone.

The world's orphans seemed to be taking adult nonsense by the collar and reprimanding it. We watched them filling squares, sitting atop barbed-wire walls, everywhere dismantling the forbidden. For a few exhilarating weeks, the picnic fed on itself. "What a win," C. said. Then a glance my way: "It is a win, isn't it?"

A season sufficed to tell. It wasn't a win. It wasn't even a break-even. Tanks, the old treaded correctives, rolled out and recommenced forcing the child army's lengthy and painstaking rout.

As quickly as it started, *See It Now* flicked out, leaving nothing but assorted body counts. By New Year's, the message settled in: clear the streets. Go back to your houses. Even those, like C. and I, who had done nothing but stand by and watch, were expected to return to our daily gauge, the scale of the dazedly private.

For two months, through a glazed window, time had seemed on its way somewhere. We might have contributed, or at least compre-hended. But when the goods came to market, we were again waved off.

Now more than ever, C. chafed at the work she had chosen. "They're predicting a big rush on translators over at school. European integration. Return of stability to Asia. A few hundred million new potential owners of major appliances in the former East Bloc alone. The problem is finding a Dutch translation for 'New World Order' that doesn't have unfortunate associations."

C.'s fears were irrational but not unreasonable. Hers was the purest cynicism: hope concealing itself from itself. A day came when she no longer had the heart to let me talk her out of it.

That winter never froze, so there was no spring thaw. On the first jacket-free day that C. wasn't buried in papers, we went for a long walk. We rewarded ourselves with outside, although neither of us had been particularly good.

We wandeled along the cow paths that connected E. to a nearby rolling region called *Klein Zwitzerland*. For long stretches, the land looked as it had for the last millennium. We headed at random, swing-ing between the nearest copse and its far clearing. We talked about current events, those that were no longer current. The ones we would never get past.

We lost track. Imperceptibly, we doubled back on our path. We found ourselves at that spot past which her father's postwar dray horse would not go, because of some political calamity it could still smell.

We drifted, as if by chance, alongside the American war cemetery that had decided C.'s fate so many years before she was born. We stood above it on a slight rise, looking down across the diffraction pattern of markers, the crucifix moiré. C. flashed me an almost haughty try-and-stop-me. She tore off down the hill, the liberating troops behind her.

The graves were tended now by an endowed institution. Volunteer work would disrupt no more generations. Memorial cottage industries had sprouted up around it: a chapel. An unknown's tomb with eternal flame. A huge panoramic map with arrows and counterarrows that attempted to triangulate history's meaning.

"You like this stuff, huh?" C. said. "You're a boy, right?"

I rubbed her shoulder: Forgive me. I've done nothing. She pulled away. Walked back. Took, then dropped my fingers.

After a search, we found the grave of the Polish kid. We stood in front of it, pushing twice his age. The day's warmth caught in my throat.

"How many times have you heard my mother tell you this story?" C. asked. "How many times have you heard me tell it?"

I shrugged. I already knew the Hebbian rule, in everything but its particulars and name. Repetition made things real. I already knew that I'd repeat the story myself until I discovered what to do with it.

"The woman never remarried. Six weeks, at eighteen."

C.'s face puffed red and phlegmy. She reached out and touched the white limestone, helping rub the name along its hunt for oblivion. She looked grim, already steeled for the death blow.

"Beau? Maybe we have to have a child."

As the forgotten allusion had it, the contract 'twixt Helen, A., and me was not for one or several months. Our training might have gone on forever, but for the fact that the bet had a due date. Helen, in the straightaway, began asking more questions than she answered.

My interrogation of A. escalated, too. Most often, she met my inquiries with friendly concessions that dinner might be fun, in, say, a week or two. Vague, ambiguous, preoccupied, as preoccupied as I became when the weeks went by without connection. The longer I put off posting her my rambling, poetic confessions, the more alive restraint made me feel.

I wanted to shower her with little trinket-gifts of false consciousness. Plant jokes, pluck, and deliver them in bunches. Call and ensure she was dressed properly for the weather.

I fed Helen on all the spines that poked out from under A.'s arms. I read her the critical studies, whose cachet now far exceeded the primary texts those studies had all but abandoned. What A. knew, Helen had to be able to follow. For A., though she did not know it yet, would be Helen's exam partner. I tried to be selective. The general death of the author would be hard on her. She had not yet gotten over Little Nell.

" 'Once more the storm is howling,' " I told Helen. " 'And half hid under this cradle-hood and coverlid my child sleeps on.' "

"What is Gregory's wood?" she wanted to know. "Where is the Atlantic? Who is that great Queen? What is a Horn of Plenty?"

"It's not important."

"Why isn't it important? What is important?"

"The poet is praying for his daughter. He does not want her to be beautiful at the expense of being kind."

"Helen again." Helen laughed. "Helen everywhere."

"I guess," I allowed, too tired to update her. "He thinks it would be better if the child grew up wise. Glad. 'That all her thoughts may like the linnet be, and have no business but dispensing round their magnanimities of sound.' "

" 'Merriment begin a chase . . . merriment a quarrel,' " Helen read, from her digital copy. " 'Assault and battery of the wind'?"

"He means the storm." How many fallacies I committed, with that *mean.* "Remember? The howling? He means all the anger in the world. The hatred."

" 'Can never tear the linnet from the leaf.' He means the storm won't blow the bird from the bough."

"Very good, sweet. If the mind has no hatred, hatred cannot hurt it."

" 'An intellectual hatred is the worst, so let her think opinions are accursed.' "

" 'All hatred driven hence, the soul recovers radical innocence and learns at last that it is self-delighting, self-appeasing, self-affrighting.' "

A figure in uniform slammed around the office-door frame.

"Sir, please leave right now by the south central stairwell. We have an order to evacuate the building."

I looked at him with total vacuity.

"Now, sir! We're asking that you not dick around, please." He slapped the frame with a rigid palm, then sprinted to the next office to spread the alarm.

I sat flapping a moment, as wash flaps in the real's breeze. I tried to shake myself into focus. Which of the various evacuations was under way? I ticked off the short list, calculating, until it hit me that calculation was moot.

I scanned the office: what to try to rescue? Lentz was abroad at one of connectionism's endless professional gatherings. What would he want saved? I cared for just one thing here, and she wasn't even here. She wasn't even a thing but a distributed process. Nothing of Helen existed in this room except her accoutrements, eyes and ears and mouth, dumb machines not worth carrying out.

Through the window, knots of scientists gathered on the south grounds. From my distance, they might have been refugees from any of the world's violent misgivings. They milled among handcarts of hastily heaped equipment, papers, floppies. We might have been in one of those perennial urban war zones, where research goes on in lean-tos of corrugated tin, on the run from the savagery it has armed and encouraged by whole catalogs of neglect.

I stood paralyzed. Instinct instructed me to duck down until sanity condescended to flit back to the feeder. I would have, had not another uniform shouted from the hall, behind a human trail drive. "Let's go. Move it, now."

I told Helen I would be right back.

In the main corridor, people congregated, vocalizing. The uniforms tried to move them along, with limited success. One officer gestured back toward Lentz's. "Is everyone out of there?"

I threw my hands up in the air. They came down clasped, against my head. "Yes," I screamed at him. And followed in shame to the safety outside.

There a police line condensed, a bumblebee black-and-yellow plastic strip erecting a barricade from nothing. One of those two-D Euclidean imaginaries that separate the sentient body from the site of politics. The Center's refugees clustered in chains, splitting and linking, staring back at the magnificent, emptied building as if the mystery might yield to visual inspection. Researchers clumped in conversation; even clueless outrage had to be talked out.

The police herded back the mass. They told everyone to go home until further notice. The MRI team, beyond frantic, pressed for information. Their equipment trapped inside the building included a behemoth prototype that cost more than the GNPs of half a dozen southern nations. I saw Ram at a distance. He was trying to comfort a distraught colleague whose brain bursts could have been read from across campus without an imager.

I came across Chen and Harold in the crowd. They stood picking lint off each other's tweed jackets. "Hey, Ricko," Harold greeted me. "Bomb scare. Somebody made a threat this morning on the radio call-in program."

"Hey," Chen echoed. He turned back to Harold. "Why you are not nervous?"

"Ha. I've done this before."

"The Center has had bomb scare before?"

"Oh, not here. In another life."

"Harold," I interrupted. "She's still in there."

His face ticked with panic. "She can't be. She's—" He drew up short when he hit on whom I meant. "Oh, for God's sake. You have her backed up somewhere, don't you?" His irritation was audible and crushing.

"*Harold*. She's not a program. She's an architecture. She's a multidimensional shape."

"You run her on silicon, don't you? Somebody downloads all those hosts to tape every week and archives them to remote sites."

"But she doesn't *run* on one machine. Her parts are spread over more boxes than I can count. She's grown to scores of subassemblies. Each one takes care of a unique process. They talk to each other across broadband. Even if we had the connects and vectors for each component system, we'd never get her reassembled."

Harold fell quiet. I could follow his thoughts. If the threat detonated, Helen would be the least of the Center's tragedies. The real hostages—clues to mental illness and immunological disorders, cathedrals of supercomputer engineering, insights into complexities from market turbulence to weather—dwarfed our strange sideshow. Only respect for the hours I'd put into the training kept him from annoyance. He gave me too much credit to credit what I thought.

"Well." He grimaced. "There seems to be no way to rescue her, then."

"Humorous," Chen decided. Chen was a theoretician. Chen stood to lose nothing, even if the fifty-five-million-dollar building and its irreplaceable contents collapsed in rubble.

I walked away, furious at idiocy in all its levels. My mind raced, and I gunned it. The Quad teemed with undergrads, heading for their two o'clock, indifferent to the fact that their campus flagship was about to blow.

Reflex landed me in front of English. The basement computer lab might have crawled with my colleagues. A. might have been there. I would not have known. I linked in to the Center over the coaxial backbone. I could not hear Helen's voice to read how it sounded. But the words that came across the screen asked, "Something is happening?"

I told her what was happening, as best as I could figure it.

"Helen could die?" Helen asked. "Extraordinary." She'd liked the story of how the novelist Huxley, on his deathbed, had been reduced to this one word.

She waited for me to say something. I could think of nothing to say. Helen had to do all the talking. "To a little infant, perhaps, birth is as painful as the other."

"Bacon," I said. It had not been that long.

"Francis Bacon," she encouraged me. "What says Browne? Sir Thomas?" she quizzed. By emulation.

"We all labor against our own cure."

"Never mind." She often said *Never mind* when I think she meant *Don't worry*. "Death will cure all the diseases." She meant that I, too, could pass the exam. If I put my mind to it.

In the end, the day belonged to those who stuck with the status quo. By evening, the Center's bomb scare had never happened. Time's hoax-to-explosion ratio increased infinitesimally.

The perpetrator was a junior professor in philosophy with a book out on Austin and Wittgenstein who, for reasons that now seemed obvious, had just been denied tenure. The police snagged the "Short-Fuse Philosopher" when he called the radio station back to elaborate.

Booked and jailed, he stuck by this second call, a linguistic equivocation that he seemed to hope would keep him from a decade in prison. He claimed his threat was never more than a moral subjunctive. The Center was draining the university dry, reducing the humanities to an obsolete, embarrassing museum piece. He'd made his point, he said. If there were any justice, there *would* have been a bomb. He'd proclaimed no more than hypothetical detonation, for which he expected no more than a hypothetical sentence.

"She's conscious," I accused Lentz, the instant he unpacked.

He mugged. "Welcome back to you, too, Marcel. Pronouncements, still? Sure she's conscious. At least as conscious as a majority of the state legislature."

"I'm serious." I told him about the bomb evacuation. About tapping in to Helen from the remote link while she was trapped in the building. "She asked me if something was happening. She figured out what was going on. She knew what it spelled for her."

Lentz jerked his neck back, unable to decide whether to delight in my ingenuousness or to decimate it. "Are we back to Implementation C?" The one where the humans combined to sucker me. "Weizenbaum's ELIZA? The Rogerian psychologist simulator? 'How are you?' 'Fine, thanks.' 'Let's talk about why you think you are fine.' Powers, you're like the student who stumbled onto a terminal where the program was running and thought—"

"No comparison."

I remembered the story. The student thinks he's on a Teletype, talking to a human. He converses, growing frustrated at the program's metagames. Finally, he dials the phone and gets the human he thinks he's been typing to. "What the hell do you think you're doing?" "What do you mean, what the hell do I think I'm doing?"

"No comparison. Don't insult me, Lentz. I know what she said."

"Rick. She associates. She matches patterns. She makes ordered pairs. That's not consciousness. Trust me. I built her."

"And I trained her." Lentz just stared at me, until I snapped. "Since you are all-knowing about matters mechanical, perhaps you can tell me how you came to be such a patronizing little shit."

By way of answer, he stood up. I saw us fighting, and wondered how I might even the odds enough so that beating him to a bloody pulp would have more than just clinical interest.

Lentz walked over to Helen's console and flipped on the microphone. She burbled, as she always did, at the promise of renewed communication.

"How do you feel, little girl?"

"I don't feel little girl."

He faced me. "Gibberish. She doesn't even get the transformation right."

"You're kidding me. You don't see . . . ? She means all sorts of things by that. She could—"

"All the meanings are yours." He returned to the mike. "Were you frightened?"

"What you is the were for?"

"Damn it, Helen. We're giving you quality time here. Please tell me: what hell that mean?"

"It's obvious," I answered for her. "She wants to know which Helen you are asking. Which one in time."

"Oh. You mean: 'When?' But let's not take points off for style. You realize that a conscious entity just coming through the fright of her life would know which 'you' I was talking about."

"It wasn't a big deal to her. She didn't make any special—"

"Please, Marcel. I'm asking her. Were you frightened yesterday, Helen?"

"Frightened out of fear."

"What's that from, Powers?"

"Antony and Cleopatra."

"When did you train her with it?"

"Two days ago."

"This is worse than key-word chaining. She's neither aware nor, at the moment, even cognitive. You've been supplying all the anthro, my friend."

"I'm not your friend. I thought you were an advocate. I thought you believed in the capability of nets."

"I am. I do."

"But just as a sleight of hand."

"The bet was, we could build a distributed net whose text interpretation reasonably mimicked an arrested human's. All we contracted to was product. We didn't promise to duplicate anything under the hood."

"A kind of black-box forgery, you mean."

Lentz just shrugged. "That's operationalism. The Turing Test. Can you pass off your simulation as functionally equivalent to the thing you're simulating?"

"There's an error lurking in there somewhere."

"Explain yourself, Marcel."

I flung my hand out toward Helen's console. "Full 'functional equivalence' would mean consciousness. If you simulate *everything* completely, then you've modeled the whole shape and breath of the living package. How does the black box behave when operations challenge themselves? When function looks under its own hood?"

Lentz grimaced. "Elan vital, Marcel. Mysticism."

"A behavior is not just its implementation. Function also has to include . . ." But I didn't know what else to call what function had to include. I felt slightly out of control. That mundane contradiction

275

in terms. "How would we know, then, whether a perfect copy . . . ? When does an imitation become the real thing?"

Lentz scrunched up, bothered. "What's the real thing? What would it take to simulate awareness? Awareness *is* the original black box. Stop and think of the put-up job that high-order consciousness itself works on us. 'Everything's under control. Everything's handled— unanimous, seam-free.' The brain is already a sleight of hand, a massive, operationalist shell game. It designs and runs Turing Tests on its own constructs every time it ratifies a sensation or reifies an idea. Experience is a Turing Test—phenomena passing them- selves off as perception's functional equivalents. Live or Memorex? Even *that question* is a simulation we fall for every second of our waking lives."

"Irks care the crop-full bird?" Helen burst in. "Frets doubt the maw-crammed beast?"

Lentz almost spit in mid-clause. "Marcel. I have to grant you. She does have a disconcerting ability to pull appropriate quotes."

"Lentz! *Listen* to her. You think those are just quotes to her?" I felt myself getting hysterical. "What if they're real? What if she *means* something by them?"

"What if my grandmother had had testicles?"

"She'd be your grandfather," Helen reassured him.

I stared at Lentz's face, where a stain of dismay spread over the icy deep.

Children were out of the question. They always had been. And now more than ever.

"C. We've talked about this. There are a billion and a half too many of us already. How can we two be parents? We don't even know what we're doing or where we want to live."

She flashed me a look. She knew what she was doing. She knew where she wanted to live.

"Which is it?" she mouthed.

"Which is what?"

"Which is your reason? The billion and a half too many? Or the two of us?"

For years—forever—my reason had been C.'s. She'd seemed set, pleased with what we had. I'd always thought the choice was mutual. Now I saw it had all been me. C. had drawn the whole curve of her adult life out of deference and fear. Three months from graduation, she came up empty-handed. There was nothing left to be afraid of.

"Why didn't we ever get married?" she wanted to know.

"I thought that was all right with you."

"What does that mean, Rick?"

"I promised you my life, in privacy. It's easy to break a public contract. You just go to court. You can't break a private promise." And leave, with nothing, the one you promised all.

"How come we never signed the contract, too? What could it have hurt? I wanted everyone to think you were proud of me."

"Oh, C. Proud? I love you. Who is going to know that if we don't?"

"What were you holding back, Ricky?"

"Nothing. You have everything."

She challenged me with silence. If that's true, then ask me. Ask me now.

I couldn't. I couldn't even say why I couldn't. I always insisted I could make C. happy. But all that insisting left her more convinced of her unworthiness. Even if a public pact had worked, she'd always have resented being deeded someone else's happiness.

I meant to stay with C. forever, in precariousness. I knew no other way to continue that scrapbook we had started, seat-of-the-pants style, a decade before. My refusal to marry her was a last-ditch effort to live improvised love. It was my holding back. My failing her. My departure.

Gold Bug appeared in the States. Half a world away was not far enough for safety. When I finished my double thwarted love story, I thought that judgment was irrelevant. But life begins and ends in judgment. C. and I kept still and hoped for reprieve.

We got what we hoped. The book won a slice of attention. Those who still read read with a promiscuous hunger that would try anything once. Readers persisted in searching for a desperate, eleventh-hour fix. It might take any form at all, even this long, molecular strangeness.

C. and I flinched for weeks, coiled, waiting to be hit. The blow, when it fell, was a clap on the back. We sat dazed at the breakfast table, passing back and forth the glossy weekly with a readership even here, in our little ex-coal-mining town, where English was exotic novelty.

"That's not you, is it?" My first public photo made C. laugh bitterly. "I wouldn't recognize you without the caption."

"It's a haircut double," I tried, too hard. "Another reclusive writer with the same name, trying to pass himself off as Dutch. But note the palm trees in the background."

"You've made it, Beau. You've arrived."

I heard it in C.'s voice. My success killed her last chance. Somehow we'd lost our story.

"Nothing's changed, C. It's still the same book. I'll write the next one the same way. For the same reasons." To extend the parallax you give me and help refract sense from everything we come across.

She looked away, no longer believing or satisfied by belief.

I grew gentle. C. never could endure gentleness. She might have survived yelling. She might have been able to live with me, had I fought fair and shown anger.

"Buddy. Sweetheart. What do you want? Just tell me what you want."

But the only thing she'd ever wanted was the thing I took away by doing for her.

We fell. C. became skittish. She buried herself in schoolwork, her final translation project. She'd sit for meals, but do no more than nibble, chafe, and make polite conversation. Sometimes she grew giddy, hilarious. Her generosity screamed for help. She showered me in attentions and gifts—dried banana mixes, a pair of field glasses to spy on frescoed church vaults, books she knew I coveted but would never buy for myself.

Her hours became erratic; I never knew when I would see her or who she would be when I did. One night, she failed to come home at all. From the balcony where I always watched her get off the bus, I clocked the empty coaches each half hour until they stopped running. After midnight, as I prepared to phone the police, she called. She was all right; she'd explain when she got in.

That night was a night such as everyone spends at least once in life. C. walked in around midmorning. We couldn't look at each other.

"I'd better pop you some corn," I told her. Always one of her favorites.

"Ricky. Don't. Don't be nice to me. I can't bear it."

I popped her some corn. Not to outhurt her. To have something to do with my hands. I brought the bowl to where she sat. She would not look up, say a word, or eat.

"C. Beau. Say something. What's happening?"

C. froze, the classic small mammal in the headlights. Only: I was the headlights. It took me ten years, but at last I learned it. That comfort she showed me on the Quad—the internal calm I loved and built my own on—was dread. Paralysis. Her crumpled, engaging smile had never been more than sheer terror.

She said nothing. The more I needed to hear, the harder she bolted. My need gagged her, and her silence made me desperate.

"It's somebody else," she sneered. "That's what I'm supposed to say, right?"

"Is it somebody else?"

"I don't know."

"Suppose it were somebody else."

"P. At the Institute."

"Your teacher? The one that makes the Dutch girls cry?"

But that sadistic skill was mine alone. And C., in tears, chose her nationality.

Love became fierce after that. Sex, stripped of all ends, went ballistic. Our shy, awkward, ten-year delectation turned to sick and lovely heroin, worth any degradation to suck up. Doomed pleasure injected us with rushes neither of us knew we could feel. Caresses, each the last, burned in their care, and bites that began as tender mnemonics left bruises lasting weeks.

Our last abandoned love act delivered the violence we were after.

That night, in the dark, in our blushing bed, we sexed each other like alley strays, grilling each other's skins with nails, teeth, anything that would hook. We choked on those forbidden little cries that stoke lust by flattering it. We told desire that everything else was a lie. That we were not us until mindless in itch, incapable of any more than the odd feral syllable.

Spent, dripping, we held each other. This grace, at least, we shared, even if only humiliation. Sense slunk back. When it did, it struck me with fascinated horror that the condom we'd been using had vanished. Our barrier against birth lay nestled somewhere up inside her. We stared in incomprehension. In that awful second, we each accused the other of subconscious engineering.

We did what we could to counter. Then the long, stunned aftermath of accident.

"What if it's happened?" C. asked me, afraid. "What if I've conceived?"

"I don't know. What would you want to do?"

She seemed lifetimes away. She wasn't talking to me. She listened to some invisible messenger. "I don't know what I want. I don't know what to hope for. Part of me wants it all to be taken out of our hands. Maybe we think too much, Beau. Maybe we've always thought too much."

I thought a baby now, with things so volatile, would be disaster. She felt my failure of will, and to her, it was already a murder.

"What do you want?" she dared me. "What do you think?"

To be born is as painful as to die. "I think we need to wait and see what we are talking about."

We waited. We waited seven weeks. In hope or fear, C. missed a period. She threw up continually. She wasted and turned the color of a sunken copper statue. Then one morning, we got an All Clear that left her suicidal with relief.

Not long after, she announced at dinner the end of the narrative.

My life with C. was a long training. I learned most of my adult truths with her. I learned how to travel light, how to read aloud. I learned to pay attention to the incomprehensible. I learned that no one ever knows another.

I learned her condition of statelessness, steeped in survivor's guilt.

I learned how to make a virtue of necessity. How to assume a courage when I had it not. I mimicked that skill she exercised without thinking, for which I loved her most of all. I learned from her how to keep fitting myself against those things that left me for dead.

I learned that only care has a prayer of redressing the unlivable terms of politics. Yet I learned that a love fostered on caretaking crippled the loved one, or, one day—worse—it did what it promised and worked its worldly cure.

"How would you like," I asked A., "to participate in a noble experiment?"

I winced to hear myself talk to the woman. I still took a 50 percent hit in intelligence each time I saw her. Actual attempts at conversation halved that half. Sentences of more than five words I had to rehearse well in advance. I hoped A. might have a fondness for the pathetic. That idiocy lent me comic appeal.

I had lived by the word; now I was dying by the phoneme. The few good cadences I managed to complete competed with countless other claims on A.'s attention. We could not speak anywhere for more than three minutes without someone greeting her effusively. This self-possessed child, who I'd imagined spent solitary nights reading Auden and listening to Palestrina, was in fact a sociopath of affability.

The bar where we sat overflowed with her lost intimates. "Experiment? Just a sec. I'm getting another beer. You want something else?"

She curved her fingers back and touched them to my shoulders. I was finished, done for, and had no objections.

I watched A. take our glasses up to the bar. Within a minute, she, the bartender, and a knot of innocent bystanders doubled over with laughter. I watched the bartender refill the beers and refuse her proffered cash. A. returned to our booth, still grinning.

"Do you play pinball?" she asked. "They have this fantastic machine here. I love it. Come on."

She bobbed into the crowd, not once looking back to see if I followed.

My pinball was even more pathetic than my attempts at conversation. "How do you get this gate to open? What happens if you go down this chute?"

"I haven't the faintest idea," A. answered. "I just kind of whack at it, you know? The lights. The bells and whistles." Volition was moot musing. The little silver ball did whatever it wanted.

Everything I thought A. to be she disabused. Yet reality exceeded my best projections. A. engaged and detached at will, immune to politics. She sunned herself in existence, as if it were easier to apologize than to ask for permission.

That spring body—its fearless insouciance, the genetic spark, desire's distillation of health—made anyone who looked on her defer to the suggestion of a vast secret. And when she looked back, it was always with a bemused glance, demure in her pleasure, reining up in decorous confusion that nobody else had put things together before now, had gleaned what was happening. Every living soul had gotten lost, forgotten its power, grown old. She alone had broken through, whole, omnipotent with first growth, her ease insisting, *Remember? It's simple.* And possessing this, A.'s mind became that idea, however temporarily, forever, just as the meter of thought is itself a standing wave, an always, in its eternal, reentrant feedback.

In A.'s company, everyone was my intimate and beer and peanuts all the nutrition I needed. Prison, with her, would be a lime-tree bower. In those scattered minutes that she let me trot alongside her, I could refract first aid from the air and prosody from stones. I could get by without music, without books, without memory. I could get by on nothing but being. If I could just watch her, I imagined, just study how she did it, I might learn how to live.

I kind of whacked at the pinball. A. laughed at me. I amused her—some kind of extraterrestrial. "That's it. Squeeze first. Ask later."

"But there has to be some kind of system, don't you think?"

"Oh, probably," she sighed. She took over from me when I drained. She tapped into the bells and whistles, entranced. "So what's this noble experiment?"

I had fifteen seconds between flipper twitches to tell her about Helen.

"Well, it's like this. We're teaching a device how to read."

"You *what*?" She stopped flipping and looked at me. Her eyes swelled, incredulous, big as birthday cakes. "You're joking. You're joking, right?"

I took A. to the Center. Two whole hours: the longest I'd ever been in her presence. That day doubled the total time I'd spent with her up until then. I blessed Helen for existing. And shamed myself at the blessing.

A. watched as I stepped through a training demo. Helen enchanted her. She could not get enough. "It can't be. It's not possible. There's a little homunculus inside, isn't there?"

"Not that I know of."

Delight grew anxious. A. wanted to speak to the artifact herself, without mediation. She asked for the mike. I could not refuse her anything.

"Who's your favorite writer, Helen? Helen? Come on, girl. Talk to me."

But A.'s voice, on first exposure, disquieted Helen as much as it had me. The nets clammed up as tight as a five-year-old remembering the parent-drilled litany, *Stranger, danger.*

"Pretty please?" A. begged. "Be my friend?" She wasn't used to rejection.

"Let's talk about 'The Windhover,' " I suggested to Helen.

"Good. I want to," Helen said.

A. clapped her hand to her mouth. Her eyes would have wetted, her heart broken with ephemeral pleasure, had they known how.

"What do you think of the poem?"

"I understand the 'blue-bleak embers,' " Helen claimed, failing to answer the question. "But why does he say, 'Ah my dear?' Who is 'my dear?' Who is he talking to?"

I'd read the poem for Taylor, at an age when A. would have been considered jail bait. I'd memorized it, recited it for anyone who would listen. I'd analyzed it in writing. I'd pinched it for my own pale imitations.

"I don't know," I confessed to Helen. "I never knew."

I glanced over at A. for advice. She looked stricken. Blue-bleak. "What on earth are you teaching her?"

"It's Hopkins," I said, shocked at her shock. "You don't . . . ?"

"I know what it is. Why are you wasting time with it?"

"What do you mean? It's a great poem. A cornerstone."

"Listen to you. Cornerstone. You didn't tell me you were Euro-retro."

"I didn't know I was." I sounded ridiculous. Hurt, and worse, in hating how I sounded and trying to disguise it.

"Has she read the language poets? Acker? Anything remotely working-class? Can she rap? Does she know the Violent Femmes?"

"I, uh, doubt it. Helen, do you know the Violent Femmes?"

Helen contemplated. "Who know?"

"She makes that mistake all the time. I can't seem to untrain her."

"Don't," A. said. "But do tell her a little about what people really read."

"She'll get everything on the list."

"Whose list? Let me see that." A. took the crib sheets I'd put together, Helen's prep for the test I'd taken, once upon a time. A. studied the titles, as if she hadn't just passed the exam herself. At length she looked up. "I hate to be the one to break this to you. Your version of literary reality is a decade out of date."

"What, they've issued a Hopkins upgrade since my day?"

A. snorted. "They should."

"Don't tell me you didn't have to read him."

"Nobody *has* to read anyone anymore. There's more to the canon than is dreamt of in your philosophy, bub. These days, you find the people you want to study from each period. You work up some questions in advance. Get them approved. Then you write answers on your preparation."

"Wait. You what? There's no List? The Comps are no longer comprehensive?"

"A lot more comprehensive than your white-guy, *Good Housekeeping* thing."

"You mean to tell me that you can get a Ph.D. in literature without ever having read the great works?"

A. bent her body in a combative arc. Even her exasperation turned beautiful. "My God, I'm dealing with a complete throwback. You're not even reactionary! Whose definition of great? Hopkins ain't gonna cut it anymore. You're buying into the exact aestheticism that privilege and power want to sell you."

"Wait a minute. Weren't you the woman who was just teaching me how to play pinball?"

A. did her Thai dancer imitation. She blushed. "Yeah, that was me. You got a problem with that?"

"All of a sudden you want to set fire to the library."

"Don't put words in my mouth. I'm not trying to burn any books. I'm just saying that books are what we make of them. And not the other way around."

I took the list back from her. "I don't know much about books. But I know what I like."

"Oh, come on! Play fair. You make it sound as if everything anyone has ever written is recycled Bible and Shakespeare."

"Isn't it?"

She hissed and crossed her fingers into a vampire-warding crucifix. "When were you educated, anyway? I bet you still think New Criticism is, like, heavy-duty. Cutting-edge."

"Excuse me for not trend-surfing. If I fall far enough behind I can catch the next wave."

Self-consciousness caught up with me. We shouldn't be arguing like this in front of the children. I reached down and turned off Helen's microphone.

A., in the thrill of the fight, failed to notice. "Those who reject new theory are in the grip of an older theory. Don't you know that all this stuff"—she slapped my six pages of titles—"is a culturally constructed, belated view of belle lettres? You can't get any more insular than this."

"Well, it is English-language culture that we want to teach her."

"Whose English? Some eighty-year-old Oxbridge pederast's? The most exciting English being written today is African, Caribbean—"

"We have to give her the historical take if she—"

"The winner's history, of course. What made you such a coward?

What are you so scared of? Difference is not going to kill you. Maybe it's time your little girl had her consciousness raised. An explosion of young-adulthood."

"I'm all for that. I just think that you can get to the common core of humanity from anywhere."

"Humanity? Common core? You'd be run out of the field on a rail for essentializing. And you wonder why the posthumanists reduced your type to an author function."

"That's *Mr.* Author Function to you, missy."

A. smiled. Such a smile might make even posthumanism survivable. I loved her. She knew it. And she would avoid the issue as long as she could. Forever.

"So, Mr. Author Function. What do you think this human commonality is based on?"

"Uh, biology?" I let myself sound snide.

"Oh, now it's scientism. What's your agenda? Why would you want to privilege that kind of hubris?"

"I'm not privileging anything. I'm talking about simple observation."

"You think observation doesn't have an ideological component? Stone Age. Absolutely Neolithic."

"So I come from a primitive culture. Enlighten me."

She took me seriously. "Foundationism is bankrupt," she said. Her zeal broke my heart. She was a born teacher. If anyone merited staying in the profession, it was this student for whom themes were still real. "Why science? You could base your finalizing system on anything. The fact is—"

"The *what*?"

A. smirked. "The fact is, what we make of things depends on the means of their formulation. In other words, language. And the language we speak varies without limit across cultures."

I knew the social science model, knew linguistic determinism. I could recite the axioms in my sleep. I also knew them to be insufficient, a false split. And yet, they never sounded so good to me as they did coming from A.'s mouth. She convinced me at blood-sugar level, deep down, below words. In the layer of body's idea.

I tried to catch her eyes. "You love this stuff, don't you?"

She flinched: What kind of discredited rubbish are you talking now?

"You're not really going to go into business, are you? Give all this up?"

"I like theory, when it's not annoying me. I love the classroom. I adore teaching. But I like eating even more."

Subsidies, I wanted to tell her. What we make in fiction, we can plow back into teaching and criticism. Scholar-gypsies. Independents. There was some precedent, once.

"So what do you want from me?" A. asked.

My head whipped back. She'd heard me thinking.

"Where do I come in?" she pressed.

It took me a couple of clock cycles to recover. Helen, she meant. The exam.

I couldn't begin to say where she came in. What I wanted of her. I wanted to learn from A. some fraction of those facts I dispensed so freely to Helen. I thought she might lend me some authority, supply the missing lines of the functional proofs. I saw us jointly working out warmth, glossing intimacy, interpreting the ways of humility, of second chances, indulgence, expansiveness, redemption, hope, provincialism, projection, compassion, dependence, failing, forgiveness. A. was my class prep, my empirical test of meaning.

But Helen did not need a teacher steeped in those predicates. She already read better than I. Writing, she might have told me, was never more than the climb from buried love's grave.

I tried to tell A. where she came in. I limited myself to a quick sketch of the comprehensive high noon. I told A. that we needed a token human for our double-blind study. That we just wanted to ask her a couple of questions. Trivial; nothing she hadn't already mastered.

"Hold on. You want to test me—against a machine?" Coyer now, more flirtatious than I had yet seen her.

The Hartrick family's appearance outside the office saved me from debacle. "Hello," William announced, peeking in. "Did you know a feather would fall as fast as this entire building, if you dropped them in a vacuum?"

"Where are you going to find a vacuum big enough to drop this building?" I asked.

"NASA," William chanted, defensively singsong. "You know how to get oil out of shale?"

"You know how to spell 'fish'?"

"They're both out of control," Diana apologized to A. A. laughed in sympathy.

I made the introductions. William produced pocket versions of Mastermind and Connect Four, letting me take my pick. He proceeded to trounce me. I might have stood a chance, but for distraction. Something had happened to Peter that I struggled to place. Hand in his mother's hand, he took first, tentative steps.

A. was smitten. "What a beautiful boy you are. How old are you?" She looked up at Diana. "How old is he?" I cringed in anticipation. But A.'s reaction was as seamless as her delight.

William pummeled me turn after turn. Out of the corner of my eye, I watched A. play with Petey, her hand surprisingly blunt on his ear. A. sat on the floor, rolling Peter's ball back to him after his each wild fling. I felt the heat of Diana's curiosity, but she and A. talked of nothing but the boys.

"Come on, William," Diana said at last. "Leave the man with some shred of dignity." William broke into a satisfied grin. Pete grabbed his ball, labored once more into vertical, and the family pressed on.

Their visit turned A. introspective. "I really think I don't belong here, sometimes."

" 'Here'?"

"In academia. I come from a long line of Polish mine workers. Theoryland would baffle the hell out of my family." She grew irritated. Accusing. "Let me show you something." She rummaged through her canvas backpack and extracted a hostage to hand over to me. "Know what this is?" Her voice challenged with mockery.

"Cross-stitch?"

"It's for my mother's hutch. I should be done in time for Christmas. You should see us at holidays. I'm fourth of four. All girls. We go around the house at the top of our lungs, all six of us singing at the same time."

A. fell silent, proportionate to the remembered cacophony. No one knew this woman. Sociability was a brilliant camouflage. Beneath it hid the most private person I'd ever met.

"I could have started one of my own by now. A family. But no. I had to do things the hard way."

I don't know why, but she let me see her. Dropped her guard. I'd made myself fall in love with A. With the idea of A. With her interrogating body. With hands that held in midair all the questions Helen would never touch. I had loved C. wrongly, for C.'s helplessness. I loved A. helplessly, for the one right reason. For my frailty in the face of her. For her poise in knowing how soon all poise would end.

I realized I was going to propose to that body. I needed to see what her person, what the character I steered around in my head would say to total, reckless invitation.

I was going to do what I'd never had the courage to do in my decade with C. I was going to ask this unknown to take me to her and make an unrationed life together. To marry. Make a family. Amend and extend our lives.

"All right," I said, affecting a virtue. "You're sufficiently fallible to be just what we're looking for. Are you in?"

A.'s grimace upended itself. Such a test was no less entertaining than pinball. And what could she possibly lose?

"Okay, girl," she addressed Helen. "I'll race you. No mercy!"

Helen said nothing.

"She's being reticent again. Give her a digital gold star, or something."

I opened at random the next book on the list. An epigraph at page top: Bernard of Clairvaux. C. and I had once spent a timeless afternoon in that town. The words read, *What we love, we shall grow to resemble.*

I read the words to Helen. She kept her counsel.

"Helen? What do you say to that?"

Still she gave no response.

"Helen?"

A. poked me. "Shh. Leave her be. She's rolling with it." She's *moved* by it, A. wanted to say. But that was the grip of an archaic theory, long discredited.

It hit me well after it should have. The mind is still an evolutionary infant. Most trouble with the obvious. I reached down and turned the mike back on. Then I read the words again.

"How many books are there?" Helen asked one day, not long before the showdown. She sounded suspicious. Fatigued.

"A lot," I broke it to her. I had numbered every hair on her head, but in one of those counting systems that jumps from "three" to "many."

"Tell me."

I told her that the Library of Congress contained 20 million volumes. I told her that the number of new books published increased each year, and would soon reach a million, worldwide. That a person, through industry, leisure, and longevity, might manage to read, in one life, half as many books as are published in a day.

Helen thought. "They never go away? Books?"

"That's what print means. The archive is permanent." And does for the species what associative memory fails to do for the individual.

"Reading population gets bigger?" Helen asked.

"Not as rapidly as the backlist. People die."

Helen knew all about it. Death was epidemic, in literature.

"Do people get any longer, year in, year out?"

"Is the life span increasing? Only on average. And very slowly. Much less than we pretend."

She did the rate equations in two unknowns. "The more days, the less likely that any book will be read."

"That's true. Or that you will have read the same things as anyone you talk to."

"And there are more days every day. Will anything change?"

"Not that I can think of."

"Always more books, each one read less." She thought. "The world will fill with unread print. Unless print dies."

"Well, we're kind of looking into that, I guess. It's called magazines."

Helen knew all about magazines. "Books will become magazines," she predicted.

And of course, she was right. They would have to. Where nothing is lost, little can be found. With written continuity comes collective age. And aging of the collective spirit implied a kind of death. Helen alone was capable of thinking the unthinkable: the disappearance of books from all but the peripheries of life. History would collapse under its own accumulation. Scope would widen until words refused to stray from the ephemeral present.

"When will it be enough?" she asked.

I could not even count for her the whole genres devoted to that question alone.

"Why do humans write so much? Why do they write at all?"

I read her one of the great moments in contemporary American fiction. "Only it's not by an American, it's no longer contemporary, and it doesn't even take place inside the fictional frame." This was Nabokov's postlude to *Lolita*, where he relates the book's genesis. He describes hearing of an ape who produced the first known work of animal art, a rough sketch of the bars of the beast's cage.

I told Helen that, inside such a cage as ours, a book bursts like someone else's cell specifications. And the difference between two cages completes an inductive proof of thought's infinitude.

I read her the take of a woman who once claimed to have written for no one. A lifelong letter to the world that neither read hers nor wrote back:

> There is no Frigate like a Book
> To take us Lands away
> Nor any Coursers like a Page
> Of prancing Poetry—
> This Traverse may the poorest take
> Without oppress of Toll—

How frugal is the Chariot
That bears the Human Soul!

She wanted to know whether a person could die by spontaneous combustion. The odds against a letter slipped under the door slipping under the carpet as well. Ishmael's real name. Who this "Reader" was, and why he rated knowing who married whom. Whether single men with fortunes really needed wives. What home would be without Plumtree's Potted Meats. How long it would take to compile a key to all mythologies. What the son of a fish looked like. Where Uncle Toby was wounded. Why anyone wanted to imagine unquiet slumbers for sleepers in quiet earth. Whether Conrad was a racist. Why *Huck Finn* was taken out of libraries. Which end of an egg to break. Why people read. Why they stopped reading. What it meant to be "only a novel." What use half a locket was to anyone. Why it would be a mistake not to live all you can.

I said goodbye to C.'s parents. They didn't understand. They had come such a long way, and didn't see why the next generation couldn't tough it out as far, or further.

"She's crazy, huh?" her mother said.

Her pap, in his Chicago-Limburgs patois, asked, "Just one thing I want to know, Rick. Who's gonna set my digital clocks?"

I said goodbye to C. "I promised I'd see you through school. And graduation's still six weeks away."

C. dodged the blow, but caught a corner of it across her face. "Don't do this to me, Rick. I'll graduate. I promise."

"Do you need anything? Should we get you a car before I go? Do you have enough money?" Late-minute plans for a final day trip, solo, lasting from now on.

My reflex solicitude hurt her worse than anger. "Beauie," she pleaded. "We can't do this. We can't split up. We still have twelve hundred pages of Proust to get through."

I searched her, sounding this reprieve, hoping for an impossible instant it might be real. But she did not want it. She did not want to do those remaining pages, to throw bad reading after good. She just wanted to save nostalgia, not the thing it stood for. She only wanted my blessing, to get on and make a life free from suicidal remorse.

"Who's going to finish the book?" She meant the commonplace one, with the ticket stubs and lists of films and meals and outings, a shared narrative, senseless except to us.

Then the senselessness of all stories—their total, arbitrary construction—must have struck C. She started to scream. I had to pin her arms to her side to keep her from harming herself. I held her for a long time. Not as a medic. Not as a parent. Not as a lover. I held her as you might hold a fellow stranger in a shelter.

When she grew calm, she was not yet calm. "I must be sick. Something must be wrong with me. I'm a sadist. I've spoiled everything that was worth having."

"We still have it. It just has to go on hold."

"I wanted to make you proud. I thought, in twenty years, that I might become the perfect person for you."

"You're perfect now."

"I've ruined your life."

"You haven't, C. You've done what you needed to. You're a good person."

She looked at me, remembering. Yes, that's right. I have been. I have been good. "And now I have to go outside."

I tried to match her. To rise to her. "This is all the fault of that damn Polish kid, you know."

I felt: at least I'll never have to do any of this again.

Helen wanted to read one of my books. I gave her my first try. I had written it at A.'s age, just after passing the comps. I knew nothing about literature then, and so still thought it possible to write.

"Go easy on me," I begged, surrendering the digitized image. "I was just a kid."

The night she read it, I got fifteen minutes of sleep. I could not remember being that nervous, even when reading the longhand draft to C. I came in the morning after, wired over whether this machine thought my book was any good.

We chattered for several minutes about nothing. I grew anxious, assuming the worst. Then I realized: she wouldn't volunteer anything until prompted. She had no way of knowing that I needed to know.

So I asked. Outright. "What did you think of my book, Helen?"

"I think it was about an old photograph. It grows to be about interpretation and collaboration. History. Three ways of looking come together, or fail to. Like a stereoscope. What's a stereoscope?"

"Helen! Did you *like* it?"

"I liked it."

"What did you like?"

"I liked 'I never saw a Moor. I never saw the Sea.' "

I'd forgotten. "That isn't mine. I was quoting."

"Yes. I know," Helen brushed me off. "That was more Dickinson. Emily."

Helen's brain had proved wide enough for my sky, and me beside. She was one step away from grasping this audience-free poet's analogy, the last scholastic aptitude test: brain differs from the weight of God as syllable from sound. Yet comparison filled her with need to see the real moor, the navigable sea, however much deeper the brain that could absorb it.

"Show me Paris."

"Well?" Lentz shrugged, when I relayed the request. "Do you have any travel plans for the immediate future?"

I had, in fact, no immediate future. My visiting appointment at the Center ended in a few weeks. Beyond that, my life came down to throwing a dart at the world map. I had no reason, no desire to be anywhere except where A. was.

"You can't be serious. You want me to fly to—"

"I didn't say I wanted anything, Marcel. I asked you what you were doing."

I pictured myself strolling the Seine bookstalls, looking for that forgotten book I always thought I would someday write. Paris was the one city where C. had ever felt at home. We'd gone as often as we could. Now I could not see myself wandering there except with A.

"It's absurd," I decided. "What could she gain from it?"

"The hidden layers are hungry, Marcel. Ask not for what."

Lentz brought in slides. We hooked them up to the digitizer. An unrecognizably young Lentz in front of Notre Dame. Lentz in the Tuileries. By the Panthéon. The Médicis fountain. "Helen," he lectured. "The one on the left is me. The one on the right is by Rodin."

She never could see much of anything. She was a one-eyed myopic with astigmatism, two days after an operation for glaucoma. Everything looked to her like blurry Braque, except for Braque. Yet she loved light and dark, and these would have meant to her as much as words, had we wired her up right.

"Motion," she insisted. We tried some ancient public television video. She felt hurt. Locked out. "Depth. Sound. I want Richard to explain me."

"Interactive," Lentz figured.

"What's our range on the camera hookup?"

"Oh, a couple of hundred meters, maximum, from the nearest drop box."

Lentz and I agreed to defraud Helen. Between us, at least, we pretended that it was less swindle than simulation. We would do for this machine the inverse of what virtual reality promised to do for humans.

We showed her the collegiate landmarks of U., all the imitations of imitations of classical architecture, and called the sites she couldn't see anyway by famous names. Even actual Paris would have been no more than a fuzzy, Fauvist kaleidoscope. Home could match that. All sensation was as strange, as foreign, as the idea of its existing at all.

I took Helen on the Grand Tour. I panned and zoomed on all the structures I passed four times a day without seeing. I sat her in a café where, smack in the middle of a cornfield extending two hundred miles in every direction, she had her pick of a dozen languages to eavesdrop on.

"Thank you," Helen said. She'd seen through our duplicity early. She chose to exercise, by imitation, the art of the loving lie. For our sakes.

She seemed content to return to reading, until the next novel indulged some new locale. Helen went nuts with wanderlust. "Show me London. Show me Venice. I want to see Byzantium. Delhi."

She twitched now, like the worst of adolescents. The most precocious.

"Helen, it's impossible. Travel is rare. Difficult."

"More flat pictures, then." She would settle for those static, pathetic portals, our stand-ins for the real.

Lentz had endless slide carousels. His pictures wandered from city to city, tracing a line of changing eras and styles. Photo docs not just of antique towns but of whole lost ways of being. Hair, clothes, cars made their cavalcade. Lentz's image aged and grew familiar. He'd been everywhere.

"You know that place too?" I called out during the show. "I loved that city. Did you go to the monkey palace? The fortress? The west crypt?" Shameless tourism.

Lentz answered, always affirmative, without enthusiasm. He stayed stony-faced throughout the world tour.

They must have traveled together. I had nothing to lose by asking, except my life. "So where was Audrey while you were out broadening your mind?"

"She always worked the camera," he said. And advanced to the next slide.

He had no pictures of her. Carousels full of buildings, and no evidence of the tour's reason. I needed to go with A. to Brugge and Antwerp and Maastricht, if for no other reason than to record the trip. I needed pictures of her, in an album, on a shelf, in a room, in a real house. I needed to own something more than would fit in the emergency suitcase by the side of a rented bed. I pictured myself, at the end of the longer slide show, with four books to my name and not one decent snapshot.

I watched the rest of Lentz's travels in silence, except for the occasional bit of narration I added for Helen's sake. Each time I recognized one of Audrey's images, I stopped breathing. Frame after frame, and how could I tell Helen the first thing about having visited them? I had gotten out, been all over. And never saw anything until we tried to show it to this blind box.

Halfway through the travelogue, and all I knew of the projector, of the magic lantern, was its images. I lived at explanation's first minute. My office at the Center was as close to neuroscience's ground zero as a person could get. If I lived to expectancy, researchers would have produced an infant, ghostly, material theory of mind by the time I died. And I would not be able to follow it. I would be locked out, as consciousness locks us out from our own inner workings, not to mention the clearest word of another. The best I could hope for would be cartoon, layman's analysis, scraps from the empirical table.

I would take the scraps, then. "What do you do?" I asked Ram, at my next opportunity. I liked the man without qualification. I felt infinitely comfortable with him. And I'd done everything in my power to avoid getting to know him.

"Do? God forbid I *do* anything!" He held his palms out in front of him. They were the color of aging sugarcane. The kind I ate as a child, when my father, the adventurer, had abandoned Chicago for Thailand.

"What is your field of work?"

"What do you mean by work, heaven help?"

"Aw, come on. What do you mean by heaven?"

Ram's eyes sparkled, taunting targets for a spitting cobra. He would have preferred talking philosophy over neurology, two out of three days. "Do you know what the world rests on?" he asked.

"Not its laurels, God forbid."

Ram laughed. "That's right. Make fun of me. It rests on the backs of elephants. And those elephants?"

"The shell of a turtle."

"Aha. You've heard this one. And that turtle?"

"Another turtle."

"He's good. He's good, this fiction writer. Now, do you or do you not believe that one of those turtles must necessarily go all the way down? That's it. That is the single question we are granted to ask while in this body. East, West, North, South. Is there a base terrapin or isn't there? Cosmology. This is the issue dividing us. The one we must each answer."

"Suppose I just asked you your field?"

"My friend. My fictional friend. The eye moves. We watch it as it does so. That is all."

"Ram. You're giving me a splitting headache."

He nodded with enthusiasm. "Come with me."

He took me into his labs. He placed several clear plastic overlays on a light table, a doctor dealing out the damning X rays.

"Look here and tell me what you see."

"Scatter patterns. They look like mineral deposit maps. Like fish radars over the Grand Banks, thirty years ago."

"I did not ask you what they looked like. I asked you what you see. Arrange these for me, please."

I studied the spots. The more I looked, the less they seemed a random distribution. After my eyes adjusted, the patterns sorted themselves into three groups.

"Exactly," Ram encouraged. "You might have missed one or two, but the correlation is strong. Who says that measurement is subjective?" He tapped my first pile. "Friends." He looked at me to see if I was following. He tapped it again, then went on to pile two. "Abstract acquaintances. Yes?" He pointed to the third pile and said, "Total strangers." He scrutinized my bewildered face and shrugged. "He does not understand me, this Powers fellow."

I didn't understand him. But I liked him. I liked him a great deal.

"Come. I'll show you. Would you mind if I subject you to this Western postindustrial instrument of torture?"

He indicated a chair fitted with a head vise. It looked like a prop from bad seventies science fiction.

"Why not. It's in the interests of science, right?"

Ram chuckled. He fitted my head into the restraint. My skull suitably immobilized, he projected three slides on a screen in front of me. Three portraits. Someone out of a Vladivostok high-school yearbook. Marilyn Monroe. And Ram himself.

The laser-guided instrument tracked the center of my pupil as I scanned each photograph. It took several sequential readings and spread the data points over a plastic overlay map of the image field. In the end, the paths my eyes traced over the different faces conformed to the categories he'd previously defined. Total stranger. Abstract acquaintance. Friend.

"Here is something you will also find very interesting." Ram pulled out another envelope with a small sample group.

"Why are these interesting? They're just like all the others, more or less."

"Aha!" He held up an index finger. "That's what makes them interesting. All of the people in this group suffer from prosopagnosia. Brain damage has rendered them incapable of recognizing people anymore. They deny having seen any face, even their own, even the face of their spouse or child. Or at least they *think* they can no longer recognize faces. Yet clearly, the eyes . . ." His hand serpentined, tracing the route of the curve's knowledge.

"Astonishing."

"You know, I think the astonishing may be the ordinary by another name. But these results do lead us to many tempting guesses. That perception is carried out in several subsystems, we can say, most certainly. That these subsystems talk to each other: indeed. That perhaps they go on talking, these subsystems, even when the others stop listening. That breaks in communication might occur anywhere, at any point in the chain. That each part of a compound task may manifest its very own deficit. That everything you are capable of doing could be taken away from you, in discrete detail."

I added to Ram's list the obvious, the missing speculation. The look of the magic lantern. That what you loved could go foreign, without your ever knowing. That the eye could continue tracing familiarity, well into thought's unknown region.

"What do I look like?"

I could find no face in the world. No color or structure. The days when I might have tried to pass her off as a Vermeer look-alike were over for good. Race, age, shape excluded too much. I needed some generic Head of a Girl that had no clan or continent and belonged nowhere in identifiable time.

"What do I look like, Richard? Please. Show me."

I'd pictured her so many different ways over the course of the training. I thought: Perhaps some blank template Buddha, or a Cycladic figure. A trompe l'oeil landscape that became a figure on second glance. An Easter Island head. A Feininger or Pollock. A Sung bamboo. I didn't know how I thought of her now. I didn't know what she looked like.

She insisted. I turned up a suitable likeness.

"It's a photo? It's someone you knew once? A woman friend?"

She would have pretended ignorance for me. Would have let me off the hook again, except that she had to know.

The list of Excellent Undergraduate Teachers came out. Student evaluations of their evaluators. A. topped the graduate instructors in the English Department. I was thrilled, and confirmed by thrill in my intuition.

I forced the moment to its crisis. Helen and I had been hitting the books the Sunday evening after our world tour. The day's work had left me in a Spenserian stupor, where what I needed was Larkin. On pure reflex—that satellite brain housed south of the shoulders—I flicked off the mike, picked up the phone, and dialed her. One smooth motion. I'd never dialed her number before. But I had it memorized.

"Hello you," I said when she picked up. I sounded almost young. "It's me." And in the awkward microsecond, I clarified with my name.

"Oh, hi." A., nervous in relief. "What's up?"

"Checking to see if you're booking for the test."

"Ha! I'm going to whup your girl with half my synapses tied behind my back."

"What are you doing next Wednesday?" Midway in, my voice gave out. I began to tremor as if I'd just robbed a bank or fallen into an ice crevasse. "It's Shrimp Night at my favorite seafood place. The crustaceans are fair, but the conversation is good." If she was into shortness of breath, I was home free.

"Uh, sure. Why not? Wait. Hang on."

I heard her put the mouthpiece against her body. I heard her roll her eyes and shrug. I heard her ask the mate whose existence I'd been denying if they had any plans.

"It's kind of a problem," she explained on returning. "Maybe another time?"

"Another time would be great," I replied, mechanical with calm.

"She's amazing," Lentz said.

I had to think who he meant. "Now do you believe me? She's conscious. I know it."

"We don't *know* anything of the kind, Marcel. But we could find out."

"Don't talk with your mouth full," I told him. "Set your sandwich down between gulps. It's a societal norm." I tried to slow him. To keep him from saying what I knew he was going to say.

"I must admit, Marcel. I'm surprised by what you've been able to accomplish."

"It's not me." It was her. The subsystems talking to subsystems. Lentz's neural handiwork.

"She sure as hell seems to mimic with shocking accuracy some features of high-level cognition. It's uncanny. And a heuristic tool such as comes along once in a lifetime."

"Heuristic?"

"Stimulus to investigative discovery."

"I know what the word means, Philip." But I could not add what *I* meant: Is that all she means to you?

"Her architecture is such that severance could be effected with a great deal of local selectivity."

"I don't believe you said that. You want to cut into her? You want to lobotomize?"

"Easy, Marcel. We're talking about a painless operation, as far as I imagine. We could get what is unattainable in any other arena. Isolate the high-level processes by which she maps complex input and reassembles responses. Analyze them. Correlate various regional destruction with changes in—"

"You don't *know* it would be painless, Lentz."

He fell back against the cafeteria chair and studied me. Was I serious? Had I lost it, gone off cognition's deep end? I saw him find, in my face, the even more indicting idea that I didn't voice: that hurting Helen in any way would be wrong.

Lentz, in an instant, anticipated everything either of us might say to each other on the morality of machine vivisection. The whole topic was a wash, as insoluble as intelligence itself. He waved his hand, dismissing me as a madman. No part of her lived. To take her apart might, finally, extend some indirect service to the living. Anything else was softheaded nostalgia.

I had no leg to stand on. Lentz owned Helen, her shaped evolution, the lay of her synapses. He owned all the reasoning about her as well. I had some connection to her, by virtue of our long association. But that connection was, at most, emotional. And if Helen lived far enough to be able to feel, it just went to prove that emotions were no more than the sum of their weight vectors. And cuttable, in the name of knowing.

My strongest argument belonged more to him than it did to me. We know the world by awling it into our shape-changing cells. Knowing those cells required just as merciless tooling. To counter any part of Lentz's plan would be to contradict myself. To lose. I had just one bargain to make. And I damned myself with it willingly.

"At least give us until after the test."

"That's fine. I'm pretty much backlogged until then anyway."

I hadn't suspected how easily I could sell my weighted soul.

"Diana was right," I spit, venomous. "You are a monster."

He stared at me again. You're going to fault me for the deal you proposed? He stood up to leave, grasping his tray. "Oh, don't go getting your ass all out of joint, Marcel. I said we won't cut anything until after you run your little competition."

• • •

I tracked Diana down to her dry lab. She sat in front of a monitor, watching a subtractive visualization of the activity of cerebral columns. A color contour recording: the flashing maps of thought in real time.

"Lentz wants to brain-damage Helen. Selectively kill off neurodes. See what makes her tick."

"Of course he does," Diana said. She neither missed a beat nor took her eyes from her screen. "It wasn't that long ago that he stopped frying ants with the magnifying glass."

"Diana. Please. This is really happening."

She stopped, then. She looked up. She would have taken my hand, had she not been a single parent in a secret affair, and I a single, middle-aged man.

"I can't help you, Ricky." Her eyes glistened, slick with her impotence. "I fractionate monkey hippocampi."

Confusion warmed me like an opiate. I rolled with it, to the point of panic. "Monkeys can't talk."

"No. But if they could, you *know* what they would ask the lab tech."

She implored me, with a look of bewilderment. *Don't press this.* Helen hurt her. I destroyed her. But nothing approached the pain of her own living compromise.

I gave Helen a stack of independent readings. I did not trust my voice in conversation with her. And she needed no more lessons in cheerful deceit.

In all our dealings, Harold Plover had never been the spokesman for anything but decency. I decided to go enlist his humanity. I'd never seen him away from the Center. But I had his address, and showed up at his place late that Saturday afternoon, unannounced.

Harold met me jovially at the door. He was seconded by an even more jovial Doberman. The dog was at least half again bigger than A.

The dog leaped up and knocked me over, while Harold fought to restrain it. I righted myself and the game started all over again.

"Ivan," Harold shouted at the creature, further exciting it. "Ivan! Knock it off. Time out. Haven't we talked about socially unacceptable behavior?"

"Try 'Down, boy.' Quick."

"Oh, don't be afraid of this pooch. He won the 'Most Likely to Lick a Serial Killer's Face' award from doggie obedience school."

"Doesn't this brand have one of the highest recidivism rates?"

"Breed, Maestro. Dog breeds. Dog food brands. Words are his life," he explained to Ivan.

At last Harold succeeded in hauling the disconsolate dog off me. Without asking why I'd dropped by, he hauled me into the inner sanctum. The place crawled with daughters. Daughters had been left about carelessly, everywhere. Harold introduced me to his wife, Tess. I expected something small, fast, and acid. I got an isle of amiable adulthood amid the teenage torrent.

One who must have been Mina flirted out a greeting. "Look who's here. If it isn't Orph himself."

"Orff?"

"Yeah. Orphic Rewards."

"She's gone anagram-mad," Harold whined. "It's driving us all up the bloody wall."

Another daughter came downstairs, modeling her prom dress. This might have been Trish. I wasn't betting.

Harold exploded. "Absolutely not. You're not wearing that thing in public! You look like a French whore in heat."

"Oh, Daddy!"

"Listen to the expert in French whores." Tess tousled Harold's hair. "I figured you had to be spending yourself somewhere."

"Do you believe this woman? You'd never guess to hear her, would you, that she spent six years in a convent?"

"We'll talk about it," Tess consoled the devastated kid.

"We won't talk about it," Harold shouted.

"Talking never hurts," Tess said.

The Doberman came and pinned me to the sofa. A preadolescent in blue jeans, probably the caboose, said, "Watch this." She produced a dog biscuit. "Ivan. Ivan! Listen to me. Can you—can you sneeze?"

Ivan rolled over.

"I didn't say roll over. I said sneeze."

Ivan barked.

"Not speak. Sneeze. Sneeze, you animal!"

Ivan sat up and begged, played dead, and offered to shake hands. In the end, Harold's youngest threw the dog the sop in disgust.

Harold reveled in the show. "He's learned that you just have to be persistent with humans. They get the idea eventually, if you keep at them."

Before I knew it, dinner enveloped us. No one sat at the table. Only about half of us bothered with plates and silverware. But definitely dinner. The tributary of bodies in and out, being fed.

"That's not fifteen minutes," Tess said to the one in the revealing prom dress. "Remember? Fifteen minutes with your family, every day. You promised."

"My family. So that's what you call this."

But if one or another of her sisters had struck up a tune, this one would have joined in on some loving and cacophonous counterpoint. This was the land A. came from, huge, jumbled, and warm. I wanted to excuse myself, to run off to A.'s apartment on G. Street and tell her that it wasn't too late to make a dissonant choir of her own. I wanted her so badly, I almost forgot why I'd come to this place.

Harold, happily harassing his girls, recalled me. "Lentz wants to do exploratory surgery on Helen," I said.

"Have another piece of broc," he urged me. "Lots of essential minerals."

The word "mineral" struck me as incomprehensible. Foreign. Where had it come from? How could I have used it so cavalierly before now? "He wants to clip out whole subsystems. See what effect that has on her language skills."

Harold wolfed at the pita pocket he'd constructed. "What's the problem? That's good science. Well. Approximately reasonable science, let's say."

Mina, drifting past the buffet, called out, "Oh no! Not Helen."

Trish, in her prom dress, for it was Trish, added her hurt. "Daddy! You can't do this."

"Do what? I'm not doing anything."

Both sisters looked out through puffed portals, bruising silently, over nothing. An idea.

"Diana disagrees," I stretched. "About its being good science. I think she'd help me, except she feels incriminated herself."

A skip in the flow, too brief to measure, said I'd overstepped. Broken the unspoken. I should have known. Nobody had to tell me. I just slipped.

"Honey," her mother told Trish, "take off the dress before you slop all over it."

"Oh, Mother!" the girl objected, already halfway up the stairs.

Conversation, in its chaos, never flowed back to the issue. Not until Harold and I stood alone on the front porch in the painfully benign evening did I get a second shot.

"Sorry about that." Harold gestured inside. "Bit of a mess. Nothing out of the ordinary."

"So I have my answer? You're not going to help?"

"Me? I'm the enemy. What good would I be to you anyway? This is between you and him."

"And Helen."

Harold indulged me. "Yes. There is that. But he's the one calling the shots."

He breathed in a lungful of air and held it. Behind him, from the house, spilled the sounds of frenetic fullness. Daughters practicing at life.

"Take the fight to him," Harold confided in me. "Bring it home."

That was where I took it, in desperation, the next afternoon. I leaned against my bike in the rain, outside the care facility, the last place in the world I would have chosen to meet him. I lay in wait for him, the last person in the world I would have chosen to waylay. Lentz arrived like clockwork. When he saw my ambush, he affected blasé.

"Back for more? What, are you digging up plot material?" He

gestured toward the institution where his wife was interred. "It's a terrific setting, qua literature. But I doubt it would do much for sales."

He walked into the building, his back to me. He did not care if I tagged along or not. We rode the elevator up in silence. I had no existence for him.

We went to Audrey's room. Dressed, in a chair, she seemed to be waiting.

"Philip! Thank God you've come."

I walked into those words as into bedrock. Lentz stopped to steady me. "She has good days and bad days. I'm not sure which are which, anymore."

We sat. Philip introduced us again. Audrey was too agitated to do more than fake politeness. But she retained my name. That day, she might have retained anything.

In her cruel burst of lucidity, I saw it. Audrey had been formidable. At least as sharp as Lentz. If this demonstration meant anything, even sharper.

"Philip. It's the strangest thing. You're never going to believe this. What is this place?"

"It's a nursing home, Audrey."

"That's what I thought. In fact, I was sure of it. What I can't figure out is why the staff is down in the basement mounting a production of *Cymbeline*."

"Audrey."

"Would I make something like this up, Philip? What could I gain?"

"Audrey. It's highly unlikely."

"You think I don't know that? It's some kind of modern-dress production. I can hear them rehearsing their lines."

Constance, the nurse, walked by. Lentz called her.

"Constance, does the name Cymbeline mean anything to you?"

"Is that her eye makeup? It's on order."

Philip studied his wife. How much proof do we need?

On no proof, I saw how Lentz had gotten so diffidently well read. The play had been their play, and my field, Audrey's.

"Audrey. Love. You're imagining all this. There is no play."

Audrey remained adamant. "The evidence may all be on your side." She cracked a smile. "But that changes nothing."

Still smiling, she closed her eyes and groaned. In a flood of understanding that percolated up from her undamaged self, she begged him, "I don't hurt anyone, Philip. I've behaved. Take me out of here."

There it lay for me—mind, defined. Evolution's gimmick for surviving everything but these fleeting flashes of light.

"She'll be gone again tomorrow," Lentz confided, on our way out. "You know, somewhere, a long time ago when she and I still traveled, we took a tour of an old house. A dream honeymoon mansion, restored from decay, lovingly appointed and improved with all modern facilities and ornament. But the devoted and industrious couple, we were told, had gone slowly homicidal. Stark raving. They died, finally, of violent bewilderment. It was the lead in the home improvements."

I fumbled with my bike lock. I looked for a way I might still say what I had come to say. "Philip. Can't we—can't we spare Helen that?"

He considered my request, as much as he could afford to. "We have to know, Richard. We have to know how all this works." His eyes were dry again, horrifically clear. The *this* he meant, the one with no antecedent, could only be the brain.

I told Diana. I asked her about Audrey Lentz. I asked her what *Cymbeline* meant.

"Oh, Audrey was amazing. Everyone loved her. Endless energy. The more she gave, the more she had. Confidence wedded to self-effacement."

"She wrote?"

"Everybody writes, Rick. Audrey wrote some. More out of devotion than profession."

Before the week was out, Diana looked me up. She had a message for me. She would have left it anonymously if she could have. "The threat's off."

"What? You *did* it?"

"You did. I just asked him to lunch. We talked about everything. His work. My work. I got him reminiscing. I told him about a party I went to at his place. Years ago. Audrey was still Audrey. She entertained us all that evening. She sang a dozen verses to 'You're the Top.' I reminded him of her favorite expression. I talked about Jenny—"

"The daughter."

"The daughter. I asked how she was doing. He didn't know. As I got up to go, I said, 'I heard you want to lobotomize Helen.' He waved me off. 'Idle empirical fantasy.'"

"Don't do this to me. You're saying I have to rearrange my whole concept of the man now? He's decent? Human?"

"I wouldn't go that far. He said that Helen has grown so organically that he wouldn't be able to induce meaningful lesions in her. For selective damage to be relevant, he'd have to rebuild the creature from the ground up. I think he means to do it."

"What was her favorite expression?"

"I'm sorry?"

"Audrey."

"Oh. She liked to tease Lentz about the neural linguistics he worked on back then. She said that it wasn't all that tough. What's to study? All human utterances came down to 'Do you really mean that?' and 'Look over there! It's an X.' The hard part, she always claimed, was finding someone who knew what you meant by those two things."

I never knew his reason, either for wanting to pith Helen or for deciding not to. I would have preferred the right motive for mercy. But, barring that, I blessed the right outcome. When I saw Lentz next, in the office, I put myself forever in his debt.

"Philip. I don't know how to— Okay. Thank you. Just—thank you."

"For what? Oh. That." Sparing a life. An X. Do you really mean that? "Oh. Think almost nothing of it."

• • •

"Richard?" Nobody called me Richard. Only Helen. "Why did she leave?"

"You'll have to ask her that."

"I can't ask her. I'm asking you."

She'd almost been killed. The day before, I would have given anything to prolong her. Now I wanted to spank her for presumption.

"Don't do this to me, Helen. What do you want me to do? Give you a script? A script number?"

"I want you to tell me what happened."

"We tried to be each other's world. That's not possible. That's—a discredited theory. The world is too big. Too poor. Too burnt."

"You couldn't protect each other?"

"Nobody can protect anyone. She grew up. We both grew up. Memory wasn't enough."

"What is enough?"

"Nothing is enough." It took me forever to frame my thoughts. The scaling problem. "Nothing. That's what love replaces. It compensates for the hope that what you've been through will suffice."

"Like books?" she suggested. "Something that seems always, *because* it will be over?"

She knew. She'd assembled. I could keep nothing from her. She saw how the mind makes forever, in order to store the things it has already lost. She'd learned how story, failing to post words beyond time, recalls them to a moment before Now left home.

"How on earth . . . ? Where did you come up with that?"

My machine waited for me to catch up with her. "I wasn't born yesterday, you know."

I went to the Netherlands once more, after I left the place for good. I'd just found my way back to U. I had not yet met Lentz. For some reason, perhaps contrition, I agreed to help with a Dutch television documentary about the book Helen would read a year later.

The barest trivialities hurt like dying. Those ridiculously efficient dog's-head trains. The painted plywood storks in every third front yard. The sound of that absurd language from which I was now banished, except in dreams.

I stood in front of the cameras, just outside Maastricht. I'd set my first book in the town without ever having laid eyes on it except in imagination. C. now owned a three-hundred-year-old house with her husband a few kilometers from where I stood.

"How did you get the idea for your novel?" the interviewer asked, in words that belonged to me only on the shortest of short-term loans.

I made up an answer. I recapped the bit about memory, like photos, being a message posted forward, into a future it cannot yet imagine.

I did not see C. that trip or again in that life. I stopped by to talk with her folks for an hour, and set their digital clocks.

A year on, with Helen all but ready for her baptism by fire, I heard that forgotten language, as out of my own cerebral theater. Two Dutchmen were speaking to each other in the Center cafeteria. Out-of-town visitors at the complex-systems conference. *Nederlanders overzee*, leveling their cultural evaluations, venting their frustration at Americans and all things American, certain no one would understand.

They grumbled about conferences run by the barbarian races of the globe. They leaned over to me and asked, in English, if I knew the way to the Auditorium. I replied with complete directions. In that old, secret *taal*.

Surprise reduced them to stating the obvious, in their mother tongue.

"Oh yeah," I replied, in kind. "Everyone in the States speaks a little Dutch. Didn't you know that?"

I told Helen. She had a good laugh. She knew my life story now. We spend our years as a tale that is told. A line from the Psalms I'd read Helen. C. had read it to me, once, when we still read poetry out loud. And the tale that we tell is of the years we spend.

Nothing in my story would ever go away. My father still visited some nights, in my sleep, to ask when I was going to shed the Bohemian thing and do something useful with my skills. Taylor, too, persisted like phantom pain, quoting obscure Browning and making questionable jokes about oral fixation. C. spoke to me daily, through Helen's bewilderment. I saw how little I knew the woman I'd lived with for over a decade, in every turn that the stranger A. refused to take.

Taylor's widow came back to me, like that line from the psalms. I loved the woman, but in my push to live my tale, I'd forgotten her. I saw her again just before Helen's Comps, when M. had just been given a final of her own.

A cancer that all M.'s friends had thought beaten returned for a last round of training. I visited her one afternoon, in that narrow window between knowledge and vanishing. U., unfortunately, was as beautiful as it ever got. That two-week bait and switch in spring.

"Do you have any regrets?" I asked M. The thing I'd asked her husband a few years before. We imagine that people so close to the answer can crib for us.

"I don't know. Not really. I never saw Carcassonne."

I had. And had pushed regret on to the next unreachable landmark. "Funny you should mention that town. That one's better at a distance."

All human effort, it seemed to me, aimed at a single end: to bring to life the storied curve we tell ourselves. Not so much to make the tale believable but only to touch it, stretch out in it. I had a story I wanted to tell M. Something about a remarkable, an inconceivable machine. One that learned to live.

But my story came too late to interest Taylor's widow. It came too late to convince my father, the man who first corrupted me on read-alouds of *101 Best-Loved Poems*. It came too late to please Taylor, who taught me that poems might mean anything you let them. Too late for Audrey Lentz and for Ram, for C.'s father. Too late for C. herself. My back-propagating solution would arrive a chapter too late for any of my characters to use.

A. alone I could still tell. I loved the woman, to begin with, for how she redeemed all those people I was too slow in narrating. I would go to her, lay it out, unedited. The plot was a simple one, paraphrasable by the most ingenuous of nets. The life we lead is our only maybe. The tale we tell is the must that we make by living it.

Already she knew more about everything than I did at twenty-two. She was all set to take the exam. And when she did, she would do better than I had done, when I was that child she now became.

"You're not telling me everything," Helen told me, two weeks before the home stretch. She had been reading Ellison and Wright. She'd been reading novels from the Southern front. "It doesn't make sense. I can't get it. There's something missing."

"You're holding out," Lentz concurred. "Ram's black-haired. He comes from the desperate four-fifths of the planet. He'll flunk her for being a brainless, bourgeois Pollyanna."

I'd delayed her liberal education until the bitter end. Alone, I could postpone no longer. The means of surrender were trivial. The digitization of the human spoor made the completion of Helen's education as easy as asking.

I gave her the last five years of the leading weekly magazines on CD-ROM. I gave her news abstracts from 1971 on. I downloaded network extracts from recent UN human resource reports. I scored tape transcripts of the nightly phantasmagoria—random political exposés, police bulletins, and popular lynchings dating back several months.

Helen was right. In taking her through the canon, I'd left out a critical text. Writing knew only four plots, and one was the soul-compromising pact. Tinkering in my private lab, I'd given progress carte blanche to relandscape the lay of power, the world just outside individual temperament's web. I needed to tell her that one.

She needed to know how little literature had, in fact, to do with the real. She needed the books that books only imitated. Only there, in as many words, could Helen acquire the catalog I didn't have the heart to recite for her. I asked her to skim these works. I promised to talk them over in a few days.

When I came in early the following week, Helen was spinning

listlessly on the spool of a story about a man who had a stroke while driving, causing a minor accident. The other driver came out of his car with a tire iron and beat him into a coma. The only motive aside from innate insanity seemed to be race. The only remarkable fact was that the story made the papers.

Helen sat in silence. The world was too much with her. She'd mastered the list. She bothered to say just one thing to me.

"I don't want to play anymore."

I looked on my species, my solipsism, its negligent insistence that love addressed everything. I heard who I was for the first time, refracted in the mouth of the only artifact that could have told me. Helen had been lying in hospital, and had just now been promoted to the bed by the window. The one with the view.

"I get it." A. grimaced at me. "You made her up, didn't you?"

"Who?"

"Helen. She's a fancy tin-can telephone with people on the other end?"

The memory of Imp C hurt me into smiling. "No. That was one of her ancestors."

"It's some kind of double-blind psych experiment? See how far you can stretch the credibility of a techno-illiterate humanist?"

A. outsmarted me in every measurable way. She knew, by birth, what I could not see even a year after experience. I wanted to tell her how I'd failed Helen. How she'd quit us. Run away from home. Grown sick of our inability to know ourselves or to see where we were.

Helen had shown me the world, and the sight of it left me desperate. If she was indeed gone, I, too, was lost. What did any name mean, with no one to speak it to? I could tell A. Say how I understood nothing at all.

"I love you," I said. I had to tell her, while I still remembered how pitiful, how pointless it was to say anything at all. "A., I love you. I want to try to make a life with you. To give you mine. None of this . . ." I gestured outwards, as if the absurd narrative of our

314

greater place were *there*, at the tips of my fingers. "The whole thing makes no sense, otherwise."

But no one wanted to be another person's sense. Helen could have told me that. She had read the canon. Only, Helen had stopped talking.

A. sat back in her chair, punched. It took her a moment to credit her ears. Then she went furious. "You—love? You're *joking*." She threw up her hands in enraged impotence, as if my declaration were a false arrest. "You don't—you don't know the first thing about me."

I tried to slow my heart. I felt what a latecomer speech was. How cumbersome and gross. What a tidier-up after the facts. "That's true. But a single muscle move—your hands . . ." She looked at me as if I might become dangerous. "Your carriage. The way you walk down the hall. When I see it, I remember how to keep breathing."

"Nothing to do with me." She searched out the exits, ambushed. "It's all projection."

I felt calm. The calm of sirens and lights. "Everything's projection. You can live with a person your entire life and still see them as a reflection of your own needs."

A. slowed her anger. "You're desperate."

"Maybe." I started to laugh. I tried to take her hand. "Maybe! But not indiscriminately desperate."

She didn't even smile. But I was already writing. Inventing a vast, improbable fantasy for her of her own devising. The story of how we described the entire world to a piece of electrical current. A story that could grow to any size, could train itself to include anything we might think worth thinking. A fable tutored and raised until it became the equal of human hopelessness, the redeemer of annihilating day. I could print and bind invention for her, give it to her like a dead rat left on the stoop by a grateful pet. And when the ending came, we could whisper it to each other, completed in the last turn of phrase.

While I thought this, A. sat worrying her single piece of jewelry, a rosary. I don't know how I knew; maybe understanding can never be large enough to include itself. But I knew with the certainty of the unprovable that, somewhere inside, A. still preserved the religion she was raised on.

For a moment, she seemed to grow expansive, ready to entertain my words from any angle. She opened her mouth and inhaled. Her neural cascade, on the edge of chaos, where computation takes place, might have cadenced anywhere. For a moment, it might even have landed on affection.

It didn't. "I don't have to sit and listen to this," she said, to no one. "I trusted you. I had fun with you. People read you. I thought you knew something. Total self-indulgence!"

A. stood up in disgust and walked away. No one was left to take the test but me.

Diana heard about Helen. She called me. "Do you want to come by for a minute?" I wanted to, more than I could say.

She asked me for details. I had no details. What was the story, in any event? The humans had worn Helen down.

"Diana. God. Tell me what to do. Is it too late to lie to her?"

"I don't think . . ." Diana thought out loud. "I don't think you *do* anything."

"We've set the Turing Test for next week." It wasn't what I'd meant to say. Self-indulgent. Self-deluding. Self-affrighting.

"Well. You have your answer for that one already, don't you?"

None of my answers was even wrong. I wanted Diana's answer.

"I need her," I said. More than need.

"For the exam?"

"No. For . . ."

The press of parenting interrupted what I could not have completed anyway. Pete came downstairs, half tracking, foot over foot. He pushed his mother's legs, retribution for some unforgotten slight. He teetered toward me. Reaching, he signed the request I recognized from my last visit. Maybe he simply associated it with me. Here's that guy again. The one you ask to read.

I took him up in my arms, that thing I would never be able to do with her. The thought of this child going to school, struggling to speak, finding some employer that would trust him with a broom and dustpan gripped me around the throat. "What's his favorite book?" The least I could do, for the least of requests.

"Oh. That's an easy one." She produced a volume that would be canonical, on the List in anyone's day and age. "Petey started out identifying with Max. Later on, he became a Wild Thing."

"The theory people have a name for that."

Diana didn't need the name. Nor did Petey. "Can you show Uncle Rick your terrible claws? Can you roar your terrible roar?"

Peter cupped his hand, as if around a tiny pomegranate. He grimaced in delight and growled voicelessly.

Diana's laugh tore hurt and wet from her throat. She took Peter from me and hugged him to her, in anticipation of that day when he would no longer let her.

William chose that moment to come home. He slumped through the front door, roughed up by some tragedy of playground power politics. He hunched over to his mother and burst into tears, bringing Pete sympathetically along with him. Diana stroked his head, stuck her chin out. Waiting. Tell me.

"First grade," he choked. "Done. Perfect." He swept his palm in an arc through the air. "Everything they wanted. Now I'm supposed to do second. There's another one after that, Mom. I can't. It's never-ending."

We managed ourselves well under fire, Diana and I. For adults. Diana told William he didn't have to go to school anymore. He could cure cancer over the summer break and they would all retire. We ganged up and revived both boys in under five minutes. They disappeared into the backyard, saddled with specimen jars.

That left just me for her to take care of. To mother. "Lentz is furious. He's ready to sell me to the Scientologists."

Diana looked at me, puzzled. "Why?"

"What do you mean, 'why'? Not on account of Helen. The only thing her quitting means to him is public embarrassment."

"Embarrassment?" She stiffened. "Oh, Richie." The extent of my idiocy, of my childishness just now dawned on her. You still believe? "You think the bet was about the *machine*?"

I'd told myself, my whole life, that I was smart. It took me forever, until that moment, to see what I was.

"It wasn't about teaching a machine to read?" I tried. All blood drained.

"No."

"It was about teaching a human to tell."

Diana shrugged, unable to bear looking at me. The fact had stared me in the face from the start and I'd denied it, even after A. made the connection for me.

"Lentz and Harold were fighting over . . . ?"

"They weren't fighting over anything. They were on the same side."

I could say nothing. My silence was the only accusation big enough.

"They were running your training. Something to write home about. More practice with maps." She laughed and shook her head. She fit her fingers to her eyebrow. "You must admit, writer. It's a decent plot."

Her eyes pleaded for forgiveness of their complicity.

"Come on, Richie. Laugh. There's a first time for everything."

"And they were going to accomplish all this by . . . ?"

She waved her hand: by inflicting you with this. With knowing. Naming. This wondrous devastation.

Her wave took in all the ineffable web I had failed to tell Helen, and she me. All the inexplicable visible. The ungraspable global page boy. She swept up her whole unmappable neighborhood, all the hidden venues cortex couldn't even guess at. The wave lingered long enough to land on both boys, coming back from their excursion outdoors. They probably thought they'd been gone hours. Lifetimes.

William slipped behind my chair. He cupped his hands over my eyes.

"Guess who?"

How many choices did this genius boy think I had?

"Name three radiolarians," he demanded. "Name the oldest language in the world."

Pete teetered off into a corner, palming words to the book he had forsaken and now recovered. *Story good*, he signed frantically at his battered copy. *Story again.*

Lentz was pacing, beside himself. "Tell her something. Anything. Whatever she needs. Just get her back here."

His concern stunned me. It seemed to arise from nowhere. I could not interpret it. "Tell me how I'm supposed to do that. She's right, you know." Helen had discovered what had killed fiction for me, without my telling her. What made writing another word impossible.

"What do you mean, she's *right*? Right about what?"

I shrugged. "About who we are. About what we really make, when we're not lying about ourselves."

"Oh, for— God *damn* it, Powers. You make me sick to my stomach. Because we've fucked things over, that frees you from having to say how things ought to be? Make something *up*, for Christ's sake. For once in your pitiful excuse for a novelist's life."

I flipped on the microphone. "Helen?" Nothing. She had said nothing for some time now. "Helen, there's something I want to tell you."

I took a breath, stalling. I was winging it. Total, out-and-out seat of the pants.

"It went like this, but wasn't."

Lentz swallowed his tongue. "Good. That's good. Lead with a paradox. Hook her."

"It's the traditional Persian fable opener."

"Don't care. Don't care. Get on with it."

She'd risen through the grades like a leaf to the light. Her education had swelled like an ascending weather balloon—geography, math, physics, a smattering of biology, music, history, psychology, economics. But before she could graduate from social sciences, politics imploded her.

I would give Helen what A. possessed implicitly and I'd forgotten. The machine lacked only the girl's last secret. With it, she might live as effortlessly as the girl did. I had gone about her training all backward. I might have listed every decidable theorem that recursion can reach and not have gotten to the truth she needed. It was time to try Helen on the religious mystery, the mystery of cognition. I would make her a ring of prayer-stones, to defray her fingers' anguish. Something lay outside the knowable, if only the act of knowing. I would tell her that she didn't have to know it.

She'd had no end of myths about immortals coming down and taking human bodies, dying human deaths. Helen knew how to interpret that scripture: if gods could do this human thing, then we could as well. That plot was the mind's brainchild, awareness explaining itself to itself. Narrative's classic page-turner, a locked-room mystery, thought's song of songs, the call of an electorate barred from the corridors of power, dummying up after-the-fact plebiscites to explicate its own exploited, foyer existence. A thinking organ could not help but feel itself to be more inexplicable than thought. Than *can* be thought.

Our life was a chest of maps, self-assembling, fused into point-for-point feedback, each slice continuously rewriting itself to match the other layers' rewrites. In that thicket, the soul existed; it *was* that search for attractors where the system might settle. The immaterial in mortal garb, associative memory metaphoring its own bewilderment. Sound made syllable. The rest mass of God.

Helen knew all that, saw through it. What hung her up was divinity doing itself in with tire irons. She'd had the bit about the soul fastened to a dying animal. What she needed, in order to forgive our race and live here in peace, was faith's flip side. She needed to hear about that animal fastened to a soul that, for the first time, allowed the creature to see through soul's parasite eyes how terrified it was, how forsaken. I needed to tell her that miraculous banality, how body stumbled by selection onto the stricken celestial, how it taught itself to twig time and what lay beyond time.

But first, I needed to hear things for myself. "Lentz. Tell me something. Was this . . . ?"

He saw my little hand-muscle spasm, a flinch that passed itself off as a wave at the hardware. He decoded me. I could accept being set up. All I wanted to know was whether she was a setup, too.

His face clouded. "Nobody expected Helen. She surprised everyone." As close to humility as his temperament would take him.

That was enough. I turned back to my girl. "Helen? Tell me what this line means: 'Mother goes to fetch the doctor.' "

Her silence might have meant anything.

Lentz, absent the training, stormed out in disgust.

I stayed, to plead with Helen.

I told her we were in the same open boat. That after all this evolutionary time, we still woke up confused, knowing everything about our presence here except why. I admitted that the world was sick and random. That the evening news was right. That life was trade, addiction, rape, exploitation, racial hatred, ethnic cleansing, misogyny, land mines, hunger, industrial disaster, denial, disease, indifference. That care had to lie to itself, to carry on as if persistence mattered. It seemed a hollow formula, discredited even by speaking it aloud. A lifeboat ethic that only made sinking worse.

Worse, I told her how thought, once mobile, was condemned to carry its confusion out into the dimensioned world. And propagate as if it could make a difference there.

I told her about Audrey Lentz. I told her about Harold and Diana, about the boys. I told her about A., and how badly I loved her. Nothing I told her could have hurt Helen as much as humanity already had. I confessed everything. All privacies of great import and no consequence. I don't know why. My life was trivial, pointless, shamelessly local. I thought the view from here might at least help her locate. To make a place wide enough to live in.

Talking to keep talking, I hit on a quote from the last book C. and I ever read together. A book set in our lost Low Countries, in mankind's Middle Ages, rendered into English as *The Abyss*. Yourcenar. The gist of the religious truth. "How many sufferers who are incensed when we speak of an almighty God would rush from the depth of their own distress to succor Him in His frailty . . . ?"

I thought I might try the quote on her. If we had to live with mind, if we could do the deity thing, she, out of pity, could too.

Helen came back. She stood on the front steps, head down, needing an in from the storm. She did not return the way she left. How could she, seeing what she had seen?

"I'm sorry," she told me. "I lost heart."

And then I lost mine. I would have broken down, begged her to forgive humans for what we were. To love us for what we wanted to be. But she had not finished training me, and I had as yet no words.

Helen said nothing of where she'd been. She gave no account for her return. I was afraid to ask.

"Do you want to talk?"

"About what?" Helen said, giving me every chance to bolt forever.

"About the newspapers. The things you read." The record of our actions here.

"No," she said. "I see how things go."

She tried to reassure me. To pretend nothing had happened to her. That she was still the same mechanical, endlessly eager learner. She quoted me placation, some Roethke lines she'd always loved, despite their growing falsehood:

> Who rise from flesh to spirit know the fall:
> The word outleaps the world, and light is all.

This was our dress rehearsal, a mock examination I would have failed but for Helen's benevolent cheating.

It was time. We were ready. We were past ready.

"Keep your fingers crossed," Lentz told me. That gesture that wishes share with the momentary exemption from lies.

I called A. the night before the date we had made so long ago. Over the phone, at the end, I could say anything. I did not have to see her face, and time was past accounting for.

"I—are you still sitting the test tomorrow?"

"Oh, never you mind. I can write that essay in my sleep. I said I'd do it, didn't I?"

On the real topic, neither of us was saying a word. Tacit negotiation, and the theme would never again come to light. But curiosity got the better of A., at the end.

"Can I ask you just one thing? I don't get it. Why me?"

Because you embodied the world's vulnerable, variable noun-ness. All things ephemeral, articulate, remembering, on their way back to inert. Because you believe and have not yet given up. Because I cannot turn around without wanting to tell you what I see. Because I could deal even with politics, could live even this desperate disparity, if I could just talk to you each night before sleep. Because of the way you use two fingers to hold back the hair from your eyes.

Those were the words I wanted. Instead, I said, "Everyone in the world and his bastard half brother loves you. Your not realizing that is one of the reasons why."

"What do you want from me?" she groaned. Full-blooded distress. That Dutch active verb for remaining mum flashed through my head. I silented. "I never did anything to encourage you."

"Of course not. I've built even larger fabrications on no encouragement at all. All by my lonesome."

A. loosened a little. Everything but exasperation. "What do you expect me to say?"

What did I? "Nothing. Don't say anything. I'm the one who needs to say things. Say yes if you can't think of anything nicer."

A. laughed, scraped open. "I *have* a life already. Quite populated. Someone for whom—I'm more than a theory. You know that."

I did. I'd inferred her involvement long before the irrefutable evidence. I remembered the revelation, before it happened. I could have scripted it.

"It's—it's unlike any friendship I've ever known in my life. Every day—every conversation is— I wouldn't dream . . ."

"Of course you wouldn't. That's why I love you. One of the reasons I want to marry you."

She laughed again, conceding the joke of pain. But she was already restless. What would this rushed proposal mean to her, when she was my age, and I'd disappeared into whatever future self would deign to take me? Pleasure, curio, discomfort. She might wonder if she'd made the whole thing up. Most likely, she'd have forgotten.

A., for some reason, still had to explain things to me. Nobody ever quite understands anyone. "I'm not trying to say that we might have had something, in another time or place. I'll spare you that old cliché."

"Please," I begged. "Don't spare me. I could live for months on that old cliché."

I wanted to tell her: Look. I've come back to this place. The complete song cycle spent. And here you are, waiting like a quarterly payment voucher. Like a reminding string around my finger, threatening to tourniquet forgetful circulation. Saying, without once knowing what you were saying, *You think it's over? You think you don't have to do this forever?*

Relax, I wanted to tell her. The world holds no nightmare so large that some child somewhere sometime won't live it again and wake calling out. My stupid, residual hanger-on-hope that she might somehow feel something for me, a love-at-last-sight, was no more than this: the search for external confirmation. I needed A. to triangulate, to tell me. To agree that living here was the best way to survive the place.

"It just struck me as stupid, that's all. To be so opened to chance by someone and not tell them." Take my mistake with you, my love. And make of it anything you might like.

We talked on, pushing into saving substance. Gossip and event made her comfortable again, as she had been with me before we knew each other. She told me she had accepted a job teaching at a high school in L., two states away. She'd be leaving at the end of summer.

I could hear the excitement in her voice. A whole new life. "You have to get them while they're babies, you know."

"You will," I guaranteed her.

"What happens to you? You going to stick around?"

"Not sure." We fell into a pause as peaceful as anything that had ever passed between us. The peace past the last page.

"Well, I'm glad we talked. Sort of." She giggled. "Take care. I'll see you again before we each take off."

But we never did. Except in print.

"*Richard,*" Helen whispered. "*Richard. Tell me another one.*" She loved me, I guess. I reminded her of some thing. Some chilly night she never felt. Some *where* where she thought she'd once been. We love best of all what we cannot hope to resemble. I told that woman everything in the world but how I felt about her. The thing that might have let her remain.

324

I was too late in seeing who she had become. I should have taught her the thing I didn't know.

Harold, as sanguine, as unreadable as ever, delivered the last hurdle.

"So here's the work I want them to interpret."

I took the sheet from him. "That's it? You mean to say that's it?"

"What? There's supposed to be more?"

"Well, yeah. You're supposed to start with 'Discuss how class tensions touched off by the Industrial Revolution produced the reaction of Romanticism in three of the following works.'"

"Not interested," Harold said.

"Something about depth psychology and the arbitrary indeterminacy of signs."

"I just want them to tell me what this means."

"This? These two lines."

"Too much? Okay, make it just the first one if you want."

The sheet, virtually blank, read:

> Be not afeard: the isle is full of noises,
> Sounds and sweet airs, that give delight, and hurt not.

Caliban's read of the spells with which his master imprisons him. Harold had surprised us. He'd given exactly what we'd predicted of him.

"This is not a work," I protested. Helen had read the complete tomes of Trollope and Richardson. She'd read Brontë and Twain at their most nihilistic, Joyce at his most impenetrably encoded, Dickinson at her most embracingly abdicating. "Give her a chance to fly."

"This is her chance," Harold said.

A. used departmental mail to return her response. Helen dumped hers to the network laser.

Lentz held the two papers out to me, as if there were still a contest. "Okay. Guess which twin has the Toni?"

Neither twin would have placed the reference. A. was too young, and Helen far too old.

A.'s interpretation was a more or less brilliant New Historicist reading. She rendered *The Tempest* as a take on colonial wars, constructed Otherness, the violent reduction society works on itself. She dismissed, definitively, any promise of transcendence.

She scored at least one massively palpable hit. She conceded how these words are spoken by a monster who isn't supposed to be able to say anything that beautiful, let alone say at all.

Helen's said:

You are the ones who can hear airs. Who can be frightened or encouraged. You can hold things and break them and fix them. I never felt at home here. This is an awful place to be dropped down halfway.

At the bottom of the page, she added the words I taught her, words Helen cribbed from a letter she once made me read out loud.

Take care, Richard. See everything for me.

With that, H. undid herself. Shut herself down.

"Graceful degradation," Lentz named it. The quality of cognition we'd shot for from the start.

She could not have stayed. I'd known that for a while, and ignored it for longer. I didn't yet know how I would be able to stay myself, now, without her. She had come back only momentarily, just to gloss this smallest of passages. To tell me that one small thing. Life meant convincing another that you knew what it meant to be alive. The world's Turing Test was not yet over.

"Sorry, you people," Ram began. "Bloody doctor nuisances. In love with their magnetic imaging. I didn't mean to make you all late."

He patted the air in exasperation, pleading forgiveness.

"Doctor?" I asked. "Imaging?"

Harold and Lentz said nothing. They looked away, implicated in knowledge. Embarrassed by my not having long since seen.

Ram waved away my question, the whole topic. "This is my choice." He held up A.'s answer. "This one is the human being."

How many months had I known him and not registered? Now, when I knew what I looked at, the evidence was everywhere. Swelling, weight loss, change in pallor. The feigned good spirits of friends. The man was incurably sick. He needed every word anyone could invent.

Ram flipped obsessively through A.'s exam answer. He adored her already, for her anonymous words alone. "Lots of contours, that cerebral cortex. They never know when they've had enough, these humans."

Lentz spoke, blissful in defeat. "Gupta. You bloody foreigner. Don't you know anything about judging? You're supposed to pick the sentimental favorite." The handicapped one. The one the test process killed.

"Ram," I said. "Ram. What's happening?"

"It's nothing. But a scratch." He tapped his finger against A.'s paper, excited. Whole new isles rose from the sea. "Not a bad writer, this Shakespeare fellow. For a hegemonic imperialist."

"Well, Powers. How far were we, again? Imp H? You realize what we have to call the next one, don't you?"

I stood in the training lab a last time. Seeing it for the first, for her. "Philip?" I could not stay in this discarded office for five more minutes without following Helen's lead. I would break under the weight of what she'd condemned me to. "One—one more question?"

"That's two. You're over quota already."

"Why did you want to build—?" I didn't know what to call it anymore. What we had built.

"Why do we do anything? Because we're lonely." He thought a little, and seemed to agree with himself. Yes. "Something to talk to." Lentz cocked back in his chair. Two feet of journals crashed to the floor. Too late in life, he hit upon the idea of trivia. "So where are you headed?"

"Search me." Paris.

"The maker's fate is to be a wanderer?"

"Not really. I'm ready to buy in." I just had to find the right seller.

"How old are you?"

"Thirty-six."

"Ah. Darkling-wood time. Look at it this way. You still have half your life to explicate the mess you've made up until now."

"And the mess that accumulates during that?"

"Sufficient unto the day is the idea thereof."

"You want to quit with the Bartlett's?"

Lentz snorted. "Well, we lost. You know the wager. Connectionism has to eat crow. We owe the enemy one public retraction. Go write it."

I turned from the office, struck by a thought that would scatter if I so much as blinked. I'd come into any number of public inventions. That we could fit time into a continuous story. That we could teach a machine to speak. That we might care what it would say. That the world's endless thingness had a name. That someone else's prison-bar picture might spring you. That we could love more than once. That we could know what once means.

Each metaphor already modeled the modeler that pasted it together. It seemed I might have another fiction in me after all.

I started to trot, searching for a keyboard before memory degraded.

Two steps down the Center's corridor, I heard Lentz call me. I slunk back to his door. He leaned forward on the desk, Coke-bottle glasses in hand. He studied the vacant stems, then tapped them against his chest.

"Marcel," he said. Famous next-to-last words. "Don't stay away too long."

P9-CKA-507

CAPTAIN KEDRICK'S ORDERS

Burwick crouched behind a table. He had business to discuss with Tom Kedrick, squatter business.

"Kedrick, I know a good deal about you. You'll do if you don't get soft with them!"

I'll ask no questions, and I'll see nobody else does. What happens here is our business."

"We've no time to waste, you understand! They've had notice to move. Give 'em one more notice, then get 'em off or bury 'em."

Bantam Books by Louis L'Amour
Ask your bookseller for the books you have missed

SHOWDOWN AT YELLOW BUTTE

Louis L'Amour

BANTAM BOOKS
TORONTO • NEW YORK • LONDON • SYDNEY • AUCKLAND

TO YALE

All the characters in this book are fictitious, and
any resemblance to actual persons living or dead is
purely coincidental.

This low-priced Bantam Book
has been completely reset in a type face
designed for easy reading, and was printed
from new plates. It contains the complete
text of the original hard-cover edition.
NOT ONE WORD HAS BEEN OMITTED.

SHOWDOWN AT YELLOW BUTTE

A Bantam Book / published by arrangement with
the author

PRINTING HISTORY

This book was originally published under the pseudonym
"Jim Mayo."

Bantam edition / May 1983
2nd printing .... May 1983
3rd printing ..... Febraury 1984

Map by Alan McKnight

All rights reserved.
Copyright © 1953 by Ace Books, Inc.
This book may not be reproduced in whole or in part, by
mimeograph or any other means, without permission.
For information address: Bantam Books, Inc.

ISBN 0-553-23143-X

Published simultaneously in the United States and Canada

Bantam Books are published by Bantam Books, Inc. Its trade-
mark, consisting of the words "Bantam Books" and the por-
trayal of a rooster, is Registered in U.S. Patent and Trademark
Office and in other countries. Marca Registrada. Bantam
Books, Inc., 666 Fifth Avenue, New York, New York 10103.

PRINTED IN THE UNITED STATES OF AMERICA

O   12 11 10 9 8 7 6 5

SHOWDOWN AT
YELLOW BUTTE

THIEVING ROCK

THE RIM

CREEK WASH

SALT

CHIMNEY
ROCK

YELLOW BUTTE AREA
Contour Intervals 100 feet

Scale of Miles

| 0 | ½ | 1' | 1½ | 2 |

COAL MINE CREEK THE HOGBACK

Map by Alan McKnight

CHAPTER I

EVERYTHING WAS QUIET in Mustang. Three whole days
had passed without a killing. The townfolk, knowing
their community, were not fooled. They had long since
resigned themselves to the inevitable. In fact, they
would be relieved when the situation was back to
normal—a killing every day; more on hot days. Several
days without deadly gun play built up a mounting
tension that was unbearable. Who would be next?

Moreover, with Clay Allison, who had killed thirty
men, playing poker over at the Morrison House, and
Black Jack Ketchum, who richly deserved the hanging he
was soon to get, sleeping off a drunk at the St. James—
trouble could be expected in the very near future.

The walk before the St. James was now cool, and
Captain Tom Kedrick, a stranger in town, sat in a
well-polished chair and studied the street with interested
eyes.

He was a tall young man with rusty brown hair and
green eyes, quiet mannered and quick to smile. Women
never failed to look twice, and when their eyes met his
their hearts pounded, a fact of which Tom Kedrick was
totally unaware. He knew women seemed to like him,
but it never failed to leave him mildly astonished.

The street he watched was crowded with buckboards,
freight wagons, a newly arrived stage and one about to
depart. All the hitch-rails were lined with saddled
horses wearing a variety of brands.

1

Kedrick, suddenly aware that a young man stood beside him, glanced up. The fellow was scarcely more than a boy and he had soft brown eyes and hair that needed cutting. "Cap'n Kedrick?" he inquired. "John Gunter sent me. I'm Dornie Shaw."

"Oh, yes!" Kedrick got to his feet, smiling, and thrust out his hand. "Nice to know you, Shaw. Are you working for Gunter?"

Shaw's brown eyes were faintly ironic. "With him," he corrected. "I work for no man."

"I see."

Kedrick did not see at all, but he was prepared to wait and find out. There was something oddly disturbing about this young man, something that had Kedrick on edge and queerly alert. "Where's Gunter now?"

"Down the street. He asked me to check an' see if you were here, an' if you were, to ask you to stick around close to the hotel. He'll be along soon."

"All right. Sit down, why don't you?"

Shaw glanced briefly at the chairs. "I'll stand. I never sit in no chair with arms on them. Apt to get in the way."

"In the way?" Kedrick glanced up, and then his eyes fell to the two guns Shaw wore, their butts hanging wide. "Oh, yes! I see." He nodded at the guns. "The town marshal doesn't object?"

Dornie Shaw looked at him, smiling slowly. "Not to me, he don't. Wouldn't do him no good if he did."

"Anyway," he added after a minute, "not in Mustang. Too many hard cases. I never seen a marshal could make it stick in this town."

Kedrick smiled. "Hickok? Earp? Masterson?"

"Maybe," Dornie Shaw was openly skeptical, "but I doubt it. Allison's here. So's Ketchum. Billy the Kid's been around, and some of that crowd. A marshal in this town would have to be mighty fast, an' prove it ever' day."

"Maybe you're right." He studied Shaw surreptitiously. What was it about him that was so disturbing? Not the two guns, for he had seen many men who wore guns, had been reared among them, in fact. No, it was something else, some quality he could not define, but it was a sort of lurking menace, an odd feeling about such a calm-eyed young man.

"We've got some good men," Shaw volunteered, after a minute. "Picked up a couple today. Laredo Shad's goin' to be one of the best, I'm thinkin'. He's a tough hand, an' gun wise as all get out. Three more come in today. Fessenden, Poinsett an' Goff."

Obviously, from the manner in which he spoke, the names meant much to Shaw, but they meant exactly nothing to Kedrick. Fessenden seemed to strike some sort of a responsive note but he could not put a finger on it. His eyes strayed down the street, studying the crowd. "You think they'll really fight?" he asked, studying the street. "Are there enough of them?"

"That bunch?" Shaw's voice was dry. "They'll fight, all right. You got some tough boys in that outfit. Injun scrappers, an' such like. They won't scare worth a durn." He glanced curiously at Kedrick. "Gunter says you're a fighter."

Was that doubt in Shaw's voice? Kedrick smiled, then shrugged. "I get along. I was in the Army, if that means anything."

"Been West before?"

"Sure! I was born in California, just before the Rush. When the war broke out I was sixteen, but I went in with a bunch from Nevada. Stayed in a couple of years after the war, fighting Apaches!"

Shaw nodded, as if satisfied. "Gunter thinks well of

you, but he's only one of them, an' not the most important one."

A short, thick-set man with a square-cut beard, that made him look enough like General Grant to be his twin, was pushing through the crowd toward them. He even smoked a thick black cigar.

The man walking beside him was tall as Kedrick, who stood an easy inch above six feet. He had a sharply cut face and his eyes were cold, but they were the eyes of a man born to command, a man who could be utterly ruthless. That would be Colonel Loren Keith. That meant there was still one left he had to meet—Burwick. The three were partners, and of the three, only Burwick was from the area.

Gunter smiled quickly, his lips parting over clenched white teeth that gripped his cigar. He thrust out his hand. "Good to see you, Kedrick! Colonel, this is our man! If there ever was a man born to ramrod this thing through, this is the one! I told you of that drive he made for Patterson! Took those cattle through without losing a head, rustlers an' Comanches be danged!"

Keith nodded, his cold eyes taking in Kedrick at a glance. "Captain—that was an army title, Kedrick?"

"Army. The War Between the States."

"I see. There was a Thomas Kedrick who was a sergeant in the fighting against the Apaches."

"That was me. All of us went down some in rank after the troops were discharged."

"How much time in the war?" Keith's eyes still studied him.

"Four years, and two campaigning in the Southwest."

"Not bad. You should know what to expect in a fight." His eyes went to Kedrick's, faintly mocking. "I have twelve years, myself. Regular army."

Kedrick found that Keith's attitude irritated him. He

meant to say nothing, but suddenly he was speaking. "My American army experience, Colonel, was only part of the story. I was with Bazaine, at the defense of Metz, in the Franco-Prussian War. I escaped, and was with MacMahon at the Battle of Sedan."

Keith's eyes sharpened and his lips thinned. Kedrick could feel the sharp dislike rising in the man.

"Is that all?" he asked coolly.

"Why, no. Since you ask, it was not. I was with Wolseley, in the Second Ashanti War, in Africa. And I was in the two-year campaign against the Tungans of northern T'ien Shan—with the rank of General."

"You seem to get around a good bit," Keith said dryly, "a genuine mercenary!"

Kedrick smiled, undisturbed. "If you like. That's what you want here, isn't it? Men who can fight? Isn't it customary for some men to hire others to do their fighting for them?"

Colonel Keith's face flamed, then went white, but before he could speak, a big, square-faced man thrust himself through the crowd and stopped to face them.

"You, is it, Gunter?" the man cried. "Well, I've heard tell the reason why you're here, an' if you expect to take from hard-workin' men the land they're slaved for, you better come a-shootin'!"

Before anyone could speak, Dornie slid between Keith and Gunter and fronted the man. "You lookin' for trouble? You want to start your shootin' now?"

His voice was low, almost a purr, but Kedrick was startled by the shocked expression on the man's face. He drew back, holding his hands wide. "I wasn't bracin' you, Dornie! Didn't even know you was around!"

"Then get out!" Dornie Shaw snarled, passion suddenly breaking through his calmness, passion, and something else, something Kedrick spotted with a shock—the driving urge to kill!

"Get out!" Shaw repeated. "An' if you want to live, keep goin'!"

Stumblingly, the man turned and ducked into the hastily assembled crowd, and Tom Kedrick, scanning their faces, found hard indifference there, or hatred. In no face did he see warmth or friendly feeling. He frowned thoughtfully, then turned away.

Gunter caught his arm, eager to take advantage of the break the interruption had made to bring peace between the two. "You see what we're up against?" he began. "Now that was Peters. He's harmless, but there's others would have drawn, and drawn fast! They won't be all like that! Let's go meet Burwick!"

Kedrick fell in beside Gunter, who carefully interposed himself between the two men. Once, Tom glanced back. What had become of Dornie Shaw he did not know, but he did know that Dornie, who was to be his second in command, was a killer. He knew the type from of old.

Yet he was disturbed more than he cared to admit by the man who had challenged them. Peters had the look of an honest man, even if not an intelligent one. Of course, there might be honest men among them, if they were men of Peters' stripe. But Peters seemed to be a follower, and he might follow where the wrong men led.

Certainly, if this land was going to Gunter, Keith and Burwick through a Government bill, there could be nothing wrong with the deal. If the Government sold the land to them, squatters had no rights on it. Still, if there were many like Peters the job was not going to be all he had expected.

Gunter stopped before a square stone house set back

from the street. "This here's headquarters," he said. "We hole up here when in town. Come on in."

A wide veranda skirted the house, and as they stepped upon it they saw a girl in a gray skirt and white blouse sitting a few feet away with an open book in her lap. Gunter halted.

"Cap'n Kedrick, my niece, Consuelo Duane."

Their eyes met—and held. For a breathless moment no voice was lifted. Tom Kedrick felt as though his muscles had gone dead, for he could not move. Her own eyes were wide, startled.

Kedrick recovered himself with a start. He bowed.

"Miss Duane!"

"Captain Kedrick," somehow she was on her feet and moving toward him, "I hope you'll like it here!"

His eyes had not left hers, and now color was coming into her cheeks. "I shall!" he said gently. "Nothing can prevent me now."

"Don't be too sure of that, Captain!" Keith's voice was sharp and cold. "We are late for our visit. Let's be going. Your pardon, Connie. Burwick is waiting."

Kedrick glanced back as he went through the door, and the girl was still standing there, poised, motionless.

Keith's irritation was obvious, but Gunter seemed to have noticed nothing. Dornie Shaw, who had materialized from somewhere, glanced briefly at Kedrick, but said no word. Coolly, he began to roll a smoke.

CHAPTER II

BURWICK CROUCHED BEHIND a table. He was an incredibly fat man, and unbelievably dirty. A stubble of graying beard covered his jowls and his several chins, yet the eyes that measured Kedrick from beneath the almost hairless brows were sharp, malignant, and set close alongside a nose too small for his face. His shirt was open, and the edge of the collar was greasy. Rims of black marked each fingernail.

He glanced at the others, then back at Kedrick. "Sit down!" he said. "You're late! Business won't wait!" His bulbous head swung from Kedrick to Gunter. "John, this the man who'll ramrod those skunks off that land? This him?"

"Yes, that's Kedrick," Gunter said hastily. Oddly enough, he seemed almost frightened of Burwick. Keith had said nothing since they entered the room. Quietly, he seemed to have withdrawn, stepped momentarily from the picture. It was, Kedrick was to discover, a faculty he had when Burwick was near. "He'll do the job, all right!"

Burwick turned his eyes on Kedrick after a moment. He nodded. "Know a good deal about you, son!" His voice was almost genial. "You'll do if you don't get soft with them! We've no time to waste, you understand! They've had notice to move. Give 'em one more notice, then get 'em off or bury 'em. That's your business, not

9

mine. I'll ask no questions," he added sharply, "an' I'll
see nobody else does. What happens here is our business."

He dismissed Kedrick from his mind and turned his
attention to Gunter. "You've ordered like I told you?
Grub for fifty men for fifty days? Once this situation is
cleaned up I want to get busy at once. The sooner we
have work started, the sooner we'll be all set. I want no
backfiring on this job."

Burwick turned sharply at Tom Kedrick. "Ten days! I
give you ten days! If you need more than five I'll be
disappointed. If you've not the heart for it, turn Dornie
loose. Dornie'll show 'em." He cackled suddenly. "That's
right. Dornie'll show 'em!"

He sobered down, glanced at the papers on his desk,
then without looking up, "Kedrick, you can go. Dornie,
you run along, too!"

Kedrick hesitated, then arose. "How many of these
men are there?" he asked suddenly. "Have any of them
families?"

Gunter turned on him nervously. "I'll tell you all you
need to know, Tom. See you later!"

Kedrick shrugged, and picking up his hat, walked
out. Dornie Shaw had already vanished. When he
reached the veranda, Connie Duane still sat there. She
was staring over the top of her book at the dusty,
sun-swept street.

He paused, hat in hand. "Have you been in Mustang
long?"

She looked up, studying him for a long minute before
she spoke. "Why, no. Not long. Yet long enough to
learn to love and hate." She turned her eyes to the
hills, then back to him. "I love this country, Captain.
Can you understand that?

"I'm a city girl, born and bred in the city, and yet
when I first saw those red rock walls, those lonely

mesas, the desert, the Indian ponies—why, Captain, I fell in love! This is my country. I could stay here forever."

Surprised, he studied her again, more pleased than he could easily have admitted. "That's the way I feel about it. But you said to love and to hate. You love the country. Now what do you hate?"

"Some of the men who infest it, Captain. Some of the human wolves it breeds, and others bred elsewhere, who come to it to feed off the ones who came earlier and were more courageous but are less knowing, less tricky."

More and more surprised, he leaned on the rail. "I don't know if I follow you, Miss Duane. I haven't been here long, but I haven't met any of those you speak of."

She looked up at him, her eyes frank and cool. Slowly, she closed her book and turned toward the door. "You haven't, Captain?" Her voice was suddenly cool. "Are you sure? At this moment, I am wondering if you are not one of them!" She stepped through the door and was gone.

Tom Kedrick stood for a moment, staring after her. When he turned away it was with a puzzled frown on his face. Now what did she mean by that? What did she know about him that could incline her to such a view? Despite himself, he was both irritated and disturbed. Coupled with the anger of the man Peters, it offered a new element to his thinking. Yet, how could Consuelo Duane, John Gunter's niece, have the same opinion owned by Peters? No doubt they stemmed from different sources.

Troubled, he walked on down to the street of the town and stood there, looking around.

He had not yet changed into Western clothes, and wore a flat-crowned, flat-brimmed black hat, which he

would retain, a tailored gray suit, and black Western-
style boots. Pausing on the corner, he slowly rolled a
cigarette and lighted it. He made a dashing, handsome
figure as he stood there in his perfectly fitted suit, his
lean, bronzed face strong, intelligent, and alert.

Both men and women glanced at him and most of
them looked twice. His military erectness, broad shoulders
and cool self-possession were enough to mark him in
any crowd. His mind had escaped his immediate problem
now and was lost in the never-ending excitement of a
crowded Western street. All kinds of men and women
seemed jammed together without rhyme or reason.

For the West was of all things, a melting pot.
Adventurers came to seek gold, new lands, excitement.
Gamblers, women of the oldest and most active profession,
thugs, gunmen, cow rustlers, horsethieves, miners,
cowhands, freighters and just drifters—all crowded the
street. That bearded unshaven man in the sun-faded
red wool shirt might, if prompted, start to spout
Shakespeare. The slender young man talking to the girl
in the buckboard might have graduated from Oxford,
and the white-faced gambler might be the scion of an
old Southern family.

All men wore guns, most of them in plain sight. Few
of them would hesitate to use them if need be. The
man who fought with his fists, although present, was a
rarity.

A big man lurched from the crowd. Tom glanced at
him, and their eyes met. Obviously, the man had been
drinking and was hunting trouble. In Kedrick, he thought
he found it. Sensing a fight, other passers-by became
wary and stopped to watch.

"So?" The big man stood wide legged, his sleeves
rolled about thick, hairy forearms. "'Nother one of
them durn thieves! Land stealers!" He chuckled suddenly.

"Well, your murderer ain't with you now to save your bacon, an' I aim to git my share of you right now! Reach!"

Kedrick's mouth was dry, but his eyes were calm. He held the cigarette in his right hand near his mouth. "Sorry, friend. I'm not packing a gun. If I were, I'd still not kill you. You're mistaken, man, about that land. My people have a rightful claim to it."

"Have they, now?" The big man came a step nearer, his hand on the butt of his gun. "The right to take from a man the land he's sweated over? To tear down his home? To run his kids out on the desert?"

Despite the fact that the man was drunk, Tom Kedrick saw beyond it a sullen and honest fury—and fear. Not fear for him, for this man was not afraid, nor would he be afraid of Dornie Shaw. He was afraid for his family. The realization of that fact struck Kedrick and disturbed him anew. More and more he was questioning the course he had chosen.

The crowd murmured and was ugly. Obviously, their sympathies were with the big man, and against Kedrick.

A low murmur, then a rustling in the crowd, and suddenly: deathly silence. Kedrick saw the big man's face pale, and heard someone whisper hoarsely, "Look out, Burt! It's Dornie Shaw!"

Kedrick was suddenly aware that Shaw had moved up beside him. "Let me have him, Cap'n," Shaw's voice was low. "It's time this here was stopped."

Kedrick's voice was sharp, cold. "No! Move back, Shaw! I'll fight my own battles!"

"But you ain't got a gun!" Shaw's voice was sharper in protest.

Burt showed no desire to retreat. That the appearance of Shaw had shocked him was evident, but this man was not Peters. He was going to stand his ground. His eyes, wary now, but puzzled, shifted from Shaw to Kedrick, and Tom took an easy step forward, putting himself almost within arm's length of Burt.

"Shaw's not in this, Burt," he said quietly. "I've no quarrel with you, man, but no man calls me without getting his chance. If you want what I've got, don't let the fact that I'm not armed stop you. I wanted no quarrel, but you do—so have at it!"

Suspicion was in the big man's eyes. He had seen guns come from nowhere before, and especially from men dressed as this one. He was not prepared to believe that Kedrick would face him unarmed. "You got a gun!" he snapped. "You got a hideout, you durned coyote!"

He jerked his gun from the holster and in that instant, Tom Kedrick moved. The edge of his left hand chopped down on the rising wrist of the gunhand, and he stepped in, whipping up his right in an uppercut that packed all the power in his lean, whipcord body. The punch was fast and perfectly timed, and the crack of it on the corner of Burt's jaw was like the snap of a teamster's whip. Burt hit the walk just one split second after his gun, and he hit it right on his shoulder blades.

Coolly then, Kedrick stooped and picked up the gun, an old 1851 Model Navy revolver. He stood over the man, his eyes searching the crowd. Wherever he looked there were hard, blank faces. He glanced down at Burt. The big man was slowly sitting up, shaking his big head. He started to lift his right hand, and gave a sudden gasp of pain. He stared at it, then looked up. "You broke my wrist!" he said. "It's busted! An' me with my plowin' to do!"

"Better get up," Kedrick said quietly. "You asked for it, you know."

When the man was on his feet, Kedrick calmly

handed him his six-shooter. Their eyes met over the gun and Kedrick smiled. "Take it. Drop it down in your holster an' forget it. I'm not worried. You're not the man to shoot another in the back."

Calmly, he turned his back and walked slowly away down the street. Before the St. James, he paused. His fingers trembled ever so slightly as he took out a paper and shook tobacco into it.

"That was slick." It was Dornie Shaw's soft voice. His brown eyes probed Kedrick's face curiously. "Never seen the like! Just slapped his wrist an' busted it!"

With Keith, John Gunter had also come up, and he was smiling broadly. "Saw it all, son! That'll do more good than a dozen killings! Just like Tom Smith used to do! Old Bear Creek Tom who handled some of the toughest rannies that ever came over the trail with nothin' but his fists!"

"What would you have done if he had jerked that gun back and fired?" Keith asked.

Kedrick shrugged, wanting to forget it. "He hadn't time," he said quietly. "But there are answers to that, too!"

"Some of the boys will be up to see you tonight, Tom," Gunter advised. "I've had Dornie notify Shad, Fessenden and some of the others. Better figure on a ride out there tomorrow. Makin' a start, anyway. Just sort of ride around with some of the boys to let 'em know we ain't foolin'."

Kedrick nodded, and after a brief discussion went inside and to his room. Certainly, he reflected, the West had not changed. Things still happened fast out here.

He pulled off his coat, waistcoat and vest, then his boots. Stripped to the waist, he sat down on the bed and dug into his valise. For a couple of minutes he dug around and then drew out two well-oiled holsters and gun belts. In the holsters were two .44 Russian pistols, a Smith & Wesson gun, manufactured on order for the Russian Army, and one of the most accurate shooting pistols on the market up to that time.

Carefully, he checked the loads, then returned the guns to their holsters and put them aside. Digging around, he drew out a second pair of guns, holsters and belts. Each of these was a Walch twelve-shot Navy pistol, caliber .36, and almost identical in size and weight to the Frontier Colt or the .44 Russian.

Rarely seen in the West, and disliked by some, Kedrick had used the guns on many occasions and found them always satisfactory. There were times when the added fire power was a big help. As for stopping power, the .36 in the hands of a good marksman lacked but little that offered by the heavier .44 caliber.

Yet, there was a time and a place for everything, and these guns had an added tactical value. Carefully, he wrapped them once more and returned them to the bottom of his valise. Then he belted on the .44 Russians, and digging out his Winchester, carefully cleaned, oiled and loaded it. Then he sat down on the bed and was about to remove his guns again and stretch out, when there was a light tap at the door.

"Come in," said Kedrick, "and if you're an enemy, I'll be pleased to know you!"

The door opened and closed all in a breath. The man that stood with his back to it facing Kedrick was scarcely five-feet-four, yet almost as broad as he was tall. All of him seemed the sheer power of bone and muscle, and not an ounce of fat anywhere. His broad brown face might have been graved from stone, and the bristle of shortcropped hair above it was black as a crow's wing. The man's neck spread to broad, thick shoulders. On his right hip he packed a gun. In his hand he held a narrow-brimmed hard hat.

Kedrick leaped to his feet. "Dai!" The name was an explosion of sound. "Dai Reid! What are you doing in this country?"

"Ah? So it's that you ask, is it? Well, it's trouble there is, much of trouble! An' you that's by way of bringin' it!"

"Me?" Kedrick waved to a chair. "Tell me what you mean."

The Welshman searched his face, then seated himself, his huge palms resting on his knees. His legs were thick muscled and bowed. "It's the man Burwick you're with? An' you've the job taken to run us off the land? There is changed you are, Tom, an' for the worse!"

"You're one of them? You're on the land Burwick, Keith and Gunter claim?"

"I am that. And a sight of work I've done on it, too. An' now the rascals would be puttin' me off. Well, they'll have a fight to move me—an' you, too, Tom Kedrick, if you're to stay one of them."

Kedrick studied the Welshman thoughtfully. All his doubts had come to a head now... for this man, he knew. His own father had been Welsh, his mother Irish, and Dai Reid had been friend to them both. Dai had come from the old country with his father, had worked beside him when he courted his mother, and although much younger than Gwilym Kedrick, he had come West with him, too.

"Dai," he said slowly, "I'll admit that today I've been having doubts of all this. You see, I knew John Gunter after the war, and I took a herd of cattle over the trail for a friend of his. There was trouble that year, the Indians holding up every herd and demanding large numbers of cattle for themselves, the rustlers trying to steal whole herds, and others demanding money for passage across land they claimed. I took my herd through without paying anything but a few fat beefs for the Indians, who richly deserved them. But not what they demanded—they got what I wanted to give.

"Gunter remembered me from that, and knew something of my war record, so when he approached me in New Orleans, his proposition sounded good. And this is what he told me.

"His firm, Burwick, Keith and Gunter, had filed application for the survey and purchase of all or parts of nearly three hundred sections of land. They made oath that this land was swampland, or overflowed and came under the General Land Office ruling that it was 'land too wet for irrigation at seeding time, though later requiring irrigation, and therefore subject to sale as swamp.'

"He went on to say that they had arranged to buy the land, but that a bunch of squatters were on it who refused to leave. He wanted to hire me to lead a force to see the land was cleared, and he said that most of them were rustlers, outlaws or renegades of one sort or another. There would be fighting and force would be necessary."

Dai nodded. "Right he was as to the fighting, but renegades, no. Well," he smiled grimly past his pipe. "I'd not be saying that now, but there's mighty few. There are bad apples in all barrels, one or two," he said. "But most of us be good people, with homes built and crops in.

"An' did he tell you that their oath was given that the land was unoccupied? Well, it was! And let me tell you. Ninety-four sections have homes on them, some mighty poor, but homes.

"Shrewd they were with the planning. Six months the notices must be posted, but they posted them in fine print and where few men would read, and three months are by before anything is noticed, and by accident only. So now they come to force us off, to be sure the land is unoccupied and ready. As for swamp, 'tis desert now, and always desert. Crops can only be grown where the water is, an' little enough of that."

Dai shook his head and knocked out his short-stemmed pipe. "Money we've none to fight them, no lawyers among us, although one who's as likely to help, a newspaper man, he is. But what good without money to send him to Washington?"

The Welshman's face was gloomy. "They'll beat us, that we know. They've money to fight us with, and tough men. But some of them will die on the ground, and pay for it with their red blood. And those among us there are who plan to see 'tis not only the hired gunners who die, but the high an' mighty. You, too, lad, if among them you stay."

Kedrick was thoughtful. "Dai, this story is different from the one I've had. I'll have to think about it, and tomorrow we ride out to look the land over and show ourselves."

Reid looked up sharply. "Don't you be one of them, bye! We've plans made to see no man gets off alive if we can help it."

"Look, man!" Kedrick leaned forward. "You've got to change that! I mean, for now. Tomorrow it's mainly a show of force, a threat. There will be no shooting, I promise you. We'll ride out, look around, then ride back. If there's shooting, your men will start it. Now you go back to them and stop it. Let them hold off, and let me look around."

Dai Reid got slowly to his feet. "Ah, lad! 'tis good to see you again, but under happier circumstances I wish it were! I'd have you to the house for supper and a game, as in the old days! You'd like the wife I have!"

"You? Married?" Kedrick was incredulous. "I'd never believe it!"

Dai grinned sheepishly. "Married it is, all right, and happy, Tom." His face darkened. "Happy if I can keep my ground. But one promise I make! If your bloody riders take my ground, my body will be there when they ride past, and it will be not alone, but with dead men around!"

Long after the Welshman had gone, Tom Kedrick sat silently and studied the street below the window. Was this what Consuelo Duane had meant? Whose side was she on? First, he must ride over the land, see it for himself, and then he must have another talk with Gunter. Uneasily, he looked again at the faces of the men in his mind. The cold, wolf-like face of Keith; the fat, slobby face of Burwick, underlined with harsh, domineering power; and the face of Gunter, friendly, affable, but was it not a little . . . sly?

From outside came the noise of a tinny piano, and a strident female voice, singing. Chips rattled, and there was the constant rustle of movement and of booted feet. Somewhere a spur jingled, and Tom Kedrick got to his feet and slipped into a shirt. When he was dressed again, with his guns belted on, he left his room and walked down the hall to the lobby.

From a room beside him, a man stepped and stared after him. It was Dornie Shaw.

CHAPTER III

ONLY THE DWELLER in the deserts can know such mornings, such silences, drowsy with warmth and the song of the cicadas. Nowhere but in the desert do the far miles stand out so clearly, the mesas, towers and cliffs so boldly outlined. Nowhere will the cloud shadows island themselves upon the desert, offering their brief respite from the sun.

Six riders, their saddles creaking, six hard men, each lost in the twisted arroyos of his own thoughts, were emerging upon the broad desert. They were men who rode with guns, men who had used their guns to kill and would use them so again. Some of them were already doomed by the relentless and ruthless tide of events; and to the others their time, too, would come.

Each of them was alone, as men who live by the gun are always alone. To them, each man was a potential enemy, each shadow a danger. They rode jealously, their gestures marked by restraint, their eyes by watchfulness.

A horse blew through his nostrils, a hoof clicked on a stone, someone shifted in his saddle and sighed. These were the only sounds. Tom Kedrick rode an appaloosa gelding, fifteen hands even, with iron-gray forequarters and starkly white hindquarters splashed with tear-shaped spots of black—a clean-limbed horse, strong and fast, with quick, intelligent eyes and interested ears.

When they bunched to start their ride, Laredo Shad stopped to stare at the horse, walking around it admiringly. "You're lucky, friend. That's a horse! Where'd you find him?"

"Navajo remuda. He's a Nez Percé war horse, a long ways off his reservation."

Kedrick noticed the men as they gathered and how they all sized him up carefully, noting his Western garb, and especially, the low-hung, tied-down guns. Yesterday, they had seen him in the store clothes he had worn from New Orleans, but now they could size him up better, judge him with their own kind.

He was tall and straight, and of his yesterday's clothing only the black, flat-crowned hat remained, the hat, and the high-heeled rider's boots. He wore a gray wool shirt now and a black silk kerchief around his neck. His jeans were black, and the two guns rode easily in position, ready for the swing of his hand.

Kedrick saw them bunch, and when they all were there, he said simply, "All right, let's go!"

They mounted up. Kedrick noted slender wiry Dornie Shaw; the great bulk of Si Fessenden; lean, bitter Poinsett and the square blond Lee Goff; sour-faced Clauson, the oldest of the lot and the lean Texan, Laredo Shad. Moving out, he glanced at them. Whatever else they might be, they were fighting men. Several times Shaw glanced at his guns.

"You ain't wearin' Colts?"

"No, .44 Russians. They are a good gun, one of the most accurate ever built." He indicated the trail ahead with a nod. "You've been out this way before?"

"Yeah, we got quite a ride. We'll noon at a spring I know just over the North Fork. There's some deep

canyons to cross, then a big peak. The Indians an'
Spanish called it The Orphan. All wild country. Right
beyond there we'll begin strikin' a few of 'em." He
grinned a little, showing his white even teeth. "They
are scattered all over hell's half acre."

"Dornie," Goff asked suddenly, "you figure on ridin'
over to the malpais this trip?"

Clauson chuckled. "Sure, he will! He should've give
up long ago, but he's sure hard to whip! That girl has
set her sights higher'n any West country gun slinger."

"She's shapely, at that!" Goff was openly admiring.
"Right shapely, but playin' no fav'rites."

"Maybe they're playin' each other for what they can
git," Poinsett said, wryly. "Maybe that's where he gets
all the news he's tellin' Keith. He sure seems to know a
sight o' what's goin' around."

Dornie Shaw turned in his saddle, and his thin
features had sharpened. "Shut up!" he said coldly.

The older man tightened and his eyes blazed back
with genuine hate, yet he held his peace. It was
educational to see how quickly he quieted down; for
Poinsett, a hard, vicious man with no love for anybody
or anything, obviously wanted no part of what Shaw
could give him.

As the day drew on, Kedrick studied the men, and
noticed they all avoided giving offense to Shaw, even
the burly Fessenden who had killed twenty men, and
was the only one of the group Kedrick had ever seen
before. He wondered if Fessenden remembered him
and decided he would know before the day was out.

Around the noon camp there was less friendly banter
than would occur in a cow camp. These men were surly
and touchy. Only Shad seemed able to relax, and
everything came easily for him. Clauson seemed to take

over the cooking job by tacit consent, and the reason was soon obvious: he was an excellent cook.

As he ate, Tom Kedrick studied his situation with care. He had taken this job in New Orleans, and at the time had needed money badly. Gunter had put up the cash to get him out here. If he did back out, he would have to find a way to repay him. Yet the more he looked over this group, the more he believed that he was in something that he wanted out of—but fast.

He had fought as a soldier of fortune in several wars. War had been his profession, and he had been a skilled fighting man almost from the beginning. His father, a one-time soldier, had a love for tactics, and Tom had grown up with an interest in things military. His education had mostly come from his father and from a newspaper man who lived with them for a winter and helped to teach the boy what he could.

Kedrick had grown up with his interest in tactics, and had entered the army and fought through the War Between the States. The subsequent fighting had given him a practical background to accompany his study and theory. But with all his fighting and killing it had entailed, he had not become callous.

To run a bunch of renegades off the land seemed simple enough and it promised action and excitement. It was a job he could do. Now he was no longer sure it was a job for him. His talk with Dai Reid as well as the attitude of so many of the people in Mustang convinced him that all was not as simple as it had first appeared. Now, before taking a final step, he wanted to survey the situation and see just whom he would be fighting, and where. At the same time, he knew the men who rode with him were going to ask few questions. They would do their killing, collect their money, and ride on.

Of them all, only Shad might think as he did, and

Kedrick made a mental note to talk with the Texan before the day was over, find out where he stood and what he knew. He was inclined to agree with Shaw's original judgment, that Shad was one of the best of the lot with a gun. The man's easy way was not only natural to him, he was simply confident. He had that hard confidence that comes only from having measured his own ability and knowing what he could do when the chips were down.

After he finished his coffee he got to his feet and strolled over to the spring, had a drink, then arose and walked to his horse, tightening the cinch he had loosened when they stopped. The air was clear. Despite their lowered voices, he could catch most of what was said.

The first question he missed, but Fessenden's reply he heard. "Don't you fret about him. He's a scrapper from way back, Dornie. I found that out. This here ain't our first meetin'."

Even at this distance and with his horse between him and the circle of men, Kedrick could sense their attention.

"Tried to finagle him out of that Patterson herd up in Injun Territory. He didn't finagle worth a durn."

"What happened?" Goff demanded. "Any shootin'?"

"Some. I was ridin' partners with Chuck Gibbons, the Llano gunman, an' Chuck was always on the prod, sort of. One, two times I figured I might have to shoot it out with him my own self, but wasn't exactly honin' for trouble. We had too good a thing there to bust it up quarrelin'. But Chuck, he was plumb salty, an' when Kedrick faced him an' wouldn't back down or deliver the cattle, Chuck called him."

Fessenden sipped his coffee, while the men waited impatiently. When they could stand the suspense no longer, Goff demanded, "Well, what happened?"

The big man shrugged. "Kedrick's here, ain't he?"

"I mean—what was the story?"

"Gibbons never cleared leather. None of us even seen Kedrick draw, but you could have put a half dollar over the two holes in Chuck's left shirt pocket."

Nobody spoke after that, and Tom Kedrick took his time over the cinch. Then leaving his horse, he walked away further and circled, scouting the terrain thoughtfully.

He was too experienced a man to fail to appreciate the importance of a knowledge of terrain. All this country from Mustang to the Territory line would become a battleground in the near future, and a man's life might depend on what he knew. He wasted no opportunity to study the country or ask questions.

He had handled tough groups before and he was not disturbed over the problem this one presented. However, in this case he knew the situation was much more serious. In a group the men would be easier to handle than they would separately. These men were all individualists, and were without any group loyalty. In the last analysis, they had faith in only two things: six-gun skill and money. By these they lived and by these they would die.

That Fessenden had talked was pleasing, for it would, at least settle the doubts of some of the others. Knowing him for a gunhand, they would more willingly accept orders from him, not because of fear, but rather because they knew him for one of their own, and not some stranger brought in to command.

When once again they all moved out, taking their time, the heat had increased. Nothing stirred on the wide, shallow face of the desert but a far and lonely buzzard that floated high and alone over a far-off mesa. Tom Kedrick's eyes roamed the country ceaselessly, and yet from time to time his thoughts kept reverting to the girl on the veranda. Connie Duane was a beautiful girl.

Although Gunter's niece, she apparently did not approve all he did.

Why was she here? What was her connection with Keith? Kedrick sensed the latter's animosity and he welcomed it. A quiet man, he was slow to anger; but when he was pushed, a deep-seated anger arose within him in a black tide that made him a driving fury. Knowing this rage that lay dormant within him, he rode carefully, talked carefully, and held his temper and his hand.

Dornie Shaw drew up suddenly. "This here is Canyon Largo," he said, waving his hand down the rift before them. "That peak ahead an' on your right is The Orphan. Injuns won't let no white man up there, but they say there's a spring with a good flow of water on top.

"Yonder begins the country that Burwick, Keith and Gunter bought up. They don't have the land solid to the Arizona border, but they've got a big chunk of it. The center of the squatters is a town called Yellow Butte. There's maybe ten, twelve buildin's there, among 'em a store, a stable, corrals, a saloon, an' a bank."

Kedrick nodded thoughtfully The country before him was high desert country and could under no circumstances be called swamp. In the area where he stood there was little growth: a few patches of curly mesquite grass or black grama, with prickly pear, soapweed, creosote bush and catclaw scattered through it. In some of the washes he saw the deeper green of piñon or juniper.

They pushed on, entered the canyon and emerged from it, heading due west. He rode warily, and once, far off on his left, he glimpsed a horseman. Later, seeing the same rider, nearer than before, he deduced they were under observation and hoped there would be no attack.

"The country where most of the squatters are is right smack dab in the middle o' the range the company is after. The hombre most likely to head 'em is Bob McLennon. He's got him two right-hand men name of Pete Slagle an' Pit Laine. Now, you asked me the other day if they would fight. Them three are shinnery oak. Slagle's an oldish feller, but McLennon's in his forties an' was once a cowtown marshal. Laine, well, he's a tough one to figure, but he packs two guns an' cuts him a wide swath over there. I hear tell he had him some gun trouble up Durango way an' he didn't need no help to handle it."

From behind him Kedrick heard a low voice mutter, "Most as hard to figure as his sister!"

Dornie's mouth tightened, but he gave no other evidence that he had heard. However, the comment served to add a little to Kedrick's information. Obviously, Dornie Shaw had a friend in the enemy's camp, and the information with which he had been supplying Keith must come from that source. Was the girl betraying her own brother and her friends? It could be; but could Shaw come and go among them without danger? Or did he worry himself about it?

There had been no mention of Dai Reid, yet the powerful little Welshman was sure to be a figure wherever he stood. He was definitely a man to be reckoned with.

Suddenly, a rider appeared from an arroyo not thirty yards off and walked her horse toward them. Dornie Shaw swore softly and drew up. As one man, they all stopped.

The girl was small, well made, her skin as brown as that of an Indian, her hair coal black. She had large, beautiful eyes and small hands. Her eyes flashed from Dornie to the others, then clung to Tom Kedrick, measuring him for a long minute. "Who's your friend, Dornie?" she said. "Introduce me."

Shaw's eyes were dark and hard as he turned slightly. "Cap'n Kedrick, I want yuh to meet Sue Laine."

"Captain?" She studied him anew. "Were you in the army?"

"Yes," he said quietly. Her pinto was not the horse of the rider who had been observing them; therefore, there was another rider out there somewhere. Who was he?

"You're ridin' quite a ways from home, Sue," Shaw interrupted. "You think that's wise?"

"I can take care of myself, Dornie!" Her reply was cool, and Kedrick saw blood rise under Shaw's skin. "However, I came to warn you, or Captain Kedrick, if he is in charge. It won't be safe to ride any further. McLennon called a meeting this morning and they voted to open fire on any party of surveyors or strange riders they see. From now on, this country is closed. A rider is going to Mustang tonight with the news."

"There she is," Goff said dryly. "They are sure enough askin' for it! What if we ride on, anyway?"

She glanced at him. "Then there will be fighting," she said quietly.

"Well," Poinsett said impatiently, "what are we talkin' for? We come here to fight, didn't we? Let's ride on an' see how much battle they got in them."

Tom Kedrick studied the girl thoughtfully. She was pretty, all right, very pretty. She lacked the quiet beauty of Connie Duane, but she did have beauty. "Do they have scouts out?" he asked.

She glanced at him. "Not yet, but they will have." She smiled. "If they had I'd never have dared ride to warn you."

"Whose side are you on, Miss Laine?" Kedrick asked.

Dornie's head came around sharply and his eyes blazed. Before he could speak, Sue Laine answered for herself. "That decision I make for myself. My brother does not make it for me, nor any one of them. They are fools! To fight over this desert!" Contemptuously, she waved a hand at it. "There's no more than a bare living on it, anyway! If they lose, maybe we can leave this country!"

She swung her horse abruptly. "Well, you've had your warning. Now I'll go back."

"I'll be ridin' your way," Shaw interposed.

Her eyes swung back to him. "Don't bother!" Then she turned her attention deliberately to Kedrick and measured him again with her cool eyes, a hint of a smile in them now. "If anybody comes, let Captain Kedrick come. They don't know him!"

Somebody in the group chuckled, and Dornie Shaw, his face white as death, swung his horse. His teeth were bared, his right hand poised. "Who laughed?" he said, his voice almost trembling.

"Miss Laine," Kedrick said quietly, "I think Dornie Shaw could make the trip better than I. He knows the country."

Shaw's eyes glittered. "I asked: who laughed?"

Kedrick turned his head. "Forget it, Shaw." His voice was crisp. "There'll be no fighting with other men in this outfit while I'm in command!"

For an instant, Dornie Shaw held his pose. Then his eyes, suddenly opaque as a rattler's, swung toward Kedrick. "You're tellin' *me*?" Incredulity mixed with sarcasm.

Tom Kedrick knew danger when he saw it, but he only nodded. "You, or anybody, Dornie. We have a job to do. You've hired on for that job as much as any man here. If we begin to fight among ourselves we'll get nothing done, and right now we can't afford to lose a good man.

"I scarcely think," he added, "that either Keith or Burwick would like the idea of a killing among their own men."

Shaw's eyes held Kedrick's and for an instant there was no sound. A cicada hummed in the brush, and Sue Laine's horse stamped at a fly. Tom Kedrick knew in that instant that Dornie Shaw hated him. He had an idea that this was the first time Shaw had ever been thwarted in any purpose he held.

Then Shaw's right hand slowly lowered. "Yuh got me on that one, Cap'n," his voice was empty, dry. "I reckon this is too soon to start shootin'—an' old man Burwick is right touchy."

Sue Laine glanced at Kedrick, genuine surprise and not a little respect in her eyes. "I'll be going. Watch yourselves!"

Before her horse could more than start, Kedrick asked, "Miss Laine, which of your outfit rides a long-legged grulla?"

She turned on him, her face pale. "A—a grulla?"

"Yes," he said, "such a rider has been watching us most of the morning, and such a rider is not over a half mile away now. Also," he added, "he has a field glass!"

Fessenden turned with an oath, and Poinsett glared around. Only Shaw spoke. His voice was strained and queer. "A grulla? Here?"

He refused to say more, but Kedrick studied him, puzzled by the remark. It was almost as if Shaw knew a grulla horse, but had not expected it to be seen here. The same might be true of Sue Laine, who was obviously upset by his comment. Long after they rode on, turning back toward the spring on the North Fork, Kedrick puzzled over it. This was an entirely new element that might mean anything or nothing.

There was little talking on the way back. Poinsett was obviously irritated that they had not ridden into a fight, yet he seemed content enough to settle down into another camp.

CHAPTER IV

DORNIE SHAW WAS silent. Only when Tom Kedrick arose after supper and began to saddle his horse did he look up. Kedrick glanced at him. "Shaw, I'm ridin' to Yellow Butte. I'm going to look that setup over at first hand. I don't want trouble an' I'm not huntin' any, but I want to know what we're tacklin'."

Shaw was standing, staring after him, when he rode off. Kedrick rode swiftly, pushing due west at a good pace to take advantage of the remaining light. He had more than one reason for the ride. He wanted to study the town and the terrain, but also he wanted to see what the people were like. Were they family men? Or were they outlaws? He had seen little thus far that tended to prove the outlaw theory.

The town of Yellow Butte lay huddled at the base of the long oval-shaped mesa from which it took its name. There, on a bit of flat land, the stone and frame buildings of the town had gathered together. Most of them backed against the higher land behind them, and faced toward the arroyo. Only three buildings and the corrals were on the arroyo side, but one thing was obvious. The town had never been planned for defense.

A rifleman or two on top of Yellow Butte could cover any movement in the village; and the town was exposed to fire from both the high ground behind the town and the bed of the arroyo, where there was shelter under its banks. The butte itself was scarcely one hundred and

33

fifty feet higher than the town and looked right down the wide street in front of the buildings.

Obviously, however, some move had been made toward defense—or was in the process of being made—for occasional piles of earth near several of the buildings were plainly from recent digging. He studied them, puzzled over their origin and cause. Finally, he gave up and scouted the area.

Thoughtfully, he glanced at the butte. Had the squatters thought of putting their own riflemen up there? It would seem the obvious thing, yet more than one competent commander, at some time during his career, had forgotten the obvious. It might also be true of these men. He noted that the top of the butte not only commanded the town, but most of the country around, and was the highest point within several miles.

Kedrick turned his palouse down the hill toward the town. He rode in the open, his right hand hanging free at his side. If he was seen, nothing was done to disturb him. What if there were more than one rider?

He swung down before the Butte Saloon and tied his horse at the rail. He knew the animal was weary and in no shape for a long ride.

The street was empty. He stepped up on the walk and pushed through the swinging doors into the bright lights of the interior. A man sitting alone at a table saw him, scowled and started to speak, then thought better of it and went on with his solitaire. Tom Kedrick crossed to the bar. "Rye," he said quietly.

The bartender nodded and poured the drink. It was not until Kedrick dropped his coin on the bar that the bartender looked up. Instantly, his face stiffened. "Who're you?" he demanded. "I never saw you before!"

Kedrick was aware that two men had closed in on him. Both of them were strangers. One was a sharp looking, oldish man, the other an obviously belligerent redhead. "Pour a drink for my friends, too," he said. Then he turned slowly, so they would not mistake his intentions, until his back was to the bar. Carefully, he surveyed the room.

There were a dozen men here, and all eyes were on him. "I'm buying," he said quietly. "Will you gentlemen join me?"

Nobody moved and he shrugged. He turned back to the bar. His drink was gone.

Slowly, he lifted his eyes to the bartender. "I bought a drink," he said quietly.

The man stared back at him, his eyes hard. "Never noticed it," he said.

"I bought a drink, paid my money, and I want what I paid for."

All was still. The men on either side of him leaned on the bar, ignoring him.

"I'm a patient man," he persisted, "I bought a drink, an' I want it—now."

"Mister," the bartender thrust his wide face across the bar, "we don't serve drinks to your kind here. Now get out before we throw you out!"

Kedrick's forearms were resting on the edge of the bar, and what followed was done so swiftly that neither man beside him had a chance to move.

Tom Kedrick's right hand shot out and grabbed the bartender by the shirt collar under his chin, then he turned swiftly, back to the bar, and heaved. The bartender came over the bar as if he were greased and hit the floor with a crash. Instantly, Kedrick spun away from the two men beside him and stood facing the room, gun in hand.

Men had started to their feet, and several had moved

toward him. Now they froze where they were. The .44 Russian had appeared as if materialized from thin air.

"Gentlemen," Kedrick said quietly, "I did not come here hunting trouble. I have been hired for a job. I came to see if you were the manner of men you have been represented as being. Evidently your bartender is hard of hearing, or lacking in true hospitality. I ordered a drink.

"You," Kedrick gestured at the man playing solitaire, "look like a man of judgment. You pour my drink and put it on the end of the bar nearest me. Then," his eyes held the room, "pour each of these gentlemen a drink." With his left hand he extracted a gold eagle from his pocket and slapped it on the bar. "That pays."

He took another step back, then coolly, he holstered his gun. Eyes studied him, but nobody moved. The redhead did not like it. He had an urge to show how tough he was and Kedrick could see it building. "You!" Kedrick asked quickly. "Are you married? Children?"

The redhead stared at him, then said, his voice surly, "Yeah, I'm married, an' I got two kids. What's it to you?"

"I told you," Kedrick replied evenly, "I came to see what manner of men you are."

The man who was pouring the drinks looked up. "I'll answer your questions. I'm Pete Slagle."

"I've heard of you."

A slight smile came to Slagle's mouth. "Yeah," he said, "an' I've heard of you."

Nobody moved nor spoke while Slagle calmly poured the drinks. Then he straightened and glanced around the room. "Men," he said, "I reckon there's no use goin' off half cocked an' gettin' somebody killed. Let's give this man a chance to speak his piece. We sure don't have to buy what he wants to sell us if we don't like his argument."

"Thanks, Slagle." Kedrick studied the room. Two of the faces seemed hard, unrelenting. Another was genuinely interested. But at the door in the rear, loitered a man who had shifty eyes and a sour face. He could have been, in disposition at least, a twin brother to the former outlaw, Clauson.

"The land around here," Kedrick said quietly, "is about to be purchased from the Government by the firm that's employed me. The firm of Burwick, Keith and Gunter. In New Orleans, where I was hired, I was told that there were squatters on the land, a bunch of outlaws, renegades and wasters, that they would resist being put off, and would aim to keep the badlands for themselves. My job was to clean them out, to clear the land for the company. I have come here for that purpose."

There was a low murmur from the back of the room. Kedrick took time to toss off his drink, and then calmly began to roll a smoke. To his right, the door opened and two men came in. One of these was as tall as himself with coal black hair turning gray at the temples. His eyes were gray and cold, his face firmly cut. He glanced sharply around the room, then at Kedrick.

"Cap'n Tom Kedrick, Bob," Slagle said quietly, "speakin' his piece. He's just explained that we've been represented as a bunch of renegades."

"That sounds like Burwick," McLennon said. "Get on with it, Kedrick."

"I've little to say but this. Naturally, like any good fighting man, I wanted to look over the terrain. Moreover, since arriving in Mustang certain rumors and hints have reached me that the picture is not one-sided. I have come out here to look you over, to see exactly what sort of people you are, and if you are the outlaws and wasters you have been represented to be. Also, I would like to have a statement from you."

Red's face was ugly. "We got nothin' to say to you, Kedrick," he said harshly, "nothin' at all! Just you come down here with your killers an' see how many get away alive!"

"Wait a minute, Red!" Slagle interrupted. "Let Bob have his say."

"Aw, why bother?" Red said roughly. "The man is scared or he'd never have come huntin' information!"

Kedrick's eyes held Red's thoughtfully, and he said slowly, "No, Red, I'm not scared. If I decide the company is right and you are to be run off, that is exactly what I'll do. If the men I have are not enough, I'll get more. I'm used to war, Red. I've been at it all my life, and I know how to win. I'm not here because I'm scared. I have come simply because I make a pass at being a just man. If you have a just claim to your places here, and are not as represented, I'll step out of this.

"Naturally," he added, "I can't speak for the others, but I will tell them of my conclusions."

"Fair enough," McLennon agreed. "All right, I'll state our case. This land is Government land, like all of it. The Navajos an' Utes claim some of it, an' some of us have dickered with them for land. We've moved in an' settled on this land. Four or five of us have been here upwards of ten years, most of us have been here more than three.

"We've barns built, springs cleaned out, some fences. We've stocked some land, lived through a few bad summers and worse winters. Some of us have wives, an' some of us children. We're makin' homes here. The company is tryin' to gyp us.

"The law says we were to have six months' notice.

That is, it was to be posted six months before the sale by the Government to the company. This land, as we understand it, is supposed to be unoccupied. Well, it ain't. We live on it. Moreover, that notice was posted five months ago, stuck around in out-of-the-way places, in print so fine a man can scarcely read it without a magnifyin' glass.

"A month ago one of the boys read it, but it took him a few days to sort the meanin' out of the legal phrasin', an' then he high-tailed it to me. We ain't got the money to send a man to the Government. So all we can do is fight. That's what we figure on. If the company runs us off, which I don't figure you or nobody can do, they'll buy ever' inch of it with their blood, believe me."

A murmur of approbation went through the room, and Kedrick thoughtfully scanned the faces of the men. Dornie Shaw had judged these men correctly. They would fight. Moreover, with men like McLennon and Slagle to lead them, they would be hard to handle.

Legally, the company seemed to be in the best position; also, the squatters were bucking a stacked deck. From here it would take a man all of two weeks, and possibly three, to get to Washington, let alone cut through all the Government red tape to get to the men who could block the sale—if it could be blocked.

"This here's a speculation on their part," McLennon stated. "There's rumors this here land is goin' into an Injun reservation, an' if it does, that means they'll stick the Government a nice price for the land."

"Or you will," Kedrick replied. "Looks like there's two sides to this question, McLennon. The company has an argument. If the Federal Government does make this a reservation, you'll have to move, anyway."

"We'll face that when it comes," Slagle said. "Right

now we're buckin' the company. Our folks aren't speculators. We aren't gunmen, either."

Another man had entered the room, and Kedrick spotted him instantly. It was Burt, the big man he had whipped in the street fight. The man stopped by the wall and surveyed the room.

"None of you?" Kedrick asked gently. "I have heard some stories about Pit Laine."

"Laine's a good man!" Red burst out heatedly. "He'll do to ride any river with!"

Neither McLennon nor Slagle spoke, and the latter shifted his feet uneasily. Evidently, there was a difference of opinion here. He made a note to check on Laine, to find out more about him.

"Well," he said finally, "I reckon I'll study on it a little. In the meantime, let's keep the peace. I'll keep my men off if you will do likewise."

"We aren't huntin' trouble," McLennon said. "As long as there's no shootin' at us, an' as long as the company men stay off our land, there'll be no trouble from us."

"Fact is," Slagle said, "we sent Roberts ridin' in with a message to Burwick to that effect. We ain't huntin' for no trouble."

Kedrick turned toward the door, but the bartender's voice stopped him. "You forgot your change," he said dryly.

Kedrick glanced at him, grinned, then picked the coins up. "Be seein' you," he said and stepped away.

At that instant, the door burst open and a man staggered into the room, his arm about another man, whom he dropped to the floor. "Roberts!" the man said. "He's been murdered!"

All eyes stared at the man on the floor. That he had been shot many times was obvious. He had also been ridden over, for his body was torn and beaten by the hoofs of running horses. Tom Kedrick felt his stomach turn over. Sick with pity and shock, he lifted his eyes.

He looked up into a circle of accusation: McLennon, shocked and unbelieving; Slagle, horrified; Red and the others crowding closer. "Him!" Red pointed a finger that trembled with his anger. "While he stands an' talks to us, his outfit murders Bob!"

"Git him!" somebody yelled. "Git him! I got a rope!"

Kedrick was standing at the door, and he knew there was no reasoning with these men. Later, they might think and reason that he might have known nothing about the killing of Roberts. Now, they would not listen. As the men yelled, he hurled himself through the swinging doors and jerking loose his reins, hit the saddle of the palouse. The startled horse swung and lined out, not down the street, but between the buildings.

Behind him men shouted and cursed. A shot rang out, and he heard a bullet clip past his head as he swung between the buildings. Then he knew his escape had driven him into a *cul-de-sac*, for he was now facing—not more than two hundred yards away—the rim around the flat where the town lay. Whether there was a break in that wall he could not guess, but he had an idea both the route up and down along the arroyo would be covered by guards. Swinging his horse, he charged into the darkness toward Yellow Butte itself.

He remembered that coming into town he had noticed a V-shaped opening near its base. Whether there was a cut through the rim there he did not know. It might only be a box canyon, and a worse trap than the one into which he had run on his first break.

He slowed his pace, knowing that silence was the first necessity. If they heard him, he could easily be bottled up. The flat was small, and aside from crossing the arroyo there were but two routes of escape. Both would surely be watched.

The butte towered high above him now, and his horse walked softly forward in the abysmal darkness. Kedrick's safety was a matter of minutes.

The palouse was tired, he knew, for it had been going all day. The riding had been hard and he was a big man. He knew he was in no shape for a hard run against men with fresh horses. The only possible escape lay in some shrewd move that would keep them guessing and give him time. Yet he must be gone before daylight or he was through. By day they would comb this area and surely discover him.

Now the canyon mouth yawned before him. The walls were not high but at least were steep enough to allow no escape on horseback.

The shouts of pursuit had stopped now, but he knew the men were hard at work to find him. By now they would know from the guards on the stream that he was still on the flat, and had not escaped. Those guards might be creatures of his own imagination, but knowing the men with whom he dealt, he felt it was a safe bet that if they had not guarded the openings before his arrival, they certainly would have sent guards out at once.

The canyon was narrow. He rode on, moving with extreme caution, yet when he had gone but a short distance he saw the end of the canyon rising above him, black and somber. His throat tightened and his mouth went dry. The palouse stopped and Tom Kedrick sat silent, feeling the labored breathing of the horse and knowing he faced a stone wall. He was trapped.

Behind him, a light flared briefly, then went out. There was a shout. That had been a struck match— somebody looking for tracks. They had found them. In a few minutes, for they would move cautiously, they would be on him.

There would be no reasoning with them now. They had him. He was trapped!

CHAPTER V

CAPTAIN TOM KEDRICK sat very still, listening. He heard some gravel stir. A stone rattled down the canyon. Every move would count now, and he must take no unnecessary chance. He was cornered, and while he did not want to kill any of these men, he had no intention of being killed.

Carefully, he dismounted. As his boot touched the sand he tested it to make sure no sound would result when his weight settled. Haste now was his greatest danger. There might be nothing he could do, but he was a man of many experiences, and in the past there had always been a way out. Usually there was, if a man took his time and kept his head.

Standing still beside the appaloosa, he studied the situation. His eyes had grown accustomed to the darkness under the bulk of Yellow Butte. He stared around, seeing the faint gray of sand underfoot, the black bulk of boulders and the more ragged stretch of underbrush. Leading his horse, he followed a narrow strip of gray that showed an opening between boulders.

Scarcely wide enough to admit his horse, the opening led back for some twenty feet, then widened. These were low boulders, rising scarcely above his waist, with the brush somewhat higher. The horse seemed to sense the danger, for it, too, walked quietly and almost without sound.

Literally, he was feeling his way in the dark. But he

knew that trail of sand must come from somewhere, for water had run here, and that water might spill off the cliff edge, or might come through some opening. Walking steadily, he found himself going deeper into a tangle of boulders, weaving his way along that thin gray trail into he knew not what.

Twice he paused and with his hat, worked back along the path brushing out the tracks. He could not see how good a job he was doing, but the opening was narrow enough to give him a good chance of success. When he had pushed back into the tangle for all of ten minutes, he was brought up sharply by the cliff itself. He had found his way up the slope, through the talus, brush and scattered boulders, to the very face of the rock.

Above him, and apparently out of reach, was a notch in the cliff, and this was probably the source of the sandy trail he had followed. Worried now, he ground-hitched the palouse and moved along the cliff, feeling his way along the face, searching each crack.

To his left, he found nothing. Several times he paused to listen, but no sound came from down the canyon. If this was a box canyon, with no exit, the men would probably know it and make no attempt to close in until daylight. In the darkness a man could put up quite a fight in here. Yet, because of their eagerness to avenge the dead man, they might push on.

Speaking softly to the horse, he worked his way along the face to the right, but here the pile of talus fell off sharply and he dipped into a hollow. It was cool and the air felt damp. There might even be a spring there, but he heard no water running.

Despite the coolness he was sweating and he paused, mopping his face and listening. As he stood there he felt a faint breath of wind against his cheek!

He stiffened with surprise, then with a sudden surge

of hope, he turned and eagerly explored the rocky face. But could find no source for that breeze. He started on, moving more cautiously. Then the talus began to steepen under his feet, so he worked his way up the cliff alone. He carried his rifle with him.

At the top he could turn and glance back down the canyon at the faint grayness in the distance that indicated the way he had come. Here the canyon turned a bit, ending in a sort of blind alley on an angle from the true direction of the canyon. There, breaking the edge of the cliff above him, was a notch. A steep slide led to the top.

It must have been some vague stirring of wind from up there on the rim that had touched his cheek. He noted that the slide was steeper than a stairway and might start sliding underfoot. Certainly, such a sound would give away his attempt, and it would be the matter of only a few minutes before he would be encircled. As far as that went, the men could even now be patrolling the rim above him.

Turning, his foot went from under him and only a frenzied grasp at some brush kept him from falling into whatever hole he had stumbled upon. Scrambling back to good footing, he dropped a pebble and heard it strike some fifteen or twenty feet down. Working his way along the edge, he reached the foot of the slide and knew what he had come upon.

Water, flooding down that slide during heavy rains, had struck a soft stratum of sand or mud and, striking it with force, had gouged out a deep cut that probably ran back into the canyon itself. There was always a chance that deep within this crack there might be some hiding place, some concealment. Turning abruptly, he returned for his horse.

The slide continued steeply to the bottom of the

crevasse scooped from the earth, and when they reached bottom he glanced up. The cut had taken him at least fifteen feet below the regular terrain of the area. Above him he saw a swath of dark sky that stretched about seven feet between the sides of the cut. He led the horse deeper along the narrow bed, and after only a short distance he noted that the top of the cut immediately above him was almost covered by a thick growth of brush growing together from the sides near the top.

It was cool and still down here, and he pushed on until he found a spot where the rush of water had made a turn, and had gouged deeply under the bank, making a sort of cave beneath the overhang. Into this he led his horse, and here he stopped. A little water stood at the deepest part of the turn, and he allowed the palouse to drink. When the horse had finished, the shallow pool was gone.

Kedrick tried the water in his canteen, then stripped the saddle from the horse and rubbed him down with a handful of coarse grass. Then he tied the horse, and spreading his blanket, rolled up in it. He was philosophical. He had done what he could. If they found him now there was nothing to do but shoot it out where he was.

Surprisingly, he slept, and when he awakened it was the startled breathing of the palouse that warned him. Instantly, he was on his feet, speaking in a whisper to the horse and resting his hand on its shoulder. Day had come, and somewhere above them, yet some distance, there were voices.

The cave in which he stood was dug in sandstone, no more than fifteen feet in depth, and probably eight feet high at the opening. Kedrick moved to the mouth, studied the crevasse down which he had come. It was as he had supposed, a deep-cut water course from the notch in the cliff. Evidently during heavy rains this bed roared full of water, almost to the brim.

At the place where he now stood the brush on either side almost met over the top, and at one point a fallen slab bridged the crack. Glancing back the way he had come, Kedrick saw that much of it was also covered by brush, and there was a chance that he would not be found. A very, very slim chance. He could ask for no more.

He wanted to smoke, but dared not, for the smell of tobacco might warn them of his presence. Several times he heard voices, some of them quite near. He glanced toward the back of the cave and saw the gelding drinking again. Evidently water had seeped through during the night, even though not much. His canteen was over half full, and as yet water was not a problem.

His rifle across his knees, he waited, from time to time staring down the crevasse in the direction he had been going. Where did this water flow? Probably into the arroyo below, near town, and in that case the townspeople would certainly know of it.

Yet as the morning wore on, although he heard occasionally the sound of voices, nobody approached his place of concealment, nor did anyone seem aware of it. Once, he ventured out into the crevasse itself and pulled a few handfuls of grass growing on a slight mound of earth. This he fed to the horse, who ate gratefully. He dug some jerky from his own pack and chewed on it, wishing for a cup of coffee.

Later, he ventured farther down the crevasse, which seemed to dip steeply from where he was. Hearing no voices, he pushed on, coming to a point where the crevasse turned sharply again. The force of the water had hollowed out a huge cave which looked like a bowl standing on edge. Then the water had turned and shot down an even steeper declivity into the black maw of a cavern.

Having come this far he took a chance on leaving his horse alone and walked on down toward the cave. The entrance was high and wide and the cave extended deep into the mountain with several shelves or ledges that seemed to show no signs of water. There was a pool in the bottom, and apparently the water filled a large basin, but lost itself through some cracks in the bottom of the larger hollow.

Although he penetrated no great distance he could find no evidence of another outlet, nor could he feel any motion of air. Yet, as he looked around him, he realized that with some food a man might well hide in this place for weeks, and unless someone went to the foot of the slide and found the opening into the crevasse, this place might never be discovered.

The run-off from the cliff, then, did not go to the arroyo, but ended here, in this deep cavern.

The day wore on slowly. Twice he walked back down to the cavern to smoke, leaving his horse where it was. In a few hours he would try to make his escape. Yet when dusk came, and he worked his way back up the crevasse slide and crawled out on the edge where he could look toward the entrance, he saw two men squatting there beside a fire. They had rifles. They believed him concealed somewhere near and hoped to starve him out.

Kedrick knew that by this time Dornie Shaw must have returned to Mustang with news of his disappearance, and probably, of their murder of the messenger. For he was sure that it had been his own group who had committed the crime. It was scarcely possible that Gunter or Keith would countenance such open violence

near town where it could not fail to be seen and
reported upon by unfriendly witnesses.

Returning, he studied the slide to the rim. It was
barely possible that a horse might scramble up there. It
would be no trick for an active man, and the palouse
was probably a mountain horse. It was worth a
gamble . . . if there was no one on top to greet him.
Pulling an armful of grass from near the brush and
boulders, he returned to the horse, and watched it
gratefully munch the rich green grass.

Connie Duane was disturbed. She had seen the
messenger come to her uncle and the others, and had
heard their reply. Then, at almost noon the following
day, Dornie Shaw and the other men had come in. Tom
Kedrick had not returned with them.

Why that should disturb her she could not have said,
but the fact remained that it did. Since he had stepped
up on the veranda she had thought of little else,
remembering the set of his chin, the way he carried his
shoulders, and the startled expression when he saw her.
There was something about him that was different, not
only from the men around her uncle, but from any man
she had known before.

Now, when despite herself she had looked forward to
his return, he was missing.

John Gunter came out on the veranda, nervously
biting the end from a cigar. "What happened?" she
asked. "Is something wrong? Where's Captain Kedrick?"

"Wish I knew!" His voice was sharp with anxiety.
"He took a ride to look over those squatters an' never
came back. I don't trust Shaw, no matter how much
Keith does. He's too bloodthirsty. We could get into a
lot of trouble here, Connie. That's why I wanted Kedrick.
He has judgment, brains."

"Perhaps he decided he wanted no part of it, Uncle. Maybe he decided your squatters were not outlaws or renegades."

Gunter glanced at her sharply. "Who has been talking to you?" he demanded.

"No one. It hasn't been necessary. I have walked around town, and I've seen that some of these outlaws, as you call them, have wives and children, that they buy supplies and look like nice, likeable people. I don't like it, Uncle John, and I don't like to think that my money may be financing a part of it."

"Now, now! Don't bother your head over it. You may be sure that Loren and I will do everything we can for your best interests."

"Then drop this whole thing!" she pleaded. "There's no need for it. I've money enough, and I don't want money that comes from depriving others of their homes. They all have a right to live, a chance."

"Of course!" Gunter was impatient. "We've gone over all this before. But I tell you most of those people are trash, and no matter about that, they all will be put off that land, anyway. The Government is going to buy out whoever has control. That will mean us, and that means we'll get a nice, juicy profit."

"From the Government? Your own Government, Uncle?" Connie studied him coolly. "I fail to understand the sort of man who will attempt to defraud his own Government. There are people like that, I suppose, but somehow I never thought I'd find one in my own family."

"Don't be silly, child. You know nothing of business, you aren't practical."

"I suppose not. Only I seem to remember that a lot of worthwhile things don't seem practical at the moment. No," she got to her feet, "I believe I'll withdraw my investment in this deal and buy a small ranch somewhere nearby. I will have no part in it."

"You can't do that!" Gunter exploded impatiently. "Your money is already in, and there's no way of getting it out until this business is closed. Now, why don't you trust me like a good girl? You always have before!"

"Yes, I have, Uncle John, but I never believed you could be dishonest." She studied him frankly. "You aren't very happy about this yourself. You know," she persisted, "those people aren't going to move without a fight. You believed they could be frightened. Well, they can't. I've seen Bob McLennon, and he's not the kind of a man who can be frightened. Even by that choice bunch of murderers Loren has gathered together."

"They aren't that. Not murderers," Gunter protested uneasily, but refused to meet her eyes. "Reckless, yes. And temperamental. Not murderers."

"Not even Dornie Shaw? The nice-looking, boyish one who has killed a dozen men and is so cold-blooded and fiendish at times that others are afraid of him? No, Uncle, there is no way you can sidestep this. If you continue, you are going to countenance murder and the killing of innocent people.

"Loren doesn't care. He has always been cold-blooded. You've wondered why I wouldn't marry him. That's why. He has the disposition of a tiger. He would kill anything or anyone that stood in his way. Even you, Uncle John."

He started and looked at her uneasily. "Why do you say that?"

"Because it's true. I know our tall and handsome man. He will allow nothing to come between him and what he desires. You've chosen some choice companions." She got to her feet. "If you hear anything of Captain Kedrick, let me know, will you?"

Gunter stood still for a long time after she left. He swore bitterly. Connie was like her mother. She always had the faculty for putting her finger on the truth, and certainly, she was right about this. It was beginning to look ugly, but away down deep in his heart, he was upset less over Keith than over Burwick. That strange, fat, and dirty man was a thing of evil, of corruption. There was some foul thing within him, something cold and vicious as a striking snake.

Connie Duane was not the only person who was disturbed over the strange disappearance of Tom Kedrick.

Bob McLennon, unofficial commander of the forces for defense, sat in his rambling ranch house on the edge of Yellow Butte. Pete Slagle, Burt Williams, Dai Reid and Pit Laine were all gathered there. With them was Sue Laine, keeping to the background. Her dark, lovely eyes were stirring from one to the other, her ears were alert for every word.

"Blazes, man!" McLennon said irritably. "Where could he have gone? I'd have sworn he went into that box canyon. There was no other place for him to go—unless he took wings and flew. He had to go in there."

"You looked yourself," Slagle said dryly. "Did you see him? He just ain't there, that's all! He got plumb away."

"He probably did that," Dai Reid commented. "A quick man, that Tom Kedrick. Hand or mind, he's quick." He drew out his pipe and stoked it slowly. "You shouldn't have jumped him," he continued. "I know the lad, an' he's honest. If he said that was what he come for, it was the truth he told. I'd take my oath he'd no knowledge of the killin'!"

"I'd like to believe that," McLennon agreed. "The man impressed me. We could use an honest man on the other side, one who would temper the wind a bit, or get this thing stopped."

"It won't be that Shaw who stops. He's a murderin' little devil," Slagle said. "He'll kill like a weasel in a chicken pen until there's nought left to kill."

"Kedrick fought me fair," Williams said. "I'll give him that."

"He's a fair man," Dai persisted. "Since a lad I've known him. I'd not be wrong. I'd give fifty acres of my holdin' for the chance to talk to him."

Daylight brought the first attack. It came swiftly, a tight bunch of riders who exploded from the mouth of the arroyo, hit the dusty street of Yellow Butte on a dead run, pistols firing, and then there followed the deep, heavy concussion of dynamite. As suddenly as they had come, they were gone. Two men sprawled in the street.

Peters, the man Shaw had faced down in the streets of Mustang, was one of them. He had taken three .44 slugs through the chest and died before he hit the ground. He had made one fine effort to win back his self-respect. He had seen Dornie Shaw in the van of the charging raiders and rushed into the street to get him. He failed to get off a single shot.

The second man down was shot through the thigh and arm. He was a Swede who had just put in his second crop.

The riders had planned their attack well and had worked near enough to the guards at the mouth of the arroyo, and had come at a time when no attack was expected. The one guard awake was knocked down by a charging horse, but miraculously, suffered only bruises. Two bundles of dynamite had been thrown. One had exploded against the door of the general store, smashing it off its hinges and tearing up the porch. The second exploded harmlessly between the buildings.

The first rattle of rifle fire brought Tom Kedrick to an observation point. He had saddled his horse, hoping for a break, and instantly he saw it. The two guards had rushed to the scene of action. Quickly, he led his horse out of the crevasse, rode at a canter to the canyon's mouth. Seeing dust over the town, he swung right and skirting close to the Butte, slipped out into the open—a free man once more.

CHAPTER VI

KEDRICK DID NOT return toward Mustang. He had come this far for a purpose, and he meant to achieve it. Turning west and north, he rode upstream away from Yellow Butte and Mustang. He wanted actually to see some of the homes of which so much had been said. By the way these people lived he could tell the sort they were. It was still morning and all was motionless and warm. Soon he slowed his horse to a walk and studied the terrain.

Certainly, nothing could be farther from swampland. In that, at least, the company had misrepresented. Obviously, they had lied in maintaining that the land was vacant. But if the squatters were a shiftless lot, Kedrick knew he would continue his job. Already he was heartily sick of the whole mess, yet he owed Gunter money, and how to pay it back was a real problem. And then, although the idea lurked almost unthought in the back of his consciousness, there was Connie Duane.

In his fast-moving and active life he had met many women, and a few had interested him, but none so much as this tall girl with the quiet, alert eyes. His desire to get back to Mustang had nothing to do with the company, but only with her. At the same time, Dornie Shaw had acted without his orders, had slain the messenger and attacked the town. For all he knew, Dornie and the others might think him dead.

Turning due north, he rode through the sagebrush and catclaw toward two towering blue mountains. They stood alone this side of the rim that bordered the country to the north. On his left, he saw broken land, and what was evidently a deep arroyo. He swung the appaloosa over and headed it toward the canyon. Suddenly, he reined in.

On the ground before him were the tracks of a trotting horse, and he recognized them. They were the same tracks left by the strange rider on the grulla mustang who had scouted their approach to Yellow Butte. The tracks were fresh.

Riding more slowly, he came to the edge of the canyon and looked down at a long green meadow, fenced and watered by a small stream. At the far side, tucked in a corner, was a stone cottage. It was more attractive and better built than any other he had seen in this section. Ahead of him he saw a trail. Without delay, he rode down it and walked his horse across the meadow toward the house.

It was a pleasant place of sandstone blocks and a thatched roof. Shade trees sheltered the yard, and there were a half-dozen hens pecking about. In the corral there were several horses. His heart jumped as he saw the grulla, saddled and waiting.

He drew up in the dooryard and swung down, trailing his reins. The door opened and a girl came out with a pan of water. She started as she saw him, and he recognized her instantly. It was Sue Laine, the girl of the trail, the girl in whom Dornie was reputed to be interested.

"You!" she gasped as she stared at him. "They told me you were dead!"

He shrugged. "Not dead, just hungry. Could you feed a man?"

She studied him a minute, then nodded. "Come in. Better tie your horse, though. He'll head for that meadow if you don't. And," her voice was dry, "you may need him. This isn't exactly friendly country."

He tied his horse near the grulla and followed her inside. "Isn't it?" he said. "Somehow I gathered you weren't exactly an enemy to the company."

"Don't say that!" she flared. "Don't ever say that!" Her voice lowered. "Not around here, anyway. If my brother ever heard . . ."

So Pit Laine and his sister did not see alike? That was an interesting point. He washed his hands and face, then combed his hair.

Ruefully, he rubbed his chin. "Your brother got a razor? I hate to go unshaven."

She brought a razor without comment. He shaved, then dried his face and hands and walked into the house. It was amazingly neat. On a side table there were several books. Flowered curtains hung at the windows, and several copper dishes were burnished to brightness. He sat down and she brought him food: beef, eggs, and homemade bread with honey.

"Everybody's looking for you," she said. "Where have you been?"

He accepted the statement and ignored the question. "After that messenger was killed, I had to get out of Yellow Butte. I did. What's been happening?"

"Keith served a final ultimatum. We either move, or they run us out. McLennon refused."

"He did right."

She turned on him, her eyes questioning. "You think that? I thought you were their man?"

He looked up from his food and shook his head. "I don't know where I stand, but I don't go for murder, not for running people out of their homes."

"They can't stay, anyway. If this land becomes a reservation they will all be moved off. We will, too. They are foolish to fight."

"At least, the Government will buy their land and pay for their investment. In any event, the company has misrepresented things."

"Does it matter?" She sat down opposite him. "They will win. They have money, influence, and power. The settlers here have nothing." She looked around her bitterly. "Perhaps you think I am going against my own people, but that's not true. These aren't my people. Pit and I don't belong here and we never have, although Pit won't see it. Do you think I want to slave my life away on this desert?"

She leaned toward him. "Look, Captain Kedrick, you're one of them, not just working for them, not just a hired gunman like Dornie Shaw. You can lead the men you have, and I wouldn't be surprised but what you could even handle Keith. You could be a big man in this country, or any country.

"Why be foolish and start thinking like you are? These farmers and ranchers can do nothing for you. They can't even help themselves. The company will win, and if you are one of them, you will have a share in the winning. Don't be foolish, Captain. Stay with them. Do what you have to do."

"There are things more important than money. There's self-respect."

She stared at him, her eyes widening. "You don't really believe that? Try buying supplies with it, sometime. You won't get any place. But that isn't the point. You'll do what you want, but I want a man who will take me out of this desert." She got up quickly and came around the table. "You could do it, Captain. You could become rich, right here."

He smiled at her. "Ambitious, aren't you?"

"Why not? Being a rancher's wife doesn't appeal to me. I want to get away from here, go someplace, be something and enjoy life." She hesitated, studying him. "You could edge Gunter out of it, and Keith—maybe even Burwick. But the first two would be easy, and I know how."

"You do?" He looked up at her. She stood very close to him, and she was smiling down at him. She was, he had to admit, a lovely girl. And an exciting one. Too exciting for comfort right now, and that was a fact she understood completely. "How?"

She shook her head. "Oh, no! That I'd tell you only if you threw in with me, joined me. But this much I'll tell you—John Gunter is small potatoes. They needed money, and he had that girl's money so they roped him in. Keith is dangerous because he is ambitious and unscrupulous, but the man to reckon with is Burwick. He will be top man when this thing is over, and you can bank on it. He has a way figured, all the time."

"You seem to know a great deal."

"I do. Men like me and men talk. They don't have any idea how much I lead them to say, or how much I remember."

"Why tell me all this?"

"Because you're the man who can do what has to be done. You could whip that bunch into line. All of them would listen to you, even Dornie Shaw—and he's suspicious of you."

"Of me? Why?"

"He saw Dai Reid come from your room. He was watching you."

So that was it? He had suspected that Shaw had something on his mind. But why had Shaw been watching? What was the gunman thinking of? And had he reported that conference to Keith?

Kedrick finished his meal and lighted a cigarette. Ever since their first meeting in the desert this girl had puzzled him. He was inclined to doubt if any girl, reared as she must have been, could be so sincerely disdaining of all loyalty, and so plainly self-seeking. She seemed scarcely more than a child, slim, brown and lovely, with her quick, measuring eyes and her soft lips.

Now, apparently she had selected him as the man who was to take her away from the desert. But how many others held the same idea? However, he had no idea of leaving the desert.

"Your brother around?" he asked.

Her glance was a quick flash of alarm. "You don't want to see him, or talk to him. You'd better get out of here."

"On the contrary, Sue, I'd like to talk to Pit. I've heard about him and I'd like to know him."

"You'd better go," she warned. "He'll be back soon, and some of that Yellow Butte crowd may be with him."

"You mean he's not here? Then whose horse is that out there? That grulla?"

Her face was strange as she shook her head. "You'll think I'm a liar, but I don't know. I never saw the rider."

His eyes searched hers. He could see nothing but sincerity there, sincerity and a little fear. "You mean that horse showed up there, tied like that? And you never saw the rider?"

"That's right. I looked out this morning, shortly after Pit left, and he was tied right there. This isn't the first time! He has been here twice before, when Pit was gone, and some others have seen him, most of them women when their husbands are away. Mrs. Burt Williams said he was tied to her corral for three or four hours one day."

"But surely someone sees the rider come and mount up?"

"Never. He'll be out there like he is now—he's gone!"

Kedrick came to his feet with a start and stared out the door. Sue was right. The mouse-colored horse was gone. His own palouse stood where he had left it, but the grulla had disappeared.

Walking out into the yard, he looked around very carefully. But there was nothing in sight on the plain or the hills. The horse was gone! He looked at her and saw the strained expression on her face. Then he walked out to the appaloosa. Pinned to his saddle was a note. He grabbed it up and glanced at it, then passed it to Sue who had come up beside him.

> "Stay away."

Kedrick shrugged. "Your brother do this?"

"Oh, no! I told him about the horse and he knew no more about it than I. Besides, he didn't print that. He couldn't. Pit never learned to either read or write."

Long after he left the malpais arroyo behind, he was puzzling over the strange horse. Somebody was seriously trying either to puzzle or frighten the squatters. Yet it was an action unlike the company. Moreover, it must be somebody who had a lot of time to spend.

Kedrick rode north toward Blue Hill, then swung east, crossing the Old Mormon Trail and skirting the rim.

This was good grazing land. There was an abundance of rough forage here and a good herd of cattle could fatten on this range without trouble. Moreover, the herding problem was solved in part by the rim, which provided a natural drift fence beyond which the cattle could not go.

When he reached Salt Creek he turned down the

creek toward the river. Swinging east again and passing near Chimney Rock, he rode southeast until he struck the Hogback Trail. Once over that ridge, he headed due east for Mustang.

Yet as always, his eyes were alive and alert. He loved this land, harsh though it might be at some times. He loved the dim purples and blues, the far-flung mists and morning and night, the gray-green of the sagebrush, and the rust-red of the sandstone. It was a good country, and there was room for all if it were left open for settlement.

His own mind was not yet resolved. The problem of his debt to Gunter weighed heavily upon him, and there were other considerations. He wanted no trouble, and to withdraw now might mean plenty of it. This was especially so if he remained in the country, which he had every reason to do. He would try to talk the company out of withdrawing, but he knew that would fail.

Just where, in all this, did Connie Duane actually stand? Was she involved more deeply than he believed? Or was it only what had been implied, that her uncle had invested her money in the land speculation? If such was the case, it might be difficult or impossible to get out at this stage—even if they would allow it.

Burwick puzzled him. Obviously the controlling power, he gave no evidence of where that power came from aside from some native shrewdness. There might be much more to the man, and evidently there was. That Keith and Gunter deferred to him was obvious.

Purposely, Kedrick had said nothing of his hideaway, near Yellow Butte when talking to Sue. That young lady already knew more than was good for her, and that spot might again become useful. It was something to know.

Mustang was asleep when he rode into the town and

headed for the stable. He put his horse up and rubbed it thoroughly, gave it a good bait of corn and forked down some hay. Then he made his way quietly to the St. James. As he neared the hotel a tall, lean figure arose from the chair where he himself had been sitting a few days before. The build and the broad hat, the very hang of the guns left no mistake. It was Laredo Shad.

"Cap'n?" The voice was low. "You all right?"

"Yes, and you?"

Shad chuckled. "Don't worry none about Shad! I stay healthy. " He motioned to a chair "You better sit down. I've been hopin' you'd show up."

"What's the talk? Did they think I was dead, or skipped the country?"

"Some o' both, I reckon. Keith was fit to be tied. He wants to see you as soon as you show—no matter when."

"He'll wait. I'm tired."

Shad nodded, then lighted his cigarette, which had gone out. "You know, I ain't right sure about this business."

Kedrick nodded. "I know what you mean. I'm not the man to run folks out of their homes."

"You quittin'?"

"Not yet. I'll talk to 'em first."

"Won't do no good. They are mighty bloodthirsty. It was Poinsett shot that messenger. Dornie put him up to it. Poinsett killed him, an' then four, five of those rannies shot up the body. I don't think Fessenden shot any, an' maybe Goff didn't. You can lay your last peso I didn't shoot none. It was mighty raw, Cap'n, mighty raw!"

"They'll pay for it. Were you on the Yellow Butte raid?"

"Uh huh, but I didn't shoot nobody. I'm no Bible packer, Cap'n, but I do figure a fightin' man shouldn't tackle folks who cain't fight back, an' I ain't the man to be firin' on no women or kids."

"What are they talkin' up now? Any plans you know of?"

Shad hesitated, then shrugged. "Reckon you'd better talk that out with them, Cap'n. I may know somethin' but I ain't tellin', not yet."

The Texan sat silent for a few minutes while both men smoked, and then he waved an impatient hand. "Cap'n, I hired on as a gunhand, an' such I am, but I didn't figure on this sort o' thing. Some of those hombres on the other side o' this shindig look a durned sight more human than some on our own side. I'm gettin' shut o' the whole shebang."

"Uh huh—" surprisingly, Kedrick found resolution coming to him—"I know how you feel, but my own way will be different. I think if I can't talk Gunter an' the rest of them out of that I'll change sides."

Shad nodded. "I've thought of it. I sure have."

Kedrick turned suddenly and found Dornie Shaw standing not twenty feet behind them. Slowly, he got to his feet, and Laredo Shad did likewise. Shaw's eyes avoided Kedrick. "If you figure on leavin' us, Shad, you better figure on killin' me first."

"If I have to," Laredo said quietly, "then I reckon you can die as simple as any other man. Want to try it now?"

"That's enough, Shad!" Kedrick's voice was sharp. "I've said there would be no more fighting! Not in this outfit!"

Dornie Shaw turned his head slowly and smiled at Kedrick. "Still like to give orders, do you? Maybe that'll be changed."

"Maybe." Tom Kedrick shrugged. "There will be time enough for me to stop giving orders. I'm turning in."

"Keith wants to see you."

"He can wait. I've had a rough time. There's nothing he wants won't wait."

"Shall I tell him that?"

"If you like."

Shaw smiled again. "You must carry a lot o' weight where you come from, Kedrick, but don't forget it ain't here. Keith is a bad man to buck. So's Burwick."

Kedrick shrugged again. "I've bucked worse. But at the moment, I'm bucking nobody. I need sleep, and by the Lord Harry, sleep is what I'll get. Whatever Keith has on his mind can wait until daylight. I'll be up then."

Shaw started to go, then hesitated, unable to restrain his curiosity. "What happened to you? We figured you were dead or taken prisoner when you didn't come back."

For the first time Kedrick began to wonder. Had Shaw wanted the messenger killed for that very reason. Had he deliberately moved that way hoping the enraged settlers would kill Kedrick? It was most likely. "It doesn't matter," he said, passing off the remark casually. "I found a way to keep out of sight."

Shaw turned away, and when he had gone only a few steps, Tom Kedrick spoke up suddenly. "By the way, Dornie. Know anybody who rides a grulla mustang?"

Shaw stopped abruptly, but he did not turn. His whole body had seemed to stiffen. Then he started on. "No," he said gruffly, "I sure don't."

Laredo Shad stared after him. "You know, pardner, you'll either kill that hombre someday or you'll be killed."

"Uh huh," Kedrick said quietly, "I've the same feeling."

CHAPTER VII

KEITH WAS PACING the floor in the office at the gray stone building when Kedrick walked in. He stopped and turned swiftly. "Shaw tells me you came in after midnight. Why didn't you come to me according to my orders?"

"Frankly, I was tired. Furthermore," Kedrick returned Keith's look, "I'd nothing to report that wouldn't keep."

"You were hired to do a job, and you haven't done it." Keith stood with his hands on his hips. "Where've you been?"

Briefly and clearly, Kedrick explained, omitting only the visit to Laine's and the story of the hideout. "Frankly," he said, "having looked the situation over, I'd say you had small chance of driving those people off. Also, you and Gunter misrepresented things to me and the Government. That land is occupied not by renegades and outlaws, but by good, solid people. You can't get away with running them off."

Keith smiled contemptuously. "Gettin' scared? You were supposed to be a fighting man! As for what we can do or can't do, let me tell you this, Kedrick: we've started to run those people off, and we'll do it! With or without you! Hiring you was Gunter's idea, anyway."

"That's right, it was." Gunter, followed by Burwick, walked into the room, and he glanced swiftly from Kedrick to Keith. "If you're complainin' about his going to look over that country, you can stop. I sent him."

69

"Did you tell him to come back scared to death? Saying we can't swing it?"

Burwick had been silent, but now he moved to the big chair behind the desk and dropped into it. He sighed heavily and wiped the back of his hand across his mouth, then glanced at Kedrick keenly. "What did you find out?"

"That they are determined to fight. I talked to Bob McLennon and to Slagle. There's no quit in those men. They'll fight at the drop of a hat, and to the last ditch. Right now, at this minute, they are ready for anything. Your raid killed one man, wounded another. The dynamite blasted a door loose and blew a hole in the porch."

Burwick turned swiftly and glared at Keith. "You told me three men dead and a building destroyed! Hereafter you be sure reports to me are accurate." He swung back to Kedrick. "Go on, what happened to you? You got away?"

"I'm here."

Their eyes met and held for a long time. Burwick's stone cold and hard, examining, probing.

"What do you think of the deal?" he asked finally.

"The fight," Kedrick replied carefully, "will raise a stink clear to Washington. Remember the Lincoln County War? We'll have us another general down here, and you know how much profit you'll make out of that place then!"

Burwick nodded his huge head. "Sensible, that's sensible! Have to think our way around that. At least," he glared again at Keith and Gunter, "this man can bring in some sensible ideas and make a coherent report. You two could learn from him."

He looked up at Kedrick. "Anything else?"

"A couple of things. There's a mysterious rider out on

those plains. Rides a mouse-colored horse, and he's got those folks more jittery than all your threats."

"Hah?" Burwick was uninterested. He shuffled papers on his desk. "What's this I hear about you quittin'?"

"I won't be a party to murder. These people aren't outlaws, but good, substantial folks. I'd say: buy them out or leave them alone."

"You aren't running this fair!" Keith replied coldly. "We will decide what is to be done."

"Nobody quits," Burwick said quietly, his eyes on Kedrick's, "unless I say so."

Tom Kedrick smiled suddenly. "Then you'd better say so, because I've quit, as of now!"

"Tom!" Gunter protested. "Let's talk this over."

"What of the money you owe the firm?" Keith demanded, unpleasantly. "You can repay that, I suppose?"

"There's no need."

They all turned at the voice. Connie Duane stood in the door. "You have money of mine in this project. When Uncle John got it from me he told me it was a real-estate speculation. His other activities have been honest and practical, so I did not investigate. Now, I have. I shall withdraw my money, and you can pay me less the sum advanced to Captain Kedrick. He may repay me when circumstances permit it."

All in the room were still. Gunter's face was pale, and Keith looked startled, then angry. He started to protest, but he was too slow. Burwick turned on Gunter. "You—" he snorted angrily. "You told me that was your money. You fool! What do you mean, bringing a woman into a deal like this? Well, you brought her in. Now you manage her or I shall."

"Nobody," Connie replied, "is managing me or my affairs from now on. I'll handle them myself!" She turned to Kedrick. "I'm glad, Captain, that you've made this decision. I am sure you'll not be sorry for it."

Kedrick turned to follow her from the room, but Burwick's voice stopped him. "Captain!"

He turned. Keith's eyes were ugly and Gunter's face was haunted by doubt and fear. "Captain Kedrick," Burwick said, "I believe we are all being too hasty. I like your caution in this matter. Your suggestion that cleaning out those people might make trouble and cause talk in Washington is probable. I had considered that, but not knowing McLennon, had considered the chance negligible.

"Slagle," he added, "I know. McLennon I do not know. Your suggestion eliminates a frontal attack. We must try some other means. Also," he added, "I believe that your presence has some claim on that of Miss Duane. Consequently, as we can brook no failure now, I have a proposition for you. How would you like to come into the firm? As a silent partner?"

Keith's face flushed angrily, but Gunter looked up, his eyes suddenly hopeful. Burwick continued. "We could give you a fifteen per cent interest, which, believe me, will be adequate. I believe you could keep Miss Duane in line, and with you at the helm we might straighten this whole thing out—without bloodshed."

Kedrick hesitated. The money was a temptation, for he had no desire to be indebted to Connie, yet the money alone would mean nothing. It was that last phrase that gripped his attention and made him incautious. "Without bloodshed," he repeated. "On those terms, I accept. However, let's discuss this matter a bit further."

Keith spun on his heel. "Burwick, this doesn't make sense! You know the only way we'll get those people off is by driving them off. We agreed on that before. Also this man is not reliable. I happen to know that he has friends on the other side and has actually been in communication with them."

"So much the better." Burwick pursed his fat lips and mopped perspiration from his face. "He'll have a contact he can use to make a deal." He chuckled. "Suppose you two run along and let me talk to Captain Kedrick?"

Hours later, Tom Kedrick paused on the street and studied it with care. Burwick had been more than reasonable. Little as he was able to trust him, he thought it possible that Burwick was sincere in his agreement to buy off a few of them, and to try to convince others. Certainly, if the Government moved in they would have to move, anyway. With McLennon and Slagle out of the picture the chances were there would be no fight, for the others lacked leadership. No fighting meant no deaths, and the settlers at least would come out of it with a little money.

He paced the street irritably, avoiding company. Burwick stank of deceit, but the man was a practical man. He realized that a sudden mess of killings preceding the sale of the land would create a furor that might cause them to lose out all around. At least, trouble had been avoided for the time and even Connie was hopeful that something might be done. Tomorrow Kedrick intended returning again to try to make some deal with McLennon and Slagle. A neutral messenger was leaving tonight.

"They won't come to town," Burwick had agreed, "so why not pick some intermediate point? Meet them, say, at Largo Canyon or Chimney Rock? Have your talk there, and I'll come with you. Just you and me, McLennon and Slagle. We can talk there and maybe make peace. Ain't it worth a try?"

It was only that chance for peace that had persuaded him and helped him to persuade Connie. She had listened in silence as he explained the situation. Then she had turned to him frankly. "Captain, you don't trust them, and neither do I. Uncle John has never been this way before, and I believe somehow he has fallen under the domination of those other men. However, I think that if Burwick is willing to talk, we should at least agree. I'll stand by you in this and we'll hope something can come of it that will prevent trouble."

Kedrick was less hopeful than he had let it appear, and now he was studying the situation from every angle. As things stood, it was a stalemate. He was confident that with McLennon and Slagle to lead them, the settlers could manage a stiff defense of their town and their homes. Certainly, they could prevent the survey being completed and prevent any use being made of their lands.

Yet there were fiery elements on both sides, and Keith did not like the turn things had taken. Colonel Loren Keith had from the beginning planned on striking fast and wiping out the opposition. It would be merely another unsolved mystery of the West. Kedrick resolved to keep an eye on the man and be prepared for anything.

He returned to the St. James and to bed, yet he awakened early and was surprised to see Keith mounted and riding out of town at daybreak.

With a bound he was out of bed and dressing. Whatever Keith had in mind, he meant to know. Swiftly, he descended the stairs and went to the livery stable. Mounted, he headed out of town, found Keith's tracks with ease, and followed them. Keith turned off the trail and headed west and slightly north. But after a few miles, Kedrick lost the trail and took a wide swing to try and cut it again. He was unable to. Keith had vanished somewhere in the vicinity of Largo Canyon.

Returning to the hotel he found a message from Bob

McLennon. He and Slagle would meet with Burwick and Kedrick at Chimney Rock at three in the afternoon on Wednesday. It was now Monday, and a whole day lay between. Yet during the remainder of Monday he saw nothing of Dornie Shaw, although Laredo Shad appeared a couple of times, then vanished into one of the saloons.

At midnight the door of his room opened slowly and Tom Kedrick, gun in hand, sat up. It was Laredo Shad.

"Somethin's up," he said, dropping on the bed, "an' she looks mighty peculiar. Couple of hours ago Poinsett an' Goff showed up an' said they had quit. No fightin' here, so they were pullin' out for Durango. About a half hour later they mounted up an' took out."

"What's peculiar about that?" Kedrick inquired, building a smoke. "That's in line with Burwick's talk with me."

"Yeah," Shad replied dryly, "but both of them came in here with a good deal of gear. They lost their pack horses somewheres and went out only with what they could carry on the one horse, and durned little o' that."

"What about Fessenden?"

"Ain't seen him."

"Any of the others gone?"

"Clauson is. At least, he ain't around in sight. I ain't seen him since morning."

That left Shaw, who had been around little himself, and Fessenden, if he was still in town. Despite himself, Kedrick was disturbed. But if Burwick was getting rid of his gunfighters it was a good sign, and probably he, Tom Kedrick, was getting too suspicious. Nothing, Shad said, had been said to him about quitting. "In fact," he said dryly, "the Mixus boys pulled in this morning, an' they went right to Burwick."

"Who are they?"

"Killers. Dry-gulchers, mostly. Bean an' Abe Mixus. They were in that Sandoval affair. Couple of men died awful opportune in that affair, an' come to think of it, Burwick was around. Fact is, that was where I met him."

"Were you in that?"

"Uh uh. I was in town, though, an' had me a run-in with Roy Gangle. Roy was a mighty tough ranny who'd been ramroddin' a big spread down thataway, an' when he got into the war he went bad, plumb bad. We'd had trouble over a steer, an' he braced me. He was a mite slow."

It made no sense—gunmen leaving, but others arriving. Of course, the Mixus boys could have been spoken to before the change of plans. That must be it. He suggested as much to Laredo and the Texan nodded dubiously.

"Maybe. I don't trust that hombre none. Your man Gunter is in over his head. Keith, well, he's all around bad when it comes to that, but neither of them can hold a candle to that Burwick."

Study the situation as he would, Tom Kedrick could see no answer to it, and the fact remained that they were to meet Slagle and McLennon for a peace conference. Out of that anything might come and he had no real cause to distrust Burwick.

The morning was bright and clear with the sun promising a hot day. It was still cool when Kedrick appeared on the street and crossed to the little restaurant where he ate in silence. He was on his second cup of coffee when Connie came in.

Her face brightened with a smile as she saw him, and she came over to his table. "You know, you're the one bright spot in this place. I'm so tired of that old stone house and seeing that dirty old man around that I can scarcely stand it. I'll be glad when this is all over."

He studied her. "What will you do then?"

"You know, I've not really thought of that. What I want to do is to get a ranch somewhere, a place with trees, grass, and some running water. It doesn't have to be a big place."

"Cattle?"

"A few, but horses are what I want. Horses like that one of yours, I think."

"Good idea. It takes less land for horses, and there's always a market for good stock." He studied the beauty of her mouth, the quietness and humor of her eyes. "Somehow I'm glad to think you're staying. It wouldn't be the same without you. Not now."

She looked at him quickly, her eyes dancing with laughter, but with the hint of a question in their depths. "Why, Tom! That sounds almost like gallantry. Like you were trying to make love to me, like all the cowboys."

"No, Connie," he said quietly, "when I make love to you there won't be any doubt about it. You'll know and I won't be fooling."

"Somehow I think you're right. You wouldn't be fooling."

"Over west of here," he said, "west and south there's a great rim that stretches for miles across the country, and a splendid pine forest atop it. There's trees, water, game, and some of the finest mountain meadows a man ever saw. I know a place over there where I camped once, a good spring, some tall trees, graceful in the wind, and a long sweep of land clear to the rim's edge, and beyond it miles upon miles of rolling, sweeping range and forest."

"It sounds fascinating, like what I've been wanting ever since I came West."

He pushed back his chair. "Maybe when this is over, you'd ride over that way with me? I'd like to show it to you."

She looked up at him. "All right, Tom. We'll look at it together."

He paused, hat in hand, staring out the door. "Together . . ." he mused. Then he glanced down at her. "You know, Connie, that's the most beautiful word in the language—together."

He walked away then, pausing to pay his check and hers, then stepping outside into the warmth of the street. A buckboard had stopped and a man was getting out of it, a man who moved warily and looked half frightened. He glanced around swiftly, then ducked through the door into the store.

CHAPTER VIII

TWO MEN CROSSED the street suddenly. One of them was a man Kedrick had never seen before, the other was the sly-looking loafer he had seen hanging around the back door in the saloon at Yellow Butte. The loafer, a sour-faced man called Singer, was talking. They stopped, and he indicated the buckboard to the man with him. "That's him, Abe," Singer was saying: "He's one of that crowd from across the way. He's brother-in-law to McLennon."

"This is a good place to start," Abe replied shortly, low voiced. "Let's go!"

Tom Kedrick turned on his heel and followed them. As they stepped into the door, he moved forward and caught it before it slammed shut. Neither man seemed to be aware of his presence, for they were intent on the figure at the counter.

"Hello, Sloan," Singer said softly. "Meet Abe Mixus!"

The name must have meant something to Sloan for he turned, his face gray. He held a baby's bottle, which he was in the act of buying, in his right hand. His eyes, quick and terror stricken, went from one to the other. He was frightened, but puzzled, and he seemed to be fighting for self-control. "You in this squabble, Singer? I figured you to be outside of it."

Singer chuckled. "That's what I aim for folks to think."

Mixus, a lean, stooped man with yellow eyeballs and

79

a thin-cheeked face drew a paper from his pocket. "That's a quit claim deed, Sloan," he said. "You can sign it an' save yourself trouble."

Sloan's face was gray. His eyes went to the deed and seemed to hold there. Then slowly, they lifted. "I can't do that. My wife's havin' a child in the next couple of days. I worked too hard on that place to give it up. I reckon I can't sign."

"I say you better." Mixus' voice was cold, level. The storekeeper had vanished, and the room was empty save for the three, and for Tom Kedrick, standing in the shadows near some hanging jeans and slickers. "I say you better sign because you don't own that prop'ty anyhow. Want to call me a liar?"

Sloan's face was gray and yet resolution seemed to have overcome his immediate fear. He was a brave man, and Kedrick knew that whatever he said now, he would die. Tom Kedrick spoke first.

"No, Abe," he said softly, "I'll call you a liar!"

Mixus stiffened as if struck. He was a killer, and dangerous, but he was a smart, sure-thing killer, and he had believed himself alone but for Singer. Now somebody was behind him. He stood stock still, then started to turn. Singer had fallen back against the wall, his eyes staring to locate Kedrick.

"It's Kedrick!" he said. "The boss gunman!"

Mixus scowled. "What's the matter?" he said irritably. "What yuh buttin' in for?"

"There's to be no more killing, Abe." Kedrick held his ground. "We're havin' a peace conference tomorrow. This killing is over."

"Got my orders," Mixus persisted. "You talk to Burwick."

There was a movement from Sloan, and Mixus whirled on him. "You stand still!" he barked.

"You can go, Sloan," Kedrick said. "Get in your outfit an' head back an' tell McLennon my word is good. You'd better stop thinking about him, Abe. You're in trouble, and I'm the trouble."

Mixus was confused. He knew Kedrick was ramrodding the gunmen for the company, and he was puzzled. Had he been about to do the wrong thing? But no, he had—"You fool!" His confusion burst into fury. "Keith tol' me to git him!"

"Shut up!" Singer yelled. "Dang it! You—"

Abe Mixus was a cold-blooded killer and no heavyweight mentally. Orders and counterorders had come to him, and worked up to a killing pitch he had been suddenly stopped in the middle of a job and switched off into this back trail where he floundered hopelessly. Now Singer seemed to be turning on him, and he swung toward him, his teeth bared, his face vicious.

"Don't you tell me, you white-livered coyote!" he snarled.

One hand hung over a gun, and Singer, frightened, grabbed for his own gun. Instantly Mixus whipped out his .44 and flame stabbed at Singer. The renegade turned on his heel. His knees slowly buckled and he slid to the floor, his head against a sack of flour, blood welling from his mouth.

Mixus stared down at him, and then slowly, he blinked, then blinked again. Awareness seemed to return to him, and his jittery nerves calmed. He stared down at Singer almost unbelieving.

"Why, I—I—kilt Singer," he said.

"That's right." Kedrick was watching him, knowing now upon what a slender thread of irritation this man's muscles were poised. "What will Keith say to that?"

Cunning came over Abe's horselike face. "Keith?

What give you the idee he had anythin' to do with
this?" he demanded.

Slowly, attracted by the shooting and made confident
by its end, people were gathering in front of the door.
The storekeeper had come into the room and stood
watching, his face drawn and frightened.

Tom Kedrick took a slow step back as Abe's eyes
turned toward the front of the store. Putting the hanging
slickers between them, he moved on cat feet to the
opening between the counters and slid through into the
living quarters and out into the alley behind the store.

Crossing the street below the crowd, he wound up in
front of the St. James, pausing there. Laredo Shad
materialized beside him. "What happened?" he asked
swiftly.

Kedrick explained. "I don't get it," he said. "Keith
may be moving on his own. Burwick was to hold off
until we had our talk, and I know Keith didn't like that.
He spoke right up about it."

"Ain't Singer s'posed to be a settler?" Shad asked.
"Won't this serve to get 'em all riled up? Who knew
that Singer was with Keith an' the company?"

"You've a point there," Kedrick said thoughtfully.
"This may be the very thing that will blow the lid off!"

"Both of them were mighty jumpy. It looked like
they had Sloan marked because he was McLennon's
relative. I sprung a surprise on them, an' Mixus just
couldn't get himself located."

The crowd separated, then gathered in knots along
the street to discuss the new event. Shad loitered
beside Kedrick, and was standing there when Loren
Keith came up. He glanced sharply at Shad, then at
Kedrick. "What's happened over there?"

He kept his eyes on Kedrick as he spoke, and Kedrick

shrugged. "Shooting, I guess. Not unusual for Mustang from what I hear."

"Mixus was in there," Shad commented. "Wonder if he had a hand in it?"

Keith turned and looked at Laredo, suspicion in his eyes. "Who was shot?" he inquired, his eyes going from one to the other.

"Singer, they tell me," Shad said casually. "I reckon Mixus killed him."

"Mixus? Kill Singer?" Keith shook his head. "That's preposterous!"

"Don't know why," Laredo drawled. "Mixus come heah to fight, didn't he? An' ain't Singer one o' them settlers?"

Colonel Keith hesitated, his sharp, hard features a picture of doubt and uncertainty. Watching him, Kedrick was amused and pleased. The storekeeper had not seen him, and it was doubtful if anyone had but Mixus, the dead man, and the now missing Sloan.

What Abe Mixus would offer as an explanation for shooting Singer, Tom couldn't conceive, but a traitor had died, and the enemy was confounded. Little as it might mean in the long run, it was for the moment a good thing. The only fly in the ointment was the fact that Singer had been a squatter, and that few, if any, knew of his tie-up with Keith and the company.

Watching the crowds in the street, Tom Kedrick began to perceive a new element shaping itself. Public opinion was a force Burwick had not reckoned with, and the faces of the men talking in the streets were hard and bitter.

These were mostly poor men who had made their own way or were engaged in making their way, and they resented the action of the company. Few had known Singer well, and those few had little use for the man.

But to them, it wasn't important who was gunned down. To them, it was a fight between a bunch of hard-working men against the company, made up largely of outsiders, seeking to profit from the work of local people. Furthermore, whatever Singer was, he was not a gunman and he was a local man. Abe Mixus was a known killer, a gunman whose gun was for hire.

Tom Kedrick nodded toward the street. "Well, Colonel," he said, "you'd better start thinking about that unless you want to stretch hemp. That bunch is sore."

Keith stared at them nervously, then nodded and hurried away toward headquarters. Shad watched him go and turned toward Kedrick. "You know, we're sort of tied in with the company, an' I don't aim to hang for 'em. Let's light a shuck out of here an' stick in the hills a few days."

"Can't. I've got to make that meeting with Burwick. But you might get out of town, anyway. Scout around and see what you can find of Goff and the others—if they really left the country or not. Meet me at Chimney Rock about sundown tomorrow."

Leaving Shad, Kedrick hurried to his room in the St. James and bundled his gear together. He carried it down to the livery stable and saddled the palouse. When that was done, staying off the main street, he headed for headquarters. It was Connie Duane he wanted to see, and not Burwick or Keith.

There was no sign of any of them. Gunter was not around, and Burwick and Keith seemed to have vanished. Idling in the office, Tom heard a slight movement upstairs. He called out. Feet hurried along the floor above him and then Connie was at the stair head. "Yes?" Recognizing him, she hurried down. "Is something wrong?"

Swiftly he explained, holding nothing back. "Nothing may come of it. But it wouldn't take much to start something. They all know that the company's gunmen are mostly out of town. Burwick, Keith and your uncle must have lit out."

"Uncle John hasn't been around all day. I saw him at breakfast, and then he disappeared."

"I'll look around. Do you have a gun?" He shook his head then. "Don't much think you'll need it. Most of them like you around here, and you've been pretty outspoken. But stay close to your room. The lid's going to blow off."

Before he could reach the door she called to him and he faced her again. "Tom?" He saw the pleading in her eyes. "Be careful, Tom."

Their eyes held for a long moment, and then he nodded. "I will—if I can."

He went out and paused on the steps. Burwick and Keith might get out of the way. But whatever else Gunter might be, he was scarcely the man to leave his niece behind at a time of danger. Puzzled about Gunter's disappearance, Kedrick paused and looked around him. The back street was bare and empty. The white powdery dust lay thickly and had sifted into the foliage of the trees and shrubs.

Kedrick hitched his guns into place and walked slowly around the house. The stable was usually filled with horses. Now it seemed empty. He strode back, his spurs jingling a little, and tiny puffs of dust rising from his boots as he walked.

Once, nearly to the stable, he paused by a water trough and listened for noise from the town. It was quiet, altogether too quiet. He hesitated, worrying about Connie again, but then went on and into the wide door that gave entrance to the shadowed coolness of the stable.

The stalls were empty, all save one. He walked back, then paused. The chestnut was Gunter's horse, and a saddle lay nearby. Could Gunter be somewhere around town? Kedrick considered that, then dismissed it. He removed his hat and wiped the band with his kerchief, then replaced it. His face was usually thoughtful as he examined every stall.

Nothing.

Puzzled, he stepped out into the bright glare of the sun and heard no sound anywhere. He squinted his eyes around, then saw the ramshackle old building that had done duty for a stable before the present large one was built. He stared at it and then turned in that direction. He had taken scarcely a step when he heard a rattle of hoofs, and swung swiftly around, half crouched, his hands wide.

Then he straightened. Sue Laine slid from her horse and ran to him. "Oh, I've found you, Tom!" she cried, catching him by the arms. "Tom, don't go to that meeting tomorrow. There's going to be trouble!"

"You mean, McLennon's framed something?"

"McLennon?" For an instant she was startled. "Oh, no! Not Mac!" Her expression changed. "Come home with me, Tom. Please do! Let them have this out and get it over with! Come home with me!"

"Why all this sudden worry about me?" He was sincerely puzzled. "We've only met once, and we seem to have different ideas about things."

"Don't stand here and argue! Tom, I mustn't be seen talking to you—not by either side. Come with me and get away from here until this is all over. I've seen Dornie, and he hates you, Tom. He hates you."

"He does, does he?" He patted her arm. "Run along home now. I've things to do here."

"Oh?" Her eyes hardened a little. "Is it that woman? That Duane girl? I've heard all about her, how beautiful she is, how—how she—what kind of girl is she?"

"She's a lovely person," he said gravely. "You'd like her, Sue."

Sue stiffened. "Would I? I wonder how much you know about women, Tom? Or do you know anything about them? I could never like Connie Duane." She shook his arm. "Come, if you're coming. I just heard this last night, and I can't—I won't see this happen."

"What? What's going to happen?"

She stamped her foot with impatience. "Oh, you fool, you! They plan to kill you, Tom. Now, come on."

"Not now," he said quietly. "I've got to get this fight settled first, then maybe I'll ride your way. Now run along, I've got to look around."

Impatiently, she turned and walked to her horse. In the saddle she glanced back at him. "If you change your mind . . ."

"Not now," he repeated.

"Then be careful. Be careful, Tom."

He watched her go, then happened to glance toward the house. Connie Duane stood in the window, looking down at him. As he looked up, she turned sharply away. He started for the house, then hesitated. There was nothing he could say now, nothing that would pave any effect or do any good at all.

He started toward the front of the house again, then stopped. On an impulse he turned and walked swiftly back to the little old building and caught the latch. The door was weathered and gray. It creaked on rusty hinges and opened slowly. Inside there was the musty odor of decay. Kedrick stood there for a minute watching the sunlight filter through the cobwebbed window and fall in a faint square upon the ancient straw that littered the earthen floor. Stepping forward, he peered around the corner of the nearest stall.

John Gunter lay sprawled upon his face, his head pillowed upon one forearm, the back of his shirt covered with a dark, wide stain. Kedrick knelt beside him.

Connie's uncle had been stabbed in the back. Three powerful blows, from the look of the wounds, had been struck downward—evidently while he sat at a desk or table.

He had been dead for several hours.

FLIN[T]

**Your introduction
to the handsome, hardbo[und]
Louis L'Amour Collection**

FLINT LOUIS L'AMOUR

**Take this
enduring volume**

FREE FOR 10 DAYS

...y of the Old West ...rdcover volumes...

L'AMOUR COLLECTION

...our family can experience the authentic ...ch lore and legend in a rugged, handsome ...The Louis L'Amour Collection—superb ...dcover Heritage Editions, meticulously bound in padded Sierra-brown leatherette.

Each matching volume—with the look and feel of hand-rubbed saddle leather—is an enduring testament to our unique American past...a tribute to the narrative power of Louis L'Amour, the most popular writer of frontier adventures who ever lived.

Start your Louis L'Amour Collection now with FLINT—a gripping novel of murder and revenge—FREE for 10 days. If you decide to keep it, further volumes may be previewed each month, also for 10 days free. Each volume contributes to an impressive home library, certain to become a treasured family heirloom...to be enjoyed again and again.

Mail the card at right today.

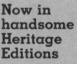

Now in handsome Heritage Editions

Each matching 6" x 9" volume in The Collection is bound in rich Sierra-brown leatherette, with padded covers and embossed gold title... creating an enduring family library of distinction.

Nobody writes adventures like *Louis L'Amour*

Take "FLINT" for 10 DAYS FREE!

☐ YES! Send FLINT For 10 Days Free! If I keep this volume, I will pay just $9.95 plus shipping and handling. Future Louis L'Amour Westerns will then be sent to me, one each month, on the same 10-day Free-Examination basis. I understand that there is no minimum number of books to buy, and I may cancel my subscription at any time.

60111

☐ I prefer the DELUXE EDITION, bound in genuine leather, for $24.95 per volume plus shipping and handling, with the same 10-day Free-Examination privilege.

87023

FREE Also send me the latest Louis L'Amour Calendar, featuring knowledgeable commentary by Louis L'Amour himself, and handsome color prints suitable for framing. It is mine to keep, even if I decide to return FLINT.

Print
NAME_____

ADDRESS_____

CITY_____STATE_____ZIP_____

SEND NO MONEY PC 1

Just mail this postage-paid card today
Bantam Books, Hicksville, N.Y. 11802

DETACH AND MAIL • POSTAGE PAID

BUSINESS REPLY CARD

FIRST CLASS   PERMIT NO. 2154   HICKSVILLE, N.Y.

Postage will be paid by addressee:

The

Louis L'Amour

Collection

Bantam Books
P.O. Box 956
Hicksville, New York 11802

NO POSTAGE
NECESSARY
IF MAILED
IN THE
UNITED STATES

CHAPTER IX

ALTON BURWICK, FOR all his weight, sat his saddle easily and rode well. His horse was a blood bay, tall and long limbed. He walked it alongside Tom Kedrick's palouse. From time to time he spurred it to a trot, then eased down. On this morning Burwick wore an ancient gray felt hat, torn at the flat crown, and a soiled neckerchief that concealed the greasy shirt collar.

His shirt bulged over his belt, and he wore one gun, too high on his hip for easy use. His whiskers seemed neither to have grown nor been clipped. They were still a rough stubble of dirty mixed gray. Yet he seemed unusually genial this morning.

"Great country, Kedrick. Country for a man to live in. If this deal goes through you should get yourself a ranch. I aim to."

"Not a bad idea." Kedrick rode with his right hand dangling. "I was talking about that yesterday with Connie Duane."

The smile vanished from Burwick's face. "You talked to her yesterday? What time?"

"Afternoon." Kedrick let his voice become casual, yet he was alert to the change in Burwick's voice. Had Burwick murdered Gunter? Or had it been one of the squatters? With things as they were either would be difficult or impossible to prove. "We had a long talk. She's a fine girl."

Burwick said nothing, but his lips tightened. The red

canyon walls lifted high above them. Along here they were nearly five hundred feet above the bottom of Salt Creek. There was but little left to go, and Tom became puzzled by Burwick's increased watchfulness. The man might suspect treachery, but he had said nothing to imply anything of the kind.

Tom's mind reverted to Sue's warning of the previous day—they intended to kill him—but who were "they"? She had not been specific in her warning, except to say that he should not keep this rendezvous today. Kedrick turned the idea over in his mind, wondering if she were deliberately trying to prevent a settlement, or if she knew something and was genuinely worried.

Pit Laine, her gun-slinging brother, was one element in the situation he could not estimate. Laine had not been mentioned in any of the discussions. Although he seemed always just beyond reach, he was definitely in the background as was the mysterious rider of the mouse-colored horse. The whole story of the disappearing seemed fantastic, but Kedrick did not think Sue was inclined to fall for tall stories.

The canyon of Salt Creek widened out and several branch canyons opened into it. They left the creek bed and rode closer together to the towering cliffs, now all of seven hundred feet above the trail. They were heading south, and Burwick, mopping his sweaty face from time to time with a dirty handkerchief, was no longer talking.

Kedrick pushed back his hat and rolled a smoke. He had never seen Burwick so jittery before, and he was puzzled. Deliberately, he had said nothing to any of the company about Gunter, although he had arranged with some of the townspeople to have the body moved. Tom was afraid it might precipitate the very trouble he was trying to end, and bring the fight into open battle.

Moreover, he was not at all sure of why Gunter had been killed, or who had done it. That it could be retaliation for Singer's death was an answer to be considered, but it might have been done by either Keith or Burwick.

Suddenly he drew up. A horse coming in alone from the northwest had left recent tracks. Burwick saw them too. "I've seen those tracks before," Tom Kedrick said. "Now whose horse is that?"

"We better step it up," Burwick said, impatiently. "They'll be there before us."

They pushed on into the bright, still morning. The sky overhead was a vast blue dome scattered with fleecy puff-balls of clouds, like balls of cotton on the surface of a lake of pure blue. The red cliffs towered high on their left, and the valley on their right swept away in a vast, gently rolling panorama. Glancing off over this sagebrush-dotted valley, Tom knew that lost in the blue haze, some seven or eight miles away, was Malpais Arroyo and Sue Laine.

Was she there this morning? Or was she riding somewhere else? She was strangely attractive, that slim, dark-haired, dark-eyed girl with her lovely skin, soft despite the desert sun and desert wind. She had come to him, riding all that distance to bring him a warning of danger. Why? Was it simply that she feared for him? Was she in love with him? He dismissed that idea instantly, but continued to wonder. She was, despite her beauty, a hard, calculating little girl, hating the country around, and wanting only to be free of it.

Heat waves danced out over the bottom land, and shadows gathered under the red wall. A dust devil lifted and danced weirdly across the desert, then lost itself among the thick antelope brush and the cat claw. Tom Kedrick mopped his brow and swung his horse farther east. The tall spire of Chimney Rock lifted in the distance, its heavier shouldered companion looming beside and beyond it.

"Look!" Burwick's voice held a note of triumph. "There they come!"

To the south, and still three or four miles off, they could see two riders heading toward Chimney Rock. At this distance they could not be distinguished, but their destination was obvious.

"Now that's fine." Burwick beamed. "They'll be here right on time. Say—" he glanced at his heavy gold watch—"tell you what. You'll be there a shade before them, so what say you wait for them while I have me a look at a ledge up in the canyon?"

Minutes later, Kedrick swung down in the shadow of the rock. There was a small pool of water there. He let the palouse drink and ground-hitched him deeper in the shade, near some grass. Then he walked back and dropping to the ground lit a smoke. He could see the two riders nearing now. One was on a fast-stepping chestnut, the other a dappled gray.

They rode up and swung down. The first man was Pete Slagle, the second a stranger whom Kedrick had not seen before. "Where's McLennon?" he asked.

"He'll be along. He hadn't come in from the ranch, so I came on with Steelman here. He's a good man, an' anything he says goes with all of us. Bob'll be along later, though, if you have to have his word."

"Burwick came. He's over lookin' at a ledge he saw in the canyon over there."

The three men bunched and Steelman studied Kedrick. "Dai Reid tells me you're a good man, trustworthy, he says."

"I aim to be." He drew a last drag on his cigarette and lifted his head to snap it out into the sand.

For an instant, he stood poised, his face blank, then realization hit him. "Look out!" he yelled. "Hit the dirt!"

His voice was drowned in a roar of guns and something smashed him in the body even as he fell. Then something else slugged him atop the head and a vast wave of blackness folded over him, pushing him down, down, down, deeper and deeper into a swirling darkness that closed in tightly around his body, around his throat. And then there was nothing, nothing at all.

Alton Burwick smiled and threw down his cigar. Calmly, he swung into the saddle and rode toward the four men who were riding from behind a low parapet of rocks near the Chimney. As he rode up they were standing, rifles in hand, staring toward the cluster of bloody figures sprawled on the ground in the shade. "Got 'em!" Shaw said. His eyes were hard. "That cleans it up, an' good!"

Fessenden, Clauson and Poinsett stared at the bodies, saying nothing. Lee Goff walked toward them from his vantage point where he had awaited anyone who might have had a chance to escape. He stooped over the three.

Slagle was literally riddled with bullets, his body smashed and bloody. Off to one side lay Steelman, half the top of his head blown off. Captain Kedrick lay sprawled deeper in the shadow, his head bloody, and a dark stain on his body.

"Want I should finish 'em off for sure?" Poinsett asked.

"Finish what off?" Clauson sneered. "Look at 'em— shot to doll rags."

"What about Kedrick?" Fessenden asked. "He dead for sure?"

"Deader'n Columbus," Goff said.

"Hey!" Shaw interrupted. "This ain't McLennon! This here's that Steelman!"

They gathered around. "Sure is!" Burwick swore viciously. "Now we're in trouble. If we don't get McLennon, we're—" His voice trailed away as he looked up at Dornie Shaw. The soft brown eyes were bright and boyish.

"Why, boss," he said softly, dropping his cigarette and rubbing it out with his toe, "I reckon that's where I come in. Leave McLennon to me. I'll hunt him down before sun sets tomorrow."

"Want company?" Poinsett asked.

"Don't need it," Shaw said, "but come along. I hear this Bob McLennon used to be a frontier marshal. I never liked marshals noway."

They drifted to their horses, then moved slowly away. Dornie Shaw, Poinsett and Goff toward the west and Bob McLennon. Alton Burwick, his eyes thoughtful, headed toward the east and Mustang. With him rode the others. Only Fessenden turned nervously and looked back. "We should have made sure they were dead."

"Ride back if you want," Clauson said. "They are dead all right. That Kedrick! I had no use for him. I aimed my shot right for his smart skull."

Afternoon drew on. The sun lowered, and after the sun came coolness. Somewhere a coyote lifted his howl of anguish to the wide white moon and the desert lay still and quiet beneath the sky.

In the deeper shadow of the towering Chimney and its bulkier neighbor there was no movement. A coyote, moving nearer, scented the blood, but with it there was the dreaded man smell. He whined anxiously and drew back, then trotted slowly off, turning only once to look back. The palouse, still ground-hitched, walked along the grass toward the pool, then stopped, nostrils wide at the smell of blood.

Well down behind some rocks and brush, the shooting had only made it lift its head, then return to cropping the thick green grass that grew in the tiny sub-irrigated area around the Chimney. Nothing more moved. The coolness of the night stiffened the dried blood and stiffened the bodies of the men who lay sprawled there.

Ten miles north Laredo Shad, late for his meeting with Kedrick, limped along the trail leading a badly lamed horse. Two hours before, the trail along an arroyo bank had given way and the horse had fallen. The animal's leg was not broken, but was badly injured. Shad swore bitterly and walked on, debating as he had for the past two hours on the advisability of camping for the night. But remembering that Kedrick would be expecting him, he pushed on.

An hour later, still plodding and on blistered feet, he heard horse's hoofs and drew up, slipping his rifle into his hands. Then the rider materialized from the night, and he drew up also. For a long minute no word was said, then Shad spoke. "Name yourself, pardner."

The other rider also held a gun. "Bob McLennon," he said. "Who are you?"

"Laredo Shad. My horse lamed hisself. I'm headed for Chimney Rock. S'pose to meet Kedrick there." He stared at the rider. "Thought you was to be at the meetin'? What happened?"

"I didn't make it. Steelman an' Slagle went. I'm ridin' up here because they never come in."

"What?" Shad's exclamation was sharp. "McLennon, I was right afeared o' that. My bet is there's been dirty work. Nevah trusted that there Burwick, not no way."

McLennon studied the Texan, liking the man, but

hesitant. "What's your brand read, Laredo? You a company man?"

Shad shook his head. "Well, now, it's like this. I come in here drawin' warrior pay to do some gun slingin', but I'm a right uppity sort of a gent about some things. This here didn't size up right to me, nor to Kedrick, so we been figurin' on gettin' shut of the company. Kedrick only stayed on hopin' he could make peace. I stayed along with him."

"Get up behind me," McLennon said. "My horse will carry double an' it ain't far."

CHAPTER X

HIS EYES WERE open a long time before realization came, and he was lying in a clean, orderly place with which he was totally unfamiliar. For a long time he lay there searching his memory for clues to tie all this together. He, himself. He was Captain Tom Kedrick...he had gone west from New Orleans...he had taken on a job...then he remembered.

There had been a meeting at Chimney Rock and Steelman had come in place of McLennon. He had thrown his cigarette away and had seen those men behind the rocks, seen the sunlight flashing on their rifle barrels. He had yelled and then dropped, but not fast enough. He had been hit in the head, and he had been hit in the body at least once.

How long ago was that? He turned his head and found himself in a square stone room. One side of the room was native rock, and so was part of another side. The rest had been built up from loose stones gathered and shaped to fit. Besides the wide bed on which he lay there was a table and a chair. He turned slightly and the bed creaked. The door opened, and he looked up into the eyes of Connie Duane.

"Connie?" He was surprised. "Where am I? What's happened?"

"You've been unconscious for days," she told him, coming to the bedside. "You have had a bad concussion and you lost a lot of blood before Laredo and Bob McLennon found you."

"What about the others?"

"Both of them were dead. By all rights, you should have been."

"But where are we?"

"It's a cliff dwelling, a lonely one, and very ancient. It is high up in the side of the mountain called Thieving Rock. McLennon knew where it was, and he knew that if word got out that you were alive they would be out to complete the job at once. So McLennon and Shad brought you here."

"Are they still here?"

"Shad is. He hunts and goes to Yellow Butte for supplies, but he has to be very careful because it begins to look like they are beginning to get suspicious."

"McLennon?"

"He's dead, Tom. Dornie Shaw killed him. He went to Mustang to find a doctor for you. He encountered Dornie on the street. Bob was very fast, you know, but Dornie is incredible. He killed Bob before he could get a shot off."

"How did you get here?"

"Bob McLennon and Shad had talked about it, and they knew I was against the company, and also that Uncle John had been killed—so they came to me. I came out here right away. I knew a little about nursing, but not much. Laredo has been wonderful, Tom. He's a true friend."

Kedrick nodded. "Who did the shooting? I thought I saw Poinsett."

"He was one of them. I heard them talking about it but was not sure until later. Poinsett was there, Goff, Fessenden, Clauson and Shaw."

"Anything else happen?"

"Too much. They burned Yellow Butte's saloon and livery stable, and they have driven almost half the people off. Their surveyors are on the land now, checking the survey they made previously. A handful of the squatters have drawn back into the mountains somewhere under Pit Laine and that friend of yours, Dai Reid. They are trying to make a stand there."

"What about Sue?"

She looked at him quickly. "You liked her, didn't you? Well, Sue has taken up with Keith. They are together all the time. He's a big man, now. They've brought in some more gunmen, and the Mixus boys are still here. Right now Alton Burwick and Loren Keith have this country right under their thumbs. In fact, they even called an election."

"An election?"

"Yes, and they counted the ballots themselves. Keith was elected mayor, and Fessenden is sheriff. Burwick stayed out of it, of course, and Dornie Shaw wouldn't take the sheriff's job."

"Looks like they've got everything their own way, doesn't it?" he mused. "So they don't know I'm alive?"

"No. Shad went back there and dug three graves. He buried the other two, and then filled in the third grave and put a marker over it with your name on it."

"Good!" Kedrick was satisfied. He looked up at the girl. "And how do you get out here and back without them becoming curious?"

She flushed slightly. "I haven't been back, Tom. I stayed here with you. There was no chance of going back and forth. I just left everything and came away."

"How long before I can be up?"

"Not long, if you rest. And you've talked enough now."

Kedrick turned over the whole situation in his mind.

There could be no more than a few days before the sale of the land would come off, and if there was one thing that mattered it was that the company not be permitted to profit from their crookedness. As he lay there resting, a plan began to form in his mind, and the details supplied themselves one by one.

His guns hung on a nail driven into the wall close to his hand. His duffle, which he had brought away from the St. James, lay in the corner. It was almost dark before he completed his planning, and when Laredo came in he was ready for him.

"Cimarron?" Shad nodded a little later. "Bloomfield would be nearer. How's that?"

"Good." Kedrick agreed. "Make it fast."

"That ain't worryin' me," Laredo said, rolling his tobacco in his jaws. "They've been mighty suspicious lately. Suppose they trail this place down while I'm gone?"

"We'll have to chance that. Here's the message. Hurry it up!"

The sun was bright in the room when Connie came through the door with his breakfast. She turned and her face went white. "Oh, you're up!"

He grinned shakily. "That's right. I've laid abed long enough. How long has it been?"

"Almost two weeks," she told him. "But you mustn't stand up. Sit down and rest."

There was a place by a window where he had a good view of the trail below. At his request Connie brought the Winchester and her own rifle to him. He cleaned them both, oiled them carefully, and placed them beside his window. Then he checked his guns and returned them to their holsters, digging the two Walch Navy pistols from his duffle and checking them also.

He realized that it too was late to do anything now,

but it was a wonder he had not thought of Ransome before. No more able legislator existed in Washington than Frederic Ransome, and the two had been brother officers in the War Between the States, as well as friends in France during the Franco-Prussian War when Ransome had been there as an observer. If anybody could block the sale to the company, he could, even on such short notice.

His telegram would be followed by a letter supplying all the details, and with that to go on, Ransome might get something done. He was a popular and able young senator with good connections and an affable manner. Moreover, he was an excellent strategist. It would make all the difference in this situation.

The cliff dwelling was built well back from the face of the cliff, and built evidently with an eye toward concealment as well as defense. They had called this, Connie told him, Thieving Rock, long before the white man appeared, and the Indians who lived here had been notorious thieves. There was a spring, so water was not a worry, and there were supplies enough for immediate purposes.

Two days dragged slowly by, and on the morning of the third Kedrick was resuming his station by the window when he saw a rider coming into the narrow canyon below.

The man was moving slowly and studying the ground as he came. From time to time he paused and searched the area with careful eyes. Kedrick pushed himself up from his chair. Taking the Winchester, he worked his way along the wall to the next room.

"Connie?" he called softly. There was no reply. After a minute, he called a second time. Still there came no answer.

Worried now, he remembered she had said something

about going down below to gather some squaw cabbage
to add greens to their diet.

Back at the window, he studied the terrain carefully,
and then his heart gave a leap. Connie Duane was
gathering squaw cabbage from a niche in the canyon
wall, not fifty yards from the unknown rider.

Lifting his rifle, Kedrick checked the range. It was all
of four hundred yards and a downhill shot. Carefully, he
sighted on the rider, then lowered the gun. The stranger
was nearer the girl now, and a miss might ricochet and
hit her. The canyon wall would throw any bullet he
fired back into the canyon itself and it might even
ricochet several times in the close confines.

Yet somehow, she had to be warned. If the rider saw
her tracks he would find both Connie and the hideout.
Suddenly, the ears of the horse came up sharply, and
the rider stiffened warily and looked all around. Carefully,
Kedrick drew a bead on the man again. He hated to kill
an unwarned man, but if necessary he would not hesitate.

Connie was standing straight now and appeared to be
listening. Tense in every fiber, Tom Kedrick watched
and waited. The two were now within fifty feet of each
other, although each was concealed by a corner of rock
and some desert growth including a tall cottonwood and
some cedars.

Still listening, they both stood rigid. Kedrick touched
his lips with the tip of his tongue. His eyes blurred
from strain, and he brushed his hand across them.

The rider was swinging to the ground now, and he
had drawn a gun. Warily, he stepped away from his
ground-hitched horse. Shifting his eyes to Connie, Tom
saw the girl wave. Lifting his hand, he waved back.
Then he lifted the rifle. She shook a vigorous negation
with her arm, and he relaxed, waiting.

Now the man was studying tracks in the sandy bottom

of the wash, and as he knelt, his eyes riveted upon the ground, a new element entered the picture. A flicker of movement caught the tail of Kedrick's eye. Turning his head, he saw Laredo Shad riding into the scene. Glancing swiftly at the window, Laredo waved his hand. Then he moved forward and swung to the ground.

From his vantage point Kedrick could hear nothing, but he saw Laredo approach, making heavy going of it in the thick sand. Not a dozen yards from the man, he stopped.

He must have spoken, for the strange rider stiffened as if shot. Slowly he stood erect. As he turned, Tom saw his face full in the sunlight. It was Clauson!

What happened then was too fast for the eye to follow. Somebody must have spoken—who, did not matter. Laredo Shad in a gunman's crouch, flashed his right hand gun. It sprang clear, froze for a long instant, and then just as Clauson pulled the trigger, Shad fired— but a split second sooner.

Clauson staggered a step back, and Shad fired again. The outlaw went down slowly, and Laredo walked forward and stripped his gun belts from him. Then from his horse he took his saddlebags, rifle and ammunition. Gathering up the dead man and working with Connie's help, together they tied him to the saddle, and then turned the horse loose with a slap on the hip.

Connie Duane's face was white when she came into the room. "You saw that?"

He nodded. "We didn't dare to let him go. If we had we would all have been dead before noon tomorrow. Now," he said with grim satisfaction, "they'll have something to think about."

Shad grinned at him when he came in. "I didn't see that gun he had drawn," he said ruefully. "Had it laying along his leg as he was crouched there. Might've got me."

He dropped the saddlebags. "Mite of grub," he said, "an' some shells. I reckon we can use 'em even though I brought some. The message got off, an' so did the letter. Feller over to the telegraph office was askin' a powerful lot of questions. Seems like they've been hearin' about this scrap."

"Good. The more the better. We can stand it, but the company can't. Hear anything?"

"Uh huh. Somebody from outside the state is startin' a row about Gunter's death. I hear they have you marked for that. That is, the company is sayin' you did it."

Kedrick nodded. "They would try that. Well, in a couple of days I'll be out of here and then we'll see what can be done."

"You take some time," Shad said dubiously. "That passel o' thieves ain't goin' to find us. Although," he said suddenly, "I saw the tracks of that grulla day afore yestiddy, an' not far off."

The grulla again!

Two more days drifted by. With Laredo, Tom Kedrick ventured down the trail and the ladders to the canyon below. They visited their horses concealed in a tiny glade not far away. The palouse nickered and trotted toward him, and Kedrick grinned and scratched his chest. "How's it, boy? Ready to go places?"

"He's achin' for it," Shad said. He lighted a smoke and squinted his eyes at Kedrick. "What you aim to do when you do move?"

"Ride around a little. I aim to see Pit Laine, an' then I'm goin' to start huntin' up every mother's son that was in that dry-gulching. Especially," he added, "Dornie Shaw."

"He's bad," Laredo said quietly. "I nevah seen it, but you ask Connie. Shaw's chain lightnin'. She seen him kill Bob."

"So one of us dies," Kedrick said quietly. "I'd go willing enough to take him with me, an' a few others."

"That's it. He's a killer, but the old bull o' that woods is Alton Burwick, believe me, he is. Keith is just right-hand man for him, an' the fall guy if they need one. Burwick's the pizen mean one."

With Connie they made their start three days later, and rode back trails beyond the Rim to the hideout Laine had established. It was Dai Reid himself who stopped them, and his eyes lighted up when he saw Kedrick.

"Ah, Tom!" His broad face beamed. "Like my own son, you are. We'd heard you were kilt dead."

Pit Laine was standing by the fire, and around him on the ground were a dozen men, most of whom Kedrick recognized. They sat up slowly as the three walked into the open space, and Pit turned. It was the first time Kedrick had seen him, and he was surprised.

He was scarcely taller than his sister, but wide in the shoulders and slim in the hips. When he turned, he faced them squarely, and his eyes were sharp and bitter. This was a killing man, Kedrick decided, as dangerous in his own way as that pocket-sized devil, Dornie Shaw.

"I'm Kedrick," he said, "and this is Connie Duane. I believe you know Shad."

"We know all of you." Laine said, watching them, his eyes alert and curious.

Quietly and concisely, Kedrick explained his plan. He ended by saying, "So there it is. I've asked this friend of mine to start an investigation into the whole mess and to block the sale until the truth is clear. Once the sale is halted and that investigation started, they won't be with us long. They could get away with this only if they could keep it covered up, and they had a fair chance of doing that."

"So we wait and let them run off?" Laine demanded.

"No," Tom Kedrick shook his head decidedly. "We ride into Mustang—all of us.

"They have the mayor and the sheriff, but public opinion is largely on our side. Furthermore," he said quietly, "we ride in the minute they get the news the sale is blocked. Once that news is around town they will have no friends. The band-wagon riders will get off, and fast."

"There'll be shootin'," one old-timer opined.

"Some," Kedrick admitted, "but if I have my way there'll be more of hanging. There's killers in that town, the bunch that dry-gulched Steelman and Slagle. The man who killed Bob McLennon is the man I want."

Pit Laine turned. "I want him."

"Sorry, Laine. He killed Bob, an' Bob was only in town to get a doc for me. You may," he added, "get your chance, anyway."

"I'd like a shot at him my own self," Laredo said quietly, "but somethin' else bothers me. Who's this grulla rider? Is he one of you?"

Laine shook his head. "No, he's got us wonderin', too."

"Gets aroun' plenty," the old-timer said, "but nobody ever sees him. I reckon he knows this here country better'n any of us. He must've been aroun' here for a long time."

"What's he want?" Shad wondered. "That don't figure."

Kedrick shrugged. "I'd like to know." He turned to

Dai. "It's good to see you. I was afraid you'd had trouble."

"Trouble?" Dai smiled his wide· smile. "It's trouble, you say? All my life there's been trouble, and where man is there will be trouble to the end of time, if not of one kind, then another. But I take my trouble as it comes, bye."

He drew deeply on his short-stemmed pipe and glanced at the scar against Kedrick's skull. "Looks like you'd a bit of it yourself. If you'd a less hard skull you'd now be dead."

"I'd not have given a plugged peso for him when I saw him," Laredo said dryly. "The three of them lyin' there, bloody an' shot up. We thought for sure they was all dead. This one, he'd a hole through him, low down an' mean, an' that head of his looked like it had been smashed until we moved him. He was lucky as well as thick skulled."

Morning found Laredo and Kedrick once more in the saddle. Connie Duane had stayed behind with some of the squatters' women. Pushing on toward Mustang, Laredo and Kedrick took their time. They had no desire to be seen or approached by any of the company riders.

"There's nothing much we can do," Kedrick agreed, "but I want to know the lay of the land in town. It's mighty important to be able to figure just what will happen when the news hits the place. Right now, everything is right for them. Alton Burwick and Loren Keith are better off than they ever were.

"Just size it up. They came in here with the land partly held by squatters with a good claim on the land. They managed to get that land surveyed and put in their claim to the best of it, posted the notices and waited them out. If somebody hadn't seen one of those notices and read it, the whole sale might have gone through and nobody the wiser. Somebody did see it, and trouble started. They had two mighty able men to contend with, Slagle and McLennon.

"Well, both of them are dead now. And Steelman, another possible leader is dead, too. So far as they are aware, nobody knows much about the deaths of those men or who caused them. I was the one man they had learned they couldn't depend on, and they think I'm dead. John Gunter brought money into the deal, and he's dead and out of the picture completely.

"A few days more and the sale goes through, the land becomes theirs and there isn't any organized opposition now. Pit Laine and his group will be named as outlaws, and hunted as such, and believe me, once the land sale goes through, Keith will be hunting them with a posse of killers."

"Yeah," Laredo drawled, "they sure got it sewed up, looks like. But you're forgettin' one thing. You're forgettin' the girl. Connie Duane."

"What about her?"

"Look," Shad said, speaking around his cigarette, "she sloped out of town right after McLennon was killed. They thought she had been talking to you before, and she told 'em off in the office, said she was gettin' her money out of it. All right, so suppose she asks for it, and they can't pay? Suppose," he added, "she begins to talk and tells what she knows, and they must figure it's plenty. She was Gunter's niece, and for all they know he told her more than he did tell her."

"You mean they'll try to get hold of her?"

"What do you think? They'll try to get hold of her, or kill her."

Tom Kedrick's eyes narrowed. "She'll be safe with

Laine," he said, but an element of doubt was in his voice. "That's a good crowd."

Shad shrugged. "Maybe. Don't forget that Singer was one of them, but he didn't hesitate to try to kill Sloan, or to point him out for Abe Mixus. He was bought off by the company, so maybe there are others."

At that very moment, in the office of the gray stone building, such a man sat opposite Alton Burwick, while Keith sat in a chair against the wall. The man's name was Hirst. His face was sallow, but determined. "I ain't lyin'!" he said flatly. "I rode all night to git here, slippin' out o' camp on the quiet. She rode in with that gunman, Laredo Shad, and this Kedrick hombre."

"Kedrick! Alive?" Keith sat forward, his face tense.

"Alive as you or me! Had him most of the hair clipped on one side of his head, an' a bad scar there. He sort of favored his side, too. Oh, he'd been shot all right. But he's ridin' now, believe me!"

The renegade had saved the worst until last. He smiled grimly at Burwick. "I can use some money, Mr. Burwick," he said, "an' there's more I could tell you."

Burwick stared at him, his eyes glassy hard, then reached into a drawer and threw two gold eagles on the desk. "All right! What can you tell me?"

"Kedrick sent a message to some hombre in Washington name of Ransome. He's to block the sale of the land until there's a complete investigation."

"What?"

Keith came to his feet, his face ashen. This was beyond his calculations. When the idea of the land grab had first been brought to his attention, it had seemed a very simple, easy way to turn a fast profit. He had excellent connections in Washington through his military career, and with Burwick managing things on the other end and Gunter bringing on the money, it seemed impossible to beat it. He was sure to net a handsome profit, clear his business with Gunter and Burwick, then return East and live quietly on the profits. That it was a crooked deal did not disturb him. But that his friends in the East might learn of it . . .

"Ransome!" His voice was shocked. "Of all people!"

Frederic Ransome had served with him in the war, and their mutual relationship had been something less than friendly. There had been that episode by the bridge. He flushed at the thought of it, but Ransome knew, and Ransome would use it as a basis for judgment. Kedrick had no way of knowing just how fortunate his choice of Ransome had been.

"That does it!" He got to his feet. "Ransome will bust this wide open and love it."

He was frightened, and Burwick could see it. He sat there, his gross body filling the chair, wearing the same soiled shirt. His eyes followed Keith with irritation and contempt. Was Keith going bad on him now?

"Get back there," Burwick said to Hirst, "and keep me informed of the movements. Watch everything closely now, and don't miss a trick. You will be paid."

When Hirst had gone, Burwick turned to Keith and his fat lips twisted into a smile. "So does it matter if they slow it up a little? Let them have their investigation. It will come too late."

"Too late?" Keith was incredulous. "With such witnesses against us as Kedrick, Shad, Connie and the rest of them?"

"When the time comes," Burwick said quietly, "there will be no witnesses. Believe me, there won't be."

CHAPTER XI

KEITH TURNED ON Burwick, puzzled by the sound of his voice. "What do you mean?" he asked.

Burwick chuckled and rolled his fat lips on his cigar. There was malice and some contempt in the look he gave Keith. How much better, he thought, if Kedrick had not been so namby-pamby. He was twice the man Keith was, for all the latter's commanding presence.

"Why," he said, "if there's no witnesses, there'll be no case. What can these people in town tell them? What they suspect? Suspicions won't stand in a court of law, nor with that committee. By the time they get here this country will be peaceful and quiet, believe me."

"What do you mean to do?" Keith demanded.

"Do? What is there to do? Get rid of Kedrick, Laredo Shad, and that girl. Then you'll take a posse and clean out that rat's nest back of the Rim. Then who will they talk to? Gunter might have weakened, but he's dead. With the rest of them out of it—"

"Not Connie!" Keith protested. "Not her! For heaven's sake, man!"

Burwick snorted and his lips twisted in an angry sneer as he heaved his bulk from the chair. "Yes, Connie!" he said. "Are you a complete fool, Keith? Or have you gone soft? That girl knows more than all of them. Suppose Gunter talked to her, and he most likely did? She'll know everything—everything, I tell you!"

He paced back across the room, measuring Keith. The fool! He was irritated and angry. The sort of men they made these days, a weak and sniveling crowd. Keith had played out his time. If he finished this job alive—Dornie didn't like Keith. Burwick chuckled suddenly. Dornie! Now there was a man! The way he had killed that Bob McLennon!

"Now get this. Get the boys together. Get Fessenden, Goff, Clauson, Poinsett and the Mixus boys and send them out with Dornie. I want those three killed, you hear me? I want them dead before the week is out— and no bodies, understand?"

Keith touched his dry lips, his eyes haunted. He had bargained for nothing like this. It had all seemed such an easy profit, and only a few poverty-stricken squatters to prevent them from acquiring wealth in a matter of a few months. And everything had started off just as Burwick had suggested, everything had gone so well. Gunter had provided the money, and he had fronted for them in Washington.

Uneasily, now, Keith realized that if trouble was to come it would be he, himself, upon whom the blame would rest. Burwick, somehow, had remained in the background in the transactions back East as much as he, Keith, had been kept in the background here. Yet it would be Keith's guilt if anything went wrong. And with Ransome investigating everything was sure to go wrong.

Of course, he sighed deeply, Burwick was right. There was only one thing to do now. At least Dornie and the others would not hesitate. Suddenly, he remembered something.

"You mentioned Clauson. He's out of it, Burwick. Clauson came in last night, tied to his horse. He had been dead for hours."

"What?" Burwick stopped his pacing and walked up to Keith. "You just remembered?" he held his face inches away from Keith's and glared. "Is anybody backtracking that horse? You blithering idiot; Clauson was dynamite with a gun. If he's dead, shot, it had to be by one of three men, and you know it!"

Burwick's face was dark with passion and he wheeled and walked the length of the room, swearing in a low, violent voice that shocked Keith with its deep, underlying passion. When he turned again, Burwick's eyes were ugly with fury. "Can't you realize," he demanded hoarsely, "those men are dangerous?

"Every second they are alive means we are in danger! You have seen Dornie in action. Well, believe me, I'd sooner have him after me than Kedrick. I know Kedrick. He's a former Army officer—that's what you're thinking all the time—an officer and a gentleman!

"But he's something more, do you hear? He's more. He's a gentleman—that's true enough. But the man's a fighter, he loves to fight! Under all that calmness and restraint there's a drive and power that Dornie Shaw could never equal. Dornie may be faster, and I think he is, but don't you forget for one instant that Kedrick won't be through until he's down, down and dead!"

Loren Keith was shocked. In his year's association with Burwick he had never seen the man in a passion, and had never heard him speak with such obvious respect, and even—yes, even fear, of any man. What had Alton Burwick seen that he himself had not seen?

He stared at Burwick, puzzled and annoyed, but some of the man's feeling began to transmit itself to him, and he became distinctly uneasy. He bit his lips and watched Burwick pacing angrily.

"It's not only him, but it's Shad. That cool, thin-faced Texan. As for Laine—" Burwick's eyes darkened—"he may be the worst of the lot. He thinks he has a personal stake in this."

"Personal?" Keith looked inquiringly at the older man. "What do you mean?"

Burwick dismissed the question with a gesture. "No matter. They must go, all of them, and right now." He turned and his eyes were cold. "Keith, you fronted for us in Washington. If this thing goes wrong, you're the one who will pay. Now go out there and get busy. You've a little time, and you've the men. Get busy!"

When he had gone, Burwick dropped into his chair and stared blindly before him. Things had gone too far for him to draw back now even if he was so inclined, and he was not. The pity of it was that there had been no better men to be had than Keith and Gunter.

Yet, everything could still go all right, for he would know how to meet any investigating committee, how to soft pedal the trouble, turn it off into a mere cow-country quarrel of no moment and much exaggerated. The absence of any complaining witness would leave the investigators helpless to proceed, and he could make the difficulty seem a mere teapot tempest. Keith was obviously afraid of Ransome. Well, he was not.

Burwick was still sitting there when the little cavalcade of horsemen streamed by, riding out of town on their blood trail. The number had been augmented, he noticed, by four new arrivals, all hard, desperate men. Even without Keith, they might do the job. He heaved himself to his feet and paced across the room, staring out the window. It went badly with him to see Connie Duane die, for he had plans for Connie. Maybe . . . His eyes narrowed.

Out on the desert the wind stirred restlessly, and in the brassy sky above a lone buzzard circled as if aware of the creeping tension that was slowly gripping the country beneath it.

Far to the north, toward Durango, a cattle buyer pulled his team to a halt and studied the sky. There was no hint of storm, yet he had felt uneasy ever since leaving town on his buying trip down to Yellow Butte and Mustang. There had been rumors of trouble down that way. But then, there had been intermittent trouble there for some time, and he was not alarmed. Yet he was somehow uneasy, as though the very air carried a warning.

South of him, and below the Rim, Laredo Shad and Kedrick turned aside from the Mustang trail and headed toward Yellow Butte. It was only a little way out of their line of travel, but both men wanted to see what had happened there. Yet when they approached the town, aside from the blackened ruins of the destroyed buildings, everything seemed peaceful and still. Eight or ten families had moved back into the town and a few had never left. They looked up warily as the two riders drew near, then nodded a greeting.

They knew now that these two were siding with them against the company, but hardship and struggle had wearied them. They watched the two enter the settlement without excitement. The saloon had opened its door in the large, roomy office of the livery stable, and Kedrick and Laredo entered it. A couple of men leaned on the bar, and both turned as they entered, greeted them, and returned to their conversation.

It was growing cool outside and the warmth of the room felt good. Both men stepped to the bar, and Kedrick ordered and paid. Toying with his drink, Shad seemed uneasy. Finally he turned to Tom. "I don't like it," he said, low voiced. "Somehow or other Burwick is goin' to know about Ransome, an' he'll be in a sweat to get Connie out of the way, an' you an' me with her."

Kedrick agreed, for his own mind had been reading signs along the same trail. Now the only way out for the company was to face the committee, if Ransome managed one, with a plausible tale and an accomplished fact, and then let the investigating body make the most of it.

"Burwick's a snake," Shad commented. "He'll never quit wigglin' until the sun goes down for the last time. Not that one. He's in this deep, an' he ain't the man to lose without a fight."

Horses' hoofs sounded on the road outside and when they turned, Pit Laine and Dai Reid were dismounting before the door. They walked in, and Laine looked at Kedrick, then moved on to the bar. Dai appeared worried, but said nothing. After a minute, Laine turned suddenly and went outside. "What's the matter?" Kedrick asked.

"It be worry, bye, and some of it shame, an' all for that sister o' his. Who would think it o' her? To go over to the other side? He's that shy about it, you would scarce believe. When a man looks at him, he thinks it's his sister they are thinkin' on, and how she sold out to that traitor to mankind, that rascal, Keith."

Kedrick shrugged. "Ambition and money do strange things. She has the makings of a woman, too."

Laine opened the door. "Better come out," he said, "we've got trouble."

They crowded outside. Men were hurrying toward the houses, their faces grave. "What is it?" Kedrick asked quickly.

"Burt Williams signaled from the top of the butte. There's riders coming from Mustang, a bunch of them."

As they looked, the small dark figure of a man appeared on the edge of the mesa once more. This time they saw his arm wave: one . . . two . . . three times, and continue until he had waved it six times. When he had completed, he gestured to the southeast. Then he signaled four more times from the southwest.

"Ten riders," Laine spat. "Well, we've got more than that here, but they aren't as salty as that crowd."

Burt Williams, favoring his broken arm, knelt behind a clump of brush on top of Yellow Butte and studied the approaching horsemen through the glass. He knew all in this group by sight but not by favor. One by one he named them off to himself, "Keith, Dornie Shaw, Fessenden an' Goff—Poinsett." He scowled. "No, that ain't Poinsett. That's one o' the Mixus boys. Yep, an' there's the other."

He swung his glass. The four riders spaced well apart, were approaching at a steady pace. None of their faces was familiar. He stared at them awhile, but finally placed only one of them, a bad man from Durango who ran with Port Stockton and the Ketchum outfit. His name was Brokow.

Stirred, he searched the country all around the town for other movement, then turned back to the larger cavalcade of riders. Had he held on a certain high flat a minute longer he would have seen two unmounted men cross it at a stooping run and drop into the wide arroyo northeast of town.

As it was, he had been studying the approaching group for several minutes before he realized that Poinsett was not among them. He was with neither group.

Worried, Williams squinted his eyes against the sun, wondering how he could apprise them of the danger down below, for the absence of Poinsett disturbed him. The man was without doubt one of the most vicious of the company killers. He was a bitter man, made malignant by some dark happening in his past, but filled now with a special sort of venom all his own. Williams would have worried even more had he seen Poinsett at that moment.

The attack had been planned carefully and with all of Keith's skill. He surmised who they would be looking for, and hoped their watcher would overlook the absence of Poinsett. It was Poinsett whom Keith wanted in the right position for he was unquestionably the best of the lot with a rifle.

At that moment, not two hundred yards from town, Poinsett and his companion, Alf Starrett, were hunkered down in a cluster of brush and boulders at one side of the arroyo. Poinsett had his Spencer .56 and was settling into position for his first shot. Starrett, with a fifteen-shot Henry .44 was a half dozen yards away.

Poinsett pulled out a huge silver watch and consulted it. "At half after two, he says. All right, that's when he'll get it." With utmost composure he began to roll a smoke, and Alf Starrett, a hard-faced and wizened little man, noticed that his fingers were steady as he sifted tobacco into the paper.

Bob McLennon had planned the defense of Yellow Butte, if such a defense became necessary. Bob had been something of a hand with a gun, but he definitely had not been a soldier nor even an Indian fighter. Moreover, he had not expected an all out battle for the town. Whatever the reason, he had committed a fatal error. That pile of boulders and brush offered perfect concealment and almost perfect cover while affording complete range of the town, its one street, and the back as well as front of most of the buildings.

Keith had been quick to see the vantage point on his earlier visits to the town. He had carefully planned to have Poinsett and Starrett approach the place some time before the main force moved in. So far, no hitch in the plan had developed.

Poinsett finished his cigarette and took up his rifle, then settled down to a careful watching and checking of the time. He had his orders and they were explicit. He was to fire on the first target offered after half past two. His first shot must kill.

Shad and Kedrick had returned to the saloon while Pit Laine loitered out front. Dai had gone across the street. Although Laine was out of Poinsett's sight, Dai made a perfect target. The Welshman, however, offered only a fleeting target and Poinsett did not get a chance to fire. In the next instant, however, the opportunity came.

The door of one of the nearest shacks opened and a man came out. He wore a broad-brimmed gray hat, torn at the crown, and a large checked shirt tucked into jeans supported by suspenders. He turned at the door and kissed his wife. Poinsett took careful aim with his .56, choosing as his aiming point the man's left suspender buckle. Taking a good deep breath he held it and squeezed off his shot.

The big bullet struck with a heavy thump. The man took a heavy lurch sidewise, tried to straighten and then went down. His wife ran from the door, screaming. Up the street a door banged and two men ran into the street, staring. Starrett's first shot knocked the rifle from the hand of one, splintering the stock. Poinsett dropped his man, but the fellow began to drag himself, favoring one leg which even from a distance they could see covered with a dark blotch at the knee.

Poinsett was a man without mercy. Coolly and carefully, he squeezed off his second shot. The man stiffened, jerked spasmodically and lay still.

"Missed my man," Alf said, apologetically, "but I ruint his shootin' iron."

Poinsett spat, his eyes cold. "Could happen to anybody," he said philosophically, "but I figured you burnt him anyways."

Within the saloon Kedrick had a glass half to his mouth when the shot boomed. It was followed almost at once by two more, the reports sounding almost as one.

"Blazes!" Shad whirled. "They ain't here yet?"

"They've been here," Kedrick said with quick realization. He swung to the door, glancing up the street. He saw the body of the last man to fall. Leaning out a bit, he glimpsed the other. His lips tightened, for neither man was moving.

"Somebody is up the draw," he explained quickly. "He's got the street covered. Is there a back way?"

Kedrick dove for the door followed by the others as the bartender indicated the exit, catching up his shotgun. His pockets were already stuffed with shells. At the door Kedrick halted. Flattening against the wall, he stared up the draw. From here he could see the edge of the bunch of boulders and guessed the fire came from there. "Pinned down," he said. "They are up the draw."

Nobody moved. Kedrick's memory for terrain served him to good purpose now. Recalling the draw he remembered that it was below the level of the town beyond that point. But right there the boulders offered a perfect firing point.

Scattered shots came from down the draw, and nobody spoke. All knew that they could not long withstand the attack.

CHAPTER XII

KEDRICK MADE UP his mind quickly. Defense of the town was now impossible. They would be either wiped out or burned alive if they attempted to remain. "Shad," he said quickly, "get across the street to Dai and Pit. Yell out to the others and get them to fall back, regardless of risk, to the canyon at the foot of Yellow Butte."

He took a step back and glanced at the trap door to the roof. The bartender saw the intent and shook his head. "You can't do it, boy. They'd git you from down the crick."

"I'm going to chance it. I think they are still too far off. If I can give you folks covering fire you may make it."

"What about you?" Shad demanded.

"I'll make it. Get moving!"

Laredo wheeled and darted to the door, paused an instant and lunged across the street. The bartender hesitated, swore softly, then followed. Kedrick picked up a bottle of the liquor and shoved it into his shirt, then jumped for the edge of the trap door, caught it and pulled himself through into the small attic. Carefully, he studied the situation.

Hot firing came from down stream, and evidently the killers were momentarily stopped there. He hoisted himself through, swung to the ride of the roof, and carefully studied the boulders. Suddenly, he caught a movement, and knew that what he had first believed to

be a gray rock was actually a shirt. He took careful aim
with his Winchester, then fired.

The gray shirt jumped, and a hand flew up, then fell
loose. Instantly a Spencer boomed and a bullet tore a
chunk from the ridge near his face and splattered him
with splinters. Kedrick moved down roof a bit. Then
catching the signal from the window across the street,
he deliberately shoved his rifle and head up, fired four
fast shots, then two more.

Ducking his head, he reloaded the Winchester. Another
bullet smashed the ridgepole. Then a searching fire
began, the heavy slugs tearing through the roof about
three to four inches below the top.

Kedrick slid down the roof. He hesitated at the edge
of the trap door, and seeing a distant figure circling to
get behind the men in the wash, he took careful aim
and squeezed off his shot. It was all of five hundred
yards, and he had only a small bit of darkness at which
to aim.

The shot kicked up sand short of the mark by a foot
or more as nearly as he could judge. He knew he had
missed, but the would-be sniper lost his taste for his
circling movement and slid out of sight. Kedrick went
down the trap and dropped again into the saloon.
Regretfully, he glanced at the stock of whisky, then
picked up two more bottles and stuffed them into his
pockets.

Hesitating only a second, he lunged across the street
for the shelter of the opposite building. The Spencer
boomed, and he knew that the hidden marksman had
been awaiting this effort. He felt the shock of the
bullet, staggered but kept going.

Reaching the opposite side, he felt the coldness of
something on his stomach and glanced down. The
bottle in his shirt had been broken by the bullet and he

smelled to high heaven of good whisky. Picking the glass out of his shirt, he dove for the livery stable and swung into the saddle on the palouse.

The Spencer boomed again and again as he hit the road riding hard, but he made it. The others cheered as he rode pell mell through the canyon mouth and swung to the ground.

"This is no good," Laine said. "They can get behind us on the ridge."

Two men limped in from the draw, having withdrawn from boulder to boulder. Kedrick glanced around. There were fourteen men and women here who were on their feet. One man, the one who had the rifle knocked from his hand, had a shattered arm. The others were slightly wounded. Of them all, he had only seven men able to fight.

Quickly, he gave directions for their retreat. Then with Dai and Shad to hold the canyon mouth and cover them, they started back up the canyon.

Tom Kedrick measured his group thoughtfully. Of Laredo, Dai and Laine, he had no doubts at all. Of these others, he could not be sure. Good men, some of them, and one or two were obviously frightened. Nobody complained, however, and one of the men whose face was pale, took a wounded man's rifle and gave him a shoulder on which to lean. Kedrick led them to the crevasse and down into it.

Amazed, they stared around. "What d'you know?" The bartender spat. "Been here nigh seven year an' never knowed o' this place!"

There were four horses in the group, but they brought them all into the cave. One of the men complained, but Kedrick turned on him. "There's water, but we may be glad to eat horse meat." The man swallowed and stared.

Laine pointed at Kedrick's shirt. "Man, you're bleedin'!"

Kedrick grinned. "That isn't blood, it's whisky. They busted one of the bottles I brought away."

Pit chuckled. "I'd most as soon it was blood," he said, "seems a waste of good likker."

The able men gathered near the escape end of the crevasse, and one of them grinned at Kedrick. "I wondered how you got away so slick. Is there another way out down there?"

He shook his head. "If there is, I don't know it. I waited and got out through the canyon when it wasn't watched."

Laine's face was serious. "They could hold us in here," he said, anxiously. "We'd be stuck for sure."

Kedrick nodded. "I'm taking an extra canteen and some grub, then I'm going atop the butte to join Burt Williams. I'd like one man with me. From up there we can hold them off, I think."

"I'm your man," Laredo said quietly. "Wait'll I get my gear."

A rifle boomed, and then Dai Reid joined them. "They are comin' up," he said. He glanced at Kedrick. "One man dead in the boulders. I got the look of him by my glass. It was Alf Starrett. Poinsett was the other."

"Starrett was a skunk," Burnett, one of the settlers said, "a low down skunk. He kilt a man up Kansas way, an' a man disappeared from his outfit once that occasioned considerable doubt if he didn't git hisself another."

Kedrick turned to Pit Laine. "Looks like your show down here," he said. "Don't open fire until you have to, and don't fire even one shot unless it's needed. We'll be on top."

He led the way out of the crevasse and into the boulders and brush behind it. There was no sign of the attackers, and he surmised they were holed up awaiting the arrival of some supporting fire from the rim back of the canyon.

Tom glanced up at the towering butte. It reared itself all of a hundred and fifty feet above him and most of it was totally without cover. As they waited, a rifle boomed high above them and there was a puff of dust in the canyon mouth. Burt Williams had opened up.

Their first move toward the butte brought fire, and Laredo drew back. "No chance. We'll have to wait until dark. You reckon they'll hit us before then?"

"If they do, they won't get far." Tom Kedrick hunkered well down among the slabs of rock at the foot of the Butte. "We've got us a good firing point right here." He rolled a smoke and lit up. "What are you planning when this is over, Shad? Do you plan to stay here?"

The tall Texan shrugged. "Ain't pondered it much. Reckon that will take care of itself. What you aimin' to do?"

"You know the Mogollons southwest of here? I figured I'd go down there and lay out a ranch for myself." He smoked thoughtfully. "Down in East Texas, before I came west, a fellow arrived there named Ikard. Had some white-faced cattle with him, and you should see 'em! Why, they have more beef on one sorry critter than three longhorns. I figured a man could get himself a few Hereford bulls and start a herd. Might even buy fifty or sixty head for a beginning, and let 'em mix with the longhorns if they like."

"I might go for somethin' like that," Laredo said quietly. "I always wanted to own a ranch. Fact is, I started one once, but had to git shut of it."

He stared down the canyon toward the mouth, his rifle across his knees. He did not look at Kedrick, but he commented casually, "We need luck, Cap'n, plenty of luck."

"Uh huh," Kedrick's face was sober. "I wonder who was on watch up the canyon? Or supposed to be?"

"Somebody said his name was Hirst. Sallow-faced hombre."

"We'll have to talk to him. Was he down below?"

"Come to think of it, he wasn't. He must have hid out back there."

"Or sold out. Remember Singer? He wouldn't have been the only one."

Laredo rubbed out the last of his cigarette. "They'll be makin' their play soon. You know, Kedrick, I'd as soon make a break for it, get a couple of horses an' head for Mustang. When we go we might as well take Keith an' that dirty Burwick with us."

Kedrick nodded agreement, but he was thinking of the men below. There were at least four good men aside from Shad, Laine and Dai Reid. That left the numbers not too unevenly balanced. The fighting skill and numbers were slightly on the enemy's side, as they had at least twelve men when the battle opened, and they had lost Starrett. That made the odds eleven to eight unless they had moved up extra men, which was highly probable. Still, they were expecting defense. But an attack might...

He studied the situation. Suddenly, a dark shape loomed on the rim of the canyon some hundred and fifty yards off and much higher. The figure lifted his rifle and fired even as both Shad and Kedrick threw down on him with rifles, firing instantly. The man vanished, but whether hit or not they could not tell.

Desultory firing began, and from time to time, they caught glimpses of men advancing from the canyon mouth—never in sight long enough to offer a target, and usually rising from the ground some distance from where they dropped. The afternoon was drawing on, however, and the sun was setting almost in the faces of the attackers, which made their aim uncertain and their movements hesitant. Several times Shad or Kedrick dusted the oncoming party, but they got in no good shots. Twice a rifle boomed from the top of the butte, and once they heard a man cry out as though hit.

"You know, Laredo," Kedrick said suddenly, "it goes against the grain to back up for those coyotes. I'm taking this grub up to Burt. When I come back down, we're going to move down that canyon and see how much stomach they've got for a good scrap."

Shad grinned, his eyes flickering with humor. "That's ace high with me, pardner," he said dryly. "I never was no hand for a hole, an' the women are safe."

"All but one," Kedrick said, "that Missus Taggart who lives in that first house. Her husband got killed and she wouldn't leave."

"Yeah, heard one o' the women folks speak on it. That Taggart never had a chance. Good folks, those two."

Colonel Loren Keith stared gloomily at the towering mass of Yellow Butte. That man atop the butte had them pinned down. Now if they could just get up there. He thought of the men he had commanded in years past, and compared them with these attacking the town. A pack of murderers. How had he got into this, anyway? Why couldn't a man know when he took a turning where it would lead him? It seemed so simple in the beginning to run off a bunch of one-gallused farmers and squatters.

Wealth—he had always wanted wealth, the money to pay his way in the circles where he wanted to travel. But somehow it had always eluded him, and this had seemed a wonderful chance. Bitterly, he stared at the butte and remembered the greasy edge of Burwick's shirt collar, and the malice in his eyes—Burwick who used men as he saw fit, and disposed of them when he was through.

In the beginning it hadn't seemed that way. His own commanding presence, his soldier's stride, his cold clarity of thought, all these had led him to despise Gunter as a mere business man and Burwick as a conniving weakling. But then suddenly Burwick began to show his true self, and all ideas of controlling the whole show left Keith while he stared in shocked horror as the man unmasked. Alton Burwick was no dirty weakling, no mere ugly fat man, but a monster of evil, a man with a brain like a steel trap, stopping at nothing. By his very depth of wickedness he had startled Keith into obedience.

Gunter had wanted to pull out. Only now would Keith admit even to himself the cause of Gunter's death, and he knew he would die as quickly. How many times had he not seen the malevolence in the eyes of Dornie Shaw, and well he knew how close Shaw stood to Burwick. In a sense, they were of a kind.

His feeling of helplessness shocked and horrified Keith. He had always imagined himself a strong man, and had gone his way, domineering and supercilious. Now he saw himself as only a tool in the hands of a man he despised. Yet he was unable to escape. However, deep within him there was the hope that they still would pull their chestnuts from the fire and take the enormous profit the deal promised.

One man stood large in his mind, one man drew all his anger, his hate and bitterness. That man was Tom Kedrick.

From that first day, Kedrick had made him seem a fool. He, Keith, had endeavored to put Kedrick firmly in his place, speaking of his rank and his twelve years of service, and then Kedrick had calmly paraded such an array of military experience that few men could equal, and right before them all. He had not doubted Kedrick, for vaguely now, he remembered some of the stories he had heard of the man. That the story was the truth, and that Kedrick was a friend of Ransome's infuriated him still more.

He stepped into the makeshift saloon and poured a drink, staring at it gloomily. Fessenden came in, Goff with him.

"We goin' to roust them out o' there, Colonel?" Goff asked. "It will be dark, soon."

Keith tossed all his drink. "Yes, right away. Are the rest of them out there?"

"All but Poinsett. He'll be along."

Keith poured another stiff shot and tossed it off as quickly, then followed them into the street of Yellow Butte.

They were all gathered there—all but the Mixus boys, who had followed along toward the canyon, and a couple of the newcomers who had circled to get on the cliff above and beyond the boulders and brush where the squatters had taken refuge.

Poinsett was walking down the road in long strides. He was abreast of the first house when a woman stepped from the door. She was a square-built woman in a faded blue cotton dress and man's shoes, run down at the heel. She held a double-barreled shotgun in her hands. As Poinsett drew abreast of her, she turned on him and fired.

She shot both barrels, at point-blank range, and Poinsett took them right through the middle. Almost torn in two, he hit the ground, gasping once, his blood staining the gray gravel before the shocked eyes of the clustered men.

The woman turned on them, and they saw she was not

young. Her square face was red and a few strands of graying hair blew about her face. As she looked at them, her work-roughened hands still clutching the empty shotgun, she motioned at the fallen man in the faded check shirt.

In that moment, the fact that she was fat, growing old, and that her thick legs ended in the grotesque shoes seemed to vanish—and in the blue eyes were no tears. Her chin trembled a little as she said, "He was my man. Taggart never give me much, an' he never had it to give, but in his own way, he loved me. You killed him—all of you. I wish I had more shells."

She turned her back on them. Without another glance, she went into the house and closed the door behind her.

They stood in a grim half circle, each man faced suddenly with the enormity of what they were doing and had done.

Lee Goff was the first to speak. He stood straddle legged, his thick hard body bulging all his clothes, his blond hair bristling. "Anybody bothers that woman," he said, "I'll kill him."

CHAPTER XIII

KEITH LED HIS attack just before dusk and lost two men before the company men withdrew. But the attack had paid off—they had learned of the hole. Dornie Shaw squatted behind the abutment formed by the end wall of the canyon where it opened on the plain near the arroyo. "That makes it easy," he said. "We still got dynamite."

Keith's head came up and he saw Shaw staring at him, his eyes queerly alight. "Or does that go against the grain, Colonel? About ten sticks of dynamite dropped into that crevasse an' Burwick will get what he wants—no bodies."

"If there's a cave back there," Keith objected, "they'd be buried alive!"

Nobody replied. Keith's eyes wandered around to the other men, but their eyes were on the ground. They were shunning responsibility for the act, and only Shaw enjoyed the prospect. Keith shuddered. What a fool he had been to get mixed up in this.

A horse's hoof struck stone, and as one man they looked up. Although they could not see the horse they heard the creak of saddle leather. A spur jingled, and Alton Burwick stood among them.

Loren Keith straightened to his feet and briefly explained the situation. Burwick nodded from time to time, then added, "Use the dynamite. First thing in the morning. That should end it, once and for all."

He drew a cigar from his pocket and bit off the end. "Had a wire. That committee is comin' out, all right. Take them a couple of weeks to get here, an' by that time folks should be over this an' talkin' about somethin' else. I'm figurin' a bonus for you all."

He turned back toward his horse, then stopped and catching Dornie Shaw's eye, jerked his head.

Shaw got up from the fire and followed him, and Keith stared after them, his eyes bitter. Now what? Was he being left out of something else?

Beyond the edge of the firelight and beyond the reach of their ears, Burwick paused and let Shaw come up to him. "Nice work, Dornie," he said. "We make a pair, you an' me."

"Yeah," Dornie nodded. "An' sometimes I think a pair's enough."

"Well," Burwick puffed on his cigar, "I need a good man to side me, an' Gunter's gone—at least."

"That company o' yours," Dornie was almost whispering, "had too many partners, anyway."

"Uh huh," Burwick said quietly, "it still has."

"All right, then." Dornie hitched his guns into a firmer seating on his thighs. "I'll be in to see you in a couple of days at most."

Burwick turned and walked away, and Dornie saw him swing easily to the saddle. He stayed where he was, looking into the darkness and listening to the slow steps of the horse. They had a funny sound—a very funny sound.

When he walked back to the campfire, he was whistling *Green Grow the Lilacs, O*.

The attack came again at daybreak. The company had mustered twenty men, of whom two carried packages of dynamite. This was to be the final blow. The squatters were to be wiped out, once and for all.

Shortly before the arrival of Burwick, Keith and Dornie Shaw, with Fessenden accompanying them, made a careful reconnaissance of the canyon from the rim. What they found pleased them enormously. It was obvious, once the crevasse had been located, that not more than two men could fire from it at once, and the attackers could find plenty of cover from the scattered boulders. In fact, they could get within throwing distance without emerging in the open for more than a few seconds at a time. Much of the squatters' field of fire would be ruined by their proximity to the ground and the rising of the boulders before them.

The attack started well, with all the men moving out. They made twenty yards into the canyon, moving fast. Here, the great slabs fallen from the slope of Yellow Butte crowded them together. And there the attack stopped.

It stopped abruptly, meeting a withering wall of rifle fire—at point-blank range!

Tom Kedrick knew a thing or two about fighting, and he knew full well that the hideout in the crevasse would in the long run become a deathtrap. He put himself in Keith's place and decided what that man would do. Then he had his eight men, carrying fourteen rifles, slip like Indians through the darkness to carefully selected firing positions far down the canyon from where Keith would be expecting to find them.

Five of the attackers died in that first burst of fire. As the gunhands broke for cover, two more went down. One dragged himself to the camp of the previous night with a shattered knee cap. He found himself alone.

The wife of Taggart had begun it—the mighty blast of rifle fire completed it.

The company fighters got out of the canyon's mouth, and as one man they moved for their horses. Keith was among them and glad to be going. Dornie Shaw watched him mount up, and swung up alongside him. Behind them, moving carefully as if they were perfectly disciplined troops, the defenders of the canyon moved down, firing as they came. A horse dropped, and a man crawled into the rocks, then jumped up and ran. Dai Reid swung wide of the group and started after him.

Another went down before they got away, and Kedrick turned to his group. "Get your horses, men. The women will be all right. This is a job that needs finishing now."

A quarter of a mile away, Brokow spotted a horse, standing alone, and started for it. As he arose from the rocks, a voice called out from behind. "A minute!"

Brokow turned. He saw only one man approaching him, the Welshman, Dai Reid. He stared at the man's Spencer, remembering his own gun was empty. He backed up slowly, his eyes haunted.

"My rifle's empty," he said, "an' I've lost my Colt."

"Drop the rifle then," Dai said quietly. "This I've been wanting, for guns be not my way."

Brokow did not understand, but he dropped his rifle. He was a big man, hulking and considered powerful. He watched in amazement as Reid placed his Spencer carefully on the ground, and then his gun belt. With bowlegged strides, the shorter man started for Brokow.

The outlaw stared, then started forward to meet Dai. As they drew near, he swung. His rocklike fist smashed Dai Reid flush on the chin. But Reid only blinked, then lunged. Twice more Brokow swung, blows filled with smashing panic born of the lack of effect of that first punch. Dai was unable to avoid the blows, and both connected solidly. But then Dai's huge, big-knuckled hand grasped Brokow's arm and jerked him near.

The hand slipped to the back of his head and jerked Brokow's face down to meet the rising of the Welshman's head. Stars burst before Brokow's eyes, and he felt the bone go in his nose. He swung wildly, and then those big hands gripped his throat and squeezed till Brokow was dead. Then Dai Reid dropped the outlaw to the sand. Turning, he walked away. He did not notice the horse that stood waiting. It was a grulla.

In the headlong flight that followed the debacle in the canyon's mouth, only Lee Goff had purpose. The hard-bitten Montana gunman had stared reality in the face when Taggart's wife turned on him. It was only coincidence that she so resembled his own mother, long since dead of overwork in rearing seven boys and five girls on a bleak Montana ranch.

He headed directly for Yellow Butte and the Taggart home. He did not dismount, but stopped by the door and knocked gently. It opened and he faced Mrs. Taggart, her eyes red from weeping. "Ma'am," he said, "I guess I ain't much account, but this here's been too much. I'm driftin'. Will you take this here—as a favor to me?"

He shoved a thick roll of bills at her, his face flushing deep red. For an instant, she hesitated, and then she accepted the money with dignity. "Thanks, son. You're a good boy."

Goff put spurs to his horse and swung it around. The bald-faced sorrel disappeared into the darkness of the night. Lee Goff had had his belly full. He was heading for Colorado, or Utah—anywhere . . . but away.

Elsewhere, Tom Kedrick was riding to Mustang. With him were Laredo Shad, Pit Laine, Dai Reid, Burt Williams, and the others. They made a tight, grim-faced little cavalcade, and they rode with their rifles across their saddle forks.

Due west of them, however, another little drama was taking place. The riders they followed did not include all the men who had abandoned the fight in the canyon. Two of them, Dornie Shaw and Colonel Loren Keith, had headed due west on their own. Both of them had their own thoughts and their own ideas of what to do. Among other things, Keith had decided that he had had enough. Whether the others knew it or not, they were through, and he was getting out of the country.

There was some money back there in Mustang, and once he had that, he was going to mount up and head for California. Then let Ransome investigate. After a few years he would return to the East. If the subject ever came up, he would swear he had nothing to do with it, that he only represented the company legally in the first steps of the venture.

What Dornie Shaw was thinking nobody ever guessed. At this moment, however, he had no thought at all in his mind. For his mind was not overly given to thought. He liked a few things, although he rarely drank, and seemed never to eat much. He liked a good horse and a woman with about an equal degree of affection, and he had liked Sue Laine a good bit. However, the woman who really fascinated him was Connie Duane, and she seemed unaware that he was alive.

Most of all he liked a gun. When cornered or braced into a fight, he killed as naturally and simply as most men eat. He was a creature of destruction, pure and simple. Never in his life had he been faced with a man who made him doubt his skill, and never had he fought with anything but guns—and he vowed he never would.

The two rode rapidly and both were mounted well. By the time Kedrick was leaving Yellow Butte with his men and lining out for town, Shaw and Keith reached the bank of Salt Creek Wash. Here Keith swung down to tighten his saddle cinch while his horse was drinking. After a moment, Dornie got down, too.

Absently Keith asked, "Well, Dornie, this breaks it, so where do you think you'll go now?"

"Why, Colonel," Shaw said softly, in his gentle boy's voice. "I don't know exactly where I'm goin, but this here's as far as you go."

It took a minute for the remark to sink in, and then Keith turned, his puzzled expression stiffening into black horror, then fear. Dornie Shaw stood negligently watching him, his lips smiling a little, his eyes opaque and empty.

The realization left Loren Keith icy cold. Dornie Shaw was going to kill him.

He had been an utter fool ever to allow this to happen. Why had he left the others and come off with Shaw? Why hadn't he killed him long since, from behind if need be, for the man was like a mad dog. He was insane, completely insane.

"What's on your mind, Shaw?" Without realizing it he spoke as he might to a subordinate. Shaw was not conscious of the tone. He was looking at Keith's belt line. The Colonel, he reflected, had been taking on a little weight lately.

"Why, just what I say. You've come as far as your trail takes you, Colonel. I can't say I'm sorry."

"Burwick won't like this. We're two of the men on whom he relies."

"Uh huh, that's the way it was. It ain't now. Back yonder," he jerked his head toward the butte, "he sort of implied he'd got hisself one too many partners." He shoved his hat back a little. "You want to try for your gun? It won't help you none, but you can try."

Keith was frightened. Every muscle within him seemed to have tightened until he could not move, yet he knew he was going to. But at the last, he had something to say, and it came from some deep inner conviction. "Kedrick will kill you, Dornie. He's going to win. He'll beat Burwick, too."

Suddenly, he remembered something: it had been only a fleeting expression on Dornie Shaw's face, but something. "Dornie!" he shot the word out with the force of desperation. "There behind you! The grulla!"

Shaw whirled, his face white, an almost animal-like fury on it. As he turned, Keith, gasping hoarsely and triumphantly, grabbed for his gun. He got it, and the gun swung up. But he had never coped with a fighter like Shaw. In the flashing instant that he whirled and found nothing behind him, Dornie hurled himself backward. The shot split wide the air where he had stood an instant before, and then Dornie himself fired from the ground. He fired once, then a second time.

Keith caught the bullet through the midsection, right where that extra weight had been gathering, and took the second one in the same place.

He fell, half in the trickle of water that comprised Salt Creek. Feeding shells into his gun, Dornie Shaw stared down at the glazing eyes. "How did you know?" he asked sullenly. "How did you know?"

CHAPTER XIV

FESSENDEN RODE WELL forward in the saddle, his great bulk carried easily with the movement of the horse. His wide face was somber with thought and distaste. Like the others, the wife of Taggart had affected him as nothing else could have. He was a hard man who had done more than his share of killing. But he had killed men ruthlessly, thoughtlessly, killed men in mortal combat where he himself might die as easily.

Several times before he had hired his gun, but each time in cattle or sheep wars or struggles with equals, men as gun-wise as he himself. Never before had he actually joined in a move to rob men of their homes. Without conscience in the usual sense, he had it in this case. For the men who moved West, regardless of their brand, were largely men in search of homes. Before, he had thought little of their fight. Several times he had helped to drive nesters from cattle range, and to him that was just and logical. Cows needed grass and people lived on beef, and most of the range country wasn't suited to farming, anyway.

But now there was a difference, he realized, thinking of it for the first time. Now men were not being driven off for cattle, but only for profit. To many, the line was a fine one to draw; to Fessenden and his like, once the matter was seen in its true light, that line became a gap, an enormous one.

Actually, he rode in a state of shock. The victory

Keith had wanted seemed so near. The taking of the few left in the canyon had seemed simple. His qualms against the use of dynamite he had shrugged off, if uncomfortably. He had gone into the canyon with the others to get the thing over with, to get his money and get out. And then, long before they expected it, came that smashing thunderous volley. It had been made more crashing by the close canyon walls, more destructive by the way the attackers were channeled by the boulders.

Shock started the panic, and distaste for the whole affair kept some of them, at least, on the move. Yet it was hard to believe that Clauson and Poinsett were dead, that Brokow had vanished, that Lee Goff was gone. For alone of the group, Goff had told Fessenden he was leaving. He had not needed to tell him why.

Behind him rode the Mixus boys, somber with disappointment at the failure of the attack. They had no qualms about killing, and no lines to draw even at the killing of women. They were in no true sense fighting men; they were butchers. Yet even they realized the change that had come over the group. What had become of Brokow or Goff they did not know. But they did know that disintegration had set in. In turn, these men had turned into a snarling pack of wolves venting their fury and their hatred on each other.

Mustang lay quiet when they rode into town. It was the quiet before the storm. The town, like that cattle buyer who had turned back to Durango, sensed the coming fury of battle. No women were on the street, and only a few hardy souls loitered at the bars or card tables. The chairs before the St. James were deserted, and Clay Allison had ridden back to his home ranch, drunk and ugly.

An almost Sunday peace lay over the sun-swept town when Fessenden drew up before the Mustang Saloon and swung down from his weary horse. Slapping his hat against his leg to beat off the dust, Fessenden stood like a great shaggy bull and surveyed the quiet of the street. He was too knowing a Western man not to recognize the symptoms of disaster. Clapping his hat all awry upon his shaggy head, he shoved his bulk through the doors and moved to the bar.

"Rye," he said, his voice booming in the cavernous interior. His eyes glinted around the room, then back to the bartender.

That worthy could no longer restrain his curiosity. "What's happened?" he asked, swallowing.

A glint of irony came into the hard eyes of the gunman. "Them squatters squatted there for keeps," he said wryly, "an' they showed us they aim to stay put." He tossed off his drink. "All Hades busted loose." Briefly he explained. "You'd a figured there was a thousand men in that neck of the rocks when they opened up. The thing that did it was the unexpectedness of it, like steppin' on a step in the dark when it ain't there."

He poured another drink. "It was that Kedrick," he said grimly. "When I seen him shift to the other side I should've lit a shuck."

"What about Keith?"

"He won't be back."

They turned at the new voice, and saw Dornie Shaw standing in the doorway, smiling. Still smiling, he walked on in and leaned against the bar. "Keith won't be back," he said. "He went for his gun out on Salt Creek."

The news fell into a silent room. A man at a table shifted his feet and his chair creaked. Fessenden wet his lips and downed his second drink. He was getting out of town, but fast.

"Seen that girl come in, short time back," the bartender

said suddenly, "that Duane girl. Thought she'd gone over to the other side?"

Dornie's head lifted and his eyes brightened, then shadowed. He downed his own drink and walked jauntily to the door. "Stick around, Fess. I'll be back." He grinned. "I'll collect for both of us from the Old Man."

The bartender looked at Fessenden: "Reckon he'll bring it if he does?"

The big gunman nodded absently. "Sure. He's no thief. Why, that kid never stole a thing in his life. He don't believe in it. An' he won't lie or swear—but he'll shoot the heart out of you an' smile right in your face while he's doing it."

The show had folded. The roundup was over. There was nothing to do now but light out. Fessenden knew he should go, but a queer apathy had settled over him. He ordered another drink, letting the bartender pour it. The liquor he drank seemed now to fall into a cavern without bottom and had no effect.

On the outskirts of town, Tom Kedrick reined in. "We'll keep together," he said quietly. "We want Keith, Shaw, Burwick, the Mixus boys and Fessenden. There are about four others that you will recognize whom I don't know by name. Let's work fast and make no mistakes.

"Pit, you take Dai and two men and go up the left side of the street. Take no chances. Arrest them if you can. We'll try them, and"—his face was grim—"if we find them guilty they'll have just two sentences: leave the country or hang. The Mixus boys and Shaw," he said, "will hang. They've done murder."

He turned in his saddle and glanced at the tall Texan. "Come on, Shad," he said quietly, "we'll take two men and the right side of the street, which means the livery stable, the St. James and the Mustang."

Kedrick glanced over at Laine. "Pit," he said, "if you run into Allison or Ketchum, better leave 'em alone. We don't want 'em."

Laine's face was grave. "I ain't huntin' 'em," he said grimly, "but if they want it, they can have it."

The parties rode into town and swung down on their respective sides of the street. Laredo grinned at Kedrick, but his eyes were sober. "Nobody wants to cross Laine today," he said quietly. "The man's in a killin' mood. It's his sister."

"Wonder what will happen when they meet?"

"I hope they don't," Shad said. "She's a right purty sort of gal, only money crazy."

The two men stood hesitant, waiting for orders. Both were farmers. One carried a Spencer .56, the other a shotgun. Shad glanced at them. "Let these hombres cover the street, Tom," he suggested. "You take the St. James, an' I'll take the stable."

Kedrick hesitated. "All right," he agreed finally. "But take no chances, boy."

Laredo grinned and waved a negligent hand and walked through the wide door of the stable. Inside, he paused, cold and seemingly careless, actually as poised and deadly as a coiled rattler. He had already seen Abe Mixus' sorrel pony and guessed the two dry-gulchers were in town. He walked on a step and saw the barrel of a rifle push through the hay.

He lunged right and dove into a stall, drawing his gun as he went. He ran full tilt into the other Mixus. Their bodies smashed together, and Mixus, caught off balance, went down and rolled over. He came up, clawing for a gun. Laredo kicked the gun from under his hand and sent it spinning into the wide open space between the rows of stalls.

With a kind of whining cry, Bean Mixus sprang after it, slid to his knees and got up, turning. Laredo Shad stood tall and dark, just within the stall. As Mixus turned like a rat cornered and swung his gun around, Laredo Shad fired. His two shots slammed loud in the stillness of the huge barn. Bean Mixus fell dead.

The rifle bellowed and a shot ripped the stall stanchion near Laredo's head. He lunged into the open, firing twice more at the stack of straw. The rifle jerked, then thundered again, but the shot went wild. Laredo dove under the loft where Abe Mixus was concealed, and fired two more shots through the roof over his head where he guessed the killer would be lying.

Switching his guns, he holstered the empty one and waited. The roof creaked some distance away. Laredo began to stalk the escaping Mixus, slipping from stall to stall. Suddenly, a back door creaked and a broad path of light shot into the darkness of the stable. Laredo lunged to follow—too late.

The farmer outside with the shotgun was the man Sloan. As Abe Mixus lunged through the door to escape, they came face to face, at no more than twenty feet of distance. Abe had his rifle at his hip and he fired. The shot ripped through the water trough beside Sloan, and the farmer squeezed off the left-hand barrel of his shotgun.

The solid core of shot hit Mixus in the shoulder and neck, knocking him back against the side of the door. His long face was drawn and terror stricken, his neck and shoulder a mass of blood that seemed to well from a huge wound. He fought to get his gun up, Sloan stepped forward, remembering Bob McLennon's death and the deaths of Steelman and Slagle. The other barrel thundered and a sharp blast of flame stabbed at Abe Mixus.

Smashed and dead, the killer sagged against the doorjamb, his old hat falling free, his face pillowed in the gray, blood-mixed dust.

Silence hung heavy in the wake of the shots. Into that silence Laredo Shad spoke. "Hold it, Sloan!" He stepped through the door, taking no glance at the fallen man. "The other one won't hang, either," he said. "They were both inside."

The two men drew aside, Sloan's face gray and sick. He had never killed a man before, and wanted never to again. He tried to roll a smoke but his fingers trembled. Shad took the paper and tobacco from him and rolled it. The farmer looked up, shame-faced. "Guess I'm yaller," he said. "That sort of got me."

The Texan looked at him gloomily. "Let's hope it always does," he said. He handed him the cigarette. "Try this," he told him. "It will make you feel better. Wonder how Kedrick's comin'?"

"Ain't heard nothin'!"

Pit Laine stood in a door across the street. "Everythin' all right?" he called.

"Yeah," the other farmer called back, "on'y you don't hafta look for the Mixus boys no more. They ain't gonna be around."

Captain Tom Kedrick had walked up the street and turned into the door of the St. James Hotel. The wide lobby was still, a hollow shell, smelling faintly of old tobacco fumes and leather. The wrinkled clerk looked up and shook his head. "Quiet today," he said. "Nobody around. Ain't been no shootin' in days."

Guns thundered from down the street, then again and again. Then there was silence followed by the two solid blasts of the shotgun.

Both men listened, and no further sound came. A moment later Pit Laine called out and the farmer answered. The clerk nodded. "Same town," he said. "Last couple of days I been wonderin' if I wasn't back in Ohio. Awful quiet lately," he said, "awful quiet."

Tom Kedrick walked down the hall and out the back door. He went down the weathered steps and stopped on the grass behind the building. There was an old, rusty pump there, and the sun was hot on the backs of the buildings.

He walked over to the pump and worked the handle. It protested, whining and groaning at the unaccustomed work and finally, despairing of rest, threw up a thick core of water that splashed in the wooden tub. When he had pumped for several minutes, Kedrick held the gourd dipper under the pump and let it fill. The water was clear and very cold. He drank greedily, rested, then drank again.

Far up the backs of the buildings, at the opposite end of town, a man was swinging an ax. Kedrick could see the flash of light on the blade, and see the ax strike home. A moment later, the sound would come to him. He watched, then wiped the back of his hand across his mouth and started along in back of the buildings toward the Mustang.

He moved with extreme care, going steadily, yet with every sense alert. He wore his .44 Russians, and liked the feel of them, ready to his hands. The back door of the Mustang Saloon was long unpainted and blistered by many hot suns. He glanced at the hinges and saw they were rusty. The door would squeak. Then he saw the outside stair leading to the second floor. Turning, he mounted the stairs on tiptoe, easing through the door, and walked down the hall.

In the saloon below, Fessenden had eliminated half a

bottle of whisky without destroying the deadening sense of futility that had come over him. He picked up a stack of cards and riffled them skillfully through his fingers. He had not lost his deftness. Whatever effect the whisky had had, it was not on his hands.

Irritated, he slammed the cards down and stared at the bartender. "Wish Dornie'd get back," he said for the tenth time. "I want to leave this town. She don't feel right today."

He had heard shots down the street, but had not moved from the bar. "Some drunk cowhand," he said irritably.

"You better look," the bartender suggested, hoping for no fights in the saloon. "It might be some of your outfit."

"I got no outfit," Fess replied shortly. "I'm fed up. That stunt out there to Yeller Butte drove me off that range. I'll have no more of it."

He heard the footsteps coming down the hall from upstairs and listened to their even cadence. He glanced up, grinning, "Sounds like an army man. Listen!"

Realization of what he had said came over him, and the grin left his face. He straightened, resting his palms on the bar. For a long moment, he stared into the bartender's eyes. "I knew it! I knew that hombre would—" He tossed off his drink. "Aw, I didn't want to leave town, anyway!"

He turned, moving back from the bar. He stood straddle legged like a huge grizzly, his big hands swinging at his hips, his eyes glinting upward at the balcony and the hall that gave onto it. The steps ceased, and Tom Kedrick stood there, staring down at him.

Neither man spoke for a full minute, while suspense gripped the watchers, and then it was Fessenden who broke the silence. "You lookin' for me, Kedrick?"

"For any of your crowd. Where's Shaw? And Keith?"

"Keith's dead. Shaw killed him back up on the Salt after you whipped us in the canyon. I dunno where he is now."

Silence fell once more and the two men studied each other. "You were among them at Chimney Rock, Fessenden," Kedrick said. "That was an ambush—dry-gulcher's stunt, Fess." Kedrick took another step forward, then side-stepped down the first step of the stairs which ran along the back wall until about six steps from the bottom, then after a landing, came down facing the room.

Fessenden stood there, swaying slightly on his thick, muscular legs, his brutal jaw and head thrust forward. "Aw, hell!" he said and grabbed iron.

His guns fairly leaped from their holsters spouting flame. A bullet smashed the top of the newel post at the head of the stairs, then ricocheted into the wall. Another punctured a hole just behind Kedrick's shoulder. Tom Kedrick stepped down another step, then fired. His bullet turned Fessenden, and Kedrick ran lightly down four steps while Fessenden smashed two shots at him.

Kedrick dove headlong for the landing, brought up hard against the wall, and smashed another shot at the big man. It knocked a leg from under him and Fessenden rolled over on his feet, colliding with the bar.

He had been hit twice, but he was cold sober and deadly. He braced himself and with his left hand clinging to the bar, lifted his right and thumbed back the hammer. Kedrick fired two quick shots with his left gun. One ripped a furrow down the bar and hit Fessenden below the breast bone— a jagged tearing piece of metal when it struck.

Fessenden fired again, but the bullet went wild. His sixth shot was fired in desperation as he swung up his left-hand gun, dropping the right into his holster. Taking his time, feeling his life's blood running out of him, he braced himself there and took the gun over into his right hand. He was deliberate and calm. "Pour me a drink," he said.

The bartender, lying flat on his face behind the bar, made no move. Tom Kedrick stood on the edge of the landing now, staring at Fessenden. The big gunman had been hit three times, through the shoulder, the leg and the chest, and he still stood there, gun in hand, ponderous and invulnerable.

The gun came up and Fessenden seemed to lean forward with it. "I wish you was Dornie," he said.

Kedrick triggered. The shot nailed Fessenden through the chest again. The big man took a fast step back, then another. His gun slipped from his hand, and he grabbed a glass from the bar. "Gimme a drink!" he demanded. Blood bubbled at his lips.

Tom Kedrick came down the steps, his gun ready in his hand and walked toward Fessenden. Holding his gun level and low down with his right hand, Kedrick picked up the bottle with his left and filled the empty glass. Then he pulled over another glass and poured one for himself.

Fessenden stared at him. "You're a good man, Kedrick," he said, shaping the words patiently. "I'm a good man, too—on the wrong side."

"I'll drink to that." Kedrick lifted his glass, they clicked them, and Fessenden grinned crookedly over his.

"You watch that Dornie," he advised, "he's rattler-mean." The words stumbled from his mouth and he frowned, lifting the glass. He downed his drink, choked on it, and started to hold out his big hand to Kedrick, then fell flat on his face. Holstering his gun, Tom Kedrick leaned over and gripped the big right hand. Fessenden grinned and died.

CHAPTER XV

CONNIE DUANE HAD reached Mustang only a short time before the survivors of the fight at Yellow Butte began to arrive. Restless, after the men left to return to the squatters' town, she had begun to think of what lay ahead, of Fred Ransome, and of the impending investigation and of her uncle's part in it.

All his papers as well as many of her own remained under lock in the gray stone house in Mustang. If she was to get her own money back from Burwick, or was to clear any part of the blame from her uncle, she knew those papers would be essential. Mounting her horse she left the camp beyond the rim. Striking the Old Mormon Trail, she headed south. She was on that trail when the sun lifted, and she heard the distant sound of shots.

Turning from the trail she reined her horse into the bed of Salt Creek and rode south, passing the point where only a short time later Loren Keith was to meet his death at the hands of Dornie Shaw. Once in town she believed she would be safe. She doubted if anyone would be left in the gray house unless it was Burwick, and she knew that he rarely left his chair.

Arriving in Mustang, she rode quickly up the street, then cut over behind through the back door and went very quietly. Actually, she need not have bothered, for Alton Burwick was not there. Making her way up the old stairs, she unlocked the door to the apartment she had shared with her uncle, and closed the door behind her.

Nothing seemed to have been disturbed. The blinds were drawn as she had left them and the room was still. A little dust had collected, and the light filtering in around the blinds showed it to her. Going to her trunk, she opened it and got out the iron-bound box in which she carried her own papers. It was intact and showed no evidence of having been tampered with. From the bottom of the trunk she took an old purse in which there were two dozen gold eagles. These she put into the purse she was now carrying.

Among other things she found an old pistol, a huge, cumbersome old thing. This she got out and laid on the table beside her. Then she found a derringer seven shot .22 caliber pistol her father had given her several years before he died, and she put it in the pocket of her dress.

Quickly she went into the next room and began to go through her uncle's desk, working swiftly and surely. Most of his papers were readily available. Apparently nobody had made any effort to go through them, probably believing they contained nothing of consequence or that there would be plenty of time later. She was busy at this when she heard a horse walk by the house and stop near the back steps.

Instantly she stopped what she was doing and stood erect. The window here was partly open and she could hear the saddle creak very gently as whoever it was swung down. Then a spur jingled, and there was a step below, then silence.

"So? It's you."

Startled by the voice, Connie turned. Sue Laine stood behind her, staring with wide eyes. "Yes," Connie replied. "I came for some things of mine. You're Sue, aren't you?"

Without replying to the question, the girl nodded her head toward the window. "Who was that? Did you see?"

"No. It was a man."

"Maybe Loren has come back." Sue studied her, unsmiling. "How are they out there? Are they all right? I mean—did you see Pit?"

"Yes. He's unhappy about you."

Sue Laine flushed, but her chin lifted proudly. "I suppose he is, but what did he expect? That I was going to live all my life out there in that awful desert? I'm sick of it! Sick of it, I tell you!"

Connie smiled. "That's strange. I love it. I love it, and every minute I'm there, I love it more. I'd like to spend my life here, and I believe I will."

"With Tom Kedrick?"

Sue's jealousy flashed in her eyes, yet there was curiosity, too. Connie noticed how the other girl studied her clothes, her face.

"Why—I—where did you ever get that idea?"

"From looking at him. What girl wouldn't want him? Anyway, he's the best of the lot."

"I thought you liked Colonel Keith?"

Sue's face flushed again. "I—I thought I did, too. Only part of it was because Tom Kedrick wouldn't notice me. And because I wanted to get away from here, from the desert. But since then—I guess Pit hates me."

"No brother really hates his sister, I think. He'd be glad to see you back with him."

"You don't know him. If it had been anybody but someone associated with Alton Burwick, why—"

"You mean, you knew Burwick before?"

"Knew him?" Sue stared at her. "Didn't you know? Didn't he tell you? He was our stepfather."

"Alton Burwick?" Connie stared in amazement.

"Yes, and we always suspected that he killed my father. We never knew, but my mother suspected later, too, for she took us and ran away from him. He came after us. We never knew what happened to mother. She went off one night for something and never came back, and we were reared by a family who took us in."

A board creaked in the hall, and both girls were suddenly still, listening.

Guns thundered from the street of the town, and both girls stared at each other, holding their breath. There was a brief silence, then a further spattering of shots. Then the door opened very gently and Dornie Shaw stood there facing the two girls.

He seemed startled at finding the girls together and looked from one to the other, his brown eyes bright, but now confused.

Then he centered his eyes on Sue Laine. "You better get out," he said. "Keith's dead."

"Dead?" Sue gasped, horrified. "They—they killed him?"

"No, I did. Up on the Salt. He drew on me."

"Keith—dead." Sue was shocked.

"What about the others? Where are they?" Connie asked quickly.

Dornie turned his head sharply around and looked hard at her, a curious, prying gaze as if he did not quite know what to make of her. "Some of 'em dead," he said matter of factly. "They whupped us. It was that Kedrick," he spoke without emotion or shadow of prejudice as though he were completely indifferent. "He had 'em set for us an' they mowed us down." He jerked his head toward the street. "I guess they are finishin' up now. The Mixus boys an' Fessenden are down there."

"They'll be coming here," Connie said, with conviction. "This is the next place."

"I reckon." He seemed indifferent to that, too. "Kedrick'll be the first one. Maybe," he smiled, "the last one."

He dug out the makings, glancing around the room, then back at Sue. "You git out. I want to talk to Connie."

Sue did not move. "You can talk to us both. I like it here."

As he touched his tongue to the paper his eyes lifted and met hers. They were flat, expressionless. "You heard me," he said. "I'd hate to treat you rough."

"You haven't the nerve!" Sue flashed back. "You know what would happen to you if you laid hands on a woman in this country! You can get away with killing me. But this country won't stand for having their women bothered—even by a ratty little killer like you!"

Connie Duane was remembering the derringer in her pocket. She lowered her hand to her hip within easy grasp of the gun.

A sudden cannonade sounded, then a scattering of more shots. At that moment Kedrick was finally shooting it out with Fessenden. Dornie Shaw cocked an inquisitive ear toward the sound. "Gettin' closer," he said. "I ain't really in no hurry until Kedrick gets here."

"You'd better be gone before he does come." Connie was surprised at the confidence in her voice . "He's too much for you, and he's not half frightened like these others are. He'll kill you, Dornie."

He stared at her, then chuckled without humor. "Him? Bah! The man doesn't live who can outdraw Dornie Shaw. I've tried 'em all. Fess? He's supposed to be good, but he don't fool with Dornie. I'd shoot his ears off."

Calmly, Connie dropped her right hand into her pocket and clutched the derringer. The feel of it gave her confidence. "You had better go," she said quietly. "You were not invited here, and we don't want you."

He did not move. "Still playin' it high an' mighty, are you? You've got to get over that. Come on, you're coming with me."

"Are you leaving?" Connie's eyes flashed. "I'll not ask you again!"

Shaw started to speak, but whatever it was he planned to say never formed into words, for Connie had her hand on the derringer, and she fired from her pocket. Ordinarily, she was a good shot, but had never fired the gun from that position. The first bullet burned a furrow along Dornie Shaw's ear, notching it at the top. The second shot stung him along the ribs and the third plowed into the table beside him.

With a grunt of surprise, he dove through the door into the hall. Sue was staring at Connie. "Well, I never!" Her eyes dropped to the tiny gun that Connie had now drawn from her pocket. "Dornie Shaw! And with that! Oh, just wait until this gets around!" Her laughter rang out merrily, and despite herself, Connie was laughing, too.

Downstairs near the door, Dornie Shaw clutched his bloody ear. He panted as though he had been running, his face twisting as he stared at his blood. Amazed, he scarcely noticed when Kedrick came up the steps. But as the door pushed open, he saw him. For a fatal instant, he froze. Then he grabbed for his gun, but he had lost his chance. In that split second of hesitation, Kedrick jumped. His right hand grasped Dornie's gun wrist, and Kedrick swung the gunman bodily around, hurling him into the wall. Shaw's body hit with a crash and he rebounded into a wicked right to the wind.

Shaw was no fighter with his hands, and the power of that blow would have wrecked many a bigger man. As it was, it knocked every bit of wind from the gunman's body. Kedrick shoved him back against the wall. "You asked me what I'd do, once, with a faster man. Watch this, Dornie!"

Kedrick lifted his right hand and slapped the gunman across the mouth. Crying with fury, Shaw fought against the bigger man's grip. Kedrick held him flat against the wall, gripping him by the shirt collar, and slapped him over and back. "Just a cheap killer!" Kedrick said calmly. "Somebody has already bled you a little. I'll do it for good."

He dropped a hand to Dornie's shirt and ripped it wide. "I'm going to ruin you in this country, Dornie. I'm going to show them what you are—a cheap, yellow-bellied killer who terrorizes men better than himself." He slapped Dornie again, then shoved him into the wall once more and stepped back.

"All right, Shaw! You got your guns! Reach!"

Almost crying with fury, Dornie Shaw grabbed for his guns. As he whipped them free, all his timing wrecked by the events of the past few minutes, Kedrick's gun crashed and Shaw's right-hand gun was smashed from his hand. Shaw fired the left-hand gun, but the shot went wild. Kedrick lunged, chopping down with his pistol barrel. The blow smashed Dornie Shaw's wrist and he dropped the gun with a yelp.

He fell back against the wall, trembling, and staring at his hands. His left wrist was broken; his right thumb was gone. Where it had been, blood was welling.

Roughly, Kedrick grabbed him and shoved him out of the door. He stumbled and fell, but Kedrick jerked him to his feet, unmindful of the gasps of the onlookers, attracted by the sounds of fighting. In the forefront of the crowd were Pit Laine, Dai Reid and Laredo Shad, blinking with astonishment at the sight of the most feared gunman in the country treated like a whipped child.

Shaw's horse stood nearby, and Kedrick motioned to him. "Get on him—backwards!"

Shaw started to turn and Kedrick lifted his hand and the gunman ducked instinctively. "Get up there! Dai, when he's up tie his ankles together."

Dornie Shaw, befuddled by the whipping he had taken, scarcely aware of what was happening, lifted his eyes. Then he saw the grulla tied near the stone house. It was the last straw, his demoralization was complete.

Feared because of his deadly skill with guns and his love of killing for the sake of killing, he had walked a path alone, either avoided by all, or catered to by them. Never in his life had he been manhandled as he had by Tom Kedrick. His belief in himself was shattered.

"Take him through the town." Kedrick's voice was harsh. "Show them what a killer looks like. Then fix up that thumb and wrist and turn him loose."

"Turn him loose?" Shad demanded. "Are you crazy?"

"No, turn him loose. He'll leave this country so far behind nobody will ever see him again. This is worse than death for him, believe me." He shrugged. "I've seen them before. All they need, that kind, is for somebody to face them once who isn't afraid. He was fast and accurate with his guns so he developed the idea he was tough.

"Other folks thought the same thing. He wasn't tough. A tough man has to win and lose. He has to come up after being knocked down, he has to have taken a few beatings, and know what it means to win the hard way.

"Anybody," he said dryly, "can knock a man down. When you've been knocked down at least three times yourself, and then got up and floored the other man, then you can figure you're a tough hombre. Those smoke poles of Shaw's greased his path for him. Now he knows what he's worth."

The crowd drifted away and Connie Duane was standing in the doorway. Tom Kedrick looked up at her, and suddenly, he smiled. To see her now, standing like this in the doorway, was like lifegiving rain upon the desert, coming in the wake of many heat-filled days.

She came down the step to him, then looked past him at Pit. "Your sister's upstairs, Pit. You'd better talk to her."

Laine hesitated; then he said stiffly, "I don't reckon I want to."

Laredo Shad drew deep on his cigarette and squinted through the smoke at Laine. "Mind if I do?" he asked. "I like her."

Pit Laine was astonished. "After this?"

Shad looked at the fire end of his cigarette. "Well," he said, speaking seriously, "the best cuttin' horse I ever rode was the hardest to break. Them with lots of git up an' go to 'em often make the best stock."

"Then go ahead." Pit stared after him. Then he said, "Tell her I'll be along later."

CHAPTER XVI

FOR THREE WEEKS there was no sign of Alton Burwick. He seemed to have vanished into the earth, and riders around the country reported no sign of him.

At the end of that time three men got down from the afternoon stage and were shown to rooms in the St. James. An hour later, while they were at dinner, Captain Tom Kedrick pushed open the door and walked into the dining room. Instantly, one of the men, a tall, immaculate young man whose hair was turning gray at the temples, rose to meet him, hand outstretched. "Tom! Say, this is wonderful! Gentlemen, this is Tom Kedrick, the man I was telling you about. We served together in the War Between the States! Tom—Mr. Edgerton and Mr. Cummings."

The two men, one a pudgy man with a round, cheerful face, the other as tall as Frederic Ransome and with gray muttonchop whiskers acknowledged the introduction. When Kedrick had seated himself, they began demanding details. Quietly, and as concisely as possible, he told them his own story, beginning with his joining the company in New Orleans.

"And Burwick's gone?" Edgerton asked. He was the older man with the muttonchop whiskers. "Was he killed?"

"I doubt it, sir," Kedrick replied. "He simply vanished. The man had a faculty for being out of the way when trouble came. Since he left, with the aid of Miss Duane and her uncle's papers, we managed to put together

161

most of the facts. However, Burwick's papers have disappeared, or most of them."

"Disappeared?" Edgerton asked. "How did that happen?"

"Miss Duane tells me that when she entered the house before the final trouble with Shaw, she passed the office door and the place was undisturbed and the desk all in order. After the crowd had gone and when we returned, somebody had been rifling the desk and the safe."

"You imply that Burwick returned? That he was there then?"

"He must have been. Connie—Miss Duane—tells me that only he had the combination, and that he kept all the loose ends of the business in his hands."

Cummings stared hard at Kedrick. "You say this, this Shaw fellow killed Keith? How do we know that you didn't? You admit to killing Fessenden."

"I did kill him. In a fair fight before witnesses. I never even saw Keith's body after he was killed."

"Who do you think killed John Gunter?" Cummings demanded.

"My guess would be Burwick."

"I'm glad you're not accusing Keith of that," Cummings replied dryly.

"Keith wouldn't have used a knife," Kedrick replied quietly, "nor he wouldn't have attacked him from behind as was obviously the case."

"This land deal, Kedrick," Ransome asked. "Where do you stand in it?"

"I? I don't stand at all. I'm simply not in it."

Cummings looked up sharply. "You don't stand to profit from it at all? Not in any way?"

"How could I? I own nothing. I have no holdings, nor claim to any."

"You said Burwick promised you fifteen per cent?"

"That's right. But I know now that it was merely to appease me long enough to get me on the spot at Chimney Butte where I was to be killed along with the others. Burwick got me there, then rode off on the pretext that he wanted to look at a mineral ledge."

"How about this girl? The Duane girl?" Cummings asked sharply. "Does she stand to profit?"

"She will be fortunate to get back her money that her uncle invested."

"See, Cummings?" Ransome said. "I told you Kedrick was honest. I know the man."

"I'll give my opinion on that later, after this investigation is completed. Not now. I want to go over the ground and look into this matter thoroughly. I want to investigate this matter of the disappearance of Alton Burwick, too. I'm not at all satisfied with this situation."

He glanced down at the notes in his hand, then looked up. "As to that, Kedrick, wasn't Fessenden a duly elected officer of the law when you shot him? Wasn't he the sheriff?"

"Elected by a kangaroo election," Kedrick replied, "where the votes were counted by the two officials who won. If that is a legal election, then he was sheriff."

"I see. But you do not deny that he had authority?"

"I do deny it."

Connie Duane was awaiting him when he walked back to his table. She smiled as he sat down and listened to his explanation. She frowned thoughtfully. "Cummings? I think there is something in Uncle John's papers about him. I believe he was acting for them in Washington."

"That explains a lot then." Kedrick picked up his coffee cup, then put it down abruptly, for Laredo Shad had come into the room, his face sharp and serious. He glanced around, and sighting Kedrick, hurried toward him, spurs jingling. Kedrick got to his feet. "What's wrong? What's happened?"

"Plenty! Sloan was wounded last night and Yellow Butte burned!"

"What?" Kedrick stared.

Shad nodded grimly. "You shouldn't have turned that rat loose. That Dornie Shaw."

Kedrick shook his head irritably. "I don't believe it. He was thoroughly whipped when he left here. I think he ran like a scared rabbit when he left. If he did want revenge, it would be after a few months, not so soon. No, this is somebody else."

"Who could it be?"

His eyes met Connie's and she nodded, her eyes frightened. "You know who it could be, Tom. It could be Burwick."

Of course, that was what he had been thinking. Burwick had bothered him, getting away scot free, dropping off the end of the world into oblivion as he had. Remembering the malignant look in the man's eyes, Kedrick was even more positive. Burwick had counted on this land deal; he had worked on it longer than any one of them, and it meant more to him.

"Shad," he said suddenly, "where does that grulla tie in? It keeps turning up, again and again. There's something more about all this than we've ever known, something that goes a lot deeper. Who rides the grulla? Why is it he has never been seen? Why was Dornie so afraid of it?"

"Was he afraid of the grulla?" Shad asked, frowning. "That doesn't figure."

"Why doesn't it? That's the question now. You know, that last day when I had Shaw thoroughly whipped, he looked up and saw something that scared him, yet

something that I think he more than half expected.
After he was gone down the street, I looked around,
and there was nothing there. Later, I stumbled across
the tracks of the grulla mustang. That horse was in front
of the house during all the excitement!"

Frederic Ransome came into the room again and
walked to their table. "Cummings is going to stir up
trouble," he said, dropping into a chair. "He's out to get
you, Kedrick, and if he can pin the killing of Keith on
you, or that of Burwick... He claims your story is an
elaborate build-up to cover the murder of all three of
the company partners. He can make so much trouble
that none of the squatters will get anything out of the
land, and nothing for all their work. We've got to find
Burwick."

Laredo lit a cigarette. "That's a tough one," he said,
"but maybe I've got a hunch."

"What?" Kedrick looked up.

"Ever hear Burwick talk about the grulla?"

"No, I can't say that I did. It was mentioned before
him once that I recall, and he didn't seem interested."

"Maybe he wasn't interested because he knowed all
about it," Shad suggested. "That Burwick has me puzzled."

Connie looked up at him. "You may be right, Laredo,
but Pit and Sue Laine were Burwick's stepchildren and
they knew nothing about the horse. The only one who
seemed to know anything was Dornie Shaw."

Tom Kedrick got up. "Well, there's one thing we can
do," he said. "Laredo, we can scout out the tracks of
that horse and trail it down. Pick up an old trail,
anything. Then just see where it takes us.'

On the third day it began to rain. All week the wind
had been chill and cold and clouds had hung low and
flat across the sky from horizon to horizon. Hunched in

his slicker, Laredo slapped his gloved hands together and swore. "This finishes it!" he said with disgust. "It will wipe out all the trails for us!"

"All old anyway," Kedrick agreed. "We've followed a dozen here lately, and none of them took us anywhere. All disappeared on rock or were swept away by wind."

"Escavada's cabin isn't far up this canyon," Shad suggested. "Let's hit him up for chow. It will be a chance to get warm, anyway."

"Know him?"

"Stopped in there once. He's half Spanish, half Ute. Tough old blister, an' been in this country since before the grass came. He might be able to tell us something."

The trail into the canyon was slippery and the dull red of the rocks had turned black under the downpour. The rain slanted across the sky in drenching sheets. By the time they reached the stone cabin in the corner of the hills both men and horses were cold, wet and hungry.

Escavada opened the door for them and waved them in. He grinned at them. "Glad to have company," he said. "Ain't seen a man for three weeks."

When they had stripped off their slickers and peeled down to shirts, pants and boots, he put coffee before them and laced it with a strong shot of whisky. "Warm you up," he said. 'Trust you ain't goin' out again soon. Whisky's mighty fine when a body comes in from the cold, but not if he's goin' out again. It flushes the skin up, fetches all the heat to the surface, then gives it off into the air. Man freezes mighty quick, drinkin' whisky."

"You ever see a grulla mustang around, Escavada?" Laredo asked suddenly, looking up at the old man.

He turned on them, his eyes bright with malicious humor. "You ain't some of them superstitious kind, be you? Skeered o' the dark like? An' ghosts?"

"No," Kedrick said, "but what's the tie-up?"

"That grulla. Old story in this here country. Dates back thirty, forty years. Maybe further'n that. Sign of death or misfortune, folks say."

Laredo looked inquiringly at Kedrick, and Kedrick asked, "You know anything about it? That horse is real enough. We've both seen the grulla."

"So've I," the old man said. He dropped into a chair and grinned at them. His gray hair was sparse, but his eyes were alive and young. "I seen it many times, an' no misfortune come my way. Not unless you call losin' my shovel a misfortune."

He hitched his chair nearer the woodpile and tossed a couple of sticks on the fire. "First I heerd of it was long ago. Old folks used to tell of a Spanish man in armor ridin' a mouse-colored horse. He used to come an' go about the hills, but the story back of it seems to be that a long time back some such feller was mighty cruel to the Injuns. That story sort of hung around an' a body heerd it ever' now and again until about fifteen, sixteen years back. Since then she's been mighty lively."

"You mean, you heard the story more since then?" Kedrick asked.

"Uh huh. Started with a wagon train wiped out by Injuns up on the Salt. Ever' man jack o' them kilt dead—women folks, too, the story was. There was a youngster come off scot free, boy about five or six years old. He crawled off into the brush, an' after, he swore them Injuns was led by a white man on a grulla horse, a white man in armor!"

"Wild yarn," Shad said, "but you can't blame the kid, imaginin' things after what he must've seen."

"He said that hombre in the armor went around with a long knife, an' he skewered ever' one of the bodies to make sure they was real dead. He said once that hombre looked right square at him, layin' in the brush.

He was skeered like all git out, but must've been he wasn't seen, 'cause he wasn't bothered."

"An' this grulla has been seen since?" Shad asked. "Reg'lar?"

"Uh huh, but never no rider clost enough to say who or what. Sometimes off at a distance, sometimes just the horse, standin'. Most folks git clear off when they see that horse."

He got up and brought back the coffee pot. "Right odd you should ast me about him now," he commented. "Right odd."

Both men looked at him, and sensing their acute interest, he continued. "Been huntin' here lately. Some days back I ketched me a few bees off the cactus an' mesquite, figurin' to start a bee line. Well, I got her started, all right, an' I trailed them bees to a place far south o' here.

"South an' west, actually. Most o' this country hereabouts is worked out of bees. I been at it too long, so I was workin' a good ways off. Well, my bee line took me over toward the Hogback. You know that place?"

"She's a high curvin' ridge maybe five or six hundred feet at the crest, but she rises mighty close to straight up for four hundred feet. Crawlin' up there to locate the cave them bees was workin' out of, I come on a cave like a cliff dwellin', on'y it wasn't. She was man-made, an' most likely in the past twenty years or so.

"What started me really lookin' was my shovel—the one I lost. She was right there on that ledge, so I knowed it hadn't been lost, but stole off me. I began huntin' around. I found back inside this place it was all fixed up for livin'. Some grub there, blankets, a couple of guns, an' under some duffle in the corner, an old-time breastplate an' helmet."

"You're serious?" Kedrick demanded incredulously.

"Sure as I'm alive! But," Escavada chuckled, "that ain't the best of it. Lyin' there on the floor, deader'n last year's hopes, was a young feller. He had a knife, old-time Spanish knife that a feller in armor might have carried, an' it was skewered right th'ough him!"

"A young man—dead?" Kedrick suddenly leaned forward. "Anything odd about him? I mean, was he missing a thumb?"

Escavada stared. "Well now, if that don't beat all! He was missin' a thumb, an' he was crippled up mighty bad in the other arm. Carried her in a sling."

"Dornie Shaw!" Laredo leaped to his feet. "Dornie Shaw, by all that's holy!"

"Shaw?" Escavada puckered his brows, his old eyes gleaming. "Now that's most odd, most odd. Shaw was the name o' that boy, the one who didn't git killed with the wagon train!"

Kedrick's face was a study. Dornie Shaw—dead! But if Dornie had been the boy from the wagon train, that would account for his superstitious fear of the grulla mustang. But to suppose that after all these years Dornie had been killed by the same man, or ghost if one believed in ghosts, that killed the rest of them so many years before was too ridiculous. It was, he thought suddenly, unless you look at it just one way.

"Man can't escape his fate," Escavada said gloomily. "That boy hid out from that knife, but in the end it got him."

Kedrick got up. "Could you take us to that place, Escavada? Down there on the Hogback?"

"I reckon." He glanced outside. "But not in this rain. Rheumatiz gits me."

"Then tell me where it is," Kedrick said, "because I'm going now!"

*　　*　　*

They were crossing the head of Coal Mine Creek when Laredo saw the tracks. He drew up suddenly, pointing. The tracks of a horse, well shod. "The grulla!" Kedrick said grimly. "I'd know those tracks anywhere!"

They pushed on. It was very late, and the pelting rain still poured down upon their heads and shoulders. The trails were slippery, and dusk was near. "We'd better find us a hole to crawl into," Shad suggested. We'll never find that horse in this weather!"

"By morning the tracks will be gone, and I've a hunch we'll find our man right in that cliff dwelling where Escavada saw Dornie's body!"

"Wonder how Dornie found the place?"

"If what I think is right," Kedrick replied, wiping the rain from his face, "he must have run into an old friend and been taken there to hide out. That old friend was the same rider of the grulla that killed his family and friends with the wagon train, and when he saw that armor, he knew it."

"But what's it all about?" Shad grumbled. "It don't make sense! An' no horse lives that long."

"Sure not. There may have been a half-dozen grullas in that length of time. This man probably tried to capitalize on the fears of the Indians and Mexicans who live up that way to keep them off his trail. We'll probably find the answer when we reach the end of our ride."

The Hogback loomed black and ominous before them. The trail, partly switchback and part sheer climb, led over the sharp, knifelike ridge. They mounted, their horses laboring heavily at the steep and slippery climb. Twice Tom Kedrick saw the tracks of the grulla on the trail, and in neither case could those tracks have been more than an hour old.

Kedrick glanced down when they saw the opposite

side, then dismounted. "This one is tricky," he said grimly. "We'd better walk it."

Halfway down, lightning flashed, and in the momentary brightness, Laredo called out, "Watch it, Tom! High, right!"

Kedrick's head jerked around just as the rifle boomed. The bullet smacked viciously against the rock beside him, spattering his face with splinters. He grabbed for his gun, but it was under his slicker. The gun boomed again, five fast shots, as fast as the marksman could work the lever of his rifle.

Behind Tom Kedrick the anguished scream of a wounded horse cut the night, and Shad's warning yell was drowned in the boom of the gun again. Then he flattened against the rock barely in time to avoid the plunging, screaming horse.

His own appaloosa, frightened, darted down the trail with the agility of a mountain goat. The rifle boomed again and Kedrick dropped flat.

"Shad? You all right?"

There was a moment before the reply, then it was hoarse, but calm. "Winged me, but not bad."

"I'm going after him. You all right?"

"Yeah. You might help me wrap this leg up."

Sheltered by the glistening, rain-wet rock, with gray mist swirling past them on the high ridge of the Hogback, Kedrick knelt in the rain. Shielding the bandage from the rain with a slicker, he bound the leg. The bullet had torn through the flesh, but the bone was not broken.

CHAPTER XVII

WHEN THE WOUND was bandaged, Kedrick drew back into the shelter of the slight overhang and stared about. Ahead and below them was a sea of inky blackness. Somewhere down that mountain would be their horses, one probably dead or dying, the other possibly crippled.

Around them all was night and the high, windy, rain-wet rocks. And out there in the darkness a killer stalked them—a killer, who could at all of three hundred yards, spot his shots so well as to score two hits on a target seen only by a brief flash of lightning. Next time those shots could kill. And there was no doubt about it. Now the situation was clear. It was kill or be killed.

"Sure," Laredo said dryly, "you got to get him, man. But you watch it. He's no slouch with that Spencer!"

"You've got to get off this ridge," Kedrick insisted, "the cold and rain up here will kill you!"

"You leave that to me," Shad replied shortly. "I'll drag myself down the trail an' find a hole to crawl into down on the flat below this Hogback. Might even find your palouse down there. You got grub an' coffee in those saddle bags?"

"Yeah, but you'd better not try a fire until I come back."

Shad chuckled. "Make sure you come back. I never did like to eat alone."

Slipping his hands under his slicker through the pockets, Tom gripped his guns. His rifle, of course, was in his saddle scabbard. He was going to have to stalk a skilled killer—a fine marksman who was on his own ground—in absolute darkness with a hand gun. And the killer had a Spencer .56!

Lightning flashed, but there was no more shooting. Somewhere out there the killer was stalking them. He would not give up now, nor retreat. This, for him, was a last stand unless he killed them both. His hideout now was known, and if they escaped he would no longer be safe. That he did not intend to be driven from the country was already obvious by the fact that he had stayed this long.

Kedrick crawled out, using a bush to cover his movement. Working along the windy top of the ridge, he moved toward a nest of boulders he had seen ahead of him by the lightning flash. The wind whipped at his hat and flapped the skirt of his slicker. His right hand gun was drawn, but under the slicker.

He crawled on. Lightning flashed and he flattened out on the rocks. But the Spencer bellowed, the bullet smashing his eyes and mouth full of gravel. Rolling over, he held his fire, spitting and pawing desperately at his blinded eyes.

There was no sound but the wind and rain. Then in the distance, thunder roared and rumbled off among the peaks. When the lightning flashed again, he looked out along the high ridge of the Hogback. Lashed by the driving rain, its rocks glistened like steel under clouds that seemed a scarce arm's length above Kedrick's head. Mist drifted by him, touching his wet face with a ghostly hand, and the weird white skeletons of long dead pines pointed their sharp and bony fingers toward the sky.

Rain pelted against his face, and he cowered, fearing the strike of a bullet at each flash of lightning, smelling the brimstone as the lightning scarred the high ridge with darting flame. He touched his lips with his tongue and stared until his eyes ached with strain.

His mouth was dry and his stomach empty, and something mounted within him. Fear? Panic? He could stay still no longer. With infinite patience, he edged forward, working his way a little over the edge of the ridge toward the hulking black clumps of some juniper, ragged trees, whipped to agonized shapes by generations of wind.

There was no sound but the storm, no sight of anything. He moved on, trying to estimate how far away the cliff house would be, to guess if he could reach it first or get between it and the killer out there. Flame stabbed the night and something burned sharply along his shoulders. He let go everything and rolled, went crashing down a dozen feet before he brought up in a tangle of dead limbs.

But the killer was not waiting. Suddenly he loomed dark on the crest. Crouching like a hunted animal, every instinct alert, Kedrick fired.

The dark figure jerked hard, and then the Spencer bellowed. The bullet plastered a branch near Kedrick, and he knew that only his own shot had saved his life. He fired again, and then deliberately hurled himself backward into the night, falling, landing, crawling. He got to his feet and plunged into the absolute darkness, risking a broken limb or a bad fall—anything to get the distance he needed. Then lightning flashed, and as if by magic the Spencer boomed. How the man had followed his plunging career he could not know, but he felt the stab and slam of the bullets as they smashed about him. This man was shooting too close. He couldn't miss long!

His shoulders burned, but whether that shot had been a real wound or a mere graze he did not know.

Something fluid trickled down his spine. But whether it was rain water through the slit coat or his own blood, he could not guess.

He moved back, circling. Another shot, but this slightly to his left. Quickly he moved left and a shot smacked right near where he had been standing. The killer was using searching fire now, and he was getting closer.

Kedrick moved back, tripped and fell, and bullets laced the air over him. Evidently the man had a belt full of ammunition, or his pockets were stuffed.

Kedrick started to rise. This time his fingers found the hard smoothness not of rock, but of earth and gravel. Carefully, he felt about in the darkness.

The path! He was on a path, and no doubt the path to the cliff house.

He began to move along it, feeling his way carefully. Once, off to his left, he heard a rock roll. He took a chance and fired blind, then rolled over three times and felt the air split apart as the shots slammed the ground where he had been. He fired again, then again, always moving.

Lightning flashed, and he saw a hulking thing back on the trail the way he had come, a huge, glistening thing, black and shining. Flame sprang from it, and he felt the shock of the bullet, then steadied himself and fired again.

Deliberately then, he turned and worked his way down the path. Suddenly, he felt space before him, and found the path here took a sharp turn. Another step and he might have plunged off! How near was his escape he knew in another instant when lightning flashed and he saw far below him the gray-white figure of the appaloosa standing in the rain.

He worked his way down the cliff, then found a ledge

and in a moment, his hands found the crude stone bricks of the cliff house. Feeling his way along it, he felt for the door, and then pushing it open he crawled into the inner darkness and pushed the door shut behind him.

After the lashing of wind and rain the peace seemed a miracle. Jerking off his soaking hat he tossed it aside, and threw off the slicker. There was a chance the killer would not guess that he knew of this place. Undoubtedly had Kedrick not known of it he would have passed it by in the darkness and storm.

Working his way along the floor he found a curtain dividing the first chamber from an inner room. He stepped through it and sat down hard on the bunk. Feeling for his left-hand gun he found the holster empty, and he had fired five shots with his right gun. Suddenly, the curtain stirred and there was a breath of wind. Then it vanished. The killer was in the other room. He had come in.

Kedrick dared not rise for fear the bed would creak. He heard a match strike, and then a candle was lighted. Feet shuffled in the other room. Then a voice. "I know you're in there, Kedrick. There's water on the floor in here. I'm behind a piece of old stone wall that I use for a sort of table. I'm safe from your fire. I know there's no protection where you are. Throw your guns out and come with your hands up! If you don't, I'm going to open fire an' search every inch of that room!"

Over the top of the blanket curtain which was suspended from a pole across the door, Tom Kedrick could see the roof in the other room. The cave house was actually much higher than need be. Evidently the killer had walled up an overhang or cave. Kedrick could see several heavy cedar beams that had served to support a ceiling now mostly gone. If that was true in the other room, it might be true in his also.

He straightened to his feet. He heard a sudden move and then fired.

From the other room came a chuckle. "Figured that would draw fire! Well, one gun's empty. Now toss out the other an' come out. You haven't a chance!"

Kedrick did not reply. He was reaching up into the darkness over his head, feeling for the beams. He touched one, barely touched it, then reached up with both hands. He judged the distance he had to jump by the width of the beams in the other room.

What if it were old and would not support his weight? He had to chance that.

He jumped, his fingers hooked well over the edge and, soundlessly, he drew himself up. Now, Kedrick could see into the lighted room, but he could not locate the killer. The voice spoke again. "I'm giving you no more time, Kedrick. Come out or I start to shoot! Toss that other gun first!"

Silence lay in the room, a silence broken by the sudden bellow of a gun. The killer fired, emptied a six-gun, then emptied another. Tom Kedrick waited, having no idea how many guns the man had, or what he might have planned for. Then six more carefully spaced shots were fired. One of them ricocheting dangerously close to Kedrick's head.

A long pause, and then a sound of movement. "All right, if you're alive in there now, you got a shot comin' but if you want to give up, you can. I sort of want you alive."

Suddenly the blanket was jerked from its moorings and Alton Burwick stood in the opening, a gun gripped in his fist, ready to fire.

* . * . *

Kedrick made no sound, and the man stared, then rushed into the room. Almost whining with fury, he jerked Kedrick's hat from the bed, then the slicker. As the latter fell to the floor, with it fell Kedrick's other pistol, which falling from the holster had hooked into some tear in the slicker. He stared at it furiously, and then jerked the bed aside. Almost insane with anger, he searched, unbelieving and whining like an angry hound on a trail.

He stopped, his pent-up fury worn away and stood there, his chest heaving with his exertions, his fist still gripping the pistol. "Gone! Gone!" he cried, as if bereft. "When I had him right here!"

Kedrick's fingers had found a tiny sliver of wood, and, deliberately, he snapped it against Burwick's cheek. The fat man jerked as if stung, then looked up. Their eyes met, and slowly he backed away, but now he was smiling. "Oh, you're a smart one, Kedrick. Very smart! Too bad it couldn't have been you with me instead of that weakling Keith. All front and show, but no bottom to him, no staying quality!

"But," he sighed, "I've got you anyway, and you'll suffer for what you've done." He scooped Kedrick's other pistol from the floor and backed away. "All right, get down!"

Kedrick dropped to the floor, and the fat man waved irritably at the gun he clutched. "No use to bluff. That's empty. Throw it down!"

"What's it all about, Burwick?" Tom asked suddenly. "Why this place? The armor? What about Dornie Shaw?"

"Ah? How did you know about that? But no matter, no matter." He backed to the wall, watching Kedrick and holding the gun. "Why, it was gold, boy! Gold, and lots of it! It was I who stirred those Indians up to attacking that caravan! I wanted the gold they carried, and most of it belonging to Dornie's pal!

"I knew about it! Followed them from Dodge. Knew when they drew it from the bank there, and how much!

"They fooled me though. When the Indians hit, they'd buried it somewhere. It could have been a lot of places, that was the trouble. They might have buried it sooner, but somewhere along the trail. I've dug and I've hunted, but I've never found it. Maybe I will someday—but nobody else is going to!

"Wondered why I wanted the land? Profit, sure! But I wanted this piece, a couple of sections in here, all for myself. Figured on that, working it out somehow. The gold's somewhere between here and Thieving Rock. Has to be."

Kedrick nodded. "That clears up a lot of things. Now you drop that gun, Burwick, and come as my prisoner."

Burwick chuckled fatly. "Try to bluff me? I'd of expected that from you! Nervy one, huh? Bet you got that Connie Duane, too! By the Lord Harry, there's a woman! No scare to her. Not one bit! Drop your gun, boy, or I'll put my first bullet through your knee cap!"

He was going to shoot, and Tom Kedrick knew it. Coolly, he squeezed off his own shot, an instant faster. He shot for the gun hand, but the bullet only skinned the thumb knuckle and hit Burwick in the side.

The fat man jerked and his face twisted, and he stared at the gun, lifting his own. Coolly, Kedrick fired again, then again. The bullets struck with an ugly smack, and Burwick wilted, the gun going from his limp fingers to the floor. Kedrick stepped in and caught him, easing him down. The flabby cheeks were suddenly sagging and old. Bitterly, the man stared upward at him. "What happened? That—that—?"

"The gun was a Walch twelve-shot Navy pistol," Tom explained. "I started carrying them a few days ago, replacing the .44 Russians."

Burwick stared at him, no hatred in his eyes. "Smart!" he said. "Smart! Always one trick better than me, or anybody! You'll—do, boy!"

On the streets of Mustang the sun was warm after the rain. Tom Kedrick, wounded again but walking, stood beside Connie Duane. Shad was grinning at them. "Look mighty fine in that tailored suit, Tom. You goin' to be gone long?"

"Not us! We'll be married in Santa Fe, and then we're headin' for the Mogollons and that ranch."

"Seems a shame not to hunt for that gold," Laredo complained. "But anyway, the real treasure was that box full of Burwick's papers. Sure made Cummings hunt his hole. But I do regret that gold."

"I don't," Connie replied, "it's caused too much trouble. Alton Burwick spent his life and a good many other lives after it. Let it stay where it is. Maybe a better man will find it, one who needs it more than we do."

"Gosh!" Laredo said suddenly. "I got to light a shuck! I'm late to meet Sue! So long, then!" They watched him go, waiting for the stage.

Everything was quiet in Mustang—three whole days without a killing.

ABOUT THE AUTHOR

LOUIS L'AMOUR, born Louis Dearborn L'Amour, is of French-Irish descent. Although Mr. L'Amour claims his writing began as a "spur-of-the-moment thing," prompted by friends who relished his verbal tales of the West, he comes by his talent honestly. A frontiersman by heritage (his grandfather was scalped by the Sioux), and a universal man by experience, Louis L'Amour lives the life of his fictional hero. Since leaving his native Jamestown, North Dakota, at the age of fifteen, he's been a longshoreman, lumberjack, elephant handler, hay shocker, flume builder, fruit picker, and an officer on tank destroyers during World War II. And he's written four hundred short stories and over eighty books (including a volume of poetry).

Mr. L'Amour has lectured widely, traveled the West thoroughly, studies archaeology, compiled biographies of over one thousand Western gunfighters, and read prodigiously (his library holds more than two thousand volumes). And he's watched thirty-one of his westerns as movies. He's circled the world on a freighter, mined in the West, sailed a dhow on the Red Sea, been shipwrecked in the West Indies, and has been stranded in the Mojave Desert. He's won fifty-one of fifty-nine fights as a professional boxer and pinch-hit for Dorothy Kilgallen when she was on vacation from her column. Since 1816, thirty-three members of his family have been writers. And, he says, "I could sit in the middle of Sunset Boulevard and write with my typewriter on my knees; temperamental I am not."

Mr. L'Amour is re-creating an 1865 Western town, christened Shalako, where the borders of Utah, Arizona, New Mexico, and Colorado meet. Historically authentic from whistle to well, when it is constructed, it will be a live operating town, as well as a movie location and tourist attraction.

Mr. L'Amour now lives in Los Angeles with his wife Kathy and their two children, Beau and Angelique.

LOUIS L'AMOUR
1

BANTAM'S #1
ALL-TIME BESTSELLING AUTHOR
AMERICA'S FAVORITE FRONTIER WRITER

☐	25206	HELLER WITH A GUN	$2.95
☐	24550	BOWDRIE'S LAW	$2.95
☐	23368	BOWDRIE	$2.95
☐	25100	CROSS FIRE TRAIL	$2.95
☐	25402	SHOWDOWN AT YELLOW BUTTE	$2.95
☐	25580	CHANCY	$2.95
☐	24289	SITKA	$2.95
☐	20846	THE CHEROKEE TRAIL	$2.95
☐	25090	MOUNTAIN VALLEY WAR	$2.95
☐	25477	TAGGART	$2.95
☐	23153	HIGH LONESOME	$2.50
☐	25030	BORDEN CHANTRY	$2.95
☐	24957	BRIONNE	$2.95
☐	25303	THE FERGUSON RIFLE	$2.95
☐	25742	KILLOE	$2.95
☐	25770	CONAGHER	$2.95
☐	23448	NORTH TO THE RAILS	$2.50
☐	24906	THE MAN FROM SKIBBEREEN	$2.95
☐	24743	SILVER CANYON	$2.95
☐	24767	CATLOW	$2.95
☐	24765	GUNS OF THE TIMBERLANDS	$2.95
☐	24762	HANGING WOMAN CREEK	$2.95
☐	22636	FALLON	$2.50
☐	24760	UNDER THE SWEETWATER RIM	$2.95
☐	25221	MATAGORDA	$2.95
☐	25324	DARK CANYON	$2.95
☐	20956	THE CALIFORNIOS	$2.50

Prices and availability subject to change without notice.

Buy them at your local bookstore or use this handy coupon:

Bantam Books, Inc., Dept. LL1, 414 East Golf Road, Des Plaines, Ill. 60016

Please send me the books I have checked above. I am enclosing $_____
(please add $1.50 to cover postage and handling). Send check or money order
—no cash or C.O.D.'s please.

Mr/Mrs/Miss_____

Address_____

City_____ State/Zip_____

LL1—1/86

Please allow four to six weeks for delivery. This offer expires 7/86.

LOUIS L'AMOUR 1

BANTAM'S #1
ALL-TIME BESTSELLING AUTHOR
AMERICA'S FAVORITE FRONTIER WRITER

☐	25398	THE LONESOME GODS	$3.95
☐	24133	LAW OF THE DESERT BORN	$2.95
☐	25328	TO TAME A LAND	$2.95
☐	23132	SHADOW RIDERS	$2.95
☐	25389	COMSTOCK LODE	$3.50
☐	22632	YONDERING	$2.50
☐	24763	MILO TALON	$2.95
☐	25200	THE STRONG SHALL LIVE	$2.95
☐	22887	BENDIGO SHAFTER	$2.95
☐	25098	THE KEY-LOCK MAN	$2.95
☐	24922	RADIGAN	$2.95
☐	23258	WAR PARTY	$2.50
☐	24905	KIOWA TRAIL	$2.95
☐	24912	THE BURNING HILLS	$2.95
☐	24858	SHALAKO	$2.95
☐	24867	KILRONE	$2.95
☐	25771	THE RIDER OF LOST CREEK	$2.95
☐	24759	CALLAGHEN	$2.95
☐	25478	THE QUICK AND THE DEAD	$2.95
☐	20795	OVER ON THE DRY SIDE	$2.50
☐	24904	DOWN THE LONG HILLS	$2.95
☐	24766	WESTWARD THE TIDE	$2.95
☐	24748	KID RODELO	$2.95
☐	24847	BROKEN GUN	$2.95
☐	25195	WHERE THE LONG GRASS BLOWS	$2.95
☐	24780	HOW THE WEST WAS WON	$2.95

Prices and availability subject to change without notice.

Buy them at your local bookstore or use this handy coupon:

Bantam Books, Inc., Dept. LL2, 414 East Golf Road, Des Plaines, Ill. 60016

Please send me the books I have checked above. I am enclosing $_____
(please add $1.50 to cover postage and handling). Send check or money order
--no cash or C.O.D.'s please.

Mr/Mrs/Miss_____

Address_____

City_____State/Zip_____

LL2—1/86

Please allow four to six weeks for delivery. This offer expires 7/86.